An Unconventional
Countess

Jenni Fletcher was born in the north of Scotland and now lives in Yorkshire with her husband and two children. She wanted to be a writer as a child but became distracted by reading instead, finally getting past her first paragraph thirty years later. She's had more jobs than she can remember but has finally found one she loves. She can be contacted on Twitter, @jenniauthor, or via her Facebook author page.

Author Note

This book was fun to write because it combined two of my favorite pastimes, reading Jane Austen and baking. It's also the start of a new series, Regency Belles of Bath, set around a biscuit shop in Bath, which will hopefully keep me in sugary snack treats for a while to come.

Biggest thanks go to my dad. He never takes any credit, and would probably delete this if he could, but everything I know about Nelson and Trafalgar I learnt from him. Also pelagic fish, but that's another story.

Finally, thank you to my friend Claudia for checking my Italian translations and for the many gifts of cheese.

For my biscuit-loving grandmothers

Historical Note

I grew up with a collector of Nelson memorabilia, so I knew it was only a matter of time before I wrote a story with a naval hero that referenced the Battle of Trafalgar.

This altercation, on the twenty-first of October 1805, proved to be one of the defining events of modern European history. The defeat of the combined French and Spanish forces by the English fleet, under the command of Vice Admiral Horatio Nelson, ensured that Wellington's soldiers were kept supplied with provisions throughout the remainder of the Napoleonic Wars and established British naval supremacy for the next hundred years—up until the start of World War I.

The ship referred to in this story, the *HMS Colossus*, really did take part in the battle. I've tried to keep the details as accurate as possible, although the actual commander was a Captain James Morris. Fighting in the very midst of the action, the *Colossus* suffered the highest casualty figures of the British fleet and sustained so much damage that it had to be towed to Gibraltar for repairs before returning to England.

I've used it as a tribute to William Wheldale, a sailor who was press-ganged from my home town of Hull in the north of England in 1803 and died aged just twenty in the battle. The details are taken from David Wheldon and Richard Turner's book *Family Connections*.

The first part of the story is set in Bath for my grandmother, who lived there for most of her life. As a teenager I stayed at her house with my sister for several weeks every summer, mainly reading Jane Austen novels. She didn't like history, but she took me to the costume museum, which I loved, and she never made a meal with fewer than three kinds of dessert, for which I will always have the greatest affection and respect.

Finally, the Water Gardens in the second half of the story were inspired by those at Studley Royal in North Yorkshire, completed in 1767 and declared a World Heritage Site in 1986. It's one of my favourite places to visit and the scene of many happy picnics. Obviously with biscuits.

Chapter One

Bath—March 1806

'"**B**elles of Bath, purveyors of the finest quality confectionery."' Captain Samuel Delaney read out the words painted on a wooden sign beside a smart yellow-and-white-striped awning, then turned to confront his companion. 'It's a *biscuit* shop.'

'Not just any biscuit shop.' The Honourable Ralph Hoxley tapped a finger against the side of his nose. 'The finest biscuit shop in the whole of England.'

'The finest...?' Samuel threw a quick look around, assuring himself that nobody else was in sight before shoving his fist none too gently into the other man's shoulder. 'Ralph, we may not be in the first flush of youth any more, but I draw the line at tea and biscuits in the middle of the afternoon.'

'Ow!' His companion rubbed his arm gingerly. 'I say,

that's no reason to attack me. The biscuits are delicious, actually, but that's not why we're here.'

'Then why are we?'

'You'll see in a minute. Now, stop complaining and come on.'

Samuel looked about him, inwardly debating whether or not to simply turn around and leave. Swainswick Crescent was less Palladian in style than most of the streets in the fashionable shopping district, though it was built in the same distinctive honey-coloured stone and had a somewhat charming aspect. It was also only a five-minute walk from the house his grandparents had rented on the Circus, but on the other hand he was bored and his curiosity was piqued. Heaving a sigh, he waited until a carriage had rolled past before crossing the street, amused to note that his companion kept just out of arm's reach until they arrived at the shop windows.

'There!' Ralph pointed through the glass triumphantly. 'Now look and tell me if she isn't the most extraordinary creature you've ever seen.'

She? Samuel rolled his eyes. He might have guessed his wayward friend would only display this much enthusiasm over a woman, yet another unsuitable paramour most likely, but since he was already there… He threw a cursory look inside and then looked again, surprised to find that, for once, Ralph was right. Usually their tastes in relation to the opposite sex were a world apart, but this time *extraordinary* was exactly the right word.

The woman standing behind the shop counter was of medium stature, slender but not too slender, with a shapely figure and a mass of dark corkscrew curls barely contained in an unruly knot on the top of her head. They gave her an attractively dishevelled aspect, as if she'd just rolled out of bed, an effect exacerbated by the presence of a frilly white apron that put him in mind of a chemise. Unfortunately she was looking downwards, her features obscured by shadow as she tied a ribbon around a barrel-shaped tin, but what he could see of her face was square-shaped and extremely pretty. He couldn't tell the colour of her eyes, but he would have hazarded a guess that they were the same coffee shade as her hair. He felt a strong urge to find out. Succeeded by an even stronger urge to shove Ralph off the pavement for seeing her first...

'Isn't she the most delectable morsel you've ever seen?' If he wasn't mistaken, Ralph actually licked his lips.

'Not bad.' Samuel stepped away from the window and folded his arms. Unlike his companion, he had absolutely no intention of drooling over a woman in public, no matter how drool-worthy she might be. 'Although it still doesn't explain why you've dragged me halfway across the city. Much as I enjoy admiring your conquests, obviously.'

'She's not one of my conquests, not yet, and she never will be without your help.'

'Really?' He quirked an eyebrow, surprised and somewhat heartened by the news. If Ralph hadn't yet managed to seduce her, then that meant... *No.* He stopped the thought in its tracks. His life was complicated enough these days without any romantic entanglements, even if she was the prettiest, most intriguing looking woman he'd set eyes on since arriving back in England four months ago. Longer than that, even. He couldn't remember ever feeling such an instant attraction to someone. 'You don't usually have problems talking to the opposite sex on your own.'

'I don't.' Ralph sniffed with irritation. 'Only I need you to distract the other one.'

'What other one?'

'The termagant who runs the place. She's over...' His companion pressed his nose up against the glass and then started indignantly. 'Wait, that *is* the other one! *She's* the termagant!'

'Her?' Samuel unfolded his arms and took another, more eager look. The coffee-haired woman didn't look much like a virago, not enough to justify the tone of disgust in his friend's voice anyway, though he had to admit there was a certain brisk, no-nonsense efficiency to her manner as she walked around the shop, serving one customer before moving on to the next. She looked self-assured and capable, qualities he personally found to be virtues rather than faults in a woman. Damned if they didn't make her even more attractive.

He let his gaze follow her while she worked. The wall behind the counter was essentially made up of just shelves, stacked with different shapes and sizes of tin and a few trays of loose biscuits. Both they and the counter were made of dark wood, oak or beech maybe, though any suggestion of gloominess was dispelled by the shafts of yellow sunlight streaming in through large, south-facing front windows. The whole place had a cosy, inviting ambience and he *was* feeling quite peckish. A biscuit at that moment sounded like a quite excellent idea.

'I'm talking about the blonde!' Ralph shot him an exasperated look.

'What blonde?'

'There!'

As if on cue a small head popped up above the counter, its owner having presumably been searching for something underneath, in a manner that put Samuel in mind of a Punch and Judy show.

'*She's* the one I brought you to see. My golden nymph.' Ralph sounded as if he were drooling again. 'Her eyes are almost as pale as yours.'

'I trust that's where the comparison ends.' Samuel threw him a sardonic look. 'Much as I like water, I doubt I'd make a very good nymph.'

'Isn't she delectable, though?'

Samuel narrowed his eyes, regarding the 'nymph' critically as she passed a small cloth bundle across to an elderly gentleman customer. She was undeniably attractive, though surely not a day above eighteen, with delicate elfin features, a minuscule waist and glossy hair swept up into an elegant chignon. Everything about her was sleek and shiny, in striking contrast to her messy-looking companion, though he found his gaze drawn inexorably back to the messiness.

'Well?' Ralph prodded him. 'What do you think?'

'About the nymph? She looks young.'

'Not that young. Eighteen.'

'Which you know because…?'

'Because I asked her the last time I was here.' Ralph pinched his lips together. 'Before the termagant told me it was none of my business and chased me away.'

'You must have made quite an impression.'

'Harumph. You'd think she was the girl's mother the way she hovers around her. As if I'm only after one thing!'

'Aren't you?'

'And now you sound like her father!' Ralph looked affronted. 'Can't a man enjoy a little casual flirtation?'

'That would depend. Specifically on whether it's the kind

of casual flirtation you enjoyed with your mother's lady's maid last month?'

'*Ex*-lady's maid now. That's why I'm banished from London, remember?'

'Exactly.'

Samuel took a step back from the window and folded his arms again. He and Ralph had been friends at school, getting into all kinds of adolescent scrapes together, right up until the morning he'd walked out and never gone back, but the intervening years had taken them in different directions, the navy for him, university and the life of a *ton* bachelor for Ralph. Inevitably they'd lost touch and now he was starting to remember why. It wasn't *just* because he'd been busy fighting Napoleon. He liked to think that he'd grown up during the past ten years, but his old friend still seemed to have few interests beyond gambling, drinking and women. If it hadn't been for Bath being so quiet at this time of year, he might have avoided renewing the acquaintance entirely.

He stifled a sigh, wishing he'd taken up Admiral Northcott's invitation to visit his house that afternoon instead. A few hours of discussing naval tactics and studying nautical charts with a retired septuagenarian sounded infinitely preferable to helping Ralph conduct yet another flirtation. If flirtation was really *all* he intended... That morning, however, Northcott's invitation had made him far too melancholy. It was bad enough feeling homesick for a ship, but the idea that his naval career might be over barely a year after he'd achieved the long sought-after rank of Captain was depressing beyond words. Maybe he oughtn't to have put his uniform aside so soon, after all. At least wearing it made him feel as if he still belonged somewhere. Instead, here he was, standing on a street in the middle of another aimless afternoon, trapped between two possible futures.

'We'll just wait for these customers to leave.' Ralph was already straightening his cravat and tugging at the lace trim of his cuffs.

'Will we?' Samuel drew his brows together, jolted back to the present. 'I don't remember agreeing to help you. What exactly are your intentions?'

'My intentions?' Ralph's expression was almost ludicrously outraged. 'I say, when did you become so passé?'

'Around the same time I learned that actions have consequences. I won't help you to ruin the girl.'

'I've no intention of ruining anyone. All I'm doing is enjoying the view, so to speak. A man has to pass the time somehow in Bath.' Ralph leered. 'Now you distract the termagant so that I can have a few minutes alone with my nymph.'

'And how do you propose that I distract her? Especially if she's as fearsome as you say?'

'Flirt with her! You used to be quite good at that as I recall, even if all you talk about these days is boats. You know, if I'd spent most of the past decade at sea, I'd want to do a lot more than flirt when I came back on shore. Isn't there any woman in Bath who interests you?'

Samuel threw a quick glance back through the shop window. Yes, there was definitely one and the thought of distracting her was distinctly, apparently irresistibly, enticing.

'Just think of it as another battle. Imagine that she's...' Ralph paused thoughtfully '...what was the name of that French Admiral you trounced again?'

'Villeneuve.'

'Right. Imagine that she's Villeneuve and you need to

keep her occupied while I break through her line like Nelson. It'll be just like Trafalgar all over again.'

Samuel felt a muscle twitch in his jaw. Comparisons to his former commanding officer aside, he had the distinct suspicion that Nelson wouldn't have approved of what they were about to do, either. On the other hand, what harm *was* there in enjoying the view? Just to pass the time for a few minutes?

'All right.' He flexed his shoulders, ignoring a prickle of conscience as he prepared for action instead. 'For King and Country...'

Chapter Two

'He's here again.' Anna Fortini waited until the shop door had closed behind the last customer before narrowing her eyes at the window and scowling.

'I know.' Her assistant Henrietta raised a hand to her head, patting non-existent stray hairs back into place and batting her eyelashes coquettishly. 'This is the third time this week.'

'Maybe we can persuade him to actually buy something this time,' Anna muttered, pushing her own very real stray hairs out of her face and wondering if she had time to carry a bucket of cold water up to the first-floor window and deposit it over the admirers below. Alas, she suspected not. In fact, she was quite certain the front door would open again the very moment she left the room and she had absolutely no intention of leaving Henrietta on her own. Tempted as she was to believe that her shop's recent popularity with the young male population of Bath was entirely due to her baking, she was well aware that it had far more to do with her new and attractive assistant. Barely a day went by when she didn't have to chase some lovesick swain or other off the premises, but this particular suitor was proving more persistent than the others. He was becoming an irritation.

'There's another gentleman with him this time,' Henrietta murmured, coming to stand close beside her.

'So I noticed. Another of your admirers, no doubt.'

'Actually, he's looking at you. Quite intently, too.' Henrietta giggled. 'He's very handsome. I wonder who he is.'

'If he's anything like his companion, then I don't care. They look like gentlemen.'

'You always say that like it's a bad thing. What do you have against gentlemen anyway?'

'Plenty! And no giving biscuits away this time. Those samples are for customers, not—stop it!' Anna looked around sharply, making a grab for her assistant's arm as she started to wave. 'You shouldn't encourage them.'

'Why not? It's just a bit of fun. There's no harm in that, is there?'

'It depends on what kind of fun you both have in mind. I very much doubt it's the same thing. Honestly, didn't you learn anything from your last employment?'

The hurt expression on the girl's face made Anna regret the words instantly. Henrietta had lost her position in a dressmaker's shop after her employer's son had formed a passionate, but unrequited, attachment towards her. She hadn't done anything to encourage him, Henrietta had assured Anna when she'd first applied for the position as her assistant, only she was afraid that she might have acted naively by not immediately rebuffing his attentions, but then she hadn't wanted to be rude, either... The inevitable result was that she'd been dismissed without references.

'I'm sorry.' Anna winced. 'I didn't mean it like that.'

'I know.' One of Henrietta's most endearing qualities was her ability to forgive and forget. 'And I'm sorry for waving, but I was only being friendly. You don't think I'd be silly enough to fall for a gentleman, do you?'

Anna dropped her gaze to the biscuit samples set out on a plate in front of her. *Yes*, she thought silently. Yes, she did think that Henrietta was capable of having her head turned by an aristocratic appearance and a few charming compliments, but she didn't want to say the words out loud. Over the past couple of months she'd become genuinely fond of the girl. She was certainly a far livelier companion than Mrs Padgett, her dour and disapproving predecessor. No one had ever come into the shop to see *her*. All in all, Henrietta's hard-working and sunny disposition would have made her the perfect employee if it hadn't been for her propensity to be *friendly* with every man who as much as glanced in her direction—and men were *always* glancing in her direction. To be fair, it would have been hard for someone so pretty not to attract male attention—Anna only hoped it wouldn't lead her into doing something foolish one day.

'Just remember that no matter how honourable they might *seem*, gentlemen like that don't regard women like us as ladies.' She threw another venomous glare in the direction of the window. 'They won't treat us like ones, either.'

'How can you be so cynical?' Henrietta made a tsking sound. 'Sometimes a gentleman really is a gentleman.'

'But most of the time he's a wolf in sheep's clothing.'

'Good gracious, anyone would think…'

Henrietta bit her lip, leaving whatever anyone would think unspoken as the bell above the shop door jingled again and the two men entered finally.

'Perhaps you could finish the window display, Henrietta?' Anna gave her assistant a none-too-subtle nudge in the ribs. 'While I deal with these customers.' Then she lifted her chin, bracing both of her hands on the countertop before putting on her brightest, most insincere smile. 'How may I help you, gentlemen?'

'Good afternoon.' The first man, the *irritant*, faltered mid-step, a lock of blond hair flopping across his face as his gaze followed Henrietta. 'My friend and I were just strolling past when we had a sudden craving for chocolate.'

'Oh, what a shame.' Anna heaved an exaggerated sigh. 'Unfortunately we don't work with chocolate, which you might have known had you asked about our merchandise on one of your previous visits. We sell biscuits, *just* biscuits. Perhaps you might try the shop on...'

'But I adore biscuits even more!' The man grinned, exposing a row of dazzlingly white teeth. *Definitely* a wolf. 'Perhaps your lovely assistant here might recommend something special?'

'I'm perfectly capable of recommending—'

'I'd like one of the big tins,' the other man interrupted before she could finish, addressing her in an amused-sounding baritone that none the less carried a distinct note of command. 'If it's not too much trouble?'

Anna turned her head to glower and then felt her stomach perform a strange kind of bouncing manoeuvre instead. She'd been so focused on the *irritant* that she'd barely spared a glance for his companion, though now she seemed unable to look away again. Henrietta was right, he was *very* handsome and yet a mass of contradictions, too, with hair the colour of mahogany and eyes so silvery pale they resembled icebergs. He might have looked austere if it hadn't been for his athletic build and a rugged aspect that seemed at odds with his finely cut and, she couldn't help but notice, perfectly tailored tailcoat, midnight-blue waistcoat and crisp white shirt. His face was lean and tanned, too, somewhat surprisingly for Somerset in March, yet despite his youthful appearance—surely he couldn't be any more than thirty?—there was already a web of fine lines around his eyes that crinkled when he smiled. Just as he was doing now, she realised, making her cheeks flush and her stomach bounce all over again.

'Trouble?' she repeated the word, trying to focus on what he'd just said. 'Of course not. If it were trouble, then I'd be in the wrong profession, sir. Just allow me a moment to fetch one.'

She turned to climb a set of steps set against the shelves, glad to avert her face for a few moments while she berated herself, or more precisely her body, for its own foolish reaction. He was a *gentleman*! Albeit a handsome one and in an attractively *un*gentlemanly sort of way, far less foppish than his friend and with an air of self-possession and authority that surely accounted for all the stomach bouncing, but *still* a gentleman, and hadn't she just been warning Henrietta about those? Besides, he could hardly have made his purpose there any more obvious if he'd had it printed across his forehead. He was a decoy, enlisted to divert her attention while his companion tried to seduce her assistant. Well, if he thought he could outwit or charm her so easily, then he could think again!

She reached for the nearest tin and started back down the steps, throwing a surreptitious glance towards the window as she descended. As expected, Henrietta was already deep in conversation with the first man, who was standing far too close for decency. Both details meant that *she* had to hurry.

'Here you are.' She deposited the rectangular-shaped tin in front of him with a clatter. 'It contains an assortment of biscuits, sixteen in total, each individually wrapped in tissue paper.'

'Just sixteen?' Her customer rested one forearm on top of the counter, regarding the tin as if it posed some kind of dilemma. 'May I see inside?'

'If you wish.' Anna removed the lid, struck with the uncharacteristic impulse to neaten her hair as he leaned closer. Not that there was any point in doing so when long experience told her the curls would only tumble straight out of her bun again, and not that she cared what this gentleman thought of her hair either, even when he was standing close enough to see every wild tendril, but something about the deep timbre of his voice made her self-conscious. She found herself tucking a stray coil behind her ear before she could stop herself.

'There you are.' She unwrapped one of the bundles of tissue paper, unveiling a cream-coloured round biscuit for his inspection, then waited in silence for several long moments until she couldn't wait any longer. 'Is something the matter?'

'Not exactly. I suppose the tin just looked bigger from a distance.' He rubbed a hand across his chin as if he were considering the problem. There were bristles there, she noticed, another ungentlemanly contradiction, though she supposed it *was* nearing the end of the day. They were the same dark auburn shade as his hair and looked softer than she would have expected bristles to look, positively strokeable, in fact... She gave a startled jolt and lifted her gaze determinedly back to his eyes, irritated that any gentleman could have such a distracting effect on her.

'I'm afraid this is the biggest tin we do.'

'Ah. Pity.' He laid his hand down flat on the counter beside hers, so close that their fingers were nearly, but not quite, touching. To her surprise, his skin was rough and weathered-looking as if, despite being a gentleman, he was used to manual labour. 'They're for a special lady, you see, and I wouldn't want to appear churlish.'

'Indeed?' She tugged her own hand away, heat rising in her cheeks. 'Then perhaps you might want to consider two tins? Or a different present altogether?'

'But these look delicious.' He seemed undeterred by her sarcasm. 'And of course some would say that quality is more important than quantity, only I'm afraid that this particular lady is rather...' he paused, lowering his voice to an intimate undertone '...*voracious* in her appetites.'

'I'm sure she'd be delighted to hear you say so.' Anna straightened her shoulders, feeling her temper start to escalate. How dare he talk to her about appetites, voracious or otherwise? No gentleman would *ever* speak to a lady in such an unguarded fashion! The words encouraged her to be indiscreet, too. 'Well, I suppose that size matters to some people. Perhaps you've disappointed her with something small before?'

She put her hands on her hips with a look of defiance, expecting him to storm out of the door in an offended rage, surprised when he burst into loud laughter instead.

'The tin it is.' He pushed himself up off the counter, eyes glinting with humour. 'And I'll just have to bear whatever criticism my lady friend makes. Are the biscuits inside all the same?'

'Only in shape.' Anna rearranged the contents and re-placed the lid quickly, trying to ignore the way his laughter seemed to vibrate through her body, like a breeze stirring ripples across a lake. It seemed to cause a strange quivering sensation in her stomach, too, lower down than before and somewhat alarming in its intensity. It made her feel even *more* agitated. If only he'd stormed out! Then she could have forgotten his existence and turned her attention back to Henrietta. Instead, annoyingly, she found herself wanting to hear him laugh again... 'We make three types of Belle. Vanilla, cinnamon and rosewater.'

'So the biscuits are called Belles?'

'Precisely.' She pushed the tin across the counter, shoot-ing a pointed look from beneath her lashes. 'You're very quick, sir.'

Despite the insult, he laughed again. 'Which is your fa-vourite?'

'None of them. I started baking when I was eight. After sixteen years, I can honestly say that I've lost my sweet tooth.'

'But if you had to choose a favourite? So that I can par-ticularly recommend one to my lady friend?'

'She's *your* lady friend.' Anna pursed her lips disapprov-ingly. 'If she's so special, then I would have thought you might know her tastes better. Here...' She picked up the plate of samples. 'Try one.'

'Thank you.' He selected the darkest-coloured biscuit and took a bite, eyebrows lifting as he chewed. 'Cinna-mon? It's delicious.'

'You sound surprised.' She lifted her own eyebrows to mirror his.

'I am. I'm not usually fond of biscuits, but I could eat a dozen of these. Definitely my favourite.'

'You haven't tried the others.'

'I don't need to.' He rapped his knuckles decisively on the countertop. 'I'll recommend this one whatever the consequences.'

'Consequences?' she couldn't resist asking. 'Are you likely to face those?'

'Oh, yes. She's quite a tyrant in her own way.'

'Of course she is.'

'But open-minded, too.' He popped the last of the biscuit into his mouth. 'I admire that in a person. Being judgemental is such an unattractive quality, don't you think?'

'I think it depends. There's a difference between being judgemental and having high standards. Now, if that's all, that will be four shillings.'

'Ribbon?'

'That costs more.'

'Ah, but she's worth it.'

'Naturally.' Anna narrowed her eyes, reaching under the counter for a roll of blue ribbon and then coughing loudly as she saw Henrietta's companion touch her elbow.

'That sounds nasty.' Her own customer sounded amused. 'Perhaps you ought to consult a physician about it.'

'I'm perfectly well, thank you.' She narrowed her eyes even further, though it was difficult to do so without actually closing them.

'I'm relieved to hear it. Otherwise I'd have to suggest a visit to the Pump Rooms to take some of the waters, and it's not an experience I'd recommend.'

'Indeed? Then I wonder what you're doing in Bath, sir?' She gave the ribbon an aggressive snip with her scissors.

'Isn't it the start of the London Season soon? Perhaps you ought to be there, preparing yourself for balls at Almack's and picnics at Vauxhall Gardens?'

'Perhaps I should be.' He gave a careless-looking shrug. 'But what can a man do when his grandmother summons him?'

'Your grandmother?' She paused in the act of curling a ribbon.

'My *special lady*, yes.' The corners of his mouth curved upwards. 'Who did you think I was talking about?'

'I...' She cleared her throat, willing the sudden onslaught of heat across her cheeks to subside. 'Your wife, perhaps?'

'Alas, I haven't found a woman willing to put up with me yet. Hard to believe, isn't it?'

'Unfathomable.' She finished curling the ribbons, trying to ignore an unwelcome frisson of excitement at the words. 'There you are. I hope that your grandmother enjoys them. They were baked fresh this morning.'

'Do you bake them yourself?' He seemed in no hurry to be leaving, extracting a few coins from his coat pocket.

'I do everything here myself. It's *my* shop.'

'You're the proprietor?' He looked impressed.

'Yes.'

'And the baker?'

'And everything else.' She lifted her chin proudly. 'I do whatever needs doing.'

'Then I compliment you, Mrs...?'

'*Miss* Fortini.'

'Miss Fortini.' He repeated her name, his eyes lingering on her face in a way that made her wish she might plunge her head into a bucket of cold water. 'Do you have a first name, too?'

'Doesn't everyone? But I share it with acquaintances, not customers.'

'Ah. In that case it's been a delight talking to you, Miss Fortini.'

'Quite.' She inclined her head and then twisted it pointedly to one side, focusing her attention back on Henrietta's companion. 'Now have you finished getting recommendations, sir, or did you only come to grace us with your presence *again*?'

'Actually I've decided I'm not so hungry, after all.' The *irritant* spun around with another wolfish grin. 'However, I've just invited your charming assistant here for a walk, what with it being such a beautiful afternoon.'

'So it is.' Anna spoke quickly before her 'charming assistant' could agree to anything. 'Unfortunately, as you may or may not have noticed, we have a business to run. Our customers can't serve themselves.'

'But we close soon,' Henrietta interjected. 'Couldn't we leave just a little bit early for once?'

'We still have cleaning up to do.' Anna shot her a warning look.

'Then perhaps I might wait and escort Miss Henrietta home? I'd be more than happy to do so.'

'I'm sure you would.' Anna gave a tight-lipped smile in return, reluctantly conceding that she'd been outwitted. Her own customer had already picked up his tin and tucked it neatly under his arm, though his expression was noticeably less triumphant than that of his friend. There was actually a small furrow between his brows as if he were displeased about something. It made a striking contrast to the way he'd smiled across the counter a few minutes before. No doubt that had just been a charming mask, one he felt able to drop now that his task as decoy was complete, but if he thought the matter was concluded, then he was very much mistaken. She wasn't defeated yet!

'Do you know...?' She walked around the counter and across the shop floor to place a protective arm around Henrietta's shoulders. 'Now that I think of it, an evening stroll sounds most pleasant, after all. We'll meet you in Sydney Gardens beside the grotto in half an hour, after we've tidied. That way we can escort Miss Gardiner home *together*.'

Chapter Three

Samuel marched up and down a picturesque-looking pathway between rows of willow and ash trees, ardently wishing that he'd been out when his old friend had called to visit him that afternoon. As amusing as he'd found his encounter with the pretty and prickly Miss Fortini, his conscience was bothering him quite considerably. No matter how tedious he found life on shore, he should never have gone along with Ralph's plan. It had felt dishonourable somehow, his behaviour that of a rake, or even worse, his father! This walk struck him as a monumentally bad idea, too, but he was involved now whether he liked it or not. To his own chagrin, it was too late to walk away.

'I say!' Ralph called out to him from the bench where he was lounging, arms thrown wide as if he hadn't a care in the world. 'Why are you in such a bad mood?'

'Because I don't appreciate being dragged into your romantic exploits, that's why!' Samuel practically exploded.

'That whole scene felt underhand. You said it was just a little harmless flirtation, nothing about walks in the park.'

'Well, I call that very ungrateful. Here I've arranged a promenade with two very attractive young ladies and all you can do is complain.'

'An hour ago you described one of them as a termagant.'

'Yes, she is, isn't she?' Ralph chuckled unrepentantly. 'I thought she was going to spit actual feathers when I offered to walk Henrietta home.'

'You don't need me to be here, too. You and the termagant can squabble over the girl together.'

'Don't you believe it. If it's just me then she'll plant herself between the two of us and I won't get a word, let alone anything else, in edgewise. You can just tell she's the sort who wants to stop everyone else having fun because she's an old maid.'

'She's hardly an old maid.'

Ralph made a snorting sound. 'I doubt she's ever had a day's excitement in her whole life.'

'Leave her alone.'

'Why? Do you like her?' His old friend draped one leg over the other and regarded him thoughtfully. 'Well, she's attractive enough, I suppose. If I wasn't so smitten with my nymph, then I might have considered her for myself. After all, her name's practically famous in Bath. She'd be quite a conquest.'

Samuel stopped pacing abruptly. *Attractive enough* wasn't exactly the phrase he would have chosen to use. *Exceedingly pretty* was more like it, with porcelain skin, a stubborn chin and eyes dark and deep enough for a man to drown in, which given his nautical background was a dangerous metaphor indeed. They'd turned out to be an even darker brown than he'd expected, only a shade away from black, and sharper than Ralph had given her credit for. She'd known perfectly well what they'd been up to from the moment they'd entered the shop, her hackles well and truly raised from the start. *He* certainly hadn't deceived or charmed her.

Truth be told, the experience had been somewhat galling. He'd never been much of a lady's man, but he'd flattered himself that he still possessed a reasonable degree of charm, on the rare occasions he chose to display it, that was. He'd favoured Miss Fortini with his most dashing smile and she hadn't been swayed for a second. Teasing hadn't worked, either. She'd given as good as she'd got and more, rebuffing his advances with flashing eyes and a dry wit that had amused him considerably. Her protective attitude towards her assistant had impressed him, too. Her concern for the girl was both laudable and touching, making him feel even guiltier by contrast. She certainly deserved better than to have to spend her time guarding against men like Ralph. It was no wonder she behaved like a termagant. Which she wasn't.

'What do you mean, famous?' he asked finally.

'Mmm?' Ralph paused in the inspection of his fingernails. 'Oh, she's Belle. *The* Belle. Anna*belle* Fortini.'

'Annabelle.' He felt inordinately pleased to discover her first name at last. 'But aren't the biscuits called Belles?'

'Yes,' Ralph yawned, 'but they were named after her. The whole shop was, in fact. Her parents set up the place just after she was born, so Henrietta says, and they named both it and the merchandise after their baby daughter. It's ironic really, such a sweet name for such a shrew.'

Samuel folded his arms, choosing to ignore the last comment. 'What happened to her parents?'

'Oh, the father died a few years ago, but the mother's still around. She doesn't work any more, something to do with ill health apparently, but *she's* even more famous than the daughter. Notorious, actually.'

'I don't listen to gossip, Ralph.'

'It's not gossip, it's fact. Do you remember the old Duke of Messi—?'

He was prevented from saying any more by the appearance of the ladies themselves, walking with varying degrees of enthusiasm along the footpath towards them. They were still dressed in their shop clothes, in matching yellow empire-line dresses, though now they both wore bonnets and shawls, too. The nymph's headwear was pink, bringing out the slight strawberry tint of her hair, while Miss Fortini's was light brown, contrasting with her dark curls to give her a coffee-and-cream appearance. Damn it if he didn't crave a cup at that moment...

The younger woman walked straight up to Ralph with a small skip in her step, taking his arm with an enthusiastic smile. Too enthusiastic, Samuel thought privately, and certainly too trusting. Her yellow dress and hair gave her the appearance of a daffodil, her golden beauty blending in perfectly with the spring foliage around them. It gave him a twinge of unease. Such innocence could so easily be stamped on by the wrong kind of person. In natural daylight, moreover, she looked even younger and more vulnerable than she had in the shop, making him wish that he'd challenged Ralph on his intentions more thoroughly.

'Shall we?' He offered an arm to Miss Fortini, but she

ignored it, sparing him only a cursory glance before starting along the path on her own.

'So your name is Belle?' he tried asking again, lengthening his stride to catch up with her quick pace.

'Annabelle.' She gave him a sharp look. 'Although, as I believe I mentioned earlier, my customers call me Miss Fortini.'

'Forgive me, I didn't intend to be over-familiar, but I only just discovered that you're the original Bath Belle.'

If he wasn't mistaken, she gave a soft sigh. 'For what it's worth, yes, I am, or at least my parents presented us both to the world around the same time. It's actually short for Annabelle Claudia Teresa Fortini, but I prefer Anna.' She glanced sideways at him, the evening sunlight bathing her face in a reddish-gold glow. 'So now you know *all* of my names, which is a great deal more than I can say about you and yours. Do you make a habit of being mysterious, sir, or am I simply not important enough to warrant an introduction?'

'Ah, forgive me again.' He drew his brows together in consternation, belatedly realising that she was right. Despite asking for her name, he hadn't mentioned his own at all. 'Captain Samuel Delaney at your service.'

'*Captain* Delaney?' Her footsteps faltered and then stopped, her prickly manner disappearing at once. 'You're a captain? In the army or navy?'

'Navy.'

'But you're not in uniform.'

'No.' He flinched at the reminder. 'I'm trying to accustom myself to not wearing it.'

'Are you on shore leave?'

'Something like that.' He shrugged as she continued to

regard him inquisitively. 'I sustained an injury during a recent skirmish and the Admiralty has no more need of me at present. I don't know when, or whether, I'll be able to return to active service.'

'It must have been serious.' Her dark eyes swept over him as if she were searching for evidence of a wound.

'Shrapnel.' He touched a hand to his collarbone, his lips twitching with amusement. He couldn't remember the last time he'd been inspected so thoroughly, especially by a woman. 'But it's mostly healed.'

'I'm glad.' She dug her top teeth into her bottom lip, a small frown puckering her brow as if she were considering telling him something. 'My brother, Sebastian, is in the navy,' she said finally.

'Indeed?' He felt strangely honoured by the confidence. 'What vessel?'

'The *Menelaus*. He's a lieutenant.'

'That's a good ship. I know Captain Marlow well.'

'You do?' Her brown eyes widened with enthusiasm, riveting on his face so intently that she didn't even notice when Ralph touched a hand to her assistant's cheek up ahead. 'Is he a good man?'

'Very. We served together on the *Asia* six years ago when we were both lieutenants. He can make buttons out of cheese and he doesn't like fish.'

'Fish?' She blinked. 'You mean to eat?'

'To do anything with, I imagine. Other than that, he's a fair man with an uncanny ability to sense bad weather. Your brother couldn't ask for a better captain.'

'Thank you. I appreciate your saying so.' For the first time since they'd met her smile didn't contain the faintest hint of sarcasm. 'You must be good, too, Captain Delaney.

To reach such a high rank by the age of…' she looked him up and down again '…thirty?'

This time he couldn't stop himself from smiling. 'You're very direct, Miss Fortini.'

'Yes, I know.' She seemed unperturbed by the comment. 'It's a failing of mine, I suppose, but the problem is that I can never understand why. If I could, then maybe I could do something about it, but as it is…' she shrugged '… I like to get to the point. It was only an observation, however. I didn't mean to offend you.'

'I'm not remotely offended, although I'm afraid your observation is slightly out. I'm a weather-beaten twenty-six, but you're correct about my rank. In peace time, it would have taken a great deal longer to gain such a promotion, but things work differently in war.'

'I suppose so.' She nodded sombrely as they started to walk again. 'Do you enjoy it? Being a sailor, I mean?'

'I do. I've always loved the water. Swimming, sailing, fishing, even looking at it, so the navy suits me. I like the routine on board ship, too. It can be tedious, but it gives me a sense of purpose and it's calming.'

'Do you often need calming?' She gave him a quizzical look.

'On a daily basis at the moment. I've been on shore for four months and it feels like an eternity. I'm afraid of losing my sea legs.'

'Sebastian loves the navy, too, but I wish he might come home for a while. The last we heard his ship was somewhere off the coast of South America, but I'm afraid of another big sea battle.'

'It's extremely unlikely. Napoleon doesn't have enough ships left to risk another naval assault and it's doubtful he'd want to anyway. Trafalgar was the longest day of my life, but at least the victory was decisive.'

'You were there?' Her head spun towards him so quickly he almost jumped. 'Is that where you were injured?'

'Yes.'

'You called it a *skirmish*!'

'A *big* skirmish.'

'A big...' She stared at him with an expression of bewilderment mixed with curiosity. 'I read that you were outnumbered. Thirty-three French and Spanish ships to twenty-seven British.'

'That's right. More than forty thousand men, all told.'

'What was the name of your ship?'

'The *Colossus*.'

'But I've heard of that!' Bewilderment turned to outright amazement. 'It was in the middle of the action.'

'Yes, unfortunately. Our yardarm locked with that of the *Argonaute*. We were trapped together for ten minutes before the sea swell drove us apart.'

'And then the *Swiftsure* surrendered to you?'

'Eventually, after we gave her a full broadside.'

'*And* the *Bahama*. You destroyed her mainmast.'

He lifted an eyebrow. 'You know your sea battles, Miss Fortini.'

'I don't see why a woman shouldn't read about such things as well as a man.'

'Neither do I, especially when that woman has a brother in the navy. Ask me anything you like.'

'All right.' She paused as if to gather her thoughts. 'What was the battle really like? The reports all make it sound so well ordered, but how do you stay in formation?'

'With many hours of practice, although what Nelson did

at Trafalgar hasn't been done often before. Instead of the fleets facing each other, he divided ours into two columns. We cut through the enemy line instead of confronting them head on. It took them by surprise and gained us the advantage.'

'Did you know you were winning?'

He shook his head. 'At close quarters, it's hard to see anything that's happening beyond your own ship. There are shards of timber and metal flying all around and you can't hear because the boom of so many cannons drowns out everything except the ringing inside your own head. You're aware of men shouting and screaming, but you can't make out the words. Meanwhile, the smoke burns your lungs so that you can't answer back, either. Most of the time, you're just fighting to stay alive.' He stopped, afraid that he might have said too much, but she seemed to be hanging on every word.

'It must have been terrifying.'

'It was. A few other words come to mind, but in essence they mean the same thing. Being responsible for so many lives is frightening enough, but I believe that every man is terrified going into battle. There's always the chance that you won't make it out again, but there's no use in showing it or giving in to the fear, either. And being with your crew and part of the fleet gives you courage.'

'Sebastian said something similar in one of his letters. He said it was like having a second family.'

'That's true. At sea, we all depend on each other for survival. You have to rely on your men to do what they've been trained for.'

'Did the fighting really last three hours?'

'It did, then the weather that night nearly finished us

off. We were in a poor enough state after the battle, but the storm was even worse. Many of us spent the night on deck, waiting to see if we'd be scuppered on the rocks. A number of ships didn't make it to morning.'

'And you'd lost your commander.'

'Yes.' He clenched his jaw at the memory. 'During the battle, Nelson refused to go below deck for safety. He wanted to fight alongside us and he said the men needed to see him. Unfortunately a French sharpshooter in the rigging of the *Redoubtable* saw him, too. The musket ball entered his left shoulder.'

'It was a great loss.'

'It was. I remember when we got word of what had happened. The whole fleet fell silent. We'd won, but it felt like defeat.'

'Maybe all battles feel like that in the end.' She sounded pensive as they emerged out of the trees and on to a wide pathway leading up to a stone pavilion. 'It all seems like such a terrible waste.'

'It was. Thousands of men died that day. The waves were red with…' He stopped mid-sentence. 'My apologies. I shouldn't have said that.'

'Why not? Because I'm a woman?' She gave him a pointed look. 'There's no need to apologise, Captain Delaney. I like to be told the truth, not be sheltered from it. I appreciate your honesty and…' she hesitated and then stopped walking again, folding her hands tightly in front of her '… if you were to hear any news of my brother's ship, good *or* bad, I would appreciate hearing about that, too.'

'Very well. If I hear anything, I'll be sure to inform you.'

'Thank you.' She cleared her throat, turning her head to

watch a squirrel as it ran about on the lawn beside them. 'I believe I owe you an apology, Captain.'

'I don't think—'

'But I do,' she interrupted him firmly. 'I behaved rudely towards you earlier. I made certain assumptions about your character, but I was mistaken. I had no idea what kind of a man you really were.'

What kind of a man...? Samuel froze, struck with a fresh pang of guilt. 'I'm not sure I understand you, Miss Fortini.'

She made an apologetic face. 'When you came into my shop earlier I assumed that you were just another bored, indolent member of the aristocracy with too much time on his hands. I didn't believe that you were really there to buy biscuits for your grandmother. I thought that you had an ulterior motive. Now I know I misjudged you. You're a gentleman who also works for his living, a man of purpose and honour and bravery.'

'Ah.' Samuel rubbed a hand around the back of his neck. Under other circumstances he might have been pleased by such a heroic portrait, but it was hard to swallow when she'd been right the first time. His earlier behaviour had been decidedly *un*heroic.

'You don't like the aristocracy, Miss Fortini?' He decided to focus on a different part of her speech.

Black lashes fanned over her cheeks as she dipped her gaze evasively. 'I'm sure there are some perfectly fine examples of gentlemen among the upper classes, but in my experience not many. Take your friend.' Her lip curled with distaste as she glanced towards Ralph. 'His sole purpose in life at the moment seems to be the pursuit of my friend.'

'I thought she was your employee?'

'Can't she be both?' Her gaze shot back to his. 'Sir, you

accused me of being direct earlier so I won't mince words. I believe that we both know what he wants from her, and that when—*if*—he gets it, he'll abandon her as he already has countless others, I'm sure. I've lived in Bath my whole life and I've seen it happen more times than I can remember. Gentlemen may visit for the Pump Rooms, but they find other ways to pass their time and they see women like us as fair game. *That's* the reason your friend feels entitled to call into my shop whenever he feels like it without buying anything, why he thinks it acceptable to ask Henrietta to walk without a chaperon, too. He would never behave in such a way with a lady.

'Well, she is *not* fair game, Captain. She's eighteen years old and far too sweet-natured to understand what he really wants and, if you're truly a man of honour as I believe you to be, I beg you to dissuade him from pursuing her.' She took a step forward and placed a hand on his arm, her tone entreating as her fingers curled gently around his wrist. 'No good can come of it.'

Samuel listened in silence. By the end of her speech she was flushed and breathless and he was feeling somewhat mortified, not by her bluntness, but by the truth behind it. Every word she'd just spoken filled him with shame, the touch of her hand on his arm like a burning hot iron. Every word was true, too, except for the part when she'd called him a man of honour. An honourable man would never have entered the shop and helped Ralph in the first place. An honourable man would have turned around and walked away. Which meant that all he could do now was try to put things right and behave like the man she thought him to be. Her impassioned speech and those soulful dark eyes made him *want* to be heroic again. Nearly as much as they made him want to kiss her, too. Quite suddenly and unexpectedly, right there in the middle of the park, in a way that *definitely* wouldn't improve her opinion of gentlemen...

'You look tired, Miss Fortini.' He pulled his arm away before he could do something he might regret. Now that they were standing so close he could see her face clearly and in truth she looked a stage beyond tired. She looked exhausted, her brown eyes ringed with dark shadows that made them appear even bigger. 'You ought to go home and rest.'

'Didn't you hear me, Captain?' She sounded dismayed.

'I did.' A new suspicion occurred to him. 'I wondered if you were speaking from personal experience?'

She took a step backwards as if he'd just threatened her, her face blanching visibly. 'What difference would it make if I was?'

He clamped his brows together. She was right. Her past experiences, whatever they were, made no difference at all to their current situation. As much as he wanted to know the answer, it was none of his business.

'Tell me, then...' he said, swallowing a different question '...does your friend usually walk home on her own at this time of evening?'

'Yes.' Her expression was guarded now. 'Although one of her brothers usually meets her on Pulteney Bridge.'

'Good. In that case, give me five minutes and I'll remember an urgent reason for myself and Mr Hoxley to be elsewhere. You have my word as a naval officer and...' he paused, resisting the urge to grimace '...a gentleman. If you'll trust me, that is, Miss Fortini?'

She didn't answer at first, holding on to his gaze for a few intense moments, her expression turning gradually from indecision to conviction to something that made his pulse start to accelerate.

'Thank you, Captain Delaney,' she said, nodding finally. 'I believe that I do trust you. Five minutes, then.' She dipped into a curtsy. 'And the next time your grandmother would like some biscuits, I'd be more than happy to deliver a tin myself.'

'I'll be sure to tell her.' He made a formal bow, but she was already turning away, waving a farewell to her friend before walking briskly towards one of the park gates.

Samuel felt an unexpectedly warm glow in his chest, followed by a pang of regret as he watched the subtle sway of her hips across the lawn. It was a pity that his future was so unsettled, otherwise she was exactly the kind of woman he would have been interested in: intelligent, capable and strong-willed. He'd *almost* fallen back into old ways that afternoon, the ones he thought he'd left behind when he'd joined the navy, but somehow Miss Fortini had stopped him. He'd been perilously close to steering off tack and she'd set him back on course. He actually felt grateful to her.

He heaved a sigh as she turned out of the gate and disappeared from view. It was *really* a pity...but it was also pointless to dwell upon what-might-have-been. Apart from anything else, she'd made her opinion of the aristocracy abundantly clear and, if she found out who he was besides a naval officer, who he *might* be anyway, then no doubt she'd walk away from him again even faster.

On the other hand, if events unfolded the way he wanted them to and he remained *plain* Captain Delaney, perhaps he might permit himself to visit her shop again one day. Not with Ralph obviously, especially since they were about to have the kind of full and frank discussion that would undoubtedly ruin their friendship for ever, but on his own and with honourable intentions this time. In another couple of months, perhaps, when the matter of his possible inheritance was settled...

In the meantime, it was probably best to keep away. He was developing an unfortunate appetite for biscuits as it was.

Chapter Four

Anna closed and latched the window shutters, drew two iron bolts across the shop door and then trudged up the back staircase to the parlour, wearily untying the ribbons of her bonnet as she went. A walk through Sydney Gardens had been the last thing she'd needed after a day that had started twelve hours before. Her neck felt stiff and her feet ached with tiredness, even more so than usual, but at least now she could rest.

From a shopkeeper's perspective, however, she couldn't complain. It had been another profitable day. She oughtn't to complain at all, she chided herself, especially when she had so much to be grateful for—an honest and reliable source of income, a warm and dry home, and independence to boot. The shop that her parents had founded almost twenty-five years earlier had become so popular with the spa visitors of Bath that they'd eventually been able to buy the whole building on Swainswick Crescent, narrow and compact as it was. There were three floors: the shop and kitchen below, a parlour in the middle and two small bedrooms in the attic. The parlour was the biggest room overall, with one large window where her mother liked to sit and watch the comings and goings on the street below. No doubt she would have seen Captain Delaney and his irritating companion earlier. Anna wondered what she'd thought of them, not to mention her and Henrietta's unprecedented early departure...

'Good evening, Mama.'

She found the scene just as she'd expected, her mother sitting in her customary armchair with an open book in her lap.

'Good evening, dear.' Elizabeth Fortini looked up from her reading with a smile. 'I was starting to wonder where you'd got to.'

'Henrietta wanted a walk in the park so I said that I'd join her.' Anna dropped down onto a sofa, telling herself that it wasn't a lie exactly, even if it wasn't the whole truth, either. 'It was nice to get some fresh air.'

'I'm surprised you had the strength after such a long day.' Her mother tipped her head to one side sympathetically. 'You work too hard, my darling. I wish I could help more.'

'It's not your fault, Mama.' Anna gestured towards her mother's swollen fingers. 'I know you're in pain.'

'It pains me to see you looking so exhausted, too.' Her mother stood up, wincing as she put weight on to her ankles. 'I'll make us some dinner.'

'It's all right, I'll do it in a few minutes.'

'You will not.' Her mother limped slowly across the room. 'I may not be much help in the shop any more, but I can still be useful in other ways. Now you have a rest and I'll be back soon.'

Anna smiled gratefully, too tired to argue. She was almost too tired to eat, although she knew that she had to. More than that, she was tired of simply *being* tired, but there seemed to be no way around it. There was always so much to *do*. When she wasn't baking, she was wrapping or stacking or cleaning or sweeping or preparing tins or doing one of the hundred other tasks that seemed to require her constant attention. Henrietta was an able assistant, but she only arrived at seven o'clock in the morning when the baking was already done and left again at four in the afternoon. Anna couldn't afford to pay longer hours, which meant that any remaining jobs fell to her and they were...*relentless*.

Yawning, she tipped her head back and closed her eyes. Things hadn't been so bad while her father was still alive. After the swelling in her mother's joints had started ten years before, first in her fingers and toes, then in her hands and feet, Anna had taken on more and more of her responsibilities in the shop and enjoyed them, too. She'd enjoyed running a business, unlike Sebastian who'd gone off in search of adventure the moment he'd turned seventeen. *She'd* been the one to suggest they start making cinnamon and rosewater-infused biscuits and to start offering tins as well as cloth-wrapped bundles.

In return, her father had taught her everything he knew, which was a great deal, but unfortunately not how to find extra hours in the day or how to go without sleep, either. His sudden heart failure had left her with a shop to run as well as an ailing, grieving mother to take care of. Not that she resented either task, but it was hard sometimes *not* to feel trapped in an endless cycle of monotonous chores. No matter how much she saved, it still wasn't enough for a holiday—just a few days, or weeks preferably, to break free of the routine and maybe travel a little. It didn't have to be far, just somewhere different. Somewhere to enjoy a little free time to read or to walk or to simply lie around daydreaming...

For some reason, the thought of daydreaming conjured up an image of Captain Delaney. His hair, somewhere between chestnut and auburn, those startling pale eyes and that deep voice that made her insides feel curiously soft and malleable, like an undercooked biscuit. He'd looked so handsome waiting for her and Henrietta in the park that she'd *almost* been tempted to take his arm when he'd offered it to her, but common sense had prevailed. She'd known better than to trust a *gentleman*.

As it turned out, however, she'd been wrong about him. She'd been so certain that he'd been trying to distract her in the shop, but apparently he really *had* been there to buy biscuits. She'd assumed the worst and discovered the exact opposite. Aristocratic though he obviously was, he was also a naval captain and not just any naval captain, but a national hero, a brave and honourable man instead of the rake she'd assumed. Their conversation in the park had been genuinely interesting and without any of the mocking undertones she'd detected earlier. Instead, his manner had been open and honest, enough that she'd felt able to appeal to his better nature to save Henrietta. Admittedly, he'd seemed somewhat taken aback by the request at first, so much so that for a few moments she'd thought he'd been offended on his friend's behalf, but to her relief his words had eventually proven otherwise.

Only the severity of his expression when he'd asked if her comments about gentlemen were based upon personal experience had unsettled her, conjuring up memories she preferred to forget. Then his gaze had seemed to bore into the back of her head, giving the uncomfortable impression that he could read all of her secrets. Thankfully he hadn't persisted in his questioning, asking her to trust him instead, and his gaze had softened then, causing a warm, tingling sensation in her chest. The feeling had actually been quite pleasant, as if some kind of unspoken communication were passing between them. It had made her decide to trust him, although she still couldn't help but wonder if she'd done the right thing by leaving Henrietta.

Whether she had or hadn't, however, she was far too tired to think about it now. But she liked his name, she thought sleepily. *Captain Samuel Delaney.* It had a nice ring to it, an authoritative ring, and it was nice to know that a few *real* gentlemen still existed in the world, even if it was unlikely that she'd ever see him again. Gentlemen who looked even more attractive when they turned out to be captains and bought biscuits for their grandmothers...

'I have a present for you.' Samuel deposited the tin he'd been carrying for the better part of two hours into his grandmother's narrow lap. 'Don't say I never give you anything.'

'Except for white hairs and anxiety, you mean?' Lady Jarrow regarded the offering with an air of suspicion. 'What is it?'

'They're Belles... *Biscuits*,' he clarified as his grandmother stared at him blankly. 'I'm told they're famous in Bath.'

'I've never heard of them in my life.'

'I have.' His grandfather's steel-rimmed spectacles peered over the top of a newspaper opposite. 'They're something of an institution, actually.'

'Do you mean to say you've eaten them before?' His

grandmother sounded as shocked as if her husband had just announced an illegitimate child.

'Dozens. I discovered them a few years ago and now I insist upon having one every morning when I'm in town. Two, sometimes.'

'Then why haven't I eaten one before?'

'I'm sure you have, my dear.' The newspaper lifted again. 'Only you were probably busy thinking about a new saddle or something.'

'Harumph.' Lady Jarrow made short work of the ribbon. 'I have a perfectly good collection of saddles, as you very well know. If anything, I'd be thinking about riding boots. I could do with a new pair.' She removed the lid and tossed it at Samuel. 'Well, this looks very pretty, I must say. I'll ring for tea. I can't abide sweet things without it.'

'I'm glad that you approve, Grandmother.'

Samuel sprawled in an armchair, looking between his grandparents with a combination of amusement and affection. Aside from his mother and half-sister in Cumberland they were the only family he had, not that he'd ever had a great many family members to speak of. Thanks to his father's notoriety in gambling, drinking and generally throwing away his inheritance, no one from the paternal side of the family had ever deigned to acknowledge Samuel, too afraid he might prove to be a chip off the old block. They'd all thought of him as tainted, refusing to budge from that opinion no matter how hard he'd tried, during the past ten years anyway, to prove otherwise.

Fortunately, his maternal relations had been made of sterner stuff, refusing to let the sins of a detested son-in-law influence their feelings for his offspring. His grandmother in particular had always been a force to be reckoned with, a renowned beauty in her youth as well as an heiress, though she'd always preferred spending time with her horses to listening to recitations of love poetry from her many admirers. She'd sat doggedly on the shelf until the shockingly great age of eight and twenty, until the day she'd set eyes on the bookish and shy Lord Jarrow. Seven years her junior, the young Baron had been as surprised as anyone by her sudden interest. Somewhat alarmed, too, since, as he frequently remarked to his grandson, when it came to a battle of wills he'd known he hadn't stood a chance. Where Georgiana had a will, she got her way. Their marriage had gone ahead with almost indecent haste and they'd immediately retired to the country to build a new block of stables and restock the library. *He'd* had his books, *she'd* had her horses, and they'd lived in perfect contentment for fifty years ever since. It was, in Samuel's opinion, an excellent example of a happy marriage. Quite unlike that of his parents.

'Have you been to the Pump Rooms today?' he enquired of the newspaper.

'Of course he has,' his grandmother answered, as was frequently the case, for her husband. 'It's the reason we're staying in this wretched city, after all.'

'There are still parks for riding in, Grandmother.'

'Pshaw! It's hardly riding when one's constantly expected to stop and make conversation. You'd think that horses were simply chairs! If people don't care about their animals, then they'd be better off using their feet.'

Samuel chuckled, though the very fact of his grandmother's presence in Bath made him uneasy. On every other occasion when his grandfather had come to take the medicinal waters she'd remained at their home in Rutland. The fact that she'd joined him this time suggested the seventy-one-year-old Baron's health was worse than either of them were letting on.

'I thought we might all go together on Monday,' his grandfather commented, folding his newspaper as the tea tray arrived. 'We could make a family outing of it, so to speak.'

'I'd be delighted, Grandfather.'

'Well, *I* wouldn't, but I will because I'm a good wife.' The Baroness lifted her eyebrows provocatively, though neither Samuel nor his grandfather were foolish enough to contradict the statement. 'But only on two conditions. One, that I don't have to drink any of that disgusting liquid. Two, that Samuel wears his uniform.'

'Grandmother...'

'Yes, I know, you're officially on sick leave, but you're still a captain until this whole inheritance matter is resolved and you look so dashing in uniform.'

'Let him be, Georgiana.' The Baron's bushy white eyebrows gave his frown a somewhat ferocious aspect. 'You know it only makes him feel worse about the whole business.'

'How anyone can feel worse about potentially inheriting an earldom is beyond me. Most reasonable people would be thrilled by the prospect.'

'Because of the entail.' His grandfather shook his head. 'It's a bad business altogether. Cruel, really. We just have to wait and see whether the widow has a boy or a girl.'

'Well, I wish that she'd hurry and make up her mind.' Lady Jarrow snorted contemptuously. 'I had a boy first and a girl second because that's what I wanted. It's all a question of mind over matter.'

'In which case, she'll have a boy for certain, my dear.'

'Only if she has a strong enough will, which I doubt. I met her once and she seemed insipid. No interest in horses at all. She hasn't even had the decency to reply to Samuel's letter.'

'What could she say, Grandmother?' Samuel shifted in his seat uncomfortably. 'The letter I sent was one of condolence.'

'She might still have acknowledged the situation. Yes, the entail makes things awkward, but you should be allowed to visit Staunton at least. If the estate turns out to be yours, then you need to know how it's run.'

'I've no wish to visit Staunton.'

'Well, somebody should. She could be undermining your inheritance as we speak.'

'Since it might be her son's, then I doubt it.'

'The whole situation is completely ridiculous. Your injury's recovered, but your life is on hold while we wait for some insipid woman to give birth.'

'It's far worse for her. She's lost her husband and now her whole future depends on the gender of her baby.' Samuel reached into the tin of biscuits with a sigh. For some reason, the rows of tissue paper looked comforting. 'I don't want the inheritance anyway. I just want everything to go back to the way it was a year ago.'

'A year ago Trafalgar hadn't happened. You'd still be blockading the English Channel and giving me new wrinkles from worry.' His grandmother sniffed. 'Personally I'm glad the Admiralty won't let you go back to sea until matters are settled. They're probably worried about drowning a peer of the realm.'

'It's not just that.' Samuel took a bite of biscuit, surprised to find that he liked rosewater flavour even more than cinnamon. 'The Admiralty thinks that the war at sea is over and all the fighting will be on land from now on. They're trying to get captains off the payroll, no matter what they say about my *duty* to Staunton.'

'None the less, I'm afraid they're right about it, my boy.' His grandfather threw him a sympathetic look. 'If you do inherit, then you have a duty to look after the estate, not to mention all the tenants who live there. You're the last man standing, so to speak, on your father's side of the family anyway.'

Samuel rubbed a hand over his forehead. 'That's what's so strange about it. My father's father and brother never wanted anything to do with me. They've practically disowned me since birth, yet now I'm the heir to some cousin I've never even met.'

'Stranger things have happened.'

'If they didn't want it to happen then they should have had more sons themselves!' There was an iron glint in his grandmother's eye. 'This is all their own doing.'

'Perhaps they oughtn't to have died either, my dear. That was rather weak-willed of them, too, don't you think?'

Samuel made a wry face as his grandfather winked at him. 'Their lawyers must have scoured the entire family tree looking for somebody else to inherit.'

'Perhaps, but the law's the law. You're the heir, whether people like it or not.'

'*If* it's a girl.'

'Well, I for one hope that it is,' his grandmother declared. 'It'll be a poke in the eye for anyone who ever cut you in society. I might not have approved of your father, which is a ludicrous understatement, but I always said that my daughter was free to make her own choices, however unutterably stupid.' Her face softened. 'But their marriage did give us you so I suppose it wasn't all bad. Now we just need to get you established and breeding heirs of your own.'

'Grandmother,' Samuel groaned. 'I'll inherit the earldom if I really must, but I draw the line at starting a dynasty.'

'You'll have to someday.'

'Not necessarily and definitely not straight away.'

'Pshaw, now you're being selfish. All I want is another little boy like you, even if I'll be too old to raise him myself this time.'

Samuel smiled affectionately. For all his grandmother's strong opinions, he couldn't have asked for a better surrogate mother. 'In that case, how can I refuse to wear my uniform on Monday? Just this once.'

'Excellent.' Lady Jarrow looked satisfied. 'And I wouldn't be surprised if the Pump Rooms are slightly busier than usual. News of a certain eligible bachelor's presence in Bath has already spread. I should imagine that several debutantes are on their way here as we speak.'

'Good grief, aren't there enough prospective husbands in London?'

'Not enough to go around, apparently. Besides, the Season hasn't started yet.'

'Well, I'm not eligible, not yet anyway.'

'True, but I imagine a few of them will want to get in the running early, just in case.'

'Then that makes them gamblers and you know how I feel about those. They remind me of Father.'

'You could always go to Staunton.'

'Grandmother...'

'Oh, all right, I'll settle for the Pump Rooms. We'll cut quite a dash with you in uniform.'

'And forget all about me, I suppose.' The Baron dipped his hand into the tin of biscuits. 'I say, all three types. It's hard to know where to begin.'

'Have one of each,' Samuel suggested.

'He will not!' His grandmother sounded outraged. 'We're here to make him fit and healthy again, not to fill him with treats.'

'I'm not a horse, my dear, and some things are a lost cause.' Her husband gave her an inscrutable look.

'Not if I have anything to do with it. You may have *one* biscuit and that's all.' She took a bite of her own, screwing her face up as if preparing to spit it out again, before nodding approvingly. 'Quite tasty. What did you say they were called again?'

'Belles. That's the name of the shop, too. It's a charming little place.'

'Indeed it is.' The Baron scooped up another biscuit before his wife could stop him. 'Have you met the eponymous Annabelle? A delightful young lady.'

Samuel lifted an eyebrow in surprise. *Was* she delightful? Prickly and forthright seemed like a more apt description, except for during those last few minutes in the park when she'd appealed to him for help. Then she'd been fairly inspiring...

On the other hand, maybe she *was* delightful in a way. If they'd met under different circumstances, then he might have thought so, too, from the start. She was definitely unique, or at least he didn't think he'd ever met anyone quite like her before. She wasn't impressed by rank, that much had been obvious by the contemptuous way she'd spoken to him and Ralph, seeming far more likely to lift her nose in the air than to bow or scrape, and she certainly knew how to stand up for herself. He liked both of those things about her, just as much as he liked her bouncy dark curls and the swirling depths of those wide coffee-brown eyes. She wasn't as obviously beautiful as the employee she called her friend, but in his personal opinion she was a hundred times more appealing. He even liked her voice, with its hint of an accent he couldn't quite place. It wasn't that of Bath, though it contained hints of the west country and even an occasional Italian inflection. It was...unique. He kept coming back to that word. It seemed like the perfect way to describe her. Not that he was about to tell his grandparents any of that.

'I met her briefly, yes,' he answered when he realised his silence had gone on a few moments too long. 'She seemed pleasant enough.'

'Aye, very pleasant. Do you know, we once talked about bees for half an hour?'

'Bees?'

'Yes, I thought that they looked like a pair of bees, her and that other girl in their yellow dresses, and that put me in mind of the hives at home. Before I knew it I was telling her all about them. I completely lost track of the time.'

'Poor girl.' The Baroness batted his hand away from the box as it drifted back again.

'She seemed interested, my dear.'

'She's a saleswoman. She had to seem interested or you might not have bought anything.'

'Ah...you may have a point. None the less, Miss Fortini makes excellent biscuits.'

'Fortini?' His grandmother's voice sharpened abruptly.

'Yes.' Samuel lifted an eyebrow. 'What's the matter with that?'

'I'm not sure. There's just something familiar...' She

pursed her lips and then shook her head. 'Well, never mind. I'm sure it'll come to me eventually. When I'm out riding most likely. In any case, I approve of her biscuits. You may bring me a tin whenever you wish.'

'I'll remember that.' Samuel popped the remainder of his own biscuit into his mouth and reached for his tea. Unfortunately, the beverage itself was disappointing. Tea was all well and good, but he still felt a powerful craving for coffee.

Chapter Five

'Are you honestly telling me that you feel better?'

Samuel winced as his grandmother's contralto tones boomed out across the Abbey courtyard. At least twenty heads turned in their direction as they emerged from the Pump Rooms and made their way towards Bath Street.

'Yes, actually.' After five decades of practice, his grandfather was unruffled by either his wife's deafening volume or her cynical pronouncements.

'I don't know how you can bear to drink something that smells so revolting.'

'It's a natural spring, my dear. That's how it smells when it comes out of the ground.'

'Well, they might try to mask the odour somehow.' The Baroness took Samuel's arm and gave him a nudge in the ribs. 'I've heard that sailors always carry a flask of rum wherever they go. I'd far rather drink some of that.'

'I'm afraid I must have forgotten mine today, Grandmother, although I do know a rather good hostelry close by. I'm sure you'd fit right in.'

'Your grandmother doesn't fit into places, my boy, you know that. She simply takes over wherever she goes. If she'd been born a man, she would have been a general the day after she joined the army.'

'Or, better still, an admiral in the navy,' Samuel pointed out. 'We could have won Trafalgar in half the time.'

'You both know very well that I would have led a cavalry regiment.' The Baroness looked down her nose at them reprovingly. 'And made a damn fine job of it, too.'

'Naturally.' Samuel started to laugh and then stopped, his attention drawn by the sight of a woman's head peering out from behind one of the pillars of the colonnade up ahead. She seemed to be hiding in the shadows, or trying to anyway, but there was something familiar about her profile and that mass of wild curls... Miss Fortini? He came to an abrupt halt, bringing his grandmother up short.

'Samuel?' The Baroness looked at him as if he were a disobedient horse. If she'd been wearing spurs, he wouldn't have been surprised to find himself prodded. 'What on earth's the matter?'

'Forgive me, Grandmother, but I've just seen an acquaintance I need to speak to. You both continue without me.'

'Will be you back at the house for luncheon?'

'I think so.'

'You *think* so?' This time she looked as if she were considering a swift kick to his flanks. 'Well, don't expect us to wait if you're late.'

'I wouldn't dream of it. Unless you'd care to take pity on me, of course.'

He grinned as she gave a contemptuous snort, waiting

until she and his grandfather were a few feet away before weaving his way through the other pedestrians, heading for the covered walkway at the side of the street and then curving around so that he approached the pillar from behind. Miss Fortini was still there, still peering out from the shadows, her hands clutching hold of the stone pillar as if she were poised and ready to dart behind it. She wasn't wearing any gloves, he noticed, or even a bonnet, just a shawl thrown haphazardly over her shoulders as if she'd come out in a rush. She was also clearly unaware of his presence, allowing him a moment to study the nape of her neck and the escaped dark ringlets framing each side of her head. They looked so soft and springy that he was tempted to curl his fingers around them.

'Miss Fortini?'

He said her name gently, though she still performed a mini-pirouette, bumping the back of her head against the pillar as she let out a startled, albeit quickly muffled shriek.

'Captain Delaney?' She put a hand over her chest, her bosom rising and falling erratically as her expression turned from surprise to relief to embarrassment in the space of a few short seconds. 'Good day.'

'Are you all right?' He started to reach for her head and then stopped himself. 'That was quite a bump. I didn't mean to startle you.'

'Oh, it's nothing.' She waved her other hand dismissively. 'I'm sure it looked worse than it felt.'

'Ah…good.' He studied her for a few moments in silence, struggling to make sense of her now guilty expression, before gesturing out at the busy street. 'It's a pleasant morning for a stroll.' He tried to sound as if there were nothing unusual about her behaviour. 'Is your shop closed today?'

'No… I mean, yes. That is, just for a few minutes. I had something important to attend to.' She lifted her chin, worrying her bottom lip between her teeth in a way that made her mouth look redder and distinctly plumper all of a sudden. Positively juicy, in fact.

'Ah.' He glanced enquiringly at the pillar and then back again. 'Anything I might assist you with?'

'Assist me?' She blinked, her dark gaze moving over his uniform as if she were just noticing it for the first time.

'Yes.' He smiled. 'You know, you remind me of my first Captain, Miss Fortini. He was a tyrant for inspections. Do I pass muster?'

'Oh.' Her eyes shot back to his, her cheeks reddening to match her swollen mouth. 'I'm sorry, I was just thinking.'

'About my offer of help? It was quite genuine, I assure you.'

'Thank you. And thank you for what you did the other night. Henrietta told me that you took Mr Hoxley away like you promised.'

'You're welcome.'

'Only… I'm afraid the situation involves her again.' She seemed to come to a decision, beckoning for him to come closer before pointing around the edge of the pillar. He looked dutifully. Her apprentice was standing next to a market stall at the far end of the street.

'She told me she was unwell. A headache.'

'And you didn't believe her?' Samuel pulled back, feeling vaguely ridiculous to be peeking out from behind a pillar in broad daylight.

'No. She's been acting strangely for days and she's a terrible liar. I could tell that she felt bad about deceiving me, too, so I knew something was going on.'

'So you closed up your shop and followed her? That doesn't sound very good for business.'

'Some things are more important.' She gave him a narrow-eyed glance. 'I expect you think that it's nothing to do with me.'

'I wouldn't say that exactly…'

He made a face. In his personal opinion, what her employee did in her own free time *was* nothing to do with her, let alone him, but if the girl was supposed to be working, then it *wasn't* strictly speaking her free time…and it *was* Miss Fortini's business that she'd been lied to. Frankly, he was starting to think that her assistant was more trouble than she was worth, but Miss Fortini obviously cared about her. Most employers would have dismissed her on the spot for lying.

'What is it that you suspect her of?'

'I think that she's come to meet someone.'

'Someone being Mr Hoxley?' He frowned, already anticipating the answer.

'Yes. He's been in the shop every day this week. I know he's your friend, but…'

She let the words trail away, although Samuel didn't finish them. Instead, he took a farther step back into the shadows, thinking. He hadn't seen Ralph since the evening he'd practically manhandled him out of Sydney Gardens, delivering a stern lecture about his behaviour on the way. He'd warned him off visiting the shop on Swainswick Crescent again, too, although he'd stopped short of actually threatening him. They'd been close companions once and he hadn't wanted to ruin the memory of their friendship entirely. Unfortunately, it seemed that he'd been too easy on him.

'I'm sure it's all perfectly innocent in Henrietta's mind,' Miss Fortini went on, 'only she has romantic ideas.'

'Is that so terrible? Surely a few romantic ideas are a good thing?'

She gave him a look that implied she'd expected better. 'I live in the real world, Captain, as I'm sure so do you. Gentlemen like Mr Hoxley don't marry girls like Henrietta. He might offer to set her up as his mistress, but that's all.'

Samuel arched an eyebrow, thinking it was a good thing he'd grown up with his grandmother or he might have been shocked to hear a woman speak about mistresses quite so openly. Not one of the well-bred young ladies he'd met in the Pump Rooms that morning would have ever contemplated using the word. Quite a few had probably never even heard of it.

Miss Fortini, on the other hand, stated it as a matter of fact, which, he had to concede, it probably was. Ralph's position as the third son of a minor baronet meant that he needed a rich wife and, unfortunately for his nymph, a shop assistant was never going to be that.

'There!' Miss Fortini uttered a sudden cry of dismay, pointing down the street to where the man in question was just now swaggering around the corner. Samuel leaned forward again, half appalled, half intrigued by the scene. Surely even Ralph wouldn't conduct a liaison in one of Bath's most famous streets? His reputation was disreputable enough, but this was outrageous even for him.

'He's walking right past her!' Miss Fortini whispered indignantly, seemingly afraid of being overheard despite there being at least ten feet and a dozen people between them and Ralph. 'Oh! He's looking this way!'

She shifted backwards, the rounded curve of her bottom

bumping forcefully against Samuel's groin before she spun around and flattened herself against the pillar, her eyes wide with a look of alarm. 'Do you think he saw me?'

'I don't think so.' Although he'd certainly see *him*, Samuel thought, if he didn't move completely into the shadows, too. He could hardly have made himself look any more conspicuous in his naval uniform. There was nothing he could do but take a step closer towards Miss Fortini, bracing his hands on the pillar on either side of her waist.

It was a slender waist, he observed, though not so slender that he was afraid she might snap in a strong wind, flaring out into perfectly proportioned hips. She was reasonably tall for a woman, too, with legs long enough that when she'd stepped back against him he'd found it momentarily hard to think straight, a flood of heat rushing straight to the lower part of his body. He was still feeling somewhat befuddled now since the front of his trousers was only a few inches away from the legs and hips in question and their close proximity was doing nothing to diminish the effect.

Fortunately, Miss Fortini appeared blissfully unaware of his body's reaction. Unaware of him altogether, in fact, so taken up with the idea of saving her friend that she seemed oblivious to the impropriety of their position. He had her pinned up against a pillar in broad daylight, for pity's sake! A swift glance over his shoulder showed there was no one else under the covered part of the colonnade, but anyone who cared to look deeper into the shadows would take *him* for the rake, not Ralph. And how he was supposed to care about that when her breasts were heaving so tantalisingly close to his chest he had no idea!

'What's happening?' she whispered, her large brown eyes

darting from side to side as if she could somehow see behind her. 'Is he going back to meet her?'

'Mmm?' For a moment, Samuel had no idea what she was talking about, his gaze transfixed by the flawless bow shape of her mouth. He hadn't paid her lips enough attention before, he chided himself, distracted by her many other attractive qualities, but now he found himself wanting to explore them in slow and intimate detail.

'Is he going back to Henrietta?'

'Oh…wait a moment.' Samuel gathered his scattered thoughts with an effort, sucking in a deep breath before stealing a look around the edge of the pillar. 'No.' He frowned. 'He's walking this way and she's following him. They must have arranged to meet like this.' His frown deepened with every word. It was typical of Ralph to flaunt his position so blatantly in front of the girl. He seemed to be stopping every few seconds to speak to some acquaintance or another, making her wait each time. It was just the kind of egotistical, self-aggrandising joke that he would enjoy.

'I need to do something!' Miss Fortini started forward, but Samuel kept his arms in place, restraining her against the pillar.

'Do what exactly?'

'Talk some sense into her!'

'Something tells me that you've already covered the subject quite thoroughly.'

The way her eyelashes fluttered confirmed it. 'Then what do you suggest I do? I can't just let her go with him!'

'No, but if you interfere now then they'll only arrange something else. You'll only delay the inevitable.'

'Then what *can* I do?'

He held on to her gaze, his whole body pulsing with an

awareness of hers. Every one of his nerve endings seemed to be tingling and straining towards her. She looked so fierce and determined that he was seized with the same near-over-whelming urge to kiss her that he'd felt in the park. Which was quite possibly the stupidest idea imaginable under the circumstances. It certainly wasn't a solution to their current problem. He had no idea what to do about that... And then he did, the answer coming to him in a blinding flash as he glanced along the street and saw that Ralph wasn't the only person who'd stopped to talk. His grandmother was holding court amid a gathering of acquaintances.

He pulled one hand away from the pillar to rub across his chin, considering. It wouldn't be the most honourable course of action, but it might be the most effective. Non-violent, too, which would save him from having to pummel some decency into his former friend.

'Stay here and don't let your assistant see you.' He took a step away from her. 'I know someone who can help us.'

'Wait!' Miss Fortini lifted a hand so quickly that it collided with his chest, her palm pressing flat over his heart. He stopped at once, feeling as if every muscle in his body had suddenly gone into spasm.

She must have felt something similar because her eyes widened and then dipped abruptly, a small gasp escaping her throat as she jerked her hand away again. 'Forgive me, it was nothing.'

Nothing. He swallowed thickly. Whatever else it was, it was definitely *not* nothing. His heart was thumping a pain-fully rapid tattoo against the walls of his ribcage and his lungs seemed incapable of dragging in enough air. The pillar, the street, the crowd of people standing just a few feet away...all of them seemed to disappear and there was only her and him and a gathering heat that seemed to sear the very air between them… His gaze focused on the delicate flutter of her pulse at the base of her throat and, without thinking, he lifted a finger to touch it, rubbing his hand gently across the silky soft skin of her neck before sliding it around the back of her head and into the dark mass of her hair. He wanted to see her curls loose, he thought, swallowing again at the feeling of luxurious spirals against his fingertips. He wanted to see them wild and free, tumbling over her naked shoulders and breasts…

He cleared his throat, surprised by the vividness of the image in his mind's eye. 'There's nothing to forgive, Miss Fortini. Leave this to me.'

Anna sagged back against the pillar, willing her breathing to return to normal and for the cold stone to have a cooling effect on her body. What had she been thinking, reaching out to Captain Delaney in such an intimate way? In that moment she hadn't even cared that he was a gentleman! She'd simply acted by instinct, not wanting him to leave despite his offer of help, pressing her fingers against the solid wall of his chest as if *she* were the one there for a private assignation!

Not that he seemed to have minded. On the contrary, he'd touched her back, the gentle caress of his fingertips against her bare skin setting off a series of small fireworks inside her body. The expression on his face hadn't been one of disapproval or disgust, either. It had been surprised, arrested…hungry?

Hungry for what?

Whatever it was, she'd wanted it, too. She *still* did, though the empty, tugging, tremulous sensation in her stomach felt more like an ache than hunger. On the other hand, maybe she was just confused. She certainly felt confused. Her skin was covered in goose pimples though she was red-hot all over and her mind was spinning so fast she felt giddy.

With a gargantuan effort she forced her mind back to the situation with Henrietta, peering out from behind the pillar again. What was Captain Delaney doing? He wasn't heading towards his friend. Instead, he was striding purposefully towards an elderly-looking couple standing arm in arm at the end of the street. The woman in particular was striking, swathed from head to toe in dark purple with white hair, an upright, confident bearing and a long aquiline nose that tilted upwards as he approached.

She threw a swift glance towards Henrietta, wondering if she'd noticed him pass by, but it seemed not. Her friend was standing a few paces behind Mr Hoxley, apparently searching in her reticule for something, though in reality waiting for him. Anna felt her cheeks burn with indignation. How dared he! Not just try to seduce her friend, but to demean her like this? Forcing her to wait in the street as if she were his servant or some other female paid to do his bidding. It was just the kind of arrogant, entitled, *aristocratic* gesture that made her blood boil!

She curled her hands into fists, tempted to march out into the street and tell him exactly what she thought of him and his whole domineering class, but Captain Delaney had told her to wait and after asking for his help she ought to at least see what he planned. Of course *he* was a member of the same upper class as his friend, but there were exceptions to every rule. *He* was a rarity, a pearl among swine, almost too good to be true and even more strikingly handsome in his uniform than he was in his everyday attire. When she'd first noticed what he was wearing she'd felt an obscure urge to salute. His white trousers were practically moulded to his legs and his dark blue tailcoat, complete with epaulets and gold embroidery around the collar, encased his broad shoulders like a second skin. It was strange that Sebastian's lieutenant's uniform had never made her feel quite so tremulous inside, but then Sebastian was her brother and Captain Delaney was... Well, there was nothing remotely brotherly about the way she'd just reacted to him.

The older woman, however, *must* have been some kind of relation because he stepped right up to her without preamble, speaking into her ear as if he were sharing some kind of confidence. As Anna watched, the woman stiffened, but he laid a hand on her arm, saying a few more words before removing it again. Whatever it was obviously did the trick. Anna had the distinct and faintly startling impression of a powerful energy being suddenly unleashed, like a lightning bolt striking down from a cloud. The moment his hand fell away the woman launched forward, waving her walking stick out in front of her like a weapon, though the martial gleam in her eye was enough to make most bystanders dart out of the way.

The only person who appeared oblivious to her wrathful approach was Mr Hoxley himself. He had his back turned towards her, laughing with a group of fashionable-looking young dandies. It was only at the last moment that he appeared to sense his impending doom and turned to find himself nose to nose with what Anna could only describe as a force of nature.

'Lady Jarrow.' Mr Hoxley attempted to make a bow, though the endeavour was thwarted by the fact that her face was so close and he could hardly do so without butting her in the head.

'Hoxley.' The woman looked him up and down in a manner that suggested he was little more than a worm beneath her feet. 'I am *appalled*!'

Anna caught her breath and then clapped a hand over her mouth, repressing a strong urge to giggle. Lady Jarrow, as he'd just called her, wasn't making the slightest attempt to be discreet, every word she uttered clearly audible to their now captivated audience. A trumpet, an entire marching band even, would have made less of an impact.

'Madam.' Mr Hoxley looked as if he'd just developed some kind of fever, his cheeks flushing a vivid shade of crimson. 'I can't imagine what I've done to offend you.'

'Can't you? Because I've been hearing rumours about you. Disturbing rumours. Lechery! Wantonness! *Debauchery!* You ought to be ashamed of yourself.'

'I can assure you…'

'And with your mother's own lady's maid! Never mind how hard it is to find decent maids these days, but I hear the poor woman was dismissed after her indiscretion with you. Have you no shame?' She lifted her stick and prodded one end into his chest. 'Well? Defend yourself if you can!'

For an infinitesimal moment, Anna felt sorry for the victim of the harangue. He was producing a series of strangled-sounding gurgles, though he appeared to have nothing coherent to say for himself.

'If I were you, Hoxley…' Lady Jarrow took another step closer, seeming to grow in height while further diminishing his, forcing him to stagger backwards '… I would go home to the country and take some time to reflect on the virtues of a quiet life. You have a reasonable head upon your shoulders, boy. You ought to try using it once in a while instead of distressing your poor mother and father and *before* you get some other poor girl into trouble.'

As she uttered the last words her gaze flickered past Hoxley towards Henrietta, whose face was even redder and more stricken than his. Anna tightened her grip on the pillar, resisting the urge to rush out and comfort her, though she could see that the woman's words were having the desired effect. Henrietta was already backing away, fleeing the scene before Hoxley could say or do anything to stop her.

'Well, now.' Lady Jarrow's lips curved into a satisfied-looking smile. 'I believe that my work here is done.'

'My lady...'

Hoxley continued to splutter ineffectually as she turned her back on him, marching away as briskly as she'd come. Anna's gaze travelled with her, past the now busily gossiping audience to where Captain Delaney stood with his shoulders rigid and arms folded in front of him. He looked... *What* did he look? Angry, regretful, sombre? Somehow his expression suggested all three at once. Judging by the furious look that Hoxley was shooting in his direction, their friendship was well and truly over. And it was *her* doing. She'd asked Captain Delaney to side with her over his friend and he had. He'd saved Henrietta for her and she had no idea why.

She was still wondering when he unfolded his arms and looked straight at her, tipping his hat in a gesture of farewell before taking the older woman's arm and walking away.

Chapter Six

'Well, now, am I allowed to enquire what all that was about?' Samuel's grandfather spoke first, his tone faintly bewildered. 'You certainly sent that fellow away with his tail between his legs.'

'I was saving a damsel in distress, Hector.' The Baroness looked eminently pleased with herself. 'Even if she wasn't aware of it.'

'A damsel who didn't know she was in distress? How extraordinary. Well then, good show I'd say.'

'I couldn't have put it better myself.' Samuel threw her a grateful look. 'You're one in a thousand, Grandmother.'

'Is that all?'

'A million, then.'

'It was rather bracing, actually.' She chuckled. 'I never did like that Hoxley boy. What on earth persuaded you to take up with him again?'

'Old times' sake, I suppose.' Samuel shrugged. 'Only it turns out we don't have a great deal in common any more.'

'I'm relieved to hear it, but now I think it's time that you explained *why* you asked me to denounce the man in public. Not that I had any objections, but you don't usually ask others to fight your battles for you.'

'No.' Samuel frowned at the reminder. 'I wouldn't have done so today, except that it struck me as the most persuasive course of action.'

'I presume it had something to do with that very pretty blonde-haired girl hovering in the background?'

'Yes. She was intent on going with Ralph and I couldn't think of any other way to stop her.'

'And why exactly is her virtue any of *your* concern?' His grandmother fixed him with an interrogatory stare. 'I hope that you don't have similar designs on the girl yourself?'

'None at all, but I was asked to intervene by an acquaintance.'

'What kind of acquaintance?'

'Just somebody I met the other day.'

'Male or female?'

Samuel heaved a sigh. His grandmother was doing her best impression of a bloodhound, which meant that there was no escaping telling her the truth now. 'Miss Fortini, the owner of Belles, if you must know.'

'The bee girl?' His grandfather perked up at once. 'I didn't see her anywhere.'

'She was hiding behind a pillar.'

'Behind a pillar?' His grandmother sounded mystified. 'Then tell me, why were you intervening on behalf of a woman you only met a few days ago?'

'Because the situation was partly my fault. It's complicated. Suffice to say, I went along with a scheme of Ralph's that I shouldn't have and it was my responsibility to put things right.'

'And this Miss Fortini is *just* an acquaintance?'

'Yes. There's really nothing more to it.'

'Pity.' His grandfather stopped to rest on his cane. 'I would have applauded your good taste if there had been.'

'Hector!' his grandmother scolded. 'Good taste or not, *she* is a shopkeeper and *Samuel* might be an earl in another two months. If you're suggesting that he conduct some kind of dalliance then I shall have no qualms about denouncing both of you in public, too. As for anything more serious, she's entirely unsuitable.'

'Oh, I wouldn't say *entirely*.' The Baron sounded unperturbed. 'Not when you consider who her mother is.'

'Who's her mother?' Samuel and his grandmother spoke at the same time.

'Oh, you know, the Duke of Messingham's youngest daughter, the one who ran off with a footman.' He scratched his head with his cane. 'It must be twenty-five years ago now. An Italian fellow, as I recall. It caused quite a scandal at the time.'

'You mean Elizabeth?' The Baroness looked confounded. 'Hector, do you mean to tell me that she's been living in Bath all this time and running a *biscuit* shop?'

'Aye, that's right, Elizabeth, that was her name. I say, you were quite close with the old Duchess once upon a time, weren't you?'

'Yes, although I thought she acted stupidly about the whole thing and I told her so. Of course she took umbrage, but I said my piece. There was no need to denounce the girl and cut her off completely. I'm sure she and that pig-headed husband of hers came to regret it, but of course, the rest of society took its cue from them.'

'Wait.' Samuel put a staying hand up. 'Are you telling me that Miss Annabelle Fortini is the granddaughter of the Duke of Messingham?'

'Oh, yes.' His grandfather nodded serenely. 'The former Duke, anyway. The new one's her uncle, I suppose, but there's no doubting the relationship. She has all those glorious curls just like her grandmother had. Her mother still has them, too, I expect, though I've only caught glimpses of her in the upstairs window.'

'And did it *never* occur to you to mention any of this before?' The Baroness sounded exasperated.

'Come to think of it, I did mean to say something once, but it must have slipped my mind. Then I probably thought I'd already told you.'

'Honestly, Hector! Where is this shop? I must go there and visit at once.'

'Why?' Samuel felt an ominous sense of dread.

'Because I want to see Elizabeth, of course. I remember her quite well, as it happens. She was a pretty young thing. Not bad on horseback at all and—'

'Grandmother,' he interrupted, trying to be tactful. 'After twenty-five years of being ostracised by society, don't you think it might be a bit of a shock if you just march in there, demanding to see her?'

'I can't see why.'

'Well...' Miss Fortini's disparaging comments about the aristocracy flitted through his mind. No wonder she'd been so emphatic '...it might be that she doesn't want anything to do with society any more.'

'Don't be preposterous!'

'It's possible.' Not to mention that if he saw Miss Fortini again then she'd probably want to thank him for what had just happened with Henrietta and his conscience wouldn't be able to stand it. Then he'd *have* to explain exactly *why* he couldn't stand it and he really didn't want to do that. Far better for their acquaintance to end with a tender moment against a pillar than for it to be ruined with the truth.

'Harumph.' His grandmother clucked her tongue. 'Well, in that case go and invite her for tea tomorrow. Both of them, the mother *and* daughter.'

'I'm not sure…'

'Samuel.' His grandmother's expression turned to granite. 'I did a favour for you. *And* Miss Fortini as it turns out. Now it's your turn to do one for me.'

He grimaced, throwing a pleading look towards his grandfather, who shrugged and dropped his eyes to the pavement. 'Oh, very well.'

'Good. Off you go, then.'

'Now?'

'Yes, Hector and I are perfectly capable of walking home by ourselves. Tell Elizabeth that tea is served at four o'clock sharp and that I shan't accept no for an answer. If she vexes me, I shall turn up on her doorstep myself.'

'And get some more biscuits while you're there!' his grandfather chimed in. 'I've already finished the last ones.'

There were three customers waiting on the doorstep when Anna got back to the shop, though fortunately, judging from the lack of any sound from upstairs, her mother was napping and unaware that anything out of the ordinary had happened. She apologised profusely, sold two small tins and one medium-sized one, then headed into the kitchen to make a cup of tea. She needed something to steady her nerves and not just because of what had *almost* happened to Henrietta. Her meeting with Captain Delaney had shaken her considerably, too, so much so that after half an hour her nerves were no closer to recovering.

She hadn't expected to *ever* see him again after their walk in the park, but particularly not when she'd been hiding behind a pillar. The idea that he'd approached specifically to talk to her had been somewhat flattering, though now she thought about it, he'd probably just wondered what she was doing. It must have looked rather as if she'd taken leave of her senses and her subsequent behaviour hadn't exactly helped. *Indiscreet* would be the polite way of describing it. And yet he'd *still* helped her, a fact that made her heart glow.

The doorbell tinkled, and she carried her cup of tea back through to the shop, her pulse jumping and then doubling in speed at the sight of Captain Delaney. *Again.* And this time there was no doubting the fact that he'd come to see her. Which was even more flattering. Positively thrilling, in fact, even if his expression was oddly sombre as he removed his bicorne hat and tucked it under one arm.

'Captain?' She smiled a welcome, smoothing one hand over her apron as she felt her cheeks flush with pleasure. 'Have you run out of biscuits already? I'd be glad to give you another tin as a thank you for your help this afternoon.'

'I don't believe that gratitude is in order.' His voice sounded stern, too.

'But it is. I'm grateful to both you and the lady. Your grandmother, I presume?'

'Yes. Lady Jarrow.'

'Please give her my thanks. The way she upbraided your friend was most impressive.'

'Upbraided…' If she wasn't mistaken, he grimaced. 'Yes, I suppose that's one way to put it.'

'Because you asked her to…' she faltered '…didn't you?'

'In a manner. That is, I explained the circumstances to her and she took the rest upon herself. As I fully expected her to, so…yes.'

'Then I'm indebted.'

'Don't be.' This time the grimace was unmistakable. 'I'm not proud of what I just did. In fact, I'm not proud of anything I've done in regard to you, Miss Fortini.' He snapped his feet together and lifted his shoulders as if he were facing a court martial. 'I've come to make a confession.'

'A confession?' She pressed a hand against her ribcage as her heart started to thump heavily inside it. Whatever he was about to say, she had the sudden, inescapable conviction that she didn't want to hear it. 'I don't understand.'

'Regarding the first time I visited your shop.' He held on to her gaze steadily. 'All of those things you said in the park the other evening about what you'd assumed about me and my motives were true. I *was* helping Mr Hoxley in his flirtation with your apprentice. I *was* attempting to distract you. I *didn't* intend to help him seduce her, but if I'd stopped to consider the matter fully…well, I ought not to have acted so irresponsibly. All I can say is that I'm ashamed of the part I played that day and I apologise for it.'

For a few horrified seconds, Anna thought that she must have misheard him. Or at least she tried to persuade herself that she had. Unfortunately it was impossible to ignore the truth. *Tricked!* She'd been tricked! *I'm ashamed of the part I played that day…* The words were accompanied by a dull thrumming sound in her ears, one that seemed to get louder and louder until it filled her whole head. Which was strange because she hadn't realised that emotions had sounds before, but that was what the thrumming surely was, a whole range of emotions all clamouring to be heard. Surprise, hurt, humiliation and a self-righteous fury that made her want to hurl the contents of her tea cup all over his smartly pressed, gleamingly spotless uniform.

Worst of all, however, was the disappointment, not just in him, but in herself. Hadn't she *known* that this was how the aristocracy behaved, gentlemen especially? Hadn't she *known* better than to trust one of them again? She'd thought she was older and wiser, but she'd been just as stupidly naive as she had been eight years ago, a fool to think any differently of this man just because he was a naval captain, too. He was just as dishonourable as his friend! Although, a small voice at the back of her mind argued, if that were truly the case then surely he wouldn't have apologised? But why on earth was she making excuses for him?

She slammed her cup down on the counter, clenching her teeth as she struggled to maintain an outward appearance of calm. 'So it was all a scheme?'

'Of sorts, yes.'

'And all those other things you said in the park? About the navy and Trafalgar? Were they all lies, too?'

'I've never lied to you, Miss Fortini.'

'No, you allowed me to deceive myself! You should at least have corrected me when I called you *honourable*!'

He inclined his head. 'Perhaps I should have, but I did attempt to make amends by separating your friend and Mr Hoxley that evening. I kept my word about that.'

She tossed her head scornfully, refusing to concede any point in his favour at all. She could feel a hot stinging sensation behind her eyes, but she'd be damned before she let herself cry in front of him. 'Very well then, you've confessed. *Now* you may leave. Forgive me if I ask you not to return.'

'As you wish, although I'm afraid there's one other matter.' He looked uncomfortable. 'I've been sent with a commission from my grandmother. It seems that she and your mother are old acquaintances.'

Anna was vaguely aware of her mouth dropping open, though it took her a few moments to close it again, then a few more to actually think up an answer.

'I doubt that.'

'Her name is Elizabeth, is it not? Lady Elizabeth Holden, the Duke of Messingham's daughter?'

'Her name is Elizabeth Fortini.'

'Of course. I meant her maiden name.'

'That was twenty-five years ago. It's not a name she cares to be associated with any more.'

'I understand, but having only just discovered her identity my grandmother is eager to see her again.' He paused. 'She'd like to invite you both to tea tomorrow afternoon.'

'*No.*'

He lifted an eyebrow at the speed of her refusal. 'You don't wish to consult your mother about it?'

'I don't need to. I know what she'll say. No.'

'I see.' He looked as if he were about to say something else and then changed his mind. 'In that case I respect your decision, Miss Fortini, but I should warn you that my grandmother isn't very good at taking no for an answer.'

'Of course she isn't.' She allowed herself a small, cynical laugh. 'She's an aristocrat. You're all used to getting your own way, aren't you, especially with people like us? Well, for once she'll have to make an exception. If she wants to see my mother then she'll have to get through me and I'm not as easily frightened as Mr Hoxley.' She folded her arms. 'My mother and I don't want anything to do with you or any member of her old life.'

'Very well.' His gaze seemed to harden. 'Whatever you might think about me, however, I believe that my grandmother means well.'

'I've no interest in what she may or may not mean.' Anna stormed towards the door, flinging it open so hard that it bounced back off the wall. 'Now if that's all you have to say...'

'Just one more comment.' He came to stand in the doorway, putting his hat back on with one firm push. 'I believe that you spoke of a debt to my grandmother earlier. This seems like a curious way of repaying it.'

'So you think you can blackmail us into visiting her?'

'No, I just wanted to remind you of your own words.'

'They were spoken under a false estimation of your character!'

'None the less, my grandmother did you a good service today. As for your friend, Mr Hoxley would have continued to pursue her whether I'd accompanied him to your shop or not. In some ways, it was my involvement that saved her.'

'You have a strange sense of logic, sir.'

'Perhaps, but the situation has been resolved, has it not?'

'*Get out!*'

'I'm leaving.' He stepped out onto the street. 'However, in case you change your mind, my grandmother is currently renting a house on the Circus. Number Twelve. Tea is at four o'clock sharp.'

'A time when many of us are still working!' Anna threw him a look that she hoped conveyed a suitable degree of contempt before slamming the door in his face.

* * *

'Don't you like your mutton?'

'Mmm?' Anna looked up from the plate where she was absently pushing her food around with a fork. 'Oh, I'm sorry, Mama, it's good. I just have something on my mind.'

'Anything I can help with?'

'I'm not sure...' She glanced towards the clock on the mantelpiece. It had been five hours since Captain Delaney had visited and revealed his true colours. Time enough to decide what to do, but her thoughts had been too much preoccupied with reliving their conversation, hearing his words over and over in her head. She still felt as angry as she had when she'd heard them the first time, but now the sense of humiliation was even worse. The horrible familiarity of it all made her feel sick.

She didn't want to mention the invitation he'd brought either, but judging by what she'd witnessed of his grandmother, she doubted she had any choice. She couldn't risk her mother being caught off guard and she could hardly barricade her upstairs if the old battle-axe came calling, which seemed a strong possibility. And she *did* owe her a debt of sorts. Perhaps just telling her mother about the invitation would be enough to discharge it...

'Mama, have you ever met Lady Jarrow?'

'My goodness, what a strange question!' Her mother lowered the fork that was halfway to her mouth. 'Yes, I knew her when I was a girl. She and my mother were friends. She used to visit the house and encourage us all to go riding. Why ever do you ask?'

'Oh...' Anna sliced a potato somewhat over-vigorously with her knife. 'I saw her today, that's all.'

'Really? I didn't think she ever came to Bath.'

'Well, she's definitely here now. She invited us to tea on the Circus tomorrow.'

'What?' Her mother looked taken aback. 'Just like that? Why?'

'It's a long story. Her grandson brought the invitation. Somehow she's found out who you are and she wants to see you again.'

'Goodness gracious.' Her mother's face brightened with a look that was both nostalgic and affectionate. 'Yes, that does sound like her. She never cared about anyone else's opinion, least of all the *ton's*. Was her grandson that man in naval uniform I saw leaving earlier? He was very handsome.'

'I didn't notice.' Anna shrugged dismissively. 'Anyway, I told him we wouldn't go.'

'But I'd be delighted to see her again!'

'What?' Anna pushed her plate away, her appetite vanishing completely. 'After the way society treated you and Father, why on earth would you want to spend time with any of them?'

'Because society as a whole might have treated us badly, but *she* didn't. She wasn't even in London at the time.'

'But won't it be upsetting to stir up old memories again?'

'*Very* old memories, dear, and I think I can manage.' Her mother reached across the table to pat one of her hands. 'I know that you've always tried to protect me from anyone I knew before my so-called disgrace, but there's really no need. I knew exactly what I was doing when I eloped *and* what the consequences would be. I'm not as delicate as you think. If I was, then your father and I would have chosen somewhere a lot less conspicuous than Bath to set up shop.'

'Yes, but...'

'Then it's decided. I'd very much like to see Georgiana again and you can close the shop early for once. If nothing else, a visit to the Baroness ought to be entertaining.'

'Baroness?'

'Yes. Didn't her grandson mention that?'

'No, he didn't.' Anna slumped down in her chair, her spirits sinking to new depths. *Of course* she'd be a baroness... 'Are you really sure about this?'

'Perfectly.' Her mother was positively beaming. 'I'm already looking forward it.'

Anna managed a wan smile in return. Her only hope was that a certain naval captain *wouldn't* be there.

Chapter Seven

'There—what did I tell you?' Lady Jarrow gave a nod of unabashed smugness at the sound of a knock on the front door. 'I've told Pearson to show them straight up, and they're on time, too, I'm pleased to say. You know how I despise tardiness.'

'I believe that you've mentioned it once or twice before.' Samuel put aside his copy of *Lyrical Ballads* with a wry smile. 'Although it might not be them.'

'Well, of course it's them. Who else would it be?'

He stood up, his gaze already travelling towards the drawing-room door. Personally he had significant doubts about the identity of the new arrivals, although he couldn't help but hope for another chance to apologise to Miss Fortini. Her refusal had been definite, to say the least, but then perhaps her mother had decided otherwise and it *did* seem unlikely to be anyone else. His grandmother's forthright opinions were notorious enough to put off all but the most thick-skinned of callers.

He'd barely had a chance to wonder, however, before the butler opened the door and Miss Fortini herself appeared. To his surprise, she looked comparatively neat for once, her dark hair scooped up into its usual high bun, though with the addition of two red bands across the top to hold stray curls in place. She was wearing a smart-looking dress, too, in the same practical style as her shop gown, but in a shade of light pink that perfectly complemented her complexion, making her skin glow with a luminous sheen.

The lady who entered behind her, meanwhile, looked nothing at all like someone who'd allegedly *ruined* herself. On the contrary, despite walking with a slight limp, she was tall and elegant, with chestnut-coloured ringlets and a remarkably youthful, unblemished countenance. She was also smiling, in contrast to her daughter, who looked as if she was only there under sufferance. Which, given her protestations of the previous day, was probably the case. Miss Fortini certainly didn't look in a very forgiving mood. He made her a formal bow, which she pointedly ignored.

'Elizabeth Holden.' As usual, his grandmother got straight to the point. 'So it is you.'

'It is, Lady Jarrow.' The older woman smiled and dipped into a stiff, but still graceful, curtsy, one that was belatedly copied with an air of reluctance and significantly less grace by the younger. 'May I present my daughter, Miss Annabelle Fortini?'

'The famous Belle, I presume?' His grandmother's gaze swept up and down appraisingly. 'I believe that you already know my grandson, Captain Samuel Delaney?'

'We've met.' Although judging by the belligerent tone of her voice, she wasn't overly thrilled by the fact.

'Lady Jarrow.' The mother spoke again, her voice sounding even warmer by contrast. 'What a pleasure it is to see you again after so many years. I was delighted to receive your invitation.'

'Indeed.' His grandmother's eyes lingered briefly on the daughter, making it obvious that her tone and reluctance to curtsy hadn't gone unnoticed. 'You must have been all of eighteen the last time I saw you.'

'I believe I was nineteen.'

'Well, take a seat beside me. We have a lot to talk about and, as you can see, tea is all ready.' Her gaze shifted back towards Miss Fortini. 'Perhaps your daughter will be good enough to pour? If she'll oblige me, that is?'

Samuel winced, struck with the ominous mental image of two bulls locking horns. One of the bulls had youth, vitality and a decidedly obstinate chin, but the other had experience, indomitability and the advantage of home territory. There was a lengthy pause before the younger finally succumbed, appearing to grit her teeth as she spoke.

'It would be my pleasure.'

'It would be my pleasure, *my lady.*'

'Miss Fortini.' Samuel stepped forward, blocking her view of his grandmother's gloating expression, though unfortunately not her words. 'I'm pleased that you chose to accept the invitation after all.'

'Yes. Who would have poured the tea otherwise?'

'*Anna.*' Her mother's murmur was reproving. 'We're guests here.'

Fortunately, before anyone else could speak, the drawing-room door opened again and his grandfather entered the room, his arrival drawing a gasp from Miss Fortini.

'The bee man!' Her confrontational attitude fell away at once.

'Miss Anna.' His grandfather made a surprisingly gallant bow. 'How delightful to see you here. Not wearing yellow today, eh?'

'No, but…' She looked between him and the Baroness with an expression of consternation. 'Forgive me, but I had no idea…'

'That such a delightful old man was married to a harridan like me?' His grandmother's tone was even more gloating than before. 'Yes, most people are surprised when they find out. Hector, come and meet Elizabeth.'

'I hope that you haven't closed your shop up especially for us?' Samuel tried interceding again.

'Of course I—' Miss Fortini stopped mid-sentence, digging her teeth into her bottom lip as if she were actually biting back words before shaking her head. 'We close at four o'clock anyway. It was only a little early.'

'None the less, we really can't ask you to serve us after you've been working all day. I believe that I'm perfectly capable of wielding a teapot.' He gestured towards a sofa, waiting until she'd sat down before proceeding to pour and hand out the teacups himself, stifling a smile as she shot a particularly pointed look across the room towards his grandmother.

'There we are.' He took the last cup for himself and then headed towards the sofa. 'May I join you, Miss Fortini?'

'It's not my house. You may sit where you like.'

'True, but I thought perhaps we might be civil to each other.' He sat down, pretending not to notice the way her body tensed beside him. 'Would you care for a piece of cake?'

'No, thank you.'

'Naturally we wanted to serve Belles, but I'm afraid

they've all been eaten. I'm not sure who ate the most, me or my grandfather.'

'Well, at least I can't fault your good taste.'

He inclined his head, wondering if she were ever going to relent. 'May I ask what changed your mind about coming today?'

'*I* didn't. It was my mother's decision.'

'Ah. Then I'm glad you told her about the invitation. I wasn't sure that you would.'

She gave him a sharp look. 'I admit I was surprised that she wanted to come, but she remembered your grandmother and thought it might be entertaining.'

'She obviously remembers her well. She likes you, by the way.'

'Who?' She looked surprised. 'Your grandmother?'

'Yes. That was her being welcoming.'

'*Welcoming?*' Her expression was so incredulous that he smiled.

'Trust me, if she didn't like you then she would have found a way to get rid of you by now. She never lets anyone she doesn't like even sit down.'

'How does she stop them? By asking them to pour tea instead?'

'Usually she talks about ticks and worms and how she thinks she might have brought them in from the stables. Or, if she's not sure about a person, she mentions fleas.'

'Are they better than ticks and worms?'

'No, but horses don't get fleas. If the person knows that, she gives them a second chance. If she's in a tolerant mood, that is.'

'How generous.' Her gaze narrowed. 'Perhaps she's just tolerating me because she wants to speak with my mother?'

'That still wouldn't stop her from throwing you out.' He tipped his head forward and lowered his voice. 'So now I know why your mother is here, but why did *you* come, Miss Fortini?'

'To give her support, of course...' her shoulders stiffened '...and to make sure that she isn't upset.'

'Ah.' He glanced across to where Mrs Fortini and his grandmother were already deep in conversation. 'Fortunately she seems quite happy at the moment. In fact, you're the only one who looks *un*happy. Is it so very terrible being invited for tea?'

'That depends. Do you think I ought to feel honoured?' She lifted her cup to her lips and took a sip. 'I concede the tea itself is quite pleasant.'

'So it's just the company you find displeasing, then?' He leaned back on the sofa, throwing one leg casually over the other. 'The indolent aristocracy in their decadent lair?'

'I never said so.' She gave him a cutting look.

'Some words don't need to be spoken aloud. Your face is remarkably vocal. And of course you gave me the full force of your opinion yesterday.'

'It's not an opinion I apply to everybody. I find your grandfather, for example, to be quite charming.'

'Yes, I believe he's rather taken with you, too. I understand that you share a common interest in bees.'

'No-o.' An almost-smile danced about the edges of her lips. 'But I've learnt a great deal from him. About butterflies, too.' She glanced sideways and the smile vanished again. 'He's a *true* gentleman.'

'Unlike myself, obviously.' Samuel made an impatient gesture. 'You might be right, but I've already admitted and apologised for my ungentlemanly conduct the other day, Miss Fortini. I prefer not to be lectured ad nauseam.'

'I don't believe that I'm keeping you here, Captain. There are several other vacant chairs.'

'Yes, but since we're talking about behaviour, you tempt me to make certain ungallant observations.'

'Such as?'

'Such as that your mother's, for instance, is *exactly* what I would expect of a lady.'

'My mother was born a lady. *I* was not.' Her eyes flashed. 'Perhaps *I* don't care whether I behave like one or not.'

'Well then, you can rest easy, but perhaps neither of us has acquitted ourselves well of late.'

'I'm perfectly at ease with *my* behaviour, Captain.'

Samuel sighed, tempted to take her advice and go and sit somewhere else instead. Apparently she had no intention of forgiving him, in which case he had better things to do than drink tea and be insulted, but he made one last attempt anyway. 'How is your assistant? I hope that she wasn't too upset after yesterday.'

She gave him a sidelong look, the combative glint in her eye fading slightly. 'I believe she was, but she seems to have recovered from the shock. She came to work early this morning to help me with the baking. I think that she feels guilty for lying.'

'She ought to. It's fortunate she isn't in the navy.'

'Why?' She sounded reluctantly interested. 'What would the punishment be?'

He took a mouthful of tea, wondering how graphic he ought to be with his answer. 'Well, that would depend on the size of the lie. Answering back to an officer, for example, is punishable with a gagging. That means tying the offender up with an iron bar in their mouth. The same would follow for a small deception, but anything bigger and they'd be clapped in irons.'

'Irons?'

'Chained to the deck for everyone to see, at the mercy of the weather and waves.'

'How cruel.'

'That's one of the most minor punishments, actually. Some captains tie men to the rigging for days. Then there's flogging and "flogging around the fleet.". That's the worst punishment of all, but it's reserved for the worst crimes, too.'

'It sounds barbaric.'

'It can be,' he agreed. 'There have been times when I wished I could have turned a blind eye to some misdemeanours, but a ship needs order.'

'You make me glad that I only run a shop. I wouldn't want to put Henrietta in irons just for one small lie. People make mistakes.'

He lifted an eyebrow, wondering if there was some hope of forgiveness for him after all. 'You know, there's a nautical term, Miss Fortini—to *parley*. It means a cessation of hostilities in order to discuss the terms of a truce. Perhaps we might consider something similar?'

She looked at him steadily for a long moment, then across the room towards her mother and his grandmother. 'Perhaps we should since they're getting along so well. Only that would imply the possibility of an eventual truce.'

'Well…' He sat forward, putting his tea aside and spreading his hands out in a conciliatory gesture. 'If we *were* to discuss terms, since we've already discussed what happened with your assistant, perhaps you might be persuaded to accept my apology?'

Her whole body seemed to bristle at the statement.

'Or...' he hurried on '...to accept that I mean it, whether you can forgive me or not?'

'All right.' She spoke slowly, as if she suspected some kind of trick. 'I can accept *that*, since you *did* make amends.'

'Thank you. In return, I shall ignore all your insults about the aristocracy.'

'You can ignore them all you want. It doesn't mean—'

'Ahem,' he interrupted her. '*Parley*, Miss Fortini.'

She pursed her lips. 'Oh, very well, but in that case we should simply agree to a state of parley *without* trying to establish an actual truce. We'll never agree on terms.'

'You might be right.' He felt a twinge of disappointment, though under the circumstances a tentative cessation of hostilities was probably the best he could hope for. Perhaps it was for the best, too. The more time he spent looking into those brown eyes, the more entrancing he found them. The more he found himself interested in her, too. Given her feelings about the aristocracy, however, he very much doubted the feeling was mutual, and if she ever found out about his possible inheritance then he suspected that even *parley* would be impossible. She'd probably turn away from him on the spot. On balance, it was probably best *not* to be entranced... 'That sounds like a compromise.'

'But I'm only agreeing for my mother's sake.'

'Naturally.' He leaned back against the sofa again. 'Speaking of your mother, I understand that she suffers from some kind of illness?'

'Yes. She has stiffness and swelling in her joints. It's not so bad at the moment, but it can be very painful for her.'

'I'm sorry to hear it.' He glanced discreetly across the room. 'I presume that she's seen a physician?'

'Yes. He tried blood-letting and leeches, all the usual things, but none of them did any good. Now he just prescribes the waters. He says that the symptoms can only be alleviated, not cured.'

'It must be very difficult for her.'

Her chin jutted upwards defensively. 'She's perfectly content, Captain. My mother has no regrets about her choices in life, even despite her condition now. My father did everything he could to make her comfortable. Contrary to everyone's expectations my parents were very much in love and happy together.'

'I'm sure they were. Your father passed away, I understand?'

'Yes, six years ago.' A wistful look came over her face. 'He and I used to do all the baking together.'

'Surely you don't do it all by yourself now?'

'Yes, first thing in the morning.'

'*Every* morning?'

'Six days a week.'

'That sounds tiring.'

'I like to keep busy.' She lifted her chin even higher, though with an air of defiance that suggested the words were more of a stock answer than the truth.

'It still sounds tiring.'

'It's just how things are. Sometimes we find ourselves in situations that we didn't expect or choose, but that we can't walk away from, either.' A small frown puckered her brow as if she were afraid she'd just said too much. 'But I do miss my father a great deal. He called us *una squadra perfetta*.'

'A perfect team?'

'Yes.' Her eyes widened with obvious surprise. 'You speak Italian?'

'I'm a sailor. In the navy, it helps to learn a little of every language, although I'm not sure I'd get very far in conversation. You're fluent, I presume?'

'Especially about biscuits. My father always made a point of speaking Italian to my brother and me so we grew up learning two languages at once.'

'Ho bisogno di una corda?'

She stared at him blankly for a few seconds. 'You need some rope?'

'Not at this precise moment, but that's the kind of subject *I* can talk about. Or if you prefer, *Dove posso comprare dieci bottiglie di vino rosso?*'

'Where can you buy ten bottles of red wine?'

'For the Captain's table, just as important as rope.' He smiled and picked up his teacup again, regarding her quizzically as he drank. She was still as prickly as a hedgehog, though under the circumstances he couldn't particularly blame her. Given the way her parents had been ostracised by society, the details of which his grandmother had expounded to him earlier, he could understand her dislike of the aristocracy, too. She'd made her prejudice abundantly obvious, yet here she was, drinking tea with a baron and a baroness in one of the grandest houses in the city. It had to feel strange.

'I say.' The Baron crossed the room to settle himself in an armchair beside them. 'I'm afraid that my wife's trying to get your mother riding again, my dear.'

'Riding?' Miss Fortini echoed as if she didn't know what the word meant.

'Yes, she was quite an accomplished horsewoman in her day, so I've been told. Repeatedly. I ought to have known that was the reason Georgiana remembered her. It's usually something to do with horses. Those creatures are the bane of my life.'

'My mother *rides*?'

'Well, of course she rides!' the Baroness answered, though bellowed would have been a more fitting description. 'Show me a lady who doesn't!'

'That doesn't mean all of them enjoy it,' Samuel cut in.

'Nonsense. If they don't enjoy it, then they're not doing it properly. What about you, Miss Fortini? Do *you* enjoy it?'

'I don't know. I've never tried.'

'You've never—' For arguably the first time in her life, his grandmother appeared to be at a loss for words. 'But how on earth is that possible?'

'Quite easily when you don't own a horse.'

'But how do you go anywhere?'

'I have two perfectly good feet.'

'Then how do you travel longer distances?'

'We don't.' It was Mrs Fortini who spoke this time. 'I'm afraid that we haven't travelled a great deal at all. My husband always wanted to take us to Italy, to show us where he grew up and introduce us to the rest of his family, but unfortunately our circumstances never allowed it.'

'Perhaps once the war is over...' The Baron's expression was kindly.

'No.' Mrs Fortini shook her head. 'It was *his* dream. We talked about it so often that it wouldn't feel right now to go without him. It would be too painful.'

'I know exactly what you mean.' His grandmother sounded uncharacteristically sympathetic. 'If I ever lost Hector, I should never set foot in a library again.'

'I can't imagine that affecting your life too badly, my dear. You hardly enter mine now.'

'Then I would never pick up another book as a matter of principle.'

'In that case I'm touched. I'd make a similar vow about stables, but we both know I'd never last a day without you.'

'Absolutely right.' His grandmother nodded vehemently, though with a tremulous note to her voice that Samuel found unsettling. Not for the first time since he'd joined them in Bath, he had the distinct impression that she was hiding something. Although if she didn't want to tell him, he knew that wild horses would never drag it from her.

'Which area of Italy was your husband from, Mrs Fortini?' he asked instead.

'From the north, an old Etruscan town close to Florence famous for olive trees, vineyards and Roman ruins. He came from a long line of bakers.' She gave a bittersweet smile. 'He used to say that he came to England for adventure, ended up as a footman, met me and went back to baking again.'

'Infinitely more interesting than being a footman, I should say.' His grandmother sniffed. 'I often wonder what they find to think about, standing around all day.'

'Perhaps you ought to let them sit down?' Miss Fortini's voice sounded altogether *too* innocent.

'I don't believe there really is much standing around,' her mother spoke gently. 'From what my husband told me, there was always work to do in a big house.'

'Hmm.' His grandmother's gaze honed in upon Miss Fortini. 'Would *you* like to visit Italy, Miss Annabelle?'

'Yes, very much. I'd like to visit Rome most of all.' Her face seemed to light up at the suggestion. 'Perhaps I ought to stow away on your ship, Captain Delaney? Or are you one of those sailors who object to having women on board?'

'Not at all. I wouldn't necessarily recommend the experience of living alongside eight hundred men, but I'll be sure to stow an extra hammock just in case.'

'That would be most obliging, thank you.'

Her lips curved and he sucked in a breath, struck by how pretty she was when she let her guard down. If she ever sheathed her prickles completely, then she might be quite beautiful. He felt unusually relaxed looking at her, too, which was curious since he'd felt almost permanently on edge ever since he'd set foot on shore; even more curious that someone so prickly could make him relax, but somehow she was doing it. Maybe it was those entrancing eyes, as dark as the sea at night and just as unfathomable. As tempestuous, too, able to leap from one emotion to another in a heartbeat. He felt as if he could gaze into them all day...

'*If* he goes back to sea, which I am determined he shall not,' his grandmother declared, breaking the mood abruptly.

'But why wouldn't he go back?' Miss Fortini seemed to give a small start, her expression arrested as she looked from him to his grandmother and back again. 'You said you loved being a sailor.'

'I do, but unfortunately my circumstances are such that it might not be possible.'

'Your injury?'

'Not exactly...' He threw a swift warning look at his grandmother, but it was too late. Her mouth was already opening and long experience told him there was no way to make it close again, or to speak over it, either. He was heading for rocks and keeling over at the same time, just when he'd thought he might make it through unscathed. In short, he was doomed.

'Because my grandson isn't just a naval captain, Miss Fortini. He's the future Earl of Staunton.'

And there it was. Shipwreck. So much for *parley*.

Chapter Eight

Anna hadn't intended to stand up, or to put it more accurately, leap out of her chair as if she'd just discovered that Captain Delaney was Napoleon in disguise. She'd had no conscious intention of moving at all, only somehow she was on her feet before her brain had a chance to catch up with her body, which seemed to have been galvanised into action by the Baroness's announcement.

The future Earl of Staunton.

She was vaguely aware of four pairs of eyes all fixed on her face, though she seemed unable to move or speak, her mind still reeling from the words. Instead, she took a deep breath, mentally reviewing all of the conversations she'd had so far with Captain Delaney, but nowhere, not once, *never* had he said anything to suggest that he was, could be, or had any intention of becoming an earl. It was a *title*, one of a collection of words that she loathed above all others in the English language. And not *just* the English language, either. In all languages. *Conte, Comte, Graf, Conde...* If she could have thought of any more examples, she would have hated them, too. It was bad enough that she was here in a house on the Circus, drinking tea with a baron and a baroness, but now one of them turned out to be an earl-in-waiting! All she wanted was to get out of the room and house as quickly as possible.

'Anna?' Her mother's expression was shocked. Which was no surprise since she was being unforgivably rude, even more than she'd been when they'd entered.

'I'm sorry, Mama, I'm just feeling...tired.' She found her voice finally. 'The shop was very busy today.'

'Oh...' Despite a valiant attempt to hide it, her mother looked embarrassed. 'I suppose we ought to be taking our leave anyway.'

'Well!' Lady Jarrow's voice conveyed exactly what she thought of her behaviour. '*You* must come again, Elizabeth.'

'I'd be delighted, my lady, and thank you for the invitation. I've enjoyed our talk very much.'

Anna watched, horrified, as her mother bent to kiss the older lady on the cheek. Meanwhile, she was acutely aware of Captain Delaney standing beside her. He'd risen to his feet at the same moment she had, though she'd kept her gaze studiously averted. Even without looking, however, she could tell that he appeared sombre. Strange that just a few moments ago she'd been *almost* enjoying his company again, enough to agree to a parley. Despite all her anger and humiliation, she'd found herself noticing little details about him, too, the fact that one of his eyes was subtly darker in colour to the other, the way he tapped his foot on the carpet as he talked, as if he were full of excess energy, and the scent of his cologne, light and citrusy, with a hint of salt that made her think of the sea. Or was she just imagining that? Now she felt as though she'd been tricked yet again, as if every time she found herself relenting towards him he revealed something else detestable...

'It's been charming to see you again, my dear.' The Baron stood and made a polite bow, causing her a sharp pang of guilt, then Captain Delaney himself stepped into her line of vision and she felt another pang of something more like regret, not for her behaviour, but for what she'd just learned about him. If it hadn't been for that...

She refused to complete the thought. If it hadn't been for that, then *nothing*. They belonged in different worlds. No matter who her mother was, or had been, *she* was a shop-keeper and she ought never to have agreed to come here. She might have known it would only lead to trouble.

'Miss Fortini.' His voice was even graver than his expression, as if he knew exactly what she was thinking. 'I believe this is goodbye.'

'Yes.' For some reason, she had difficulty uttering the word. It sounded so final, yet it *had* to be final, didn't it?

'Thank you for coming.'

'It was my pleasure,' she lied, so obviously and blatantly that his lips actually twitched upwards.

'I think not.'

'My mother's, then, Capt—' She corrected herself. 'My lord.'

'Not yet.' His smile reverted to a frown instantly. 'And perhaps never. Whether I inherit the earldom at all remains to be seen. There's still one significant matter to be decided.'

'Oh?' She tried not to sound too hopeful. 'What's that?'

He quirked an eyebrow, as if he were surprised by the question. Even for her, she was aware it was too direct. Impertinent, even. Whatever the matter was it was absolutely none of her business and it wasn't as if it would make any difference to her anyway. Yet for some reason she still wanted to know.

'Such as the gender of the former Earl's unborn child. I'm the Earl presumptive, but since the estate is entailed it's being held in abeyance. Nothing can be formally decided until the baby is born. If it's a boy, he inherits. If it's a girl...'

'Then you do?' She felt genuinely shocked. 'I didn't know such a thing was possible.'

'Neither did I until a few months ago. Frankly, I wish I didn't know it now, but that's the law. So, you see, it's not as simple as *just* going back to sea. Sometimes we find ourselves in situations we didn't expect or choose, but that we can't run away from, either. Wouldn't you agree, Miss Fortini?'

His expression seemed far too pointed suddenly, so much so that she couldn't think of an answer. Instead, she turned on her heel and fled.

'What on earth...?'

'I know, Mama.' Anna put her hands up the moment they were outside on the street. 'You don't have to say it.'

'I might not have to, but I'm your parent and I *will* say it!' To her surprise, her mother stormed on ahead without taking her arm. 'Your behaviour was appalling! We were there as their guests! Whatever must they think of me now?'

'There was nothing the matter with you!'

'Your behaviour reflects on me. They'll think I taught you no manners at all!'

'I never wanted to go there in the first place! You knew that.'

'That's still no excuse.' Her mother whirled around angrily. 'Your father would have been ashamed of you!'

'What?' Anna sucked in a breath of dismay. 'That's not true. Father hated the aristocracy!'

'No, he hated the way my family treated me. He resented all the whispering and gossip from people who came into the shop, too, but he would never have behaved so rudely to anyone and as his daughter you represent him. You just reinforced all the mean-spirited, snobbish comments anyone ever made about us!'

'But...'

'I shall walk on my own, thank you very much. The Baroness offered her carriage to take us home, but I declined. I don't believe that we deserve it.'

'What about your ankles? You'll hurt yourself if you're not careful.'

'I'll manage somehow. At this precise moment, I'm far too angry to care!'

Anna stood on the pavement gaping after her usually serene and calm-natured mother for a full minute before remembering where she was. The Circus itself was intimidating enough with its three curved terraces forming a perfect circle, but the thought of all the eyes behind the windows made her feel even more self-conscious. Barons, earls, *dukes*...those were the sorts of people who lived here and she ought never to have come. Now look what had happened! She'd never seen or heard her mother so angry, though it took her several increasingly mortified laps of the central garden to concede that her accusations were true. She *had* behaved shamefully.

Unfortunately, that also meant there was only one thing she could do to make it right, though it took her another five minutes to summon the nerve. If she wasn't careful someone would call a constable to shoo her away, she thought with bleak amusement as she finally trudged back across the road and stopped back outside the gold-hued frontage of Number Twelve.

The black door looked even bigger and more looming than it had the first time, the Palladian style more striking, too. The style of the house actually varied from floor to floor, Doric on ground level, Ionic in the middle and Corinthian on top, as if any one of those styles on its own wasn't impressive enough! Even the butler who opened the door seemed more menacing than before, though he showed no sign of surprise and made no comment as he let her back into the hallway to wait while he checked whether the family she'd just left were still at home. Part of her hoped they decided they weren't, but a few moments later he returned, allowing her to precede him back up the staircase.

The inhabitants of the drawing room were positioned almost exactly as she'd left them. Only Captain Delaney had moved to the window, standing with his face half-averted and his arms clasped behind his back. He didn't bother to look around as she entered and she baulked at the idea that he might have witnessed her quarrel with her mother, but there was nothing for it now but to continue.

'Miss Fortini? Have you forgotten something, my dear?' The Baron greeted her with his usual kindly manner, and she dropped into a low, and this time sincere, curtsy.

'Yes.' She fixed her eyes on the carpet, deciding to get the worst of it over with. 'My manners. I misplaced them earlier. In fact, I think I might have left them behind in the shop. My behaviour this afternoon was rude and ungrateful and I've come to apologise. I beg that you don't take my actions as a reflection on either of my parents.'

She lifted her gaze slowly when she'd finished, surprised to find that Lady Jarrow had already risen to her feet.

'Miss Fortini...' the Baroness's tone was stentorian '... I've never thought it fair to judge children by their parents or vice versa and you strike me in particular as being very much your own person. I would never hold your mother responsible for your behaviour, ungrateful or otherwise. Come here and let me look at you.'

Anna took a few steps forward obediently, letting the older woman study her face in silence for a few seconds.

'You must take after your father in looks, although there's something of the Holdens about you, too. It's the curls, I suppose, *and* the stubborn streak. Still, I'm glad to see you have some spirit.'

'I still shouldn't have behaved so badly.'

The Baroness made a dismissive gesture. 'It was most diverting. I can't abide polite conversation. So many words and so little gets said. I presume that your mother just gave you a set-down? Well, if it makes you feel any better, I've had one, too. My grandson has just finished scolding me for chasing you away. He thinks that *I* behaved badly, if you can believe that.'

'Oh.' Anna glanced towards the window. Captain Delaney had finally turned around and was giving his grandmother a look that suggested his opinion on the subject hadn't much altered, though there was a glint of dark humour in his eyes, too. It made him look faintly sardonic, making her breath catch and the hairs on the back of her neck rise in a new and startling fashion.

'Perhaps we ought to agree that neither of us was at fault just to disprove them?' The Baroness gave her a nudge with one bony, but surprisingly powerful, elbow. 'Then we should become friends to spite them, eh?'

'I...' Anna felt her lips twitch despite herself. Being friends with a baroness wasn't something she'd ever imagined, but it was hard to resist the idea of this woman as an ally. 'I think that sounds like an excellent idea.'

'Good, then it's settled. We may consider ourselves friends. Although in that case, you'll have to learn to how to ride. All of my friends ride. I insist upon it.'

'But...'

'I'll provide lessons, of course.'

'Thank you, my lady...' Anna hastened to protest, 'but I'm afraid that it would be impossible. I have a shop to run and no free time for lessons.'

'Then we'll just have to make you some time.' The Baroness tossed her head imperiously. 'Mornings would probably be best.'

'I start baking at five o'clock, my lady.'

'Then I'll send a couple of my kitchen maids to you tomorrow. You can tell them what to do and then your mother can supervise, I suppose?'

'Well, ye-es.' Anna was surprised to find the idea decidedly tempting. She stole another glance towards the window, but Captain Delaney's expression was inscrutable. She had no idea what he thought of his grandmother's plan. Not that she cared about his opinion, either. It had nothing to do with him. With any luck she'd never have to see *him* again. He made her feel altogether too confused and distracted...

'But I wouldn't want to impose upon you.'

'Don't be ridiculous. I never allow anybody to impose, but if you *want* to be my friend...' the baroness gave her a look that dared her to contradict it '...then you must learn

to ride or I shall refuse to receive you again. Now come to
the house tomorrow morning at six o'clock sharp. You can
have your first lesson and then tell me how you got on at
breakfast.'

'Won't you be teaching me?'

'Good gracious, no. I have no patience with amateurs.'
Lady Jarrow's eyes glittered with an expression that looked
a lot like triumph. 'Samuel will teach you.'

Chapter Nine

'I can't.' Miss Fortini stared at the placid and sleepy-looking mount before her as if it were some kind of fire-breathing dragon.

'She's the most mild-mannered horse in the stables,' Samuel attempted to reassure her.

'I still can't.' She gestured at her skirts. 'I'm not properly dressed.'

He ran a hand over his chin and cleared his throat noncommittally. There was really no disputing the statement, though he took the opportunity to steal a glance at her lower body anyway. Her dress was practical enough, but nothing like a riding habit, though it looked as if someone had attached some extra material to the skirts in a half-hearted attempt to conceal the fact. Of course if she didn't ride then presumably she didn't own a proper habit; something that he, or his grandmother anyway, ought to have considered.

'Horses don't care what you're wearing.' He looked up again before his staring became obvious. 'And we won't go outside the mews this morning. Today is just about getting you comfortable on horseback.'

'Today is a mistake.' She glared at the horse and then him. 'Surely your grandmother wasn't serious about what she said?'

'Does she strike you as a person who makes idle threats? She definitely won't receive you again if you don't even try.'

'Well, if this is some kind of punishment then it's not fair.'

He shrugged, though personally he was inclined to agree. It wasn't fair on *either* of them. Impressed though he'd been by her apology, which must have taken some considerable degree of courage, he hadn't been thrilled by the prospect of teaching her to ride, particularly after the way she'd reacted to the news of his possible inheritance. She'd seemed downright horrified at the time and apparently *still* was. She'd seemed determined to avoid looking him in the eye when they'd met on the Circus that morning, barely speaking a word until they'd reached the stables. Well, since she obviously found the company of an earl, even a potential one, so odious, the last thing he wanted to do was waste his time with teaching her. As usual, however, there was no gainsaying his grandmother, especially when she challenged him about *what else* he had to do. And when a small, contrary part of him still wanted to spend time with her... He shook his head at his own foolishness. If he searched the whole of England, he could hardly have found a woman more likely to reject him.

'Here, just stroke her. She won't bite.'

'How do you know?' Miss Fortini shot him a glance that suggested *she* might, though she did as he suggested anyway, placing her hand nervously on the mare's nose.

'That's it.' He nodded approvingly. 'Her name's Bramble and she's a sweet old thing.'

'How old?'

'Around thirty, I should think. I used to ride her when I was a boy before my grandmother insisted I have my own horse.'

For the first time that morning she looked him straight in the eye, her own curious. 'You seem very close to your grandparents.'

'I am. They practically raised me.'

'What happened to your parents?'

'Lots of things.' He gave her a pointed look. 'Don't think I don't know what you're doing. Stop trying to delay the inevitable.' He slotted his fingers together to make a step, putting an end to the subject of his parents. 'Now lean your shoulder against the saddle, put your foot in my hands and take it slowly.'

'Do you *promise* she's docile?'

'I doubt you could find a more docile creature in the whole of Bath. She's practically asleep on her feet right now.'

'All right…' Miss Fortini gave him a dubious look and then placed her right foot in his hands, exposing a length of shapely, be-stockinged calf all the way up from her ankle to her knee. Samuel looked before he could stop himself, so impressed that for an unguarded moment he was actually tempted to reach out and stroke *it*, too, though he had a feeling that would cause both her *and* the horse to bolt…

'There.' She placed one shoulder against the side saddle like he'd told her, sounding particularly pleased with herself despite the fact that one of her feet was still planted firmly on the ground. 'Now what?'

'Now grab hold of the pommel, keep your legs as straight as possible and pull yourself up.'

'Into the saddle?'

'That would be the general idea. I'll give your foot a push, too.' He lifted an eyebrow when she didn't move. 'Or I could just lift you if you prefer?'

'No.' Her answer came even quicker than he'd expected. 'I can do it.'

She closed her eyes, taking a deep breath before hoisting herself inelegantly into the saddle, exposing both of her calves and one thigh this time as she struggled to rearrange herself.

'Good.' Samuel made a show of adjusting the bridle, pretending not to have noticed. 'Now give her a nudge and we'll walk to the gate.'

'I thought you said we weren't going anywhere!'

'Miss Fortini.' He gritted his teeth, starting to lose patience. '*Must* we dispute every single detail? I said *to* the gate, not beyond it.'

'Oh… All right. How do I tell it which way to go?'

'*It* is a *her* and don't worry, I'll hold on to the bridle for now.' He handed over the reins, wrapping his fingers around hers for a brief, somewhat unnecessary moment, before leading them casually towards the gate. A quick sideways glance revealed Miss Fortini's expression to be one of sheer terror.

'Try to relax.' He rubbed a hand over Bramble's neck in case she sensed her rider's fear. 'And don't hold on to the reins too tightly.'

'I don't like being so high up.'

'You're really not.'

'I don't like wobbling from side to side, either.'

'You'll get used to it after a while. Try rolling with the movement. Imagine you're on a boat.'

'I've never been on a boat either and I *still* think this is unfair.' She sounded belligerent again. 'I apologised to your grandmother, I shouldn't have to risk my life, too.'

'You're not going to die, I promise.'

'What if I fall and break my legs? I suppose your grandmother *still* wouldn't receive me out of principle?'

'No one's ever accused her of being fair and reasonable.'

She made a harumphing sound. 'What about you? Are *you* fair and reasonable on board your ship, Captain?'

He looked around, surprised by the question. 'I hope so. I try to be.'

'Will you tell me more about life at sea?'

'What would you like to know?'

'Anything to distract me. Sebastian's a terrible correspondent.'

'Well, a lot of what we do can be quite monotonous and repetitive. Take the last two years, for example. We've spent most of the time blockading the French ports, stopping enemy ships from getting in or out, which meant a lot of time doing drills and preparing for battle, but not much real action.' They reached the gate and he started to lead them around in a half-circle. 'Although it paid off in the end. When it came to the battle, we were ten times better at reloading and aiming the cannons.'

'Wait!' Miss Fortini reached a hand out to stay him. 'We can keep going. Out of the mews, I mean.'

'Are you sure? I thought you were afraid of breaking your legs?'

'I still am, but if you can bear to live on a floating collection of planks for months on end then I can manage a short, *very short*, ride.' She looked down and then adjusted her skirts again. 'Just as long as you promise I'm not making a public spectacle of myself.'

'Not at all.'

'All right, then, let's go around to the Circus. If I can make it to the front door, then maybe your grandmother will say I've done enough.'

Samuel repressed a smile. If she thought that, then she really didn't know his grandmother very well. On the other hand, he had to admire her courage, *again*, although he really wished that he didn't. He glanced up as they turned out on to the street, just in time to see her twist her face away, a faint crease between her brows as if she'd just been studying him. The two of them must make a curious sight, he thought in amusement, her sitting stiff as a poker on horseback, him walking alongside like her groom, with one of his grandmother's maids following as a chaperon several feet behind. Not that he cared what anyone might think. He was just pleased that they weren't arguing any more. It felt like parley again, as if they might eventually come to terms after all...

'You're perfectly safe, Miss Fortini,' he reassured her. 'As for those floating planks, they're very well constructed.'

'That's what Sebastian tells me.'

'What made your brother join the navy?'

'The spirit of adventure, I suppose. He said he wanted to travel like our father had.' She smiled. 'Not that our father travelled *so* far, but Seb and I always loved listening to his stories when we were children. It was a sad day when we realised the ones about giants and dragons probably weren't true.'

'Didn't you crave adventure, as well?'

There was a significant pause. 'I'm a realist.'

'That wasn't the question.'

'It's my answer.' She jutted her chin into the air. 'What about you? Why did you join the navy? Was it a family career?'

'No, I'd never been to sea before I enlisted.'

'Neither had Sebastian. It didn't seem to worry him, but how could you possibly know whether or not you'd like it?'

'I didn't. I regretted the decision the moment we got out into open water.'

'Why?'

'Seasickness.'

She gave him an incredulous look. 'You get seasick?'

'Not any more, but to begin with...' he shook his head at the memory '... I was tempted to throw myself overboard a few times.'

'But how did you perform your duties? What did your Captain say?'

'Thankfully he was sympathetic. He said that he went through the same thing when he joined. A lot of sailors do. Even Nelson got seasick. It takes about three days, but eventually it settles down.'

'So if I stay on this horse for three days I'll start to feel better, too?'

'Perhaps, but I wouldn't put ideas into my grandmother's head if I were you.'

'Good point. She seems to think you won't go back to sea.'

'Only because she doesn't want me to. She was horrified when I joined the navy. I believe that my grandfather actually had to restrain her from visiting the Admiralty and demanding they release me.'

'So why *did* you join? If you didn't know whether you'd like it and your grandmother objected, why do it? It can't just be because water makes you feel calm.'

'No.' He looked around, surprised that she'd remembered that particular detail, though his other motives weren't something he particularly wanted to talk about. On the other hand, he had a feeling she wasn't about to drop the subject and he felt surprisingly comfortable talking to her. 'But I wanted a purpose in life and I was determined to make my own fortune. Which I did.'

'And now you might be an earl.' She was silent for a few moments. 'Why didn't you tell me about your situation before?'

'Why didn't you tell me your grandfather was a duke?' he rejoined. 'We all have secrets, Miss Fortini. Often they're things we don't care to discuss.'

Anna looked down at the reins twisted tight between her fingers. Captain Delaney was right, everyone had secrets and subjects they didn't like to talk about. She had no right to pry into his. She'd barely known him a week, after all, and yet somehow she couldn't seem to stop herself and it wasn't *just* to distract from the fact that she was sitting several feet above the ground...

'Don't you want the inheritance?' She couldn't seem to take her gaze off his face, either. 'You didn't sound very happy about it the other day.'

If she wasn't mistaken, his jaw clenched at the question. 'No, I don't want it.'

'Because you'd still prefer to make your own fortune?'

'Because of a lot of reasons.'

'What do the rest of your family think about it?'

He threw her an exasperated look. 'You ask a lot of questions, Miss Fortini.'

'I'm trying not to think about the horse.'

He rolled his eyes. 'Oh, very well. My grandparents *are* my family, all I've really known of it anyway. I have an uncle, too, my mother's older brother, but he spends most of his time in London. As for my parents, my father died when I was eleven and my mother married again a year later.'

'So you were never close to your father's family? That must be the side you've inherited from.'

'Yes, ironically, since they never wanted anything to do with me.'

'Why not?'

He sighed heavily. 'Because my father was the black sheep of his family. For very good reasons, I might add.'

'What were they?'

'Gambling and drinking mostly. Other vices, too, but I shan't offend your ears by listing them all. Suffice to say, he and Ralph have certain interests in common. His family disinherited him before he even met my mother.'

'Oh.' She tried not to sound too shocked. 'But she married him anyway?'

'He was very charming by all accounts. It was a whirlwind romance, though things soured quickly after the wedding. They had a very loud marriage.'

'Loud?'

'Turbulent. All of my earliest memories seem to involve shouting. It was a long time before I realised that wasn't how most people communicated. Eventually their marriage broke down and I barely saw him.'

'Did you miss him?'

'A great deal. He was my hero.' He glanced back over

his shoulder. 'You have to understand, to a growing boy he was the best father you could possibly imagine, always ready to play games and make jokes. Completely irresponsible games, of course, and often dangerous, too, but I was happy. It was only much later that I realised his amusement came at the expense of everyone else around him. At the time, however, it was fun. There were no rules or constraints, so I ran wild.'

'What happened to him?'

'He ran away with another woman. Somebody else's woman, unfortunately. When the husband found them he challenged him to a duel. It was my father's fifth, but the first time he lost. He bled to death on Hampstead Heath all on his own.'

'I'm sorry.'

'So was I. In retrospect it was amazing he survived as long as he did, but at the time I was inconsolable. I decided the best way to pay tribute to my father was to emulate his bad behaviour so my mother packed me off to boarding school, which I hated.'

'How sad.' She gave him a sidelong look, sympathy now mingling with suspicion. His answers had become longer as he'd talked, as if once he'd started, he'd wanted to keep going. Overall she was starting to feel as though she understood him a bit better. As if she *liked* him more, too. The differences between him and Henrietta's would-be seducer were becoming more and more obvious, but he was *still* a gentleman. A possible earl, even if he didn't act in the way she expected.

'School is where I met Ralph,' he said, as if he'd somehow guessed the direction of her thoughts. 'We were close companions growing up.'

'I see.' She paused. 'In that case, I'm sorry for what I asked of you the other day.'

'It was the right thing to do for your friend.' He shrugged. 'In any case, I've barely seen him over the past ten years. One day I walked out of school and never went back.'

'You ran away?'

'I was sixteen and a barely average student. I doubt they cared very much. I went to London, but unfortunately I found that a life of dissipation didn't suit me. I didn't even enjoy it very much. Which is a long and roundabout way of explaining why I joined the navy.' He smiled. 'I've been a model of good behaviour ever since. Most of the time anyway.'

'What happened to your mother?'

He shook his head. 'You really *do* ask a lot of questions, don't you?'

'I'm interested. Families interest me.'

'She married again and moved to Cumberland to start a new family.'

'Brothers and sisters?'

'One half-sister, Susan.'

They rounded the corner of the Circus, and Anna looked up in surprise. Somehow their conversation had managed to distract her after all. So much so that she almost regretted it was coming to an end.

'Here we are.' Captain Delaney put a hand on Bramble's nose, bringing them to a halt. 'Without a single broken bone.'

'Only a few ragged nerves.' She smiled down at him. 'You do an excellent job of distracting a person, Captain.'

'With my tale of woe?' He raised an eyebrow ironically.

'It *is* a tale of woe,' she scolded him back. 'You may

make light of it, but I know how terrible it is to be estranged from your family. I've seen how the experience affected my mother. I'm truly sorry for the situation with yours.'

'Thank you. Maybe we have something in common after all?' He held on to her gaze for so long that she felt heat start to spread up her throat and over her cheeks.

'Perhaps.' She tried to sound brisk. 'Now, how do I get down?'

'Here…' he reached a hand up, his voice husky '…jump down.'

'Just jump?' She slid her feet out of the stirrups, grabbing hold of his fingers and trying not to crush them.

'I'll catch you.'

'All right.' She launched herself into the air, flinging herself against him with such force that her bonnet smacked into his forehead.

'*Oomph.* I meant down, not outwards.'

'I'm sorry…but you said jump!' She clamped her arms around his neck as he staggered backwards.

'Maybe slide would have been a better word.' He laughed as he lowered her to her feet. 'Never mind, no harm done.'

She looked into his face, shocked by the sensation of his hard body against hers. She could feel the muscles of his neck and shoulders beneath her fingertips, large and thick and corded, *definitely not* parts of him she ought to be touching!

'Thank you, Captain.' She sprang backwards, remembering how many windows were facing towards them.

'You're welcome.' He bowed, though there was a look of something like regret on his face.

'I expect that your grandmother is waiting for me.' She shuffled one foot on the ground awkwardly.

'She doesn't wait for anybody. She's probably halfway through her bacon and eggs by now.'

'Will you be joining us?'

'I'll take Bramble back to the mews, but then I'll come and submit to coffee and a rigorous questioning. I ate breakfast an hour ago.'

'You must have been up early.'

'You're not the only one with an early rising profession, Miss Fortini.'

'Oh, yes, of course.' She felt her cheeks flush a vivid shade of crimson. 'Well, thank you for the lesson.' She started towards the front door, eager to get away before she looked like a beetroot. 'It was most instructive.'

'Miss Fortini?'

'Yes?' She turned back as he called after her, surprised to see a deep furrow between his brows.

'There's something I think you ought to know.' He paused as if he were giving her time to brace herself. 'My grandmother intends to reintroduce your mother into society.'

'What?' Her lips parted in surprise. 'How?'

'She intends to ask her to visit the Pump Rooms with her later this week.'

'But the scandal with my father...?'

'That was a quarter of a century ago. I believe that my grandmother intends to make a public show of accepting her and woe betide anyone who gets in the way.'

'Meaning me?'

'I hope not.' He gave her a searching look. 'No doubt she'll tell you herself at breakfast, but I wanted to forewarn you. If your mother accepts, then it's likely that word will get back to her—*your*—family, including the Dowager Duchess. From what I understand, she was never happy about the estrangement.'

'I see.' She swallowed, feeling as though all of her muscles were stiffening with tension. 'You mean you think that it might lead to a reconciliation?'

'It's a possibility. Although, considering that your mother accepted my grandmother's invitation to tea yesterday, it might be what she wants.'

'If it is, then I'll be happy for her.' Even to her own ears, the words sounded insincere.

'I'm sure your relatives would like to meet you, too.' His voice softened. 'You just said that estrangement was a terrible thing. Maybe it's a chance for you all to be reconciled.'

'Never!' she shot back before she could stop herself. 'They're aristocrats. I told you I don't want anything to do with any of them!'

'You already *are* one of *them*. You're more aristocratic than I am.' His eyes took on a hard gleam. 'As far as I'm aware, there are no dukes in my lineage.'

'How dare you?'

'You know, if you'd been paying attention, Miss Fortini, then you'd understand that I have about as much interest in being a part of the aristocracy as you do.' He spoke over her as she started to splutter. '*Unlike* you, however, I don't choose to dismiss a whole group of people out of stubbornness and prejudice.' He strode back to the mare, throwing the words over his shoulder as he walked away. 'Tell my grandmother I *won't* be joining you for coffee after all. As it turns out, I have better things to do.'

Chapter Ten

It wasn't that she resented her mother, Anna told herself, repeatedly and at great length, over the course of the following two weeks. She was glad to see her looking happy again, happier than she'd looked in years, in fact. Now she wondered if perhaps her mother had been lonely and *she'd* simply been too busy in the shop to notice. The change in her demeanour was striking. Elizabeth Fortini seemed like a whole new woman, a physically stiffer, but mentally refreshed version of her old self. She visited the Pump Rooms with the Baroness most days, took tea with her every afternoon and had even dined at the Circus on several occasions.

Anna had chosen *not* to accompany them. Firstly, because she had a business to run. Secondly, because she had a point to prove, even if it was hard to prove anything to a man she hadn't seen since he'd announced he had 'better things to do' and then abandoned her on his grandmother's doorstep. He hadn't visited the shop or given her any more lessons since, though as she hadn't gone back to the mews either she supposed she could hardly blame him for that.

It was as if he'd simply forgotten her existence. Which was *exactly* what she ought to do in return, Anna thought bitterly, except that her mind seemed to be working against her. Much as she hated to admit it, she already thought about him far too often for comfort. It was bad enough at night when her dreams were haunted by the image of a man with auburn hair and silvery eyes, but every time she sold a big tin or caught a glimpse of a naval uniform outside the shop window she found herself feeling alarmingly nostalgic.

It didn't help that her mother mentioned him quite so frequently, making it obvious that she *was* seeing him. *Such* a kind gentleman, *so* dashing and thoughtful and polite, and *such* a hero, too! Had she heard the story of his daring manoeuvre at Trafalgar? And what a bizarre situation to find himself in, especially when he yearned to go back to sea! But *surely* he'd make a very competent earl if it came to it... Anna listened with every outward appearance of composure, secretly thinking that if she heard the name Captain Samuel Delaney one more time, she would scream.

'Lady Jarrow intends to throw an evening party next week,' her mother finally announced one morning in the kitchen.

'Does she?' Anna paused in the act of spearing bread on to a toasting fork.

'Yes.' There was a telling pause. 'We're both invited.'

'Oh.'

'She's rather domineering, I admit, but her heart's in the right place.'

'Mmm...' Anna murmured non-committally. She hadn't seen the Baroness since that first breakfast when, still shaking with anger over Captain Delaney's accusations, she'd announced that she'd had enough of horses for ever. To her surprise, instead of delivering a dressing-down, Lady Jarrow had simply told her to come back when she was ready.

'I'm grateful for all the attention that she's shown me over the past couple of weeks,' her mother continued. 'I'd like to attend.'

'Then you should.'

'*With* you.'

'Mama...'

'Just wait a moment.' Her mother lifted a hand. 'I *know* what you think of the aristocracy. You have a lot of ideas about who you are and where you belong. It's hardly surprising given our family's circumstances, but I'm afraid you may have become overly prejudiced, my dear.'

Anna lowered the toasting fork slowly. *Prejudiced.* It was what Captain Delaney had called her before he'd stormed away... She'd resented the accusation then and it still rankled. Not because it wasn't true, but because nobody, not even her mother, knew the real reasons behind it. As much as she resented the way her parents had been treated by society, she hadn't *always* detested the aristocracy, but eight years ago she'd learnt better than to trust them...

'If I am, then they deserve it.' She answered stubbornly.

'Do you forget that I was born *Lady* Elizabeth Holden?'

'You're different. You ran away from all that.'

'I still loved my family a great deal. It broke my heart to leave them, but I knew it was the only way I could be with your father. I only wish there had been another way. I miss them even now.'

'Mama, they disowned you!'

'That doesn't mean they were happy about it. My father

was a proud man. I never expected him to accept or forgive what I did, but I do believe that he loved me, and continued to love me, in his own way. I wanted to go to his funeral, but your Uncle Anthony would have been horrified. They were always very alike.'

Anna lifted the toasting fork again, holding it close to the fireplace. 'What about my other uncle, your youngest brother?'

'Tobias? Oh, he was more like our mother. I think he would have forgiven me. With him and her, I think there might still be a chance of reconciliation, even after all these years.'

'So you *want* to see them again?'

'Yes.' Her mother didn't hesitate. 'Yes, I do.'

'What about Father? If you go back to that life, then it'll be like he never existed.'

'Except that I have you and Sebastian and many years of happy marriage to remember him by.' Her mother's gaze warmed. 'It's not a betrayal of your father to move on. He always felt bad about the rift with my family and if he were still here then I know he'd want me to be happy.' Her mother's hand curled around her arm, drawing the fork back before the toast burned. 'He would have wanted you and Sebastian to be reconciled with my family, as well. He always wanted to give you more in life.'

'He gave us everything we needed. You both did.'

'Yes, but there are other ways that my family could help you.' Her mother smiled hopefully. 'Come to the evening party with me. Let yourself have some fun. You work too hard.'

'I don't know…'

'Anna.' Her mother's voice turned slightly chiding.

'Sometimes it's easier to stay in our own little worlds than venture out, but prejudice has a way of shrinking the opportunities around us. If you aren't careful the person you end up hurting is yourself. Bitterness and resentment aren't very attractive qualities.'

'Maybe I like my life the way it is.'

'You can still like it and come to the party, too. Please, as a favour for me.'

Anna groaned, dropping the piece of toast on to a plate. Doing a favour for her mother was all well and good, but the thought of spending an evening with a group of people she'd spent years resenting gave her the shudders. On the other hand, maybe she *had* become too prejudiced. Maybe she'd let her feelings about what had happened eight years ago control her to the point that she really *had* become afraid to leave her 'own little world' as her mother called it? Maybe she'd overreacted when Captain Delaney had told her about his grandmother's plan, even if it hadn't been for the reasons he'd thought? Maybe that was why she'd refused to forgive him for his behaviour when they'd first met despite his apology, too? And maybe she was holding him accountable for the sins of a man he'd never met and knew nothing about?

The memory of a letter and an innocent walk and an alleyway floated into her mind before she buried it quickly, deep down where it belonged.

'What would I even wear, Mama?' She tried a different tack instead. 'I don't want to waste money on a gown that I'll only wear once and, before you say anything, I don't want the Baroness's charity.'

'Neither do I.'

'So unless I can persuade someone to purchase a year's supply of biscuits in one go…'

'You won't need to. I have some money saved.'

'Not for a dress, Mama.'

'Yes, for a dress. We'll buy some material and make something new.'

'How? Your hands are too swollen for you to sew and I'm terrible at it.'

'I'm not.' Henrietta stuck her head around the doorway that led to the shop. 'I'm sorry, I wasn't eavesdropping, but I couldn't help but overhear. *I* could make you a dress.'

'I couldn't ask you to…'

'You're not. I'm offering and I'm good at making clothes. Please let me. I want to make amends.'

'What for?' Anna offered her a piece of toast, but Henrietta only looked contrite.

'For something foolish I did a while ago. I lied to you about it, but I learnt my lesson and I'll never do it again. I want to make something of myself, just like you.' She took a deep breath, as if she were summoning her nerve for something. 'And you know that my brother's wife is having another baby? Well, it's getting crowded at their house and I wondered whether you might let me move in here with you? I don't mean upstairs. I could make a bed up in the kitchen every night so that I'd be here to help you bake in the mornings. If you can forgive me for lying, that is?'

'Of course I forgive you…' Anna smiled '…but I'm afraid I don't have any spare money to pay you.'

'You don't have to. Just letting me stay would be enough. And I have some new ideas for the shop we could try, like taking a basket out every morning and selling biscuits outside the Pump Rooms or on Pulteney Bridge? Or inventing a new variety and making a big announcement about its arrival?'

'Well...' Anna looked from Henrietta to her mother and back again '...in that case, what can I say except yes? *And* no. That is, yes, you can stay here, but, no, you can't sleep in the kitchen. You can share my room.'

'Really?' Henrietta hugged her so enthusiastically that Anna had to drop the toasting fork in order to avoid a painful accident. 'Thank you. You won't regret it, I promise.'

'Of course we won't.' Her mother nodded approvingly. 'And we'll make the dress together. I'm sure there are still some tasks I can do.'

'We'll make the most beautiful dress you've ever set eyes on.' Henrietta clasped her hands together dreamily. 'It sounds just like a fairy tale. You're going to a ball.'

'An evening party, not a ball.' Anna felt a fresh burst of anxiety at the thought. 'What if someone recognises me from the shop?'

'Then you'll do as I do. Hold your head up high and be proud of who you are.' Her mother tossed her curls as if to illustrate the point. 'You'll say that your name is Miss Annabelle Fortini, owner of a *very* successful confectionery business.'

'They might say there's a bad smell in the air.'

'If they do, then *I* shall tell them what I think of them.' Her mother's eyes took on a martial gleam. 'Then I'll set Lady Jarrow on them, just for fun.'

'I still don't know...' Anna bit down on her bottom lip. She wasn't ashamed of who she was and she wasn't *really* afraid of being insulted, not in the Baroness's own house, but it all seemed so unbelievable. She was being invited back into society along with her mother. It was the opposite of anything she'd ever expected to happen, but perhaps her mother was right and she was only hurting herself by holding on to the past. Perhaps it *was* time to move on. And perhaps she wanted to see Captain Delaney again. Perhaps she could trust him, too?

Her heart gave a little leap at the thought.

Chapter Eleven

An evening party... Samuel groaned, his already depressed spirits sinking even lower as he descended the stairs of his grandparents' house on the Circus. It wasn't that he was inherently misanthropic, he reminded himself, just that he was altogether *too* aware of the whispers and curious glances that followed him whenever he appeared in public. As his grandmother had predicted, a number of ambitious parents had recently experienced an impulse to visit Bath before the start of the London Season, making a point of introducing him to their young and unattached daughters, all of whom expressed a profound admiration for the navy while being unable to name a single ship.

His mood that day hadn't been helped by the receipt of two letters, one from his lawyer advising him, yet again, to visit Staunton, the other from his friend Harry Cartwright telling him, somewhat apologetically, that he'd just been awarded a new command and was preparing to sail from Plymouth. As happy as he'd been for his old comrade, to whom he'd immediately sent a letter of congratulation, Samuel still couldn't help but feel jealous. If it hadn't been for the whole damnable situation over his possible inheritance, then he might have been in a similar position, about to leave England on his own command, but the chances of that *ever* happening were receding more each day.

He'd spent most of the afternoon riding over the Downs, trying to ease the feeling of restlessness that had seemed to grow stronger over the past couple of weeks. The purposeless hours were becoming harder and harder to bear, especially when his thoughts drifted so often towards a pair of brown eyes that both entranced and infuriated him in equal measure. Since he didn't want to waste his days with idle pursuits and there was only so much reading a man could take, he'd started trying to fill them with exercise instead, though unfortunately, today's ride had done nothing to soothe his spirits or distract his thoughts. He couldn't even call himself tired. He felt trapped between two lives, two paths and purposes, and there was nothing at all he could do about any of it for another month and a half but wait.

He crossed the hall with the enthusiasm of a man about to run the gauntlet. By the sound of it, most of the guests had already arrived, a hundred of them at least, all apparently talking at once. When his grandmother decided to do something, she did it properly and she was relaunching the Fortinis back into society with a vengeance. Mrs Fortini, whom he liked and admired, and Miss Fortini, whom he did not.

Strictly speaking, of course, that wasn't true. He *did* like her, only her prejudiced, prickly behaviour made it impossible to enjoy her company for long. As for admiring, well, obviously it was different from the way he admired her mother. *Very* different, in fact, and with a very different effect. The last time he'd seen her, he'd admired her legs and that brief glimpse of thigh so much that he'd found them impossible to forget. Typical that the one woman he was interested in was also the one most likely to spurn him!

He took a deep, fortifying breath outside the drawing room and then stopped abruptly, struck by the sight of the very legs in question. They were covered up, of course, but the light from the vast candelabrum behind her outlined the contours of what he now realised was a quite spectacular body. The gown she was wearing made a striking contrast to her practical shop clothes, in periwinkle-blue and with a fashionably high waist, a low scooped neckline, short puffed sleeves and wisps of delicate lace around the hem. Her arms, meanwhile, were encased in white, tight-fitting gloves and a pair of turquoise earrings hung suspended from her ears. With her dark hair fastened into a low knot at the back of her neck, though still with corkscrew ringlets framing the sides of her face, she somehow managed to look understated, ethereal and stunningly attractive all at the same time.

What the hell had he been thinking, avoiding her company for three whole weeks?

He cleared his throat, willing himself to look away, but his eyes refused to so much as blink. In a room filled with dozens upon dozens of people, he seemed unable to focus on anyone but her. His heart was hammering so fast he actually felt slightly winded, panting with a sudden onslaught of desire.

Despite that, he was aware of a feeling of irritation, too. After everything she'd said about the aristocracy, she ap-

peared to be deep in conversation with Augustus Lambert—
a marquess, no less. Not only that, but she was actually
looking him in the eye and smiling. As if she were *enjoying* his company! As if she weren't determined to argue at
every available opportunity! As if she could smile at a marquess but not at a potential earl!

Her gaze shifted towards him suddenly, as if she'd somehow sensed the words in his head, her lips forming a small
O shape and her skin flushing a dusky and becoming shade
of pink. Even the tops of her breasts appeared to be blushing, he noticed, not that he ought to have noticed, except
that somehow he couldn't help it. He felt as if his eyes were
being dragged of their own volition down to the swell of her
usually covered bosom. If he hadn't known how he wanted
to spend his free time before, he certainly did now and it
involved taking her straight upstairs...

'Samuel!' For once he was glad of his grandmother's
booming voice, bringing him back to his senses. 'Have your
feet stopped working?'

'Apologies, Grandmother.' He forced himself to smile,
though it was hard to know what expression to adopt when
his body was strung so tight. 'I thought you said this was a
party, not a squash. No doubt the evening will be declared
a great success.'

'Harumph.' His grandmother looked disgruntled by the
compliment. Her own fashion choices were the direct opposite of understatement, a vision of copper-coloured fabric,
diamond jewellery and tall peacock feathers. 'I had no idea
so much work was involved. I've had to clear out nearly all
of my furniture, pull up the carpets and spend a small fortune on food and wine. And *plants*!'

'Plants?'

'My housekeeper informed me that plants were a must. Why, I have no idea, but as you can see, for once I capitulated. It looks like a forest in here.'

'Yes.' He glanced around, noticing a surprising new abundance of shrubbery. 'It certainly looks greener than usual.'

'It's ridiculous. Goodness knows what I'm supposed to do with it all afterwards. I certainly shan't be throwing another party in a hurry.' She fixed him with a steely look. 'I expected you here earlier.'

'I went for a ride and stayed out longer than I intended.'

'If that's supposed to be an excuse, then I don't accept it. You ought to have been here on the receiving line.'

'My apologies. I didn't think that you'd need me.'

'Honestly, Samuel, you're getting as bad as your grandfather.' She gave him an exasperated look. 'Fortunately, despite your absence, things have been going well. Even Miss Fortini appears to be on her best behaviour.'

'Indeed?'

'Yes, she's barely rolled her eyes all evening. She's been much admired, too, although most of the gentlemen have been more discreet about it than you, I'm pleased to say. I was afraid your gaze might burn a hole in her dress.'

'Tactfully put, as always, Grandmother, but you're right, I shouldn't have stared. I was just surprised to see her.'

'Really?' His grandmother's voice was blatantly sceptical. 'Then I shall have to take care not to startle you in the future, Samuel, if that's the effect.'

'You stopped surprising me a good twenty years ago, Grandmother. Now if you'll excuse me, I ought to go and apologise.'

'Do that and fix whatever squabble you two have had while you're there.'

He tipped his head, refusing to either acknowledge or contradict the comment, before making a beeline straight across the room.

'Miss Fortini.' He bowed gallantly. 'I've just been admonished for staring. May I say how lovely you look this evening?'

'Thank you, Captain.' She bobbed a small curtsy in return, her pupils widening a fraction as their eyes met, then to his surprise extended a gloved hand. He accepted it at once and pressed his lips lightly against her fingers, better prepared this time for the surge of desire that immediately raced through his body. It was like an oncoming tide, building in strength the closer he got to her. He wanted to get closer still, to touch a lot more than her hand, too, to gather her into his arms and...

'Lambert.' He let her go again reluctantly, turning towards her companion with gritted teeth and a forced smile. 'How do you do?'

'Very well, Delaney.' Fortunately the Marquess seemed unaware of any tension. 'But how could I not be in such charming company?'

'Indeed. Miss Fortini is very charming.'

'She's just been telling me that she's Belle. *The* Belle.'

'Just Belle.' The lady in question looked faintly embarrassed, though her gaze never wavered from the Marquess. 'Although I've always preferred the name Anna.'

'But that's far too plain!' Lambert put a hand over his heart. 'A beautiful woman should have a beautiful name and you're quite the most exquisite diamond in the room this evening, Miss Fortini.'

'I'd keep my voice down if I were you.' Samuel felt a primitive urge to raise his fists. The way Lambert was looking at her was altogether too appreciative. 'My grandmother takes offence very easily.'

'Ah.' The other man's gaze flickered with alarm towards the Baroness. 'Well, naturally I didn't mean to offend...'

'Your grandmother said you were out riding.' Miss Fortini came to the Marquess's rescue.

'Yes, over the Downs. It was such a beautiful day, I couldn't resist the sunshine.' He paused, waiting for some disparaging comment about the luxury of not having to work, but she only smiled.

'Then I'm glad you made it back in time for the party. It's nice to see a familiar face.'

'A friendly one, too, I hope?' He smiled back, suppressing a look of surprise. After the way they'd parted the last time, he'd expected her to still be angry with him. Or aloof at the very least. Instead, she seemed to have sheathed all her prickles, actually looking pleased to see him, as pleased as he was to see her. He was struck with the realisation that he really *had* missed her. Those gorgeous brown eyes, that low voice capable of leaping into sudden animation, that rarely bestowed smile, although she seemed to have been bestowing it quite liberally this evening... He felt an unwonted pang of jealousy.

'Of course a friendly one.' A mischievous gleam appeared in her eyes. 'I just thought you might have had something better to do.'

That time he had to stifle a laugh. 'At this precise moment, I can't think of anything else I'd rather be doing. Perhaps you'd care to join me for a stroll about the room?' He held an arm out, not that there was much possibility of strolling anywhere in such a crush, but he felt suddenly determined to separate her from Lambert.

'I'd be delighted, Captain. Excuse me, my lord.' Her black eyelashes fluttered as she dipped into another curtsy and then threaded her hand through his arm, allowing him to draw her along the side of the room.

'You seem different, Miss Fortini.' Samuel tilted his head towards hers as they walked, his lips grazing inadvertently against one of her curls, though he still had to raise his voice to be heard above the crowd.

'That's because I made up my mind to enjoy myself. According to my mother I don't do it often enough so I've decided to get out of my shop and start.'

'I'm glad to hear it. How are the riding lessons going?'

She gave him a startled look, as if she hadn't expected him to broach the subject. 'Your grandmother didn't tell you?'

'Tell me what?'

'That I never came back after...well, the last time. Only for some reason she still insists on sending her maids to help me with the baking every morning. I've told them they don't need to, but they say they daren't not.'

'Do you blame them?'

'Not at all. To be honest, it's quite pleasant. We get the work done in half the time, then we all sit around the table and eat breakfast.'

'Then I'm pleased you're enjoying a rest.'

'I am and I have to admit the extra sleep has been very nice.' Her expression turned faintly guilty. 'The other morning I stayed in bed until seven o'clock.'

'Well, Miss Fortini, I'm shocked...' He smiled, although the mention of bed made his breeches feel somewhat tighter. 'And how was the experience?'

'Wonderful.' Her lips widened and he felt a glow in his

chest, as if her smile were actually warming his insides in several different locations now.

'In that case, I'm glad my grandmother is so domineering. Just this once.'

'Talking about me again?' The Baroness swooped down on them suddenly, peacock feathers waving on top of her elaborately arranged hairstyle.

'Only in the nicest possible terms, Grandmother.'

'I don't believe it.' She dipped a feather towards his companion. 'He's been in a perfectly foul temper for the past three weeks. I would have sent him away from Bath if I hadn't thought he'd take it as an opportunity to run back to sea again.'

'Well, he's being perfectly charming now.' Miss Fortini smiled. To his surprise, despite the fact that she claimed to have spurned further riding lessons, there didn't appear to be any friction between her and his grandmother.

'Then it must be thanks to your company. I insist upon the pair of you sitting together at supper.'

'Oh, I don't know...' She glanced towards him uncertainly.

'Unless you're promised elsewhere?' He lifted an eyebrow, almost wishing that he'd punched Lambert when he'd had the chance.

'No, but I wouldn't want you to feel obligated.'

'I'd be honoured.'

'Good. Then it's settled,' the Baroness announced with an air of finality. 'Now, where is your grandfather? If he's hiding in his library, then we shall have words.'

Samuel watched as she sallied forth again, struck with the distinct impression that his grandmother was matchmaking. Which was a ridiculous idea given the uncertainty of his current circumstances, only on this particular occasion he didn't seem to mind...

'Miss Fortini.' He took the opportunity to draw her into an alcove half-hidden behind a tall potted palm. 'I believe that I owe you an apology for the way we parted three weeks ago.'

'Anna,' she corrected him. 'You can call me Anna and I believe I owe you one, too. In fact, I owe you two. One for my behaviour that morning and one for not accepting your last apology about Henrietta. I should have forgiven you.'

The words caught him by surprise. 'Well then, perhaps our apologies cancel each other out? And *my* name, incidentally, is Samuel.'

'Samuel.' Her eyelashes fluttered. 'I thought about some of the things you said and I realised that you were right. I *have* been too prejudiced.'

'I still shouldn't have spoken so bluntly.'

'Yes, you should have. I'd be a hypocrite if I objected to plain speaking just because it was about me.'

'Are you suggesting some kind of parley, Miss Forti— *Anna*?'

'No.' She shook her head though her eyes were soft. 'I'm suggesting a formal declaration of truce, if you'll agree to one?'

'Then a truce it is, but I'm still sorry.'

'Apology accepted. And, while we're apologising to each other, I'm sorry if you've had a difficult time since. It must be very hard, waiting to find out whether or not you're going to inherit.'

'It is. I like visiting my grandparents, but my ship is my home. I miss having a sense of purpose, too. Waiting around like this makes me feel...'

'Adrift?'

'Something like that.' He made a wry face. 'Forgive me, I don't mean to complain, especially when my position is in many respects so enviable.'

'But it can be hard to remember how we *ought* to feel.' She put a hand on his forearm, her tone earnest. 'I do understand what you mean. Everyone wants to have control over their own life. I *have* a sense of belonging and purpose. My parents actually *gave* me a shop and yet sometimes I feel as if I'm drifting along, too, in a current I can't escape.'

'How so?' He let his gaze drift over her face. They were standing so close that if he moved his own forward just a little...

'Sometimes I wish I could have chosen a role for myself, as you did with the navy.'

'Indeed? What is it that you would have chosen?'

She lifted her shoulders and then dropped them again with a sigh. 'I don't know. I suppose I don't let myself think about it because there's nothing I can do to change anything. It was always just presumed that I would take over Belles, but if there was one thing I could change...' She stopped and bit her lip.

'Yes?'

'Nothing. It's not important.'

'It is to me.'

'Well...' She threw a quick glance over her shoulder as if she were afraid of someone overhearing. '*Baking!* I detest it. If I could avoid it, then I'd never bake another biscuit again in my life!'

'Baking?' He gaped at her in astonishment for a few seconds and then burst out laughing.

'Shh!' She gave his sleeve an admonishing tug. 'People will wonder what we're talking about.'

'But they'll never guess. Who *would* guess that the famous Belle of Bath doesn't like baking?'

'I can't help it. I never particularly enjoyed it, but I liked helping to run the shop with my father. Only after he died, my mother's hands were already too stiff for baking and I felt so…trapped, somehow. I know it sounds ungrateful, but it felt like more of a burden than a gift.'

He sobered instantly. 'Does your mother know how you feel about it?'

'No!' She looked shocked by the idea. 'She already worries about me. I've never told anyone else, not even Sebastian.'

'Then I'm honoured that you chose to tell me.' He pressed a hand over the one resting on his arm. 'Your secret is safe, I promise.'

'Thank you.'

'Anna…' He seemed to enjoy saying her name now, especially when he was staring deep into her eyes. They looked very big all of a sudden, even darker and more enticing than usual. So enticing that he felt as though he were being drawn towards them. Towards those full rosebud lips, too, the same shade of pink as her cheeks…

'Time for some music!' His grandmother's voice broke the spell, reverberating around the room with the force of a small cannon.

'Do you play the pianoforte?' He jerked upright again, surprised to find how close his head had just come to hers.

'I'm afraid not.' If he wasn't mistaken, she pulled away at the same moment. 'Or sing either, although my mother has a beautiful voice.'

'Is that true, Mrs Fortini?' Samuel led Anna out of the alcove, calling across the room to where her mother was standing in a crowd of what appeared to be gentlemen admirers. 'Do you sing? Shall we perform a duet?'

'It's been a while since I performed for anyone.' Mrs Fortini looked more than a little daunted by the idea.

'For me, too, but perhaps we can muddle through together? If you'll permit me to accompany you, that is?'

'Oh...' The look of determination that crossed Elizabeth Fortini's face at that moment was identical to that of her daughter. 'I'd be delighted, Captain Delaney.'

Chapter Twelve

Anna watched with a smile as her mother went to stand beside Captain Delaney—*Samuel*—at the piano. She was surprised by how well the evening was going. Even standing in the receiving line alongside the Baron and Baroness hadn't been as bad as she'd feared. A few of the guests were customers she'd recognised, but all had greeted her politely and her mother had seemed to enjoy herself immensely, even recognising a few friends from her youth.

The only blot on the evening had been Samuel's absence. After the first half hour she'd started to fear he wasn't coming at all, though when he finally *had* arrived, she'd felt oddly tongue-tied and light-headed. She still did. Since she'd decided to let go of the past and put her prejudices aside she'd been forced to admit to herself just how attractive she found him. It was positively alarming how handsome he looked tonight in formal evening attire, the silvery shade of his jacket, enhanced by a diamond pin in his elegantly tied white cravat, emphasising the vibrant paleness of his eyes.

Now, to top it all off, he was playing the piano and singing, his voice a rich baritone to her mother's clear and sweet-sounding soprano. Singing duets had been one of her parents' favourite pastimes, though her mother had barely sung a note since her father's death. Now Anna was glad to hear her voice again, albeit somewhat irrationally jealous. It made her wish that she'd inherited some of her parents' musical ability, but unfortunately that had all passed to her brother.

Irrational jealousy aside, however, Samuel and her mother made a fine pair, holding their audience's attention to the very last note.

'You have a beautiful voice, Mrs Fortini.' He was the first to offer his compliments, too, as the rest of the room started clapping. 'How about this as an encore?'

He tinkled a few more bars and Anna felt as if her heart had just clenched. It was an old Italian folksong, one that her father had often sung around the shop, the words as familiar to her as the alphabet. For a moment she didn't know whether to smile or cry, but then, seeing the look of mischievous enthusiasm on her mother's face, she laughed instead. It was a joke to everyone present, a good one, acknowledging who they were without making any apology for it. And Samuel had thought of it. She felt so delighted, she could have kissed him.

The thought made the smile freeze on her face. It wasn't *just* a thought, either. It was an image, too, and not a very discreet one. She wasn't envisaging a chaste peck on the cheek. On the contrary, it was far more intimate than that, all lips and bare skin and hands, all joined together and searching, exploring, feeling… Her heartbeat stuttered and then quickened with a burst of pure longing. If it hadn't been for the room full of people, she thought she might actually have acted upon it, might have marched across the room and thrown her arms around him.

That was the moment he chose to look up. Just as a tremor of excitement coursed through her body, he looked straight at her, his eyes flashing with surprise followed by recognition.

For a few seconds, she thought that something must have happened to the room. All of the candles seemed to flare at the same moment, making it hotter and brighter and so airless that she could feel her breath coming in soft pants. Yet despite the heat, she shivered, as if they were sharing some kind of intimate moment, her whole body feeling tighter and more exposed somehow.

The song came to an end while he was still looking at her, his gaze never wavering despite the applause that erupted around them. Anna gave a start, the rest of the room coming back into focus with a jolt, feeling as if she'd just been shaken to her core.

'What a clever idea for your mother to sing in Italian.' The Baroness appeared at her side again. 'She always was very talented.'

'Yes.' Anna stood up a little straighter, afraid of what the other woman might have just witnessed. 'Very talented.'

'Would you do an old woman a favour and escort me outside for some air? It's so stifling in here I can hardly breathe.'

'Of course, my lady.'

They made their way out onto the terrace at the back of the house, Lady Jarrow leaning on her arm for support, not that Anna was fooled by the performance. She'd never met anyone less frail. There had to be some ulterior motive behind the request and if the Baroness *had* just witnessed the look that had passed between her and her grandson, then doubtless it was connected with that. She was probably about to admonish her for looking at a possible earl in such an intimate way...

'Do you know why I'm in Bath, Miss Fortini?' Lady Jarrow dropped her arm the moment they were a few feet from the house, half-swathed in darkness.

'Why?' Anna blinked. It wasn't how she'd expected her to begin. 'I understood that it was for the Baron's health, my lady.'

'Quite so. It's far worse than people know. Hector is very ill, although he hides it well, even from Samuel and me.'

'You mean he hasn't told you he's ill?'

'No.' The Baroness fixed her with a hard stare. 'I imagine that when you look at us you see a curious pair, two very different individuals living separate lives under the same roof, but the truth is that I love my husband deeply. We understand each other. He suspects that I know about his health, of course, but if he doesn't wish to tell me outright then I respect his decision. It's the way he wants it to be.'

'So you think that he's...?' Anna couldn't bring herself to finish the sentence.

'Dying? Yes.' Lady Jarrow nodded firmly. 'I know that he is. He's weaker now than when we arrived in Bath.'

'I'm sorry, my lady. I don't know what to say.'

'There's nothing *to* say, or to be done about it, either. I'm telling you in the strictest confidence, as a secret from Samuel especially, not for sympathy, but because I want you to understand why I *cannot* leave Bath. Otherwise I would have marched my grandson to Staunton a long time ago. He ought to go, but he refuses.'

'Staunton?' Anna drew her brows together. Nothing about this conversation was going the way she'd expected. 'That's the estate he might inherit?'

'Yes. In Derbyshire, a good two days away by coach.'

'But surely it's his choice whether or not he wishes to visit?'

'Pshaw.' The Baroness rolled her eyes. 'It's an earldom, Miss Fortini, not something he can just walk into. If the baby turns out to be a girl, then he will be thrown, quite literally, to the wolves. He needs to learn about the estate and his duties and responsibilities beforehand and without interference. The only reason he hasn't been overwhelmed with sycophants and even more matchmakers already is that they're waiting to see what happens.' She made a disgusted face. 'I cannot bear the idea of my grandson with some fortune-hunting debutante, but if this baby's a girl, they'll all pounce together. He'll probably end up marrying one just to get rid of the rest. In short, he needs to stop wasting his time here, pull himself together and get ready.'

'I suppose so.' Anna regarded the Baroness with trepidation. It made sense from a practical perspective, but why tell her?

'Naturally I've given him my opinion on all of this, but he refuses to disturb Clarissa, Percival's widow. It's some notion of gentlemanly propriety, I suppose, and if he finds out about his grandfather then he definitely won't go, but it won't do. And *she* doesn't help, the foolish woman. She ought to write and invite him directly, but since she won't, he needs to be convinced to go himself.'

'I understand, my lady, but what does it have to do with me?'

Lady Jarrow gave her a look that implied a great deal, but for once she said nothing.

'If you think that I have some power to persuade him, then I'm afraid—'

'I do.' The Baroness forestalled her protest. 'I saw the way that you were looking at each other just now. You may have more influence than you think.'

'I don't know what you mean.' Anna lifted her chin. 'I haven't even seen Captain Delaney for the past three weeks. Whatever you think you saw, I'm afraid you're mistaken.'

'If you say so.' The Baroness pursed her lips unconvincingly. 'By the way, I had a communication from your grandmother this morning.'

'What?' Anna drew in a sharp intake of breath. It was becoming hard to keep up with all the changes in subject. 'You mean the Dowager Duchess?'

'Yes. Ottoline and I were great friends once upon a time. She wrote to tell me that she'd be very glad to see her daughter again. *And* to meet her granddaughter.'

'Me?' Anna's mouth fell open. 'Wait, have you told my mother this?'

'No, I thought she had enough to deal with this evening, but I intend to tell her later.'

'Oh.' Anna drew her brows together, her thoughts whirling. Samuel had warned her that it might happen, but it had only been three weeks. How could gossip have travelled so fast? Unless... A new suspicion stole across her mind. 'It all seems to have happened very quickly, my lady. I mean, for news about my mother to reach my grandmother and then for her to contact you and extend such an offer... Which one of you exactly began the correspondence?'

The Baroness made a clucking sound. 'Details, my dear.

What matters is that there is one. I'm quite certain that Ottoline would have heard about it and contacted me eventually, but when you get to my age, waiting is so tedious. I wrote to inform her of my contact with your mother after the first time you came for tea and she replied at once. She's most eager to see her again.'

'So she's coming here?'

'No. At her age such a journey would be inadvisable. I told her that you'd visit.'

'You told her *what*?' Anna burst out, resisting the urge to put her hands on her hips. 'That's out of the question. I have a shop to run.'

'Nonsense. My girls know what they're doing there now.'

Anna shook her head, annoyed with herself for having been so blind to the Baroness's machinations. 'That's why you sent them to me every morning? So that they could learn to take over?'

'I thought it might come in useful at some point.'

'I still can't go running off to…where does she live?'

'With your youngest uncle at his estate in the southern part of Yorkshire.'

'I am *not* going to stay with my grandmother in Yorkshire!'

'I never said that you should. No, these things probably ought to be done in stages.'

'Then where do you expect us to…?' Anna stopped midsentence as the answer occurred to her. 'Wait, the *southern* part of Yorkshire?'

'Very close to the border with Derbyshire, yes.' Lady Jarrow nodded placidly. 'Now the details have still to be arranged, but naturally I can't let you and your mother travel alone and Samuel has nothing else to do at present.'

'You seem to have it all worked out, my lady.'

'I usually do. And you have to agree that this works in everyone's favour. Samuel will be your escort and you'll be his chaperon at Staunton.'

'His *chaperon*? That might be the most ridiculous thing I've ever heard.'

'It may well be, but he can hardly stay in a house with Clarissa all on his own. Your being there will make the whole thing look perfectly respectable.'

Anna pressed her lips into a thin line, impressed despite herself. 'I thought that you truly wanted to help my mother?'

'If you're suggesting that I've been using her, then I take offence. I would have introduced her back into society anyway, though I admit the two purposes have dovetailed nicely. However, I took that as a positive sign.'

'And what about a chaperon for me? Don't you think it might start rumours if your grandson is seen to be escorting my mother and me around the country?' She lifted an eyebrow. 'People might talk.'

'Let them.'

'So you won't mind if your grandson, a possible earl, is spoken of in connection with a shopkeeper?'

'Who also happens to be a duke's granddaughter.'

'*And* a shopkeeper!'

Lady Jarrow let out an exasperated-sounding sigh. 'Do you know, the first time I set eyes on my husband was at an evening party like this one. He was the only man in the room with absolutely no interest in either my looks or my inheritance. It was the most exceedingly attractive quality. I decided to marry him right there and then.'

'Did you ever ask what *he* wanted?'

To her surprise, the Baroness laughed. 'I hardly remember, but it all worked out in the end. I'd like a similar partner for my grandson, a woman with her own mind, who doesn't care whether he inherits an earldom or not. In my personal opinion, you'd be a most excellent match for Samuel.' She held a hand up as Anna started to protest. 'Oh, for goodness sake, I'm not saying that you *have* to marry my grandson. I'm only asking you to travel with him to Staunton. Surely that's not so much to ask?'

'No, but...' She stopped as the other woman's gaze moved past her shoulder suddenly, towards the sound of approaching footsteps.

'Honestly, Samuel.' Lady Jarrow put a hand to her chest. 'You oughtn't to sneak up on people in the dark. You just frightened me half out of my wits.'

Chapter Thirteen

'I doubt it's so easy, Grandmother.' Samuel folded his arms over his chest, his eyes narrowing suspiciously as he took in the scene. 'I came to tell you it's time for supper, if you've quite finished scheming out here. What's going on?'

'I resent the word *scheming*.' Lady Jarrow drew herself up stiffly. 'I was just telling Miss Fortini about a letter I've received from the Dowager Duchess of Messingham. She's hoping for a reconciliation.'

'Your grandmother?' His gaze softened to one of concern as he turned towards Anna. 'I hope it hasn't upset you?'

'No-o.' She was touched by the almost tender expression in his eyes. He looked as if he genuinely meant it. 'If it makes my mother happy, then it makes me happy, too.' She paused ironically. 'I mean it this time.'

'I'm glad.'

'Only apparently she isn't well enough to travel to Bath so we have to go to her.'

'We?' He sounded surprised. 'Then you intend to go, too?'

'I think it's what my mother will want…'

'And I insist that they need an escort.' Lady Jarrow chimed in.

'Naturally. I'd be happy to accompany you wherever you need to go.'

Anna winced, catching a glimpse of the Baroness's gloating expression. 'I wouldn't speak too soon if I were you.'

'Why? Where does she live? The Outer Hebrides?'

'Close to Derbyshire.'

'Ah.' There was an extended moment of silence before his gaze slid slowly back to his grandmother. 'What a coincidence.'

'Isn't it?' The Baroness tossed her head imperiously. 'In fact, the estate is only a matter of miles from Staunton, but naturally a reconciliation takes time. These things shouldn't be rushed. Personally, I think it would be best for all concerned if Miss Fortini and her mother stayed with you at Staunton Manor for the duration of their visit. You'll be doing a service for each other.'

'But only if you're willing.' Anna threw a pointed look at the Baroness. 'If you really object, then my mother and I can stay at an inn. We're perfectly capable.'

'I shan't hear of it.' The Baroness stiffened indignantly. 'Not when…'

'Stay with me at Staunton Manor?' Samuel's voice was like granite. 'After I've told you, *repeatedly*, that I have no intention of visiting.'

'And I've told you not to be so foolish. Honestly, anyone would think that I meddled for fun and not for your own good. Now, I ought to return to my guests. In the meantime, I'll leave Miss Fortini to talk some sense into you.'

Anna clenched her jaw, waiting until the older woman

had gone back inside before slowing sighing out a breath. 'I'm sorry. I'm not sure what just happened.'

'My grandmother just happened. It's not your fault.' Samuel twisted his head to one side as if he were trying to ease a crick in his neck. 'Are you really sure you want to go and visit yours? I'm starting to think they're overrated as a relation.'

She gave a soft laugh. 'I don't want to, no, but my mother will and I need to go with her.' She paused. 'Only I get the strange feeling that your grandmother's been planning all this from the start.'

'I wouldn't put it past her.'

'Although she might be right about your visiting Staunton.'

'You're *agreeing* with her?' His eyes glinted dangerously.

'Not necessarily, but I think she has a point about your learning about the estate beforehand, just in case.'

'While my cousin's widow is still in residence? You don't think that would be monstrously tactless?'

'It's…unfortunate, but it's not as if you'd be asking to see the accounts. You're just going to see the place so it won't be such a shock if you *do* inherit. I understand your reservations, but perhaps it's a necessary evil.'

He held on to her gaze for several long seconds before rubbing a hand over his face. 'Maybe it is, but if I had my way, I'd never set eyes on the place at all.'

'Why?' She took a step towards him. 'Why are you so against the idea?'

'I told you, that side of the family never wanted me. The idea of me being the one to inherit their name and estates was their worst nightmare. And maybe they were right to fear it. Maybe *you* were right, too, not about the aristocracy in general, but about some of us.' He frowned. 'My father was the worst kind of aristocrat. What were the words you used? Indolent and debauched. Well, that was him. He gambled and drank away every shilling he ever had and I have his blood. What if I turn out to be just as dissolute? What if I *can't* be trusted to inherit?'

'Oh.' She wasn't sure which part of his statement to address first. '*Do* you drink and gamble?'

'In moderation and never.' He ran a hand through his hair. 'I don't even play whist.'

'Then why are you worried about that?'

'Because I haven't always shown good judgement. Do you know why I accompanied Mr Hoxley to your shop that first afternoon? Because I was bored. I'd spent months on dry land drinking tea and making calls and I was bored to tears. What if I inherit Staunton and I can't bear that, either?'

'If you inherit, then I doubt you'll have time to get bored. From what I understand, it takes a lot of work to run an estate.'

'Are you defending the aristocracy now?'

'No, just you, and you're not your father. You're a captain in the Navy. If you were so easily led astray, then you would never have made it to that rank.' She frowned. 'And it can't be boredom that really worries you. You said yourself that the navy was boring at times. No…' she shook her head '…there has to be another reason.'

He quirked an eyebrow. 'You think you know me so well?'

'It just doesn't make sense that you'd be afraid of turning into your father. You already know that you're not really.'

The skin across his jaw seemed to stretch with tension. 'Well, then, maybe some things can't be explained.'

'Or maybe you know, but you don't want to admit it?'

'Anna…'

'I could call your grandmother back out here.'

A flash of anger animated his face 'All right, maybe it's *not* because I'm afraid of turning into my father. Maybe it's because I don't see why I shouldn't! His family never even acknowledged my existence, let alone wanted to meet me. I'm the heir that nobody wanted, but if I inherit then I'm expected to just give up the life I built for myself, a life that I love, out of some kind of familial loyalty? Why should I? I never asked for their money and I sure as hell don't want it now. Why *shouldn't* I drink and gamble it all away just to spite them? How can I ever belong in a place where I was never wanted?'

She took another step towards him, feeling a burst of sympathy at the look of heartfelt anguish on his face. 'For what it's worth, I think it was your family's loss not to know you.'

'I could say the same thing about your grandfather, the Duke.' He looked deep into her eyes, his expression arrested and faintly wondering. 'It's strange, but you might be the only person in the world who *can* understand.'

She felt her pulse quicken at the words. It was the same thing she'd thought when she'd told him how she felt trapped, as if they truly *could* understand each other. As if maybe, despite everything, they might be a good match after all, just as the Baroness had said. The way he was looking at her now suggested he thought so, too, but how could that be possible? She was a shopkeeper and he was an earl…*maybe*. Or maybe not. There was an equal chance that he might remain a captain.

'I do understand.' She tried to keep her voice normal.

'Only my mother told me recently that bitterness and resentment weren't very attractive qualities. Shall I repeat her lecture?'

'Did it make you feel any better?'

'No, but it did make me think. Now I want to let go of the past and move on, wherever it leads me.'

'Wherever...?' He echoed the word as he lifted a hand to the side of her face, his fingers sliding gently across the curve of her cheek and beneath her chin, tilting it upwards. The touch sent a thrill of heat coursing through her body, making her feel as if every inch of her skin was blushing. Thank goodness they were outside in the dark. Although they really shouldn't be. Not together and certainly not touching like this. No matter what he said about understanding each other, there were still too many obstacles between them. Only it was becoming hard to hold on to that thought.

'We ought to go in.' She swallowed nervously. 'You said it was time for supper.'

'Did I?' He moved closer, his jacket brushing against the front of her dress. 'I can't remember.'

'Yes. I don't think...'

Her words faltered as his arms closed around her waist, enveloping her in a feeling of strong masculine warmth. She didn't move or resist, too surprised to do anything as he leaned in towards her, his mouth moving slowly towards and then hovering above hers, so tantalisingly close that it was hard to believe they weren't already touching. She could feel the warmth of his breath as it skimmed across her cheek...and then there was a sensation of cold air as he moved to one side, gently grazing the edge of her mouth.

She gave a small jolt of surprise, vaguely wondering if he'd missed, though it was hard to imagine how that could be possible at such a close distance. Not that the sensation was unpleasant. On the contrary, her cheek seemed to be throbbing beneath the caress of his lips. No, he hadn't missed, she realised, as his mouth drifted down her neck and into the dip at the base of her throat, his tongue darting out in a way that made her breathing come to an abrupt and ragged halt. She lifted her hands to his shoulders to steady herself, her pulse accelerating to a dizzyingly rapid tempo as her fingers curled around the hard, solid mass of the muscles beneath his jacket. Was the whole of his body like this? she wondered. There was only one way to find out...

Tentatively, she lowered her hands, dragging them slowly over his chest, her breath returning in a series of too-loud, too-rapid gasps. Yes, she realised, he *was* the same all over. Emphatically so. Hard and honed and muscular. And *she* was touching him. Fondling him almost as his lips and tongue continued to trail a path over her throat. She tipped her head back and closed her eyes, mortified by her own behaviour and yet powerless to do anything to stop it. Her whole body was in thrall, alive with so many sensations that it was hard to hold on to reality. All she wanted was to keep on touching him like this, to keep on being touched, too...but they *had* to go back inside. If anyone found them like this, they'd be well and truly compromised...

One of his hands pressed against the small of her back, smoothing its way up the length of her spine until it cupped the back of her head. She opened her eyes to find his only a short distance away. They were watching her intently, possessed with the same look of hunger she'd seen when she'd reached out to him in the colonnade. Did she look the same? Probably. She could feel the same ache she'd felt that day, too, that odd empty, yearning sensation low down in her stomach.

Now, surely now, he was going to kiss her? She hoped so. Maybe then the ache would be satisfied and go away. Just one quick kiss and they could go back inside the house and nobody would be any the wiser. In the meantime, all her senses felt in danger of being overwhelmed. The silvery light of his eyes, the husky sound of his breathing, the warm touch of his fingers, the citrusy scent of his cologne... There was only taste left and, more than anything at that moment, she wanted to taste his lips, just to see what they would be like. She felt her own part in anticipation and saw his gaze follow the movement.

'Samuel?' She spoke his name in a whisper.

He answered by moulding his lips against hers, plundering her mouth with an intensity that only made her want more. So much for one quick kiss. If anything the aching sensation seemed to be getting stronger, but that couldn't be right, could it? This was nothing like the first time she'd been kissed. She'd never even imagined that a kiss could be so completely destabilising.

'Anna...' He pulled away again after a few moments, breathing as rapidly as if he'd been running.

'Yes?'

'If this is your idea of talking some sense into me, then I'm convinced.'

'Then you'll come with us?' The prospect seemed ten times more exciting all of a sudden.

'I will.' There was a sound of a gong being struck and he nudged his lips against hers one last time. 'Just as long as you know this conversation isn't over.'

Chapter Fourteen

He wished it were raining.

Samuel pulled the brim of his hat down over his face and scowled, silently resenting the sunshine that seemed determined to accompany them all the way on their journey from Bath to Derbyshire. It felt wrong to be arriving in Staunton on such a beautiful spring day when all he could feel was dread. There ought to be clouds. Big grey stormy ones preferably, filled with torrential rain and lightning and hailstones for good measure.

He threw a swift glance towards the carriage where Anna and her mother were ensconced while he rode on horseback. After two days of near-constant travel, they were both probably sick of the sight of the interior, but at least they were safely out of range of his thunderous glares. He'd joined them for some of the journey, but it had only made his mood worse. Sitting opposite Anna without being able to touch her had been more than his patience could bear. They hadn't been alone since his grandmother's evening party, but every time he looked at her he found himself wanting to kiss her again. Just the memory of her lips made his own tingle. Not to mention other parts of him. He wondered if she felt the same way, half-afraid that she might have changed her mind after the party, but unfortunately there had been no opportunities to find out...

'Is that Staunton?'

He looked around to see Anna's head poking out of the carriage window, one of her arms gesturing into the distance. His next impulse was to turn his horse and ride south again without looking, but since he couldn't do that, he braced himself to look in the direction of her hand instead.

He already knew the answer, of course. They'd passed through Staunton village a couple of minutes before so there was really only one house it *could* be. Her question was surely rhetorical, though the amazement in her voice suggested an element of disbelief, too.

Slowly, he looked up and understood why. Staunton Manor put even his grandparents' hall in Rutland to shame, though in fact there was not one, but two Staunton Manors, a huge red-brick mansion standing beside the ruins of a smaller, much older-looking stone building. Set amid perfectly maintained lawns and woodland, the old and the new were located side by side at the top of a south-facing incline that looked out over rolling hills towards a range of peaks in the distance. He'd been told the new building was Tudor, built during the latter half of the sixteenth century in a then-popular Renaissance style, but what it lacked in modernity, it more than made up for in extravagance. From their vantage point on the drive the afternoon sun reflected off a row of large, vertical windows, ten on each of the four levels by the look of it, making the whole frontage seem to sparkle.

He let his gaze roam over the assorted towers and cupolas and projecting bays, each of them emblazoned with intricate patterns of heraldic symbols and crests. It was impossible not to admire the attention to detail. Even the drive was impressive, lined with topiary in intriguing, though not always recognisable, shapes, all leading towards a large gravelled area in front of the house. The whole place exuded rank and ostentation, as he imagined it was supposed to, not to mention wealth and power, yet somehow it had all come down to *him*. Briefly, he wondered what its original owner would have thought about that. Nothing that bore repeating, he imagined.

To his horror, however, worse was to come. As they drew closer, he saw literally dozens of people start to gather on the front steps—the entire household staff, by the look of it—led by the butler and housekeeper, though there was no sign of anyone resembling the lady of the house. Which was one small mercy, at least. The last thing he wanted was an audience to watch his meeting with Percival's widow, though he couldn't help but wonder why she was absent.

Unfortunately, there was nowhere to go but forward and no way to arrive unobtrusively, either. He smothered a few choice swear words and jumped down from his horse reluctantly.

'Captain Delaney.' The butler executed a bow so low that his nose almost scraped along the gravel. 'It's an honour to meet you, sir. We received your request to prepare rooms for yourself and two others. May I present the staff?'

Samuel's first thought was no. No, he could *not* present the staff. The staff, for all he cared, could all go and take leaps into the nearest lake, but they were all staring expectantly at him...

'I'm not sure that would be appropriate.' He glanced towards one of the upper windows, where he thought he noticed a flicker of movement. 'Considering Lady Staunton.'

'It was her order, sir.' The butler looked embarrassed. 'She was most particular about it.'

'Ah. I see. Very well, then.'

He gritted his teeth, following the butler along an interminable line of staff and giving nods at appropriate places until the housekeeper finally came to his rescue.

'Perhaps yourself and your guests would care for some tea in the drawing room, Captain?'

'That would be most welcome, Mrs...' He racked his memory for the name he'd just been given.

'Minty.' Anna's voice murmured behind him.

'Minty,' he echoed. 'Will Lady Staunton be joining us?'

'I'm afraid that her ladyship has a headache.' The housekeeper's eyes dropped to the floor, though not before he saw a definite flash of panic. 'She said that she'll see you at dinner, Captain.'

'Ah. I see.' He glanced back at Anna with a look of gratitude and relief, extending an arm before leading her up the front steps towards a door set at a right angle in one of the projecting bays.

'The drawing room is just through here.' The housekeeper led them through a cavernous, stone-floored hallway, empty except for a collection of wooden chairs by the fireplace, then along a side corridor and into a large, oak-panelled room. 'I'll attend to the tea.'

'You did very well.' Anna squeezed his arm once the housekeeper had departed. 'That can't have been easy.'

He gave a tight smile. 'At least I'm used to inspections.'

'That's true.' She let him go and wandered across to one of the tall sash windows. 'I suppose that managing a large household is a bit like running a ship. And maybe an estate is like a fleet.' She glanced back at him thoughtfully. 'That would make you an admiral.'

'I appreciate the confidence.' He looked around at the elegantly decorated, cream-coloured drawing room. 'So here we are. It's a beautiful house.'

'It is.'

'You could fit a whole ship into that hallway.'

'And still have room for my shop in one corner.'

'Where's your mother?' Samuel twisted around, acutely aware that they were finally alone together.

'She said she wanted a stroll through the gardens after being cooped up for so long. I think she's nervous about tomorrow.'

'What about you?' He found his gaze riveted on her slender figure as she stood, bathed in sunshine in the window. 'Are you nervous, too?'

'A little, but now that we're here, I'm glad. It's nice to get away.' She looked apologetic. 'Sorry.'

'Don't be. I'm glad that one of us is enjoying themselves.'

She gave him a sympathetic smile. 'Thank you for bringing us. I know that you didn't really want to.'

'You persuaded me, remember?'

'Oh, yes.' She bit her lip as the air between them seemed to become charged suddenly. 'So I did.'

He sat down in an armchair to stop himself from going to her. The urge to take her in his arms was as strong as ever, but somehow being in this house, a house he'd never wanted to see, let alone visit, made him doubly afraid that she might have changed her mind about him. It seemed so unlikely that she was here at all *or* that she'd altered her thinking about the aristocracy. He was half-afraid to believe it was true. Besides, the housekeeper, not to mention her mother, would be back any minute.

'I suppose the tea will be here soon.' She seemed to be thinking the same thing.

'I'd prefer rum.'

'It's too early for rum.'

'Maybe a little.' He sighed. 'Do you suppose that Lady Staunton really has a headache?'

'I can't judge that before I meet her. It *might* be true.'

'Or she might just be appalled at my poor manners in coming here?'

'You're not doing anything wrong.' She walked back towards him, stopping just in front of his chair. 'You've given her plenty of time. Her baby's due next month, isn't it?'

'Yes, although I don't know if that makes my behaviour better or worse.'

'It is what it is. It's the intention that matters and you didn't come here with the intention of hurting anyone.'

'Thank you, Anna.' He dug his fingernails into the arms of the chair, resisting the urge to pull her down onto his lap. 'I'm starting to wonder what I would do without you.'

The next morning dawned as bright as the last, the sky a breathtaking pastel orange and blue as the three of them sat down for breakfast, the earliness of which appeared to both shock and scandalise some of the staff.

Anna sipped at a cup of hot chocolate, looking between Samuel and her mother with a feeling of helplessness. Despite their outward appearances of calm, it was hard to tell which of them was more nervous. Her mother was drumming her fingers rhythmically on the tablecloth and Samuel's gaze kept drifting in the direction of the doorway as if he expected Lady Staunton to make an appearance, though since she hadn't come down to dinner, after all, sending another message to say she was still feeling unwell, Anna doubted they'd see her at breakfast, either. Her own sympathy for the woman was starting to wear thin. No matter how much she was grieving, she might still have shown her face, even briefly. Her continued absence only made Samuel feel worse.

There hadn't been any opportunity for them to resume the *conversation* they'd begun at his grandmother's evening party. Which was a good thing, she told herself, since it wasn't one that *ought* to be continued, no matter how enjoyable she'd found it at the time. It was undoubtedly better to wait and find out what the future would bring before resuming *anything*, even if the look on his face when he'd said he didn't know what he'd do without her the previous afternoon made her wish otherwise...

They made their way to her uncle's estate early, too, her and her mother in an open-topped barouche with Samuel riding alongside. She'd told him that he didn't need to accompany them any further, but he'd insisted, looking visibly relieved as they'd drawn away from Staunton Manor, seemingly engrossed in his own thoughts as they travelled in silence the miles between the two houses.

It took just over an hour to reach her uncle's house at Feversham. Compared to Staunton, it looked like the very height of modernity, built in an elegant Palladian style that seemed to spring up like a natural extension of the parkland around it. Anna felt her lips curl with self-mocking amusement. Up until a few weeks ago, she'd never been inside anything resembling a mansion before, yet now she seemed to be making a habit of it.

'This is it, Mama.' She clutched her mother's hand supportively.

'Yes.' Her mother's fingers trembled. 'I just hope I'm doing the right thing.'

'Of course you are. They invited you, remember?'

'Yes, but what if…?' Her mother leaned forward suddenly. 'Oh!'

'What's the—? *Oh!*' Anna echoed as she turned her head to see two people waiting for them on the drive, a small, silver-haired lady holding a cane beside a gentleman with greying curly hair. Her grandmother and uncle, she presumed. Even at a distance she could see they both bore a striking resemblance to her mother.

Samuel dismounted before the carriage had stopped, opening the carriage door and lowering the steps without waiting for a servant to help him.

'Mrs Fortini?' He offered a hand and her mother clutched it, descending the steps with a look of unmistakable trepidation. As her feet touched the gravel there was a heavy moment of stillness, disturbed only by the sound of a blackbird trilling in the background, followed by a sudden flurry of activity as she and the grey-haired man both moved at the same time, each of them throwing their arms around the other.

Anna watched, fighting a swell in her throat. Samuel held out his arm and she took it, stepping down onto the drive to find herself face to face with the silver-haired lady.

'You must be Annabelle.' To her surprise, the woman had tears in her eyes. 'I'm so delighted to meet you, my dear.'

'I'm pleased to meet you, too, your Grace.' She dipped into a curtsy.

'Curls!' The older woman peered under her bonnet. 'You have *my* curls!'

'Oh…yes.' Anna lifted her shoulders and then dropped them again, unsure how else to respond as the woman gave a stifled sob and then pressed a handkerchief to her face, bursting into a flurry of tears. Thankfully, her mother and the grey-haired man walked quickly to join them.

'I didn't say anything terrible, I promise…' Anna looked at her mother apologetically.

'I know, dear.'

'It's not your fault,' the man hastened to reassure her. His expression was kindly, though his eyes looked moist, too, she noticed. 'I'm afraid that my mother's been feeling some-what overwrought this morning. You must be my niece.'

'Yes.' Anna nodded, feeling as though she were in some kind of bizarre dream. 'I suppose I must be.'

'I'm your uncle, Tobias Holden.' He extended a hand. 'Welcome to Feversham, Miss Annabelle. How do you do?'

'I…' She had the impression that her tongue was stuck to the roof of her mouth.

'Captain Samuel Delaney,' Samuel interceded, taking her uncle's proffered hand when she didn't move and shaking it warmly. 'Perhaps Miss Fortini and I might take a walk around your gardens while you and your sister get reac-quainted? I'm sure that you have a lot to catch up on.'

'That sounds like a good idea.' Her uncle agreed tactfully. 'Though I'd very much like to talk with my niece afterwards. If that's agreeable to you, of course, Miss Annabelle?'

'Anna, and yes.' She finally managed a strained smile, clutching hold of Samuel's arm as if her life depended on it. 'Just give me an hour. Or two.'

Chapter Fifteen

To Anna's immense relief, Samuel led the way, drawing her around the side of the house as the rest of her family, as unlikely as it sounded to call them that, went inside.

'Thank you,' Anna said when her tongue felt normal again. 'I didn't know how to react when he offered me his hand. I felt as though my arm had just frozen.'

'I'm sure he'll understand. It's not an easy situation for any of you, but it seems to be going well.'

'Yes.' She drew in a deep breath and then expelled it again slowly. 'I don't know what I expected, but it definitely wasn't that.'

'Not how you pictured them?'

'I've never tried to picture them. I've always avoided thinking about them at all. But they seem quite…normal.'

'I suppose it just goes to show.' He sounded philosophical and she lifted her face towards him curiously.

'Show what?'

'Just that things aren't always as they seem. Perhaps your grandmother really did regret the estrangement.'

'She might have said so at the time.'

The pressure of his arm against hers tightened. 'Not everyone is as forthright as you. Some people are afraid to say what they think. And who's to say that she didn't? Maybe she just couldn't defy your grandfather.'

'Maybe.' She pursed her lips. 'I suppose it does make you think about things differently. Maybe not everyone in your father's family wanted to shun him, either.'

'I'm afraid in my father's case he did a pretty effective job of alienating everybody.'

'Then maybe not everyone wanted to shun *you*?'

'Ah.' He was silent for a long moment. 'Maybe not all of them, no, but there's no way of knowing now. Most of my family are gone.'

They lapsed into silence, wandering along a side terrace and into a walled kitchen garden. Most of the flowerbeds were empty, waiting for warmer weather, all except for one long row of herbs that still defied the night-time frosts. The day itself, however, was cloudless, the chill of the breeze tempered by the heat of the sun. As long as they kept out of the shadows, it was a near-perfect temperature.

Anna closed her eyes, her nostrils filled with the scent of sage and rosemary, and began to relax. It was incredible how much her life had changed over the course of the past few weeks. It was bizarre enough that she was here, visiting the home of the family she'd always despised, even more bizarre to be in the company of a possible earl whom she'd kissed. But here she was, alone with him again. It felt as if the whole world had turned upside down.

'It's fortunate that your uncle's estate is so close to

Staunton,' Samuel spoke again after a little while. 'You and your mother should be able to visit often.'

'Yes.' She reached a hand out, skimming her fingers along the branch of a honeysuckle. 'Although we've never discussed how long we'll be staying.'

'I thought I'd see how Lady Staunton responded to our arrival.' He gave her an ironic look. 'I'll have to let you know when I find out. In any case, we ought to leave before the baby arrives.'

'That would probably be tactful...' she nodded in agreement '...and I shouldn't stay away too long or else your grandmother might knock down my shop and turned it into a stables.'

'It's a possibility.' He laughed. 'She'll need a new project now that your mother's left. It's amazing she's stayed in Bath as long as she already has. Usually she hates the place.'

'Mmm.' Anna pretended to study a clematis on the wall to hide her expression of guilt. It was obvious that Samuel had no idea of the seriousness of his grandfather's condition and, since his grandmother had told her in confidence, she could hardly reveal it. Besides, telling him would only send him riding headlong back to Bath, the last thing either of his grandparents wanted.

'What's the matter?' He seemed to sense the conflict in her.

'Oh, nothing.' She forced a smile. 'It's just been a busy month, that's all. So much has happened.'

'For me, too. I thought that I'd put off seeing Staunton until I had to, *if* I had to, but I suppose my grandmother was right about preparing myself just in case. Not that I'll ever admit that to her.'

'I think she's trying to protect you.'

'From social climbers and debutantes? I know. She seems to think I'll be mobbed if I inherit. It's quite insulting how little she trusts me to defend myself from marriage traps.'

'I'm not sure I blame her. Fighting Napoleon is one thing, but debutantes can be very unscrupulous.'

He snorted. 'Then you agree that evasive action is called for?'

'Well...' She made a show of looking around, as if there might be fortune hunters hiding in the bushes. 'You ought to be safe enough here and at Staunton, but I wouldn't go anywhere else without a chaperon if I were you.'

'I thought that you were my chaperon?'

'Oh, yes, so I am. You're perfectly safe, then.'

'I wouldn't say that.' He gave her a significant look. 'About that conversation we started the other evening... Have *you* ever thought about marriage?'

'Me?' Her heart gave an unusually heavy thump, making her fingers clench inadvertently over his forearm.

'Yes. You must have thought about it.'

'Must I? Not every woman dreams of marriage.'

'No, but I can't believe you haven't had suitors. Not unless there's something in Bath's spa water that clouds men's minds.'

'Now you're trying to flatter me.'

'Only because I'm trying to get answers.' He tilted his head towards hers, his voice huskier than usual.

'Well...' She felt her stomach quiver in response. 'I suppose there *have* been a couple.'

'But no proposals?'

'Four.'

'Four?' He stopped walking abruptly. 'You just said a *couple* of suitors.'

'Because the proposals were all from the same man, Mr Etton. He owns the shop next to mine.'

'He sounds tenacious. What kind of shop is it?'

'General goods. Sugar, flour, all the baking essentials. That's how we met.'

'But you turned down his proposals?'

'No, I married him...' She giggled. 'What do *you* think?'

His expression turned faintly petulant. 'You might have told him to come back in a year after you'd thought about it.'

'Four times? That sounds cruel.'

'So why did you say no?'

'*Why?*' She lifted an eyebrow at the question. 'Didn't you just accuse *him* of being tenacious?'

'Humour me. Didn't you like him?'

'Oh, I liked him well enough. He's very good natured.'

'Too old?'

'No. He was thirty-one the first time he proposed and that was five years ago so I suppose now he's...'

'Thirty-six.' There was a hard edge to Samuel's voice this time. 'Then what *is* wrong with him?'

'Nothing, I just didn't want to marry him. To be honest, I think he sees me more as a business proposition than a bride. He's never remotely bothered when I refuse him. He just says the offer's open if I ever change my mind.' She sighed. 'I suppose I could be Mrs Etton in a month if I wanted, but that wouldn't be a very romantic story to tell the grandchildren.'

'Hmmm. What about the other one?'

'What?' Her heart thumped again, even harder than before, though for a different reason.

'Your other suitor. What happened to him?'

'Oh.' She placed a hand over her stomach, turning queasy at the memory. 'That's not a very romantic story, either.'

'Anna?' Samuel's gruffness was replaced by instant concern. 'Are you all right? You've gone pale.'

'Yes...' She drew her arm away from his, going to sit on a small wooden bench set beside the wall. Her *other* suitor wasn't a subject she'd ever talked about with anyone and yet, now that Samuel asked, she found herself wanting to tell him.

'I'm sorry.' He crouched down in front of her. 'I didn't mean to upset you. I shouldn't have asked so many questions. It's just hard not to feel jealous.'

'Jealous?'

'Yes.' He gave a self-deprecating smile. 'That tends to happen after you've kissed someone, especially when you can't stop thinking about them.'

'Oh...'

His smile wavered. 'But if you don't feel the same way then I understand.'

'It's not that. There's just something I need to tell you.' She looked into his face, watching intently for his reaction. 'Do you remember that first day in Sydney Gardens when you asked if my attitude towards Henrietta and Mr Hoxley was based on personal experience? Well, you were right, it was.'

'A bad experience?' His brows lowered.

'Yes.' She nodded stiffly. 'It was the summer I turned sixteen. There was a gentleman who used to visit the shop every morning. He was the youngest son of...well, an important person. He was always so charming and polite and friendly, I could never understand why my father didn't like him. Then one day he passed a note to me across the counter. It said that he was in love with me, obsessed with me even, that he could barely sleep because his heart ached so badly. Then it asked me to meet him that afternoon, to go for a walk in the park and spend some time together.' She couldn't bear to look at Samuel any longer, twisting her face to one side. 'Stupidly, I decided to go.'

'Didn't your father stop you?'

'I didn't tell him. I said I had some errands to run and went off in my best dress and bonnet.' She swallowed against a tight, burning sensation in her throat. 'I was so excited.'

Samuel stood up abruptly, placing one foot on the bench beside her as if he were bracing himself. 'What happened?'

'Nothing at first. We met at the end of the street like he'd suggested, only he took me in a different direction from the park. I thought he must have made a mistake, but when I asked where we were going he just gave me a funny look and said he was taking me to meet his family.'

'But you didn't believe him?'

'I'm not *that* naive. I told him I wanted to go back home, but he wouldn't listen. He got angrier and angrier, accusing me of flirting with him and saying that I'd led him to expect certain…things.'

'Did he touch you?'

She jerked her chin up, alarmed by the note of raw anger in his voice. His expression was furious, his jaw clenched so tight that she could see the pulse of a vein in his neck.

'Yes.' She dropped her gaze again, feeling a rush of shame as she remembered the way he'd grabbed and fondled her breasts. 'But he didn't get what he wanted. I knew where to kick him so I did. As hard as I could.'

'Good.'

'Then I ran.' She shook her head, trying to remove the memory of that run, thinking that her heart might actually burst with panic, that he might catch up with her at any second. 'I was terrified for days afterwards that he'd come back to the shop, but thankfully he didn't. I never saw him again at all. Then, after the fear had passed, I felt so stupid and humiliated and dirty. I'd thought that he'd genuinely liked me, but he barely saw me as a person.' She gave a bitter laugh. 'So you see, when you accused me of blind prejudice it wasn't strictly true. There was a reason. I didn't always hate gentlemen, either. I was just scared of being tricked and deceived again.'

'And I tricked you that first day...' Samuel dropped his boot back to the ground, muttering a series of barely distinguishable oaths before sitting down beside her. 'Anna, I'm so sorry.'

'What you did was different.'

'Not *that* different. I'll never deceive you again, I promise.'

'I know. I trust you and I accepted your apology, remember?'

He reached for her hand, folding his fingers around it. 'If I'd known, I would never have accused you of being prejudiced.'

'But you were right. I blamed the whole of the aristocracy just because I couldn't blame him. I couldn't tell anyone.'

'You didn't tell your parents?'

'No. I knew that my father would have done something foolish and Sebastian would probably have joined him. Then they'd both have been hanged.'

'So you never told anyone?'

'It was too shameful.' She tried to pull her fingers away,

but he wouldn't let her, his own tightening as she tried to withdraw.

'You've no reason to feel that way. He's the one who ought to feel ashamed of himself.'

'I know, or at least my head knows that. It's just hard convincing the rest of me sometimes.' She looked up at him anxiously. The lines on his face showed he was still tense, though he seemed to be looking inward rather than out. 'Don't you judge me?'

'For being an innocent young woman who thought she was going for a walk?' His gaze softened. 'You trusted the wrong person, but you've nothing to blame yourself for.'

'Thank you.'

He lifted her hand, pulling her fingers gently to his lips and holding them there. 'What was his name?'

'What?' She gave him a startled glance. 'Why?'

'I want to know.'

'So you can do what?'

'Ever hear of running the gauntlet?'

'Ye-es.' She opened her eyes wide. The horrible practice of leading a man at sword-point between two rows of sailors while they whipped at him with frayed pieces of rope had made her doubly afraid for Sebastian when he'd joined the navy. As if storms and cannons hadn't been enough to worry about... 'But I thought the practice was banned now?'

'I could make an exception.'

She let out a shuddering laugh. 'I appreciate the thought, but I've put what happened behind me. It took a long time, but I have.'

'You shouldn't *have* to just put it behind you. He should be made to pay for his behaviour.'

'He did. There was a scandal involving another woman

a few months later and he was sent off to the army. I've no idea what happened to him, but I should think going to war was sufficient punishment.'

'Still not enough.'

'Samuel.' She pulled her thumb free from his grasp, rubbing it gently across the tops of his fingers. 'It spoiled my life for a long time, but I don't want to think of it any more. I didn't tell you so that you could take some kind of revenge. I told you because...' she hesitated '...well, because I wanted to explain why I felt the way I did about the aristocracy.'

'All right.' He nodded slowly. 'No revenge, if that's truly what you want.'

'It is.' She lifted her spare hand to her face, swiping away the tears that seemed to have leaked out from the corners of her eyes. 'So, in answer to your original question, no, I've never seriously thought about marriage. I don't want to marry just for business reasons and I'm fortunate that I don't need a husband to take care of me. My shop gives me independence and security.'

'But you don't enjoy it.'

'I never said that.'

'You said you'd be happy if you never baked another biscuit in your whole life.'

'Well...yes...but I *do* enjoy the business side of it.'

'Doing accounts?' He looked sceptical.

'Yes. I like working with figures. Accounts, prices, haggling, all of that. It's just the baking that doesn't suit me.'

'So what if you had a baker to do that part for you? Then you could just do the things you enjoy.'

'I'd have to pay a baker.'

'But if you had a husband who was willing to help you?

One who didn't see you as a business proposition, but wanted you to be happy?'

'I don't know.' She felt colour wash over her cheeks. 'I told you I've never really considered marriage.'

'Neither have I until recently. Only now I can't seem to stop thinking about it. It's a curious feeling.'

'Samuel...'

'Do you know what else is curious?' he went on, looking down at their still-joined hands. 'That I spent my first four months on shore wishing I were back at sea again and yet recently I've thought about it less and less. Hardly at all for the past few days.'

'Oh.' She felt her pulse flutter at the implication.

'The only reason I can think of is you.'

'We weren't even talking to each other a week ago!'

'But we are now.' The side of his thigh nudged against her leg. 'You're the most honest and loyal woman I've ever met. You're also the only person who understands how I feel about my family and this inheritance. It makes me wonder whether we might be compatible in other ways, too. I think we would be.'

Anna caught her breath at the words. They made her wonder, too. *Could* they be a good match? But surely he couldn't be suggesting what it sounded as though he was suggesting, especially when so much was still undecided... She felt her temperature rise and then plummet again abruptly.

'Wait, is this because of your grandmother?'

He looked confused. 'What do you mean?'

'All this talk about marriage. Did *she* suggest that you ought to propose to me?'

'No. Why? Did she suggest it to you?'

'She said that she thought it was a good idea.'

'Oh, for pity's sake… When I get back to Bath, she and I are going to have a serious talk.'

'She did add that I didn't *have* to marry you.'

'How decent of her.' He sounded terse. 'I'm sorry.'

'It's all right. It was actually nice to know that she approves, although I told her I'd be completely unsuitable. I mean, maybe not for a captain, but if you inherit, how could *I* ever be a countess?'

'Haven't we been over this? How could I be an earl?'

'Exactly! One of us at least ought to know what we're doing.'

'But if I were a captain you would consider it?' He rested his forearms on his knees and gave her a long look.

'I don't know…perhaps.' She was surprised by her own answer. 'But what would you do? Go back to the navy and leave me behind?'

'Not necessarily. Maybe I'll decide on a career in baking instead. That's something we would decide together. I've saved a reasonable amount of prize money over the years so I wouldn't have to go back if you didn't want me to.'

'But I thought you said you belonged there?'

'I said that it gave me a sense of belonging, but maybe belonging doesn't have to be with a ship.' His gaze latched on to hers. 'Maybe it could mean with a person instead. Maybe it already does.'

'You should still wait and see what happens.'

'Why? If we belong together, then what does it matter who I am or where we are?'

Anna clenched her jaw, refusing to consider the possibility. 'Are you always so impulsive?'

'I joined the navy on impulse. That was the best decision I ever made.'

'Well, I like to think things through.'

'That's why we're perfect together.'

'Except that you don't love me.' She spoke the words softly, trying her hardest to make them into a statement and not a question. She didn't want to sound as if she were trying to force him into a declaration. He hadn't said that he loved her, although his words were tantalisingly close. Did she love him? Everything had happened so fast that she hadn't had a chance to consider. Maybe it was *too* fast? What had he said about his parents' whirlwind romance? Maybe there was a danger of them repeating the same mistake. She didn't know. All she knew was that her blood was coursing so heavily that she could hear the rapid thud of her own heartbeat.

'Don't I?' He rubbed a hand thoughtfully over his chin. 'I've never considered the idea in a great deal of depth before. How would I know if I did?'

'I don't think I'm the person to ask. I've never considered it in depth before, either.'

'Then maybe we both ought to start considering.' He lifted his hands to either side of her face, twisting it slowly towards him and lowering his mouth against hers. His touch was featherlight and gentle, stroking and caressing rather than possessing. His lips were warm and soft, too, making her feel as if she were slipping into some kind of trance. Her mind, that was, since her body felt the exact opposite, thrumming with vibrations that seemed to reach down to her very core. Briefly, she thought of the piano he'd played in Bath, feeling as though she were the instrument. His hands seemed to be playing her just as skilfully, trailing a slow path over her throat, down her shoulders and around her back, down to the base of her spine, making every part of her quiver.

They came apart finally and he looked deep into her eyes, his own heavy-lidded with what, even to her inexperienced mind, looked like desire. Desire for her. The thought made her even more light-headed. If she wasn't careful, she might lose her grasp on reality altogether. She might forget who she was and where she came from and start to think that she belonged with him, too. And then what might she say...and do? It was madness to even consider marrying him and yet...she was.

'It's just something to think about.' He touched his forehead lightly against hers before moving away. 'You don't have to give an answer. Not yet.'

Chapter Sixteen

Samuel waited outside for an hour while Anna went to meet her family. It gave him some time to think about what had happened in the herb garden, which he had to admit, in retrospect, might have been somewhat misguided. They'd both been through enough emotional turmoil over the past few days without him bringing up the subject of marriage. He probably should have waited. On the other hand, he couldn't bring himself to regret it, either. The fact that she hadn't refused outright made him optimistic, too.

'I'm sorry for keeping you waiting,' a voice called out from behind. 'I hope you don't feel banished out here.'

'Not at all.' He turned to find Tobias Holden walking towards him. 'I'm sure you had a lot to talk about.'

'Twenty-five years' worth and we're not finished yet. I just wanted to thank you again for bringing my sister and niece back to us.'

'They were coming anyway.'

'But you came with them. My mother and I are both grateful.'

'Then you're welcome.' Samuel inclined his head with a smile. The other man had a kind face, a lot like his sister's, and greying curls that seemed determined to stand upright rather than flat on his head.

'We've wasted so many years.' Tobias sounded regretful. 'I always thought that Elizabeth must hate us for what happened.'

'I don't think she's the kind of person who hates.'

'Neither is our mother, although I'm afraid she never had the courage to stand up to our father. Neither did I, unfortunately, and after he died... Well, we assumed it was too late for a reconciliation.'

'Was he such a tyrant?'

'He wasn't a bad man, but he was very proud. Once he found out who my sister had eloped with, he forbade us from ever speaking about her again.'

'Did he know she lived in Bath?'

'I believe so. He had terrible gout, but he refused to go anywhere near the city.'

'And your older brother? What will he think about all this?'

'Anthony can think what he wishes. I won't let him spoil things.' The other man's expression turned resolute. 'Now, will you stay and have luncheon with us?'

'I don't wish to intrude. Perhaps I ought to leave the ladies here and return later?'

'I won't hear of it, Captain.' Mrs Fortini emerged out onto the terrace at that moment, Anna on one arm and the

Dowager Duchess on the other. 'There'll be no more tears, I promise. We'll all be perfectly composed for the rest of the day.'

'Well, then...' Samuel smiled, though his eyes felt like magnets, drawn inevitably straight towards Anna '...how can I refuse?'

Mrs Fortini was as good as her word, Samuel reflected, as he, Tobias and Anna strolled in the grounds later that afternoon. The mood during luncheon had been warm and light-hearted, without any tears at all, as if nothing untoward had happened during the past twenty-five years. Even Anna had started to smile and relax in her new family's company, though she seemed subdued, too, as if her thoughts were elsewhere...

Her uncle Tobias, as it turned out, was another kind of seafarer, a member of the Royal Academy who'd been a member of several scientific expeditions to study ichthyology around northern Europe. It was a topic he enthused about over luncheon, insisting on taking Samuel and Anna to see what he referred to as his 'pride and joy' afterwards.

'There it is.' Tobias stopped beside a lake, around a hundred feet in length and only slightly less in breadth. 'Stocked with the finest examples of trout and perch I could find.'

'It's a beautiful prospect.' Samuel smiled as his gaze fell upon a small wooden jetty. 'You have a rowing boat.'

'Yes, I like a day's fishing now and again.'

'She looks like a sturdy vessel. Do you think I might be permitted to borrow it?'

'Of course.' Tobias looked surprised. 'Do you want to go fishing?'

'Not today, but I've been pining for the water over the

past few months.' He exchanged a swift glance with Anna, wondering if he could convince her to join him. There was only one way to find out... 'And I'd like to show Miss Fortini here my navigational skills.'

'On a lake?' Her eyes lit up with amusement.

'At least you can be sure we won't get lost.' He grabbed her hand before she could argue, pulling her towards the jetty.

'Samuel!' Anna gave him a remonstrative look as they reached the boat. 'There's only one bench.'

'Then you'll just have to sit in the stern. It looks dry enough, but here...' He shrugged out of his jacket and laid it flat in the bottom of the boat. 'Use this.'

She lifted an eyebrow. 'Something tells me you wouldn't ask a real lady to sit there.'

'You *are* a real lady, although if you mean some timid debutante just out of the schoolroom then you're right, I wouldn't. But then I wouldn't have asked her to come with me in the first place.' He held out a hand and gave her a quick wink. 'Fortunately, I know you're not likely to have a fit of the vapours.'

'I might surprise you.'

He grinned as she accepted his hand and stepped down from the jetty, staggering against him slightly as she made her way to the stern.

'It's very wobbly.' She sounded anxious.

'I won't let you fall, I promise.'

'So far, so good.' She settled herself on his coat, rearranging her skirts and then opening up the parasol that her grandmother had insisted she carry in the sunshine. 'Do I have to address you as Captain now we're on the water?'

'Naturally. Unless you want to be put in the brig for insubordination.' He untied the rope that held them to the jetty and jerked his head towards the other end of the boat. 'It's over there and there's no coat to sit on.'

'Oh, dear.' She laughed. 'Well, then, whatever you say, Captain.'

Samuel looked away quickly, using one of the oars to push them off as a bolt of desire shot through his body. She looked so pretty leaning backwards, one hand trailing in the water while she twirled her parasol in the other, completely relaxed, too, definitely more than she had been at luncheon, as if she were happy that it was just the two of them again. Considering what they'd discussed that morning he took that as a good sign.

'What are you thinking about?' he asked as they glided out into the middle of the lake.

'Just that I could get used to this. It's so peaceful. All I can hear are birds singing and water lapping against the oars. Is this how it is at sea?'

'Not exactly.' He laughed at the idea. 'Ships are noisy places, especially ships with cannons and squadrons of marines on board. There isn't much time for quiet reflection.'

'I suppose not.' She gave him a quizzical glance. 'You look happy.'

'I told you, I like water.'

'Does Staunton have a lake?'

'I've no idea.'

'You ought to find out just in case you *do* inherit. What self-respecting captain can have a house without a lake?'

'I'd be a retired captain, but you're absolutely right. If there isn't, then I'll make it my first order of business to dig one. *If* I inherit.'

'I think you'd make a very good earl.'

'Based on?'

'On my own vast experience of running country estates, naturally.' She paused, her expression turning serious. 'And because you're a good man.'

'For a *gentleman*?'

'For any man.'

He felt a fresh stirring of desire, his blood heating at the words. 'You ought to be careful, Anna. That kind of praise might go to my head.'

'I've said enough insulting things about you. It's about time I redressed the balance a little.'

'Is that why you let me kiss you this morning? To redress the balance?'

'No.' A delicate pink flush suffused her cheeks. 'I let you kiss me because I liked it.'

'I liked it, too. If I thought I could get away with it, I'd do it again.' His gaze dropped to her lips. They were slightly parted and temptingly moist-looking. 'You know the far shore is a long way from the house. I could take you there and kiss you properly. No one would see. Not without a telescope anyway.'

'They still might wonder what we were up to. I don't want my uncle and grandmother thinking I have loose morals on the first day I meet them. Besides, we don't need a distant shore. I have this parasol. If we hide behind it, then nobody will see.'

'Is that an invitation?' His heart leapt at the thought. 'Does this mean you're considering my proposal?'

'I didn't say that.' Her lashes fluttered downwards for a second, obscuring his view of her eyes. 'But it might help me to decide.'

'Well, in that case...' He rested the oars on his lap and leaned forward, bringing his face down to hers.

'I *am* considering it.' She spoke softly, tilting the parasol so that they were both sheltered from any view of the house. 'Only I can't promise anything, not yet.'

'I understand.' He rubbed his nose lightly against hers. 'It's a big decision.'

'Not to mention sudden and impetuous and reckless. And anyone watching is going to get very suspicious if I keep my parasol here for much longer. You ought to hurry up and kiss me, Captain Delaney, or I'll have to do it myself.'

'Go ahead.' The words made him positively feverish. 'I'm not going anywhere.'

Brown eyes seemed to spark briefly before she kissed him, closing the remaining distance between them without hesitation or trepidation or the faintest hint of reticence. Her lips were soft and silky, tasting of the wine they'd drunk at lunchtime, intoxicating his senses more than a whole bottle of rum could have done. He kissed her back, sliding his tongue past the smooth line of her lips. She moaned softly and he went deeper, cupping one hand around the back of her head as he tasted the inside of her mouth. He could feel each of their heartbeats accelerating through both layers of their clothing, could feel the gasp of her breath as his own emerged in increasingly short bursts. Unfortunately, he could also feel the oars slipping away from his lap.

'You're a fast learner.' He ended the kiss reluctantly, making a grab for the oars before they fell into the water.

'You're a good teacher, Captain.' She tipped the parasol back behind her head, her cheeks pinker than ever. 'I'm almost tempted to let you take me ashore, after all. Except that then I'd *have* to marry you.'

'If I thought you could be compromised so easily, then we'd be there already.' He arched an eyebrow. 'But something tells me you wouldn't let me get away with that.'

'You're right. Unlike ladies, shopkeepers are allowed to be slightly scandalous. It might actually sell more biscuits, especially if you *do* turn out to be an earl.'

'Well, in that case...'

'No!'

'Just as long as you're thinking about it.'

'I am.' She leaned back again, a smile dancing about her kiss-swollen lips. '*I am* thinking about it, Captain.'

Chapter Seventeen

Anna pulled back the green-velvet brocade of her bedroom curtains to look out at the dawn. The park around Staunton was shrouded in a thin layer of mist, but spring was in full flush, making the whole world look vibrant and sparkling and *green*. Not just one shade of green either, but at least twenty different shades all merging seamlessly together. It made her feel alive and happy and rejuvenated.

Now that she was at liberty to sleep in, she found she didn't want to. She was eager to start the day, to see Samuel again, too. Unconsciously, she lifted a hand to her mouth, remembering the feeling of his lips against hers. Telling him about what had happened eight years ago, not to mention meeting her uncle and grandmother, had made her feel as if several weights had been lifted from her shoulders all at once. And the boat ride afterwards had been quite… enlightening. Kissing Samuel behind her parasol had felt wicked and thrilling at the same time. She'd told him she could get used to this kind of life and, surprisingly, she'd actually meant it. Not lounging around in boats all day, of course, but a life in the countryside. It was all so unexpectedly peaceful. And surely a countess would have a purpose in life, too. It wouldn't all be entertaining neighbours and arranging dinner parties and picnics. She could do some good for the estate and the people who lived there. She could…

She let the curtain fall abruptly. She was getting ahead of herself. She'd agreed to think about marriage, but there was no hurry, especially when so much was still undecided. Samuel had implied that he wanted an answer *before* he knew what his future would be, but there wasn't just his potential inheritance to consider. There was the matter of his grandfather's health, too. She couldn't marry him while she was keeping such a big secret. It would be disloyal, especially after he'd called her honest and loyal. Perhaps she ought to write to the Baroness and ask permission to tell him?

She started towards the writing desk in one corner and then stopped at the sound of a light tap on the door. At such an early hour of the morning she assumed it could only be her mother, opening her door and feeling a thrill of excitement at the sight of Samuel instead.

'I thought you might be up already.' He smiled, his gaze skimming over her nightgown in a way that made the skin beneath tingle. 'Did you sleep well?'

'Yes, thank you.' She clutched the neck of her nightgown self-consciously. It was warm enough that she hadn't felt the need for a wrap and the top ribbon must have come undone while she slept, letting the edges fall open. By contrast, Samuel was already dressed, albeit casually, in a loose-fitting shirt and trousers paired with Hessian boots. Judging by the swathe of dark stubble on his chin, he hadn't shaved yet, either. 'What about you?'

'Surprisingly well, all things considered.' He pressed one hand against the door frame. 'I had quite lucid dreams.'

'Oh?'

'You might be better not knowing,' he teased. 'But I'm here with an invitation. I met with the estate steward last night and he told me something you might be interested in. It's in the gardens so I thought we could go and see if it's true together. Meet me in the hall in ten minutes?'

'Sooner than that.' She didn't even pause to consider. 'Give me five.'

Hurriedly, she closed the door, divesting herself of her nightgown and replacing it with a plain blue muslin dress and woollen shawl. Her hair was already impossible, most of it having escaped from its braid to surround her face with a mass of tight, bouncy curls, but she was in too much of a hurry now to do anything about it.

'I'm ready.' She hurried down to the hall where Samuel was waiting, speaking in a loud whisper so as not to disturb the rest of the household.

'I'm impressed. I know sailors who take longer when we beat to quarters.'

He gave her a conspiratorial grin, opened the front door and they crept out together. There was still a chill in the air, accompanied by a faint smell of dampness, but as they walked around the east side of the house and out of the shadows, she was enveloped in a burst of morning sunshine.

'Now can you tell me where we're going?' she asked as they hurried across the lawn.

'You'll see in a few minutes. According to the steward there's a path leading through the woods.'

They found it easily, though it was less of a path than a trail, meandering lazily back and forth beneath a canopy of silver birch and oak. The trees were mostly leafless, but the ground beneath was carpeted with old leaves and branches.

'Wait.' Samuel came to a halt as the trees started to thin again. 'Close your eyes.'

'Close my *eyes*?' She gave him a sceptical look. 'That doesn't seem like a very intelligent thing to do in a wood. What if I walk into a trunk or trip over a root?'

'I won't let you, I promise. Take my hand and I'll lead the way.'

'All right.' She did as he asked, every nerve ending quivering as his fingers closed around hers. Neither of them were wearing any gloves and the touch of skin against skin sent a thrill of excitement racing down her spine.

'It's just a few more steps. Here we are.' Samuel sounded distinctly proud of himself when they stopped walking again. 'You can open them now.'

Anna opened her eyes and gasped. They were standing on the rim of a dip in the tree-lined hillside that contained a spectacular water garden. There was a waterfall at one end, about ten feet in height, pouring into a river that ran in a perfectly straight line down the valley. To her delight there was even a bridge and some stepping stones connecting the two banks of the river, on both sides of which were a series of circular and semi-circular pools, each with a statue in the centre.

'It's beautiful.' She breathed a sigh of admiration and then laughed. 'And I was afraid that you'd miss being close to the water! Can we go down for a closer look?'

He grinned, as if he'd been hoping for such a response, and led her down a series of small wooden steps. He was still holding on to her hand, she noticed, though she made no attempt to pull hers away, either. Somehow it felt right, as if their fingers were meant to be entwined.

'It's like a secret garden,' she marvelled as they wandered slowly towards the river.

'It's supposed to be. The steward said that my cousin had it built about eighteen years ago. The river used to be wider, but he had it reshaped and channelled into these ponds. Apparently, he wanted it hidden away so he could surprise visitors.'

'He succeeded in that. What are the statues?'

'They're mostly Grecian, I believe. This one, for example, appears to be two sirens.'

'You really *must* feel at home.'

'I'm not sure sirens are a good sign. I was fortunate enough never to meet any at sea.' His fingers tightened subtly. 'Only on shore.'

She gave him a chiding look. 'I'm not a siren.'

'*No?* You lure men into your shop with sugary treats.'

'You make them sound like horses. They're perfectly at liberty to walk past.' She stopped halfway across the bridge and looked around. 'This is stunning.'

'It is...' He kept his gaze on her as he spoke. 'But there's one more thing I want to show you.'

'More than all of this?'

'*This* is impractical. Beautiful, yes, but not even knee-deep by the look of it. No use at all for swimming.'

'I can't swim.'

'Then you're in good company.' He grinned and tugged on her hand again, leading her up the side of the waterfall and back into the trees. 'Neither can most of the men in the King's Navy.'

'Isn't that dangerous?'

'Not as long as they stay on board their ships, but it's a good idea to learn.'

'Not today, thank you.'

'I had a feeling you'd say that, but you can still plunge.'

'I can do what?' She stared at the waterfall with trepidation. 'Surely you don't want me to jump off?'

'Not the waterfall, no. In there.' He gestured towards a small, square-shaped pool set off to one side. 'It's called a plunge pool. Very good for the circulation.'

'An outdoor bath?' She crouched down, dipping her fingers into the water and then jolting upright again. 'It's freezing!'

'That's why it's good for the circulation.'

'I am *not* jumping in there.'

'You don't have to literally jump. There's a ladder.'

'Absolutely not. A morning stroll is one thing, *plunging* is quite another.'

'Suit yourself.' He started to unbutton his coat. 'But you'll feel better if you do, trust me.'

'I feel perfectly fine now.' Her jaw dropped as his overcoat fell to the ground. 'You mean you intend to…?'

'I'm afraid so.'

'Samuel!' She spun around as he hoisted his shirt up over his head, though not before she caught a glimpse of a taut stomach and muscular chest, liberally sprinkled with dark hair. 'Is this how you wash on board ship? You just plunge into the ocean?'

'It depends where we are. The English Channel is generally too cold so we use barrels on deck, but a dip in the Caribbean can be quite pleasant.'

'What about sharks?'

'We use sails to make an enclosed pool over the side. It's a relief to have everyone smelling fresh again, believe me.'

'Oh.' She closed her eyes at the sound of more rustling. 'Please tell me you're not taking your trousers off.'

'Not just them.' She could hear the laughter in his voice. 'I can hardly go back to the house in wet clothes. People will think you pushed me into the river.'

'Better that than them thinking you undressed in front of me!'

'*Behind* you and I thought you said you weren't bothered about being compromised.'

'That doesn't mean I want to see you naked!'

'Ah, that's where we differ, then.' His voice turned decidedly wicked. 'Because I'm rather curious about seeing you.'

There was an abrupt splash, followed by a spray of water on to the back of her dress.

'Ow!' She clutched at her skirts.

'*Ow?*' That time he laughed outright. 'Did the water hurt?'

'No, but you've got me wet.'

'So I have. Perhaps you ought to let your dress dry in the sun and join me?'

'I am *not* bathing outdoors!' She lifted her chin pointedly. 'How is it?'

'Like I'm back where I belong.' There was a taunting pause. 'Surely you're not scared of a little water?'

'If you think that goading me will work then you're mistaken. I'm not afraid, just...modest.'

'Spoken like a true lady.'

'A la—!' She whirled around on the spot, putting her hands on her hips to glare at him and then blushing all the way from the top of her head to the tips of her toes. He was standing in the middle of the pool, his biceps bulging visibly as he pushed his hands through slicked-back, soaking wet hair. As he moved towards her water cascaded over his shoulders and the almost impossibly sculpted-looking muscles of his chest, making his skin seem to glisten. She couldn't see any further down, but having grown up in close quarters with a younger brother, she knew what was there.

'I...' She felt at a momentary loss for words, wishing she hadn't spun around quite so fast after all. Now she felt more than a little breathless.

'Changed your mind?' He lifted an eyebrow.

'Only if you look the other way.' Somehow she forced the words out. Having turned around simply to argue with him, it was the only way she could now think of to make him turn away since her own eyes and feet seemed incapable of moving. Not to mention the fact that a cold dip suddenly seemed like a very good, very practical idea.

He turned his back obediently and she wriggled out of her gown, hesitating briefly over her undergarments before conceding that he was right and there really *was* no point in getting them wet. If she didn't remove them, they'd only make her dress damp afterwards, which someone would be bound to notice...

'Wait.' She paused with her chemise halfway over her hips. 'What are we going to dry ourselves on afterwards?'

'A few laps around the garden ought to do the trick.' There was laughter in his voice again. 'Or you can use my shirt if you'd rather the swans didn't watch you.'

'Very funny.' She tugged off her drawers and stockings, folding them neatly on the side of the pool before dipping her toes nervously into the water, keeping her eyes fixed on his back the whole time.

'It's best to get it over with.' He half turned his head, causing her to drop down into a crouching position. 'It'll be a shock for a moment, but you'll get used to it soon enough.'

'I don't want to catch a chill.'

'You're more likely to if you stand there dithering on the edge. Sometimes you need to stop thinking and let go, Anna.'

Somehow those words did the trick. Before she knew what she was doing she'd placed her palms down flat on the ground beside her and pushed herself over the edge, dropping quickly into the pool and spluttering with shock as ice-cold water enveloped her body.

'Feels good, doesn't it?' Samuel started to turn around again.

'Wait!' Instinctively, she lifted her hands to cover her breasts. 'Don't look!'

'Why not?' He kept turning, though he slowed his pace. 'You're under the water. I can barely see anything.'

'Barely?' Despite the cold, she dipped lower under the surface, wondering how she could still be blushing when all her extremities felt as if they were about to fall off.

'I wasn't sure that you'd do it.' He grinned, looking boyish and genuinely pleased. 'You should dip your head under, too. Now that you've come this far...'

'I don't want...'

'Just take a deep breath like this.' He puffed his cheeks out, making a deliberately comical expression as he ducked under the surface and then sprang up again, shaking his head like a dog.

'Well, I might as well now.' She covered her face with her hands as water flew in every direction. 'Since you've made me wet enough already. Oh, bother, I'd better untie my hair or it'll end up in more knots.' She reached for the ribbon at the end of her braid, pulling it away and running her fingers through the lengths so that it unravelled in a mass of ringlets. As usual, they seemed to spring sideways, rather than downwards.

'They're like spirals.' Samuel's gaze was arrested. 'May I?'

She nodded, and he reached for one of the curls, smoothing it gently between his fingers. 'You're beautiful, Anna.'

Immediately, she opened her mouth to deny it and then stopped. Something in his voice told her he meant it. He really *did* think she was beautiful. She'd never thought of herself as a person who needed compliments before, but now the words made her feel warm and tingly inside. Which was ironic considering how cold the rest of her felt and it was about to get colder...

She drew in a deep breath, bent her knees and then dipped under the surface, screwing her eyes shut as her ears filled with a whooshing sound.

'Oomph!' she exclaimed as she burst out of the water again, making a point of shaking her head at him. 'Take that!'

'Spoken like a true siren.' He laughed, unperturbed. 'Now, tell me the truth—doesn't that feel better?'

'Yes' she agreed in surprise. Now that her body was getting used to the cold, it was actually invigorating.

'I hate to say I told you so.' He bobbed closer towards her.

'Then don't. Gloating doesn't become you, Captain.' She found herself taking another deep breath as she stared back at him. They were standing far too close together, less than an arm's length apart, although considering the fact that they were both naked, proximity was really the least of her worries. Oddly enough, however, she *wasn't* worried. The whole situation felt intimate and natural, as if the water itself was trying to sweep them together. She felt a powerful urge to reach out and touch him, to find out if his chest felt as solid as it looked.

'You know, I've been thinking about our conversation yesterday.' His gaze darkened, as if he were feeling the same impulse to touch her.

'Oh?' Her heartbeat quickened at the reminder. 'Which part?'

'About love and what it feels like. I even went to the library to look it up.'

'Love?'

He nodded, grazing his fingers lightly against the sides of her shoulders. 'According to Dr Johnson there are several definitions, but essentially it means "to regard with passionate affection". That struck me as fitting.'

'I suppose so.' Her lips and throat felt very dry all of a sudden.

'Then I read a few poems to be sure. They were slightly more dramatic, but the gist was the same.' He paused, his gaze profound and yet wondering at the same time. 'Which led me to only one conclusion.'

'Oh?'

'Yes.' His hands curled gently around her upper arms, drawing her towards him. 'Then it struck me that my first proposal wasn't very romantic, so...'

'Samuel!' she shrieked, grabbing hold of his shoulders as he started to lower himself back under the water. 'What are you doing?'

'Going down on bended knee.'

'You can't do that in a pool!'

'Why not? Apart from anything else, it gives me a chance to look at you properly.'

'That's what I'm afraid of.'

'Are you?' His voice sounded guttural. 'Are you afraid of me, Anna?'

'Not you, but...' she gestured at their surroundings '...all of *this*.'

'I know.' He stood up again, turning sombre. 'I know that it's not what you or I want, but it's made me think about what I *do* want and that's you. I'm in love with you, Anna-belle Claudia Teresa Fortini, and I want to be with you no matter what the future holds. But...' he winced guiltily '...I promised you time to think about it.'

'I don't need time.' She lifted her hands to his chest. 'I love you, too, and I want to be with you...' she swallowed '...no matter what the future holds.'

It must have been the cold, she thought, making her say crazy, impulsive things. To her numb ears it sounded as if she'd just accepted his proposal—a proposal she would have considered out of the question just a few days before, which meant turning her whole life upside down, leaving her shop and becoming a countess if he inherited the estate. She didn't know which was crazier, the fact that she'd just agreed or that she meant it.

'Is that a yes?' He looked taken aback, as if he thought she were toying with him.

'I...' She took a few seconds to make sure that she wasn't delirious. 'Yes. Yes, it is. I'll marry you, whoever you are—'

She didn't get any further as he caught her around the waist, dragging the whole length of her body tightly against his and crushing his lips to hers. His body was substantially warmer than the pool, she noticed, encouraging her to slide her arms around his neck and push herself even closer, kissing him back even when his tongue slid between her lips. *That* was warm, too. Warm and soft and searching, heating her up from the inside as if he were determined to explore every part of her mouth. The water between them made their bodies slick, moulding her breasts to his chest as heat stoked and scorched between them. Her legs seemed to float up from the bottom of the pool of their own accord, wrapping around his waist as if it were the most natural position in the world.

The water was seething around them now, splashing over the edge as Samuel curled his hands beneath her thighs and lifted her higher, dragging his mouth away from hers to run it over her throat and each of her breasts. She let out a low moan, excited by the combination of hot kisses and cold water, her whole body aching with a quivering, yearning sensation deep in her abdomen.

'Breakfast.' He broke away abruptly, setting her apart and lowering her gently back into the water.

'What?' For a moment, she couldn't make sense of the word. 'Are you hungry?'

'Not for that.' His gaze still burned with heat. 'But we should get back. The others will be getting up.'

'Oh!' She felt a sudden rush of blood to the head. He was right. If they weren't careful, the whole household would see them traipsing back to the house together in broad daylight and it would be hard to look anything other than guilty. Not that it necessarily mattered now they were engaged...though the very idea seemed to make her feel dizzy.

'Where's the ladder?' She looked around the edge of the pool.

'Over here.' He led her towards the rungs and then proceeded to ignore them himself, using his arms to hoist his body out of the pool with ease. Anna started to climb out, too, and then stopped self-consciously. It was one thing to be engaged, another for them to see each other completely naked. Which seemed ridiculous considering where her legs had just been, but she still didn't dare to peek upwards, no matter how great the temptation.

'Here.' He passed his jacket across to her and then turned away, seeming to sense her unease. 'I won't look, I promise.'

'Thank you.' She climbed out and then rubbed herself down quickly, wringing the moisture out of her sopping wet hair before wriggling back into her clothes. It was strange to feel shy again, but she did. She'd never behaved so outrageously in her whole life—or at least not since she'd accepted an invitation to go walking eight years ago... That thought alone gave her pause, but she didn't want to think about that, not any more. She wanted to do what her heart told her and her heart wanted Samuel.

She loved him, she trusted him and she was going to marry him, no matter what the future held.

Chapter Eighteen

Samuel waited until the sound of rustling clothes had finished and then reached out a hand, clasping hers tight as they made their way back through the water garden and up through the woods. This time he looked around at the trees as they walked. Somehow the world looked even more beautiful now than it had earlier. The birds were chirruping, the sun was shining and isolated clusters of primroses and daffodils were bursting up from the woodland floor like a yellow carpet. It was perfect.

He stole a sidelong glance towards Anna. She looked perfect, too. Bright eyed, pink-cheeked and thoroughly bedraggled, her dark hair already starting to curl into ringlets over her shoulders. Tempted as he was, he didn't dare to put his arm around her. Just the touch of her fingers reminded him of how her body had felt in the pool. He'd managed to let go of her then, though not without a considerable effort, and the after-effects were still wearing off. For the first time since they'd arrived at Staunton he felt almost light-hearted. For the first time in a long time, in fact. From the moment the steward had told him about the water gardens he'd wanted to go and see them for himself, but he'd wanted to go with Anna, to see it for the first time with *her*. Waiting until the morning had been hard, but it had paid off. He hadn't expected her to accept his proposal so soon or so suddenly. Maybe they *could* both belong there, after all?

'I'll ride to London this morning.'

'What?' Her head spun towards him. 'Why?'

'For a special licence. We're not residents of this parish so an ordinary one won't suffice.'

'But you only got here two days ago. You can't leave without seeing Lady Staunton.'

'Something tells me she's not particularly keen to see me.'

'That's not the point. Why rush?'

'Because I don't want to wait.'

'Do you think that I'll change my mind?' She threw him a suspicious look. 'Don't you trust me?'

'It's not that.'

'What then?'

'I just showed you why. You can't expect me to keep my hands off you for much longer.'

'Who said you had to?'

'I do.' He felt his body tighten at the implication. 'If I inherit, then there'll be enough gossip about the pair of us. I don't want to provide any more fodder for the rumour mill.' He edged closer, pressing a kiss into her hair. 'I shouldn't have kept you out so long this morning as it is. I might have some explaining to do to your mother.'

'Don't worry, I'll talk to her.'

'*We'll* talk to her.'

'All right, *we* will, but I'd like to be married in Bath.' Her voice wavered slightly. 'Your grandparents are there and I'd like for Henrietta to be a bridesmaid.'

'If that's what you want,' he agreed reluctantly. 'But in that case, we're going back as soon as possible.'

'Thank you.' She squeezed his hand and then released it as they emerged out of the woodland, running her palms over her gown to smooth the creases and then tying her hair back in a loose, though still unruly ponytail. She looked so adorable that he couldn't resist the temptation to pull her back into his arms as they crept through the front door and into the deserted hallway, kissing her full on the lips.

'*Samuel!* Someone will see!' She giggled, kissing him back and then darting away, throwing a mischievous smile over her shoulder as she started towards the dining room and then froze.

'What's the matter?' He nearly walked into the back of her, following her gaze into the room ahead. Her mother was sitting there, he noticed first, *without* her usual smile, although it wasn't that which alarmed him. That was the presence of another woman in the room, a woman he'd never seen before, sitting ramrod straight at the head of the table with an expression that could only be described as ferocious. He'd seen less hatred on the faces of the French sailors at Trafalgar.

'Captain Delaney, I presume.' Her voice, when she finally spoke, was clipped and positively dripping with loathing. 'I see that you're making yourself at home.'

'Lady Staunton.' Samuel made a formal bow, not that there was any point in trying to impress the woman now, he thought with a grimace. That proverbial ship had well and truly sailed. Into the sunset and over the horizon. 'I'm delighted to meet you at last.'

'Indeed?' The Countess's tone suggested she was a long way from sharing the sentiment.

'Allow me to present Miss Annabelle Fortini.' He took hold of Anna's elbow and steered her into the room. 'My—'

'It's an honour to meet you, my lady,' Anna interrupted, making a stiff curtsy before he could announce their engagement, though the Countess merely lifted her eyebrows disapprovingly.

'Have the two of you been for a morning walk?' Her mother sounded as if she were trying to ease the heavy atmosphere of tension.

'Yes, Mama.' Anna took the seat a footman held out for her, appearing not to notice the Countess's slight. 'Captain Delaney wanted to show me the water garden. It was quite beautiful. We'll have to go…'

The sound of a fist banging down onto the table made them all start.

'*My* water garden.' The muscles of Lady Staunton's throat strained with tension. 'My husband commissioned it as a wedding present for *me*.'

There were a few seconds of silence, none of them knowing quite how to respond before Mrs Fortini came to the rescue again.

'What a charming gift. I'd like to go for a walk there myself later—with your permission, of course, Countess?'

'*You* may.' Lady Staunton twisted her head sharply to one side. 'I wish I could go myself, but I find myself so often indisposed these days.'

'I understand. I was always exhausted when I was carrying my children. Your housekeeper told us that you've been suffering from headaches, too. I hope that you're feeling better this morning?'

'A little, although my head still pains me a great deal.'

'Have you seen a physician?'

'A physician cannot heal what I suffer from. It is a malady of the soul and spirits.'

'Of course, but perhaps you ought to try to get some fresh air for the baby's sake?'

'Perhaps, though the water gardens would likely still be too painful. My husband and I used to walk there every day when we were first married.'

Samuel cleared his throat, taking a seat at the opposite end of the table. 'I was very sorry to receive word of his death. I understand it was a wasting disease. My sincere condolences, my lady.'

'I've no interest in *your* condolences.' Lady Staunton's eyes narrowed perceptibly. 'He would have been horrified by your presence here.'

'I know it's a difficult situation, but I assure you...'

'Horrified!' she repeated. 'He remembered your father as a boy and he knew all about him as an adult, too. All about his debauchery and licentiousness. It appalled him that the son of such a man could be his heir! All he ever wanted was to have a son, to be sure that the future of Staunton was in safe hands, but I...' Her voice trailed away for a few seconds and then returned again, even more vehemently. 'To think of your whole distinguished family line coming down to a man like *you*!'

'Quite.' Samuel braced his hands on the table, resisting the impulse to get up and walk out. 'I've had similar thoughts myself.'

'It's monstrous. A disgrace! You'll ruin the estate before the year is out!'

'I'm not my father, Lady Staunton.'

'No?' She looked accusingly between him and Anna. 'Your behaviour seems quite similar in some respects.'

'I assure you that my intentions towards Miss Fortini are perfectly honourable. In fact...'

'Captain Delaney is the most honourable gentleman I've ever met...' Anna interrupted again, her voice just as vehement as the Countess's '...and I resent any insinuation to the contrary.'

'And what exactly would you know about gentlemen?' The Countess's gaze flickered. 'From what I understand you're in trade.'

'Yes, I'm a shopkeeper,' Anna replied before Samuel could say anything. 'As well as a baker. I make and sell biscuits. Often to gentlemen.'

'*Biscuits?*' The Countess put a hand to her throat with a shiver.

'They're quite famous in Bath, actually.'

'I don't care for Bath. I spent a winter there five years ago.'

'No, I believe it's rather out of fashion now, but it's home to me.'

'Then let us hope you can return there *soon*, Miss Fortini.'

'Yes, let's.' Anna's tone was now openly belligerent. 'Believe me, nothing would make me happier.'

'Well!' The Countess's eyes narrowed to slits. 'I seem to have lost my appetite. I shall return to my rooms.'

'As you wish, my lady.' Samuel got to his feet with relief, waiting until the sound of indignant footsteps had receded before slumping back into his chair. 'That went well.'

'Dear me.' Mrs Fortini picked up the marmalade spoon with a sigh.

"'Dear me?'" Anna echoed angrily. 'Didn't you hear what she just said about Samuel?'

'Yes, that was very unfair of her.' Mrs Fortini threw him a sympathetic look. 'But we still ought to make allowances. Think of how the poor woman has suffered. She's lashing out, but it's understandable. She's lost her husband and, if her baby's a girl, then she might lose her home and position, too. Her whole future is out of her control. Just remember that.'

'Yes, Mama.' Anna still sounded aggrieved. 'But she had no right to talk about Samuel or his father like that.'

'It's all right.' Samuel smiled, touched by her indignation. 'I've heard much worse, I can assure you.'

'That's very forgiving of you, Captain, but now perhaps the two of you can explain your behaviour this morning. You must have left the house very early.' Mrs Fortini looked pointedly at Samuel, her tone faintly accusing, as if she suspected him of having debauched her daughter among the trees. 'It wasn't very discreet.'

'No, it wasn't.' Samuel exchanged a quick glance with Anna. She'd stopped him from mentioning their engagement twice already and he had no intention of being stopped a third time. To his relief, however, she smiled excitedly.

'We really *did* go to see the water garden, Mama, but we have something else to tell you, too. Samuel and I are engaged.'

'Engaged?' Her mother's eyes widened.

'Yes. He asked me yesterday and I accepted this morning.'

'As long as you approve?' he interjected, alarmed by the sombre expression on Mrs Fortini's face.

'Of course.' She nodded, though with a hint of uncertainty. 'I would never stand in the way of any suitor my daughter chose.'

'But surely you don't have any objections, Mama?'

'None at all. If you care for each other, then I'm delighted for both of you, but...you know it will be quite a change if Samuel inherits?'

'We know that and we hope that he doesn't. But if he does...' Anna lifted her chin '...we'll deal with it together.'

'Well then, come here and let me embrace you, Samuel.'

'With pleasure.' He walked around the table, kissing her on both cheeks before going to stand behind Anna's chair. 'We've decided to marry as soon as we return to Bath. Which, given our recent reception, might be sooner rather than later.'

Her mother's expression turned startled again. 'But surely you'll stay for a few days, at least?'

'I don't think the Countess wants us here.'

'Perhaps not at the moment, but give her time. You might regret it later if you don't try.'

'A few days, then. Until the end of the week if it pleases you.'

'Thank you.' Her answering smile faltered.

'It's all right if you want to stay at Feversham for longer, Mama,' Anna hastened to reassure her. 'It might be best for your health, too.'

'I admit I would like to,' her mother conceded. 'Your Uncle Tobias invited us both to stay for as long as we wish, but you can't travel without a chaperon.'

'Yes, we can. You can send a maid with us, too, if you want, but we intend to marry as soon as possible so there won't be any scandal. You can trust me, Mama.'

'I do trust you. Both of you.' Mrs Fortini looked between

them and smiled. 'And I suppose I shouldn't be surprised when the apple falls so close to the tree. I know there's no point in arguing once you've made up your mind. I wish you both joy.'

'Thank you, Mama. There's just one other thing.' Anna glanced towards Samuel for confirmation. 'I think that we ought to keep our engagement a secret from the Countess. You're right about this being a difficult time for her. No matter how offensive her comments, we don't want to make the situation any worse if we can help it.'

'Good idea,' Mrs Fortini nodded. 'In that case, I shan't make any mention of your engagement at Feversham either, not until I receive word from you in Bath.'

Chapter Nineteen

Over the next few days, Samuel had the distinct impression that the two main women in his life, neither of whom he'd met a month ago, were trying to torture him. Being so close to Anna meant that he'd had to make several solitary trips to the plunge pool just to dampen his ardour, whereas living under the same roof as Lady Staunton, infrequent as her appearances were, was like living inside a beehive filled with a swarm of particularly angry bees. Between Anna's smiles and the Countess's stings, he didn't know which was worse, only that he was counting down the hours until they could leave for Bath.

Meanwhile, his days had settled into a kind of routine. He, Anna and her mother breakfasted together before the women travelled to Feversham and he paid several discreet visits to the estate office. Contrary to his expectations the steward seemed glad, even eager, to teach him, so that he was gradually forming a clearer picture of the size and demands of the estate. It was even bigger than he'd imagined, though it helped to think of it the way Anna had suggested, as a ship in need of a captain.

He met her again in the late afternoons, when they continued their riding lessons or strolled in the park, telling each other stories about their lives. She told him all about her father and her childhood, teaching him a few more words of Italian, while he talked about his life at sea, deliberately avoiding any mention of his own family.

One day he came across a gallery in the top of the house where the family portraits were displayed along one long wall. There they all were, generations of Delaneys and their families. He found his grandfather as both a boy and a man, his uncle and cousin, too, though of his father there was no sign. He seemed to have been rubbed out of the family altogether, a dark smudge everyone preferred to forget. Overall, he supposed he couldn't particularly blame them. If his father *had* inherited the earldom, then it was highly likely that he would have gambled it all away in a year, but the exclusion still felt jarring. Wrong somehow, too, to keep on punishing a man after death. He'd have a portrait commissioned, Samuel decided, if he inherited. It shouldn't be too difficult to recreate his father considering how similar they were in appearance. He'd get one of Anna, too. She'd probably pose in her yellow shop dress just to make a point, but then why not? Maybe he'd pose next to her in his uniform. It would be a reminder of who they'd both been when they'd met, who they might still be, depending...

It was strange, but there were times when his career at sea felt so distant it was like another lifetime. Trafalgar seemed like years rather than months ago. Would he still go back to that life if he didn't inherit? The thought of spending long periods of time away from Anna made him feel preemptively heartsore. He missed her just during the days when she was at Feversham. How would he ever cope with months at sea?

A year ago, he would have laughed at the idea of feeling this way about a woman, but now there was no denying the strength of his feelings. He didn't need Johnson's dictionary to define them any more, either. Friendship, admiration and attraction had grown into love. He'd started to fall in love with her that first day in her shop and now it was too late to do anything about it. He'd come to rely on her, too, on her honesty and loyalty, as if she were an anchor holding him in place. He had the unnerving suspicion that she'd become indispensable to his very existence. Which made the days until their wedding drag even more.

'Are you glad to be leaving?' Anna asked him as they walked along the terrace on the morning of their departure. They'd finished breakfast and waved a cheerful goodbye to her mother as she'd departed with her belongings for a longer stay at Feversham.

'I'm glad that I came...' he replied, wrapping an arm tight around her shoulders and pulling her close. 'But I'm *overjoyed* to be leaving.'

'It's a pity about Lady Staunton. I thought she might thaw a little while we were here, but something tells me she'd be more than happy for us to leave without saying goodbye. I thought she'd at least have breakfast with us today.'

'Every time I've approached her she's run away as if I'm her worst enemy.'

'She ought to have given you a chance.'

'Unfortunately my father's reputation precedes me.'

'But it's not fair.' Anna shook her head. 'It can't be good

for her to be so bitter and angry in her condition, either. And if the baby *does* turn out to be a girl, think how much angrier she'll be. That won't be good for either of them.'

'I know, but I don't think there's anything more I can say or do. I've tried talking to her. I've told her that she won't be homeless if I inherit, but she won't listen. She doesn't want my assurances.' Samuel shrugged his shoulders regretfully. 'I suppose we'll just have to wait and see what happens and take everything one step at a time.'

'And keep hoping for a boy.'

'That, too. It won't be long now before we find out.' He stopped walking to wrap both of his arms around her. 'You know I could stand like this all day, but the sooner we get to Bath, the sooner we can be married.'

'About that...' She looked up into his face, her own anxious. 'It doesn't have to be a big event, does it? I'll have Henrietta and a few other acquaintances, but it might look odd if you have a hundred people on your side.'

'I can't think of a quarter of that number to invite. Most of my friends are at sea or in Portsmouth waiting for billets. Frankly, I'd be happy with just the two of us...' he kissed the tip of her nose and then rubbed his own against it '... and a ten-cannon salute, of course.'

'No cannons!' She laughed. 'And I only have the gown I wore to your grandmother's party. Will you mind?'

'You can wear a sack for all I care, but I'd be happy to buy you something new if you like. I think a captain's salary can just about stretch to a gown.'

'No. I don't care what I wear, either.' Her brow puckered. 'I suppose most people have a rough idea of which it will be when they say for richer or poorer, only in our case it could go either way. For better *or* worse.'

'We might be the only two people in England who think of an earldom as worse, but you're right. We don't know what the future will bring, just that we'll face it together. Now, I have a few things left to pack. Shall I have the carriage brought round in half an hour?'

'That sounds perfect. I thought I'd take one last walk around the water gardens since I'm going to be cooped up for the rest of the day.'

'Fancy a plunge?'

'Not this morning, thank you.' She gave him a coy look. 'Now hurry up and pack, Captain. We have a wedding to get to.'

Anna heaved a contented sigh as Samuel walked away. Despite the tension of living under the same roof as Lady Staunton, it was amazing how comfortable she felt with Samuel now. Even his smell was reassuring. Musky yet fresh-smelling with that distinctive hint of citrus. It made her wonder whether Henrietta was right and they ought to bring out a new type of biscuit. Lemon would be delicious.

She descended the terrace steps and wandered across the lawn and into the woodland. It was another gorgeous day, more like summer than spring. She'd have to dress lightly in the carriage or the heat would be stifling. It was going to be an arduous enough journey without having anyone to talk to and Samuel could hardly ride inside with her unchaperoned, no matter how appealing the idea sounded. She suspected that kissing him would pass the time quite quickly...

There was a sound of snapping twigs and she stopped at the sight of a woman walking among the trees up ahead. From a distance it looked like Clarissa, but there was something different about her, something about the way she held herself and moved. She seemed faster and more upright than usual…as if it were Clarissa and yet *not* Clarissa. A suspicion tugged at the edge of Anna's mind, unbelievable at first, but gaining in strength the longer she watched. But it couldn't be possible…could it? Surely she wouldn't be so conniving?

She stepped hastily behind one of the trees, concealing herself as Clarissa passed by and then stepped out on to the lawn. As she did so, her whole posture seemed to change, her shoulders sagging forward and her steps slowing as if she were ageing ten years before Anna's eyes.

She felt her stomach plummet to the floor, almost too shocked to be angry, waiting a few minutes to calm herself before following the other woman's steps back to the house and through the terrace doors. To her surprise, Clarissa was sitting just inside the drawing room on a low chair, sobbing into a handkerchief.

'Lady Staunton?' Anna closed the terrace door softly behind her and leaned against it for support. 'Can I help?'

'*You?*' The other woman gave a start at her sudden appearance, glaring at her through swollen, red-rimmed eyes. 'Go away!'

'I wish I could.' Anna ignored her. 'But I think that we need to talk.'

'I've no desire to—'

'You're not pregnant, are you?' Anna spoke quickly, willing the words not to be true, though she couldn't think of any other explanation that made sense.

'Of course I am!' Lady Staunton's expression registered both shock and guilt as she gestured frantically at her stomach. 'Look!'

'It would be easy enough to fasten some padding there, I

would imagine.' Anna lifted an eyebrow sceptically. 'I saw you walking in the woods just now. You were moving too fast for a pregnant woman.'

For a moment, she thought that the Countess might actually throw something at her. She looked furious enough for anything, though fortunately there were no weapons to hand. Then her whole face seemed to crumple, anger turning to anguish.

'No!' She shook her head, her narrow shoulders heaving. 'Almost twenty years of marriage and I've never once been with child. I tried everything. I've been examined by so many doctors, tried all kinds of medicines. Nothing ever worked.'

'I'm sorry.' Anna sat down on a sofa opposite, not knowing what else to say. She wasn't entirely sure what to feel, either. Indignant as she was about the Countess's deception, she couldn't help but feel sympathy for her obvious heartache. 'That must have been very hard.'

'It was the *one thing* I had to do, the one purpose in my whole life. Just give him a son, my mother told me on my wedding day, give him an heir and everything will be all right. That was the reason he married me, you know, and my parents as good as promised him that I'd be fertile...' She put her head in her hands. 'I was only seventeen and it sounded like such an easy thing to do. I assumed I'd be a mother by the end of the year. And then when it didn't happen, month after month...'

'Was he cruel to you?'

Lady Staunton twisted her face to one side. 'No. He was very loving to me at first. I told you, he built me those gardens as a gift.'

'But later?'

'He was never cruel, but he became…distant. Cold. Having a son became an obsession.'

'Because he didn't want Samuel to inherit?' Anna tried not to sound too accusing.

Lady Staunton sniffed and nodded. 'He was so afraid that he'd be like his father and gamble the estate away. He hired lawyers to try to do something about the entail, but it was no use.' She screwed her handkerchief up into a ball. 'You've no idea what it was like. We barely spoke to each other during the last few years of our marriage.'

'You're right, I don't know what it was like.' Anna placed a hand tentatively on her shoulder. 'But why on earth did you tell everyone you were pregnant? Why pretend?'

'Because this is my home!' the other woman wailed. 'I've nowhere else to go.'

'What about your family?'

'They think I'm a failure. My mother says it was a good thing my sisters were married off early or I would have damaged their prospects.' She gave a bitter laugh. 'And they've all had children. Sons!'

'That doesn't make you a failure.'

'It does to them. And if I go back now and tell them it was all a lie…'

'But you must have known they'd find out eventually.'

'Yes.' Lady Staunton's head fell forward. 'I don't know why I did it. I wasn't thinking clearly. At the funeral everyone just kept telling me that it was *such* a shame, that *if only* I'd had a son… I felt as though I were being hit in the face every time. Finally I couldn't bear it any longer. The words were out before I knew what I was saying and then everyone's behaviour changed, too. I wasn't a disappointment any more.'

'But…'

'I know, but once I'd said it I couldn't go back. And I told myself that I was doing it for my husband, that it was what he would have wanted and I was making things up to him.' She paused. 'I know it was reckless.'

'Very.' Anna made a face. 'You've been keeping Samuel's inheritance unlawfully.'

'Yes.' Lady Staunton had the decency to look guilty.

'And as for the way you've been treating him…'

'I know.'

'You have to tell him the truth.'

'I *was* going to, I truly was. I told myself that I'd admit everything when you first arrived, but I didn't know how to begin. So I kept putting it off and off. Then that morning when the two of you came into breakfast looking so happy and in love after you'd been walking in *my* water gardens, I felt jealous. It's no excuse, I know, but it made me so angry.' She drew her shoulders back. 'But I'm truly sorry for the way I've behaved. I have to admit, from what I've seen of him, Captain Delaney doesn't seem like the sort of man who'd gamble everything away.'

'He's not.' Anna jutted her chin out indignantly. 'Your husband would have known that, too, if he'd given him a chance.'

'You're right. He should have met him at least. Then none of this would have happened.' Lady Staunton toyed miserably with the ends of her handkerchief. 'Can you forgive me?'

Anna took a deep breath. *Could* she forgive her? She *could* understand, but she felt as though a bucket of cold water had just been poured over her head. If only she and Samuel had left for Bath already, she could have remained in blissful ignorance, still consoling herself with the possibility that he *wouldn't* inherit. Facing an uncertain future with him was one thing. Facing an earldom, on the other hand...

'Yes.' She tried to swallow a feeling of rising panic.

'Do you think that Captain Delaney will let me stay in the dower house after this?' The Countess's tone was faintly pleading. 'I don't want to go back to my family and be treated like a failure for the rest of my life.'

'I don't know.' Anna felt as if her insides were churning. 'You'll probably need to give him some time to think about it. He'll understand why you did it eventually, but it's going to be a big shock.'

'You don't seem very pleased, either.' Lady Staunton gave her a quizzical look. 'You're going to be the next Countess. You ought to be happy.'

Anna blinked. 'You know about our engagement?'

'I assumed. It's obvious how you feel about each other.'

'Yes, but...why *should* I be happy?' Anna drew her brows together. 'You were right about what you said the other day. I'm a shopkeeper. No matter who my grandparents were, I haven't been raised for this kind of life.'

'But I have.' To her surprise, Lady Staunton actually sounded supportive. 'And I can teach you.'

'You mean like an apprentice?'

'Why not? It'll give me a chance to make amends.' The other woman reached under her skirts, fumbling around for a few moments before drawing out a small cushion. 'I don't suppose I'll be needing this any more.'

'No... Are you all right?'

'I will be.' Lady Staunton gave a loud sniff and then hic-cupped. 'Do you know, this is the first time I've cried since before the funeral. It feels good.'

'Then cry as much as you want to. Howl at the sky if it makes you feel better.'

'I can't do that.'

'Why not? Because you were raised to be quiet and polite?' Anna gave her an exasperated look. 'Personally I've always thought that lady-like behaviour was overrated. Why be quiet if you want to roar? We can do it together if you like?'

'What will the servants think?'

'Maybe they'll think it's about time.'

'Oh... Will you start us off?'

'If you like.' Anna rose to her feet, sucking in a deep breath and then letting it out again in a roar.

'There.' She folded her arms. 'That's how you do it.'

Lady Staunton looked impressed, rubbing her nose vigorously with the handkerchief before standing up, tipping back her head and screaming so loudly that Anna had to steel herself not to wince. It was a wonder the windows didn't all crack at the sound.

'Very good.' She lifted an eyebrow once her ears had stopped ringing. 'Feel better?'

'*Yes.*' The other woman started to smile and then clutched Anna's hand at the sound of running footsteps in the hall. 'Oh, dear. Maybe that wasn't such a good idea, after all...'

Chapter Twenty

Samuel stood in the doorway, gaping in amazement at the sight of Anna and Lady Staunton standing side by side, holding hands. Neither of them appeared to be in any pain, as he'd assumed when he'd first heard the blood-curdling screams emanating from the drawing room, though their expressions weren't particularly reassuring, either.

'Samuel?' Anna spoke first, the look on her face turning from anxious to determined. 'Lady Staunton has something she needs to tell you.'

'Wha—?' His voice faltered as he noticed the cushion tucked under Clarissa's arm, then her noticeably flatter stomach.

'You're not pregnant.' A rush of horror slammed into him like a fist. Suddenly, he wished himself a thousand miles away, in the middle of the Atlantic Ocean preferably.

'I'm sorry.' Clarissa looked genuinely shame-faced. 'I never meant for it to go this far.'

'You're not pregnant.' He repeated the words, as if they might make more sense to him the second time.

'No.'

'You've been pretending this whole time?'

She nodded, her voice falling to a low whisper. 'I know it was wrong.'

'You *lied* to me!' He didn't intend to raise his voice, but he couldn't stop himself. Five minutes ago he'd been happily anticipating leaving Staunton. Two minutes ago he'd been running down the stairs in alarm. Now...*now* he felt several stages beyond furious. She'd lied! On top of everything else his family had done, she'd lied just to keep him *out* of the family! As if everything about him were so objectionable! Worse even than that, though, was the shock. He'd thought that he had another month to prepare for the possibility of becoming an earl, a month to spend with Anna, but now that future had been stolen away from him. His fate was sealed. He was the Earl of Staunton, his father's son, the unwanted but last surviving male heir from a jaded line of a once-illustrious family. There was no fighting that legacy any longer. He felt so disorientated that he had to clutch the door to stop the world from spinning around him. It was like sea sickness, only without the sea.

And now Anna, the one person he'd thought understood how he felt, was standing alongside the woman who'd deceived him, as if she wasn't angry at all. As if she'd sided with his family against him, too!

'Samuel?' Anna advanced towards him, her expression concerned. 'Perhaps you should sit down? You don't look well.'

'No.' He lifted a hand, preventing her from coming any closer as he narrowed his eyes at Lady Staunton instead.

'Your maids. They must have known. They must have helped you.'

'Ye-es.' He was pleased to see her face register panic. 'But only because they're loyal to me.'

'According to the law, they were *my* staff, not yours.' His voice sounded different even to him. Hard and grating and implacable. 'That kind of disobedience is grounds for dismissal.'

'Samuel!' Anna gasped. 'You wouldn't!'

'Why not?' He couldn't bring himself to look at her. 'I'm the Earl now, aren't I? That means I can dismiss whoever I want and I *want* to be rid of everyone who knew about this.'

'They only helped me because I begged them to.'

'Well, now you can tell them the consequences.'

Lady Staunton's whole body started shaking, though whether from shock or anger he couldn't tell. 'In that case, they can accompany me to the dower house.'

'I think not.' He turned on his heel, too angry to be in the same room with either of them any longer. 'You can find somewhere else to live, Countess. I want you gone from Staunton by tonight.'

'If I thought you'd meant any of that, I'd shove you in right now.'

Anna found Samuel standing by the side of the river, his back towards her as he hurled stones into the water.

'What makes you so sure that I didn't?' He didn't turn around, only pulling his arm back for another throw.

'Because you're an honourable man and Clarissa wants to stay here. It's her home.'

'Not any more. Legally it hasn't been her home since her husband died. It was my inheritance and I don't give a damn what she wants.' He flung a stone so far down the river that she could barely see the splash. 'She ought to be grateful I'm not summoning the magistrate.'

'She knows she acted badly.'

'Badly?' He spun around finally, his face blazing with anger. 'Is that all you can say? You *know* how miserable I've been waiting to find out what my future would be. I've spent five months on shore twiddling my thumbs!'

'I know, but she's been miserable, too, and she'll be even more miserable if you force her to leave.'

'I'm sure she has family she can go to.'

'A family who call her a failure.'

His expression relented slightly. 'What do you mean?'

'Because she never provided her husband with an heir. They've made her feel like a disappointment so much that she's afraid to go back to them. I think a lot of her anger has been about that, not you.'

'That doesn't make it all right.'

'No, but think how much worse they'll treat her if she goes home and admits the truth.' Anna took a step closer. 'I'm not defending what she's done, but there *are* reasons. I think she was desperate after the funeral and didn't really know what she was doing. Then she didn't know how to stop it.'

'None of which is my concern.' His jaw clenched again. 'Whose side are you on?'

'It's not a question of sides.'

'But you think I ought to just forgive and forget? I put my life on hold for *months* and she was lying the whole time!'

'I know.'

'All to stop *me* from inheriting! Because she thought I

was the same as my father, just like...' He stopped, a pained expression passing over his face.

'Samuel?' Something about that expression made her want to wrap her arms around him.

'Like all the rest of my family,' he finished saying, twisting his face to one side.

'She thought she was fulfilling her husband's wishes, but she's sorry for it now.'

'She even convinced her servants to keep secrets from me.'

'Yes.'

His shoulders slumped as the anger drained from his face suddenly. 'And sending them away won't make me feel any better, will it?'

'No. *Or* her. She's spent the last few months feeling angry and bitter and scared. Now she needs time to grieve properly.'

'All right. Tell her she can do whatever she wants.' He let out a heavy sigh. 'You know, I never really let myself believe it would actually happen. I kept telling myself that she'd have a son, that it wouldn't be long until I'd be free, but there's no escaping all this now, is there? I don't have a choice.'

'No.' She reached a hand up to his face, turning it gently back towards her. 'But you're not the man your family thought you were. You're better than them.'

He tipped his cheek into her palm, closing his eyes for a moment before opening them again with a look of determination. 'Then I'll do my duty. I'll do it properly and prove them all wrong, be the Earl my father could never have been. I'll find a way to belong at Staunton, too.'

'I know you will.'

'But I'll need my Countess by my side.' He clasped his hands around her waist. 'Come with me to Scotland, Anna. We can go to Gretna Green and be married tomorrow.'

'Scotland?' She stiffened at the suggestion. 'But why rush? We might have to delay our immediate plans, but we can still be married in Bath. Nothing about that needs to change.'

'Everything's already changed.' His grip tightened. 'We've spent too much time together. If we don't marry soon, then people will talk.'

'I don't care what people say.'

'But I do.' His tone was too vehement, his gaze too bright, in the grip of some new fervour. 'I want to do everything right from now on, start as I mean to go on. Besides, there's no reason for us to return to Bath now. Your mother's already here and I'm going to have a mountain of estate business to attend to.'

'Ye-es, but...' She bit her teeth into her bottom lip, trying to think of a reason to stall. He was right. If he was the new Earl, then Scotland was a far better idea from a practical perspective. They could be there and back in a matter of days. There was no reason for him to return to Bath except to see his grandparents, but since he didn't know about his grandfather's ill health there was no impetus for that. She'd sent a letter to his grandmother asking for permission to tell Samuel, but as yet she hadn't received any answer. All she knew was that she *had* to tell him before they were married.

'Anna?' He frowned when she didn't answer.

'It's just... I need to go back to my shop. I can't do anything until I've settled things there.'

'Why not? We can do all of that later.'

'But it's my responsibility. It matters to me. Please, Samuel, I want to be married in Bath. We can get a common licence there and...'

'You've changed your mind?' He dropped his hands from her waist abruptly.

'I never said that!'

'Then prove it. Come with me to Scotland today. We're already packed and the carriage is waiting. We can leave right now.'

'No.' She took a step backwards, annoyed by his dictatorial tone. He sounded as if he were issuing orders, as if he were turning into an arrogant aristocrat right before her eyes. 'I told you, I want to settle my affairs first.'

'You've changed your mind.' His whole face seemed to shut down as he spoke, his eyes looking paler and sharper than she'd ever seen them, like jagged shards of glass.

'That's not true, but I won't be *told* what to do. Just because you're an earl doesn't give you the right...'

'If you love me, then you'll come with me now!'

'If you love me, then you won't insist!'

'I should have known you'd take their side, too.' He gave a harsh laugh and turned away, heading towards the bridge. 'Goodbye, Anna.'

Samuel sat in a corner of the taproom at Staunton's somewhat dilapidated alehouse, his forearms resting on the table in front of him, staring broodingly into a tankard. He hadn't drunk more than a few mouthfuls, tempted though he was to drown his sorrows, but now that he'd finally calmed down after storming away from Anna, all he felt was empty.

Lady Staunton's deception had come as a shock to say the least, but the sight of Anna at her side and defending her had made it even worse, making him feel as though the anchor he'd been holding on to had come loose. Her following him to the water gardens afterwards had given him new hope, briefly allowing him to imagine that doing his duty and becoming the consummate Earl in defiance of his family's expectations might ease the crushing sense of entrapment, but then Anna had distanced herself again. Maybe suggesting an elopement hadn't been the best idea, but he'd wanted to make everything official and to do it all properly, to start his new life with her at his side. On top of that, he'd needed to know whether the fact of his inheritance had changed her mind about marrying him and to his horror, it had. If she'd *truly* wanted to marry him, then she would have agreed to go to Gretna Green instead of making up some excuse about needing to return to Bath. He'd thought that they'd come to an understanding. He'd thought that he could trust her, too, but as it turned out, her prejudices were stronger than her feelings for him. And he'd been a damned fool, falling in love with the one woman most likely to reject him. It had been madness to think that they might belong together, that they might make a home at Staunton, either. Of course she denied going back on her word, but what else would she say?

On the other hand, a tiny part of him argued, Clarissa's deception had been a shock for Anna, too. Maybe he ought to have given her the benefit of the doubt. Maybe he shouldn't have been quite so demanding, either…

'You look like you've been in the wars.' The voice of the innkeeper came from close by. 'Trouble with love, I'll wager?'

Samuel looked up, assuming the comments were addressed to him, surprised to find them directed at a young, fair-haired man sitting at the next table instead. In the mostly deserted taproom he hadn't noticed the man's presence before, but now he had the uncanny impression of looking into a mirror. The other's position, even down to his expression of brooding melancholy, was remarkably similar to his own.

'Aye…' The man sighed. 'Dora says she can't marry me. Her father will never agree.'

'Old Turner? No, he's a funny one.' The innkeeper gave a sage nod. 'You'd best watch he doesn't catch you wi' her either or he'll have your guts.'

'Then what do I do?'

'Find yourself someone else.'

'But I don't want someone else!'

'Why won't her father agree to the match?' Samuel interjected, unable to contain his curiosity.

The man gave him a swift glance and then heaved a sigh. 'He says I'm just a farmhand and that I'll never amount to anything.'

'Then make something of yourself to show him he's wrong. If she loves you, then she'll wait.' He frowned at the words. Wasn't *waiting* exactly what he'd just refused to do for Anna?

'And how am I supposed to do that when them at the manor do nothing but put up rents and never help us with—? Ow!' He stopped as the innkeeper gave his chair a none-too-subtle kick.

'This gentleman might know them at the manor.'

'Oh.' The man's expression turned to one of alarm. 'Pardon me, sir, I didn't know I was talking to a gentleman. Too much ale.'

'I shouldn't have been eavesdropping in the first place.'

Samuel picked up his tankard and stood, the similarity in their situations making him doubly curious. 'Do you mind if I join you?'

'If you want, sir.' The man exchanged a dubious look with the innkeeper.

'Thank you. Now...' Samuel took a seat again opposite '...does she love you, this woman?'

'Dora? She says she does, only she won't go against her father. She said our last kiss was goodbye.'

'You've kissed her?' The innkeeper gave a low whistle. 'You'd better hope Turner doesn't find out.'

'I don't care if he does.'

'You will when he pummels you. He's twice your size and then some. I once saw him flatten—'

'Maybe I can help?' Samuel interrupted before the innkeeper could go into any more lurid detail.

'How?'

'Tell me what it is you need to prove yourself. Your own farm?'

The other man stared at him suspiciously for a moment and then burst out laughing. 'Aye, that ought to do it. I don't reckon there's any lying around spare, though.'

'Maybe not spare, but there must be something we can do.' Samuel nodded at the innkeeper and then gestured at their tankards. 'Two more of these and one for yourself. Then we can put our heads together and think.'

'Th-thank you, sir.' The man looked confused. 'But if you don't mind my asking, who are you?'

'Me?' Samuel took one last mouthful of ale before answering, 'I'm Captain Samuel Delaney, the new Earl of Staunton.'

Chapter Twenty-One

'Lady Staunton?' Anna found the Countess where she'd left her in the drawing room, lying on a sofa and weeping.

'Oh.' Clarissa pulled herself up with an effort. 'I'm sorry. It's just that now I've started crying, I can't seem to stop.'

'Oh, dear.' Anna came and took a seat beside her. 'It'll be all right, I promise.'

'He said I have to leave.'

'He didn't mean it.'

'He *didn't*?'

'Well, yes, he did at the time, but now he says you can go or stay as you like. He was just upset.' She gave her a meaningful look. 'It might be a good idea to stay out of sight for a few days.'

'I will.' Clarissa nodded eagerly. 'Where is he now?'

'I've no idea.' Anna leaned back against the cushions with a sigh. 'He stormed off when I said I wouldn't go to Scotland with him. He thinks I've changed my mind about his proposal.'

'Have you?'

'No!' She was surprised by the strength of her own conviction. 'I love Samuel. I want to marry him, no matter who he is.'

'Thank you for defending me.' Clarissa looked genuinely grateful. 'I know I didn't deserve it.'

Anna pursed her lips, the words causing her a sharp pang of guilt. She'd handled the whole situation badly. She'd been trying to help and be conciliatory, but maybe she'd jumped to Clarissa's defence a little too quickly. In Samuel's eyes, it must have looked as though she'd been siding with her over him. Going after him to the water gardens had been a mistake, too. She ought to have given him a chance to get over the shock and calm down first. Perhaps then he wouldn't have been so adamant about Scotland.

'You deserved having someone to stand up for you.' Anna smiled reassuringly. 'No one should be made to feel the way you have, especially not by their families. You need a chance to work out what to do with the rest of your life.'

'What do you mean?'

'You'll want to do something, surely?'

'But there's nothing *to* do.' Clarissa sounded confused. 'Nobody will want to marry me now, especially when I tell the truth. They'll think that I'm barren.'

'There's more to life than marriage and babies. You're free to do whatever you want.'

'But my family won't approve of my *doing* something.'

'I'm not suggesting you take to the stage…' Anna rolled her eyes '…although that would be quite exciting. As for your family, they don't get to decide, especially after the way they've treated you. It's your life, Clarissa, *you* should decide how to live it.'

* * *

It was all very well, Anna thought, pacing up and down the hallway some time later, her telling Clarissa that she was a free agent. If only she could say the same! Instead, she'd spent the past three hours twisting her hands together, anxiously awaiting some sign of her fiancé's return. She hadn't bothered with luncheon, since Clarissa had gone to lie down and the continued worry meant that she'd lost her appetite anyway.

Finally, she couldn't bear the pacing any longer, scooping up her bonnet and cloak and marching back out of the house instead. If Samuel wasn't coming back, then she'd have to go and find him, if only to make sure that he was all right. Hopefully then she could reassure him and maybe hint a little about his grandfather, as much as she could anyway. Not the exact details, but the fact that she'd been sworn to secrecy. Maybe then he'd understand that her reticence about Scotland wasn't because she'd changed her mind.

She strode determinedly across the lawns and through the woods to the water gardens, crossing the bridge and following the path he'd taken that morning. It was still early afternoon and she found herself wishing that she'd had something to drink before leaving. The sun was high in the sky and she was getting thirstier by the minute. If memory served, however, the path led to the village less than a mile away, which fortunately proved to be correct. As she approached the houses, she saw the welcome sight of a tavern on the outskirts. There were loud voices coming from inside, but surely she could get a quiet glass of water, too?

She entered the tavern by the side door, making her way along a dark, wood-lined corridor into a taproom. The voices were coming from around the corner, where a group of men were singing at the top of their lungs. From what she could gather it was a kind of sea shanty, a not particularly polite story about a young woman called Kitty...

Her jaw dropped as they embarked on the chorus and not just because of the lyrics. A *sea* shanty? They were more than a hundred miles from the sea. Why would they be singing one of those unless... She crept around the side of the bar, her heart stalling at the sight of a familiar face. *Samuel?* To her horror, he was standing in the middle, his arms draped around two other men's shoulders, swaying from side to side and making enough noise for a dozen drunk sailors.

She stiffened, grinding her teeth at the sight. The only positive was that at least he didn't look angry any more. On the contrary, he seemed completely relaxed, a broad smile on his face as if he hadn't a care in the world. And after she'd been so worried about him, not to mention the guilt! She hadn't expected the transformation to happen so quickly, but apparently it didn't take long to change from responsible sea captain into debauched aristocrat!

She took a few steps backwards without looking and collided with someone coming the other way. There was a muffled exclamation, followed by commotion as a tray of drinks fell to the floor with a clatter.

'Anna?'

She looked up as she heard Samuel call out her name, their eyes meeting briefly before another voice bellowed from the direction of the front door and a large man, flanked by two only slightly smaller, younger men, burst into the taproom, towing an extremely nervous-looking woman behind them.

'You!' The large man lunged forward at the same moment

as one of Samuel's singing companions lowered his head and charged and then all hell seemed to break loose. Fists started flailing, chairs flew through the air, wood splintered and more cups clattered onto the flagstones. Anna didn't wait to see how it would end, fleeing out onto the street and back towards Staunton.

How could he? Tears blurred her vision as she ran across the fields and through the woodland. It had been barely four hours since Samuel had inherited the title and already he was drunk and brawling. So much for not wanting to follow in his father's footsteps! So much for honourable behaviour! The scene was everything she'd been afraid of and worse. He wasn't the man she'd thought he was and she'd been tricked again! Well, he'd accused her of changing her mind about his proposal and now she had—and she had no intention of staying around to discuss it with him, either. She was going to go back to Bath and her shop as quickly as possible and forget any notion of being a countess. It had been a ridiculous daydream from the start! She would be Mrs Etton instead, the person she might have been already if she'd been using her common sense. If she'd only agreed to his proposal in the first or second or even fourth place then she would never have spent any time with Samuel, never been so foolish as to trust him, never fallen in love or felt as wretched as she did now.

Samuel rolled onto his back and clapped a hand to his forehead. What the hell had happened to him? He felt as if he were back at Trafalgar with the after-effects of the smoke and noise from hundreds of guns still assaulting his senses. His eyes stung, his head ached and his throat felt as raw as if he'd just drunk a bucketful of seawater.

Reluctantly, he opened his eyes, wincing at the onslaught of daylight, and then pushed himself up to a sitting position. According to his aching head it was entirely the wrong thing to do, but at least it gave him a better opportunity to survey his surroundings. Not that that helped since he still had no idea where he was.

He clambered off the bed—what was he doing in bed?—climbed shakily to his feet and stumbled across to sit on the windowsill. Judging by the scene of activity on the street below he was in some kind of tavern. Which made sense because he vaguely remembered having entered such a place after...

After what? For some reason just thinking about *why* he'd come there made him wince again. Something had happened. Something he'd wanted to forget. Something about... He groaned, memory returning with horrible clarity. Lady Staunton had deceived him. There was no baby, no other heir, no way to hide from the fact that he was now the Earl of Staunton and...

Anna. A bolt of panic shot through the nausea. He'd argued with Anna and then stormed away from her. Worse than that, he'd seen her here afterwards while he'd been singing a less than salubrious sea shanty. He'd seen the disappointment on her face, too. It had been a long time since he'd had it directed at him, but he'd recognised the look at once. His mother had looked at him like that repeatedly over the years, usually right before she turned away.

In this case, however, it hadn't been entirely fair. As bad as drinking and carousing in the daytime must have looked, he'd barely touched his second tankard of ale and, after offering a job to his new friend, it had seemed only fitting to celebrate the occasion through song. All of which he would have explained to Anna if Turner hadn't arrived at exactly the same moment to avenge the honour of his daughter, which had led to a scuffle and then…what then? He wasn't sure, but the dizzy feeling and bump on his head were starting to give him an idea.

'Evening, sir.' The innkeeper came into the room, accompanied by a man in a sombre black suit. 'The doctor's back to see you like he promised.'

'Did he?' Samuel looked at the man in surprise. He had no memory of seeing him before.

'I'm afraid you were somewhat delirious the last time, my lord.' The doctor made a stiff bow. 'How are you feeling now?'

'Like I've had a chair smashed over my head. Or was it a table?'

'Aye.' The innkeeper rubbed a hand around the back of his neck uncomfortably. 'It was something like that. 'Course they had no idea who you were, but they're all locked up now.'

'Who?'

'Turner and his sons and anyone else who was there for good measure. They'll be brought before the magistrate tomorrow.'

Samuel groaned. 'There's no need for that. Tell the constable to let them all go.'

'But I must protest!' The doctor looked indignant. 'They caused a severe breach of the peace. Perhaps you ought to wait until your head…'

'No. I won't bring any charges…' Samuel smiled with a sudden burst of inspiration '…but only on condition that Turner agrees to the marriage.'

'I think he will now he knows who you are, sir.' The inn-keeper grinned back.

'Good. Tell him I'll pay for the wedding even. Now help me up.'

'Absolutely not.' The doctor was adamant this time. 'You shouldn't be going anywhere in your condition.'

'I have to get back to Staunton.'

'Not today. You've taken a nasty blow to the head. To-morrow, if you're not feeling sick or dizzy, but today you need to rest.'

'Try to stop me.'

'Forgive me, my lord, but I believe that your head might do that for itself.'

Samuel swung to his feet, growled an oath, then dropped down again, annoyed to find that the doctor was right. The room tilted so violently he could almost believe he was back on board his old ship again.

'Now...' the doctor's tone was infuriatingly smug '... I suggest that you drink some water and go back to sleep. I'll escort you back to Staunton tomorrow myself.'

Fortunately for Samuel, his head appeared to have com-pletely recovered by the time he woke the next morning. *Un*fortunately, it took nearly another full hour to escape from the tavern as the innkeeper, along with Turner, his sons and the new prospective bride and groom, wanted to thank him, apologise and say farewell at the same time. By the time the doctor arrived he was raring to go, only to find that his escort believed in taking life at a sedate, some would have said glacial, pace. The result was that it was past eleven o'clock before they finally arrived at Staunton and Samuel was able to run up the front steps and into the hall, headlong into Clarissa.

'Oh!' Her eyes widened in panic when she saw him. 'Captain Dela— I mean, my lord, I was just looking for my embroidery.' She glanced towards the stairs as if she were considering making a run for it. 'I'm sorry, I'll go back to my room.'

'You don't need to apologise.' Samuel shook his head quickly. 'Or hide in your room for that matter. But while we're at it, I'm sorry, too. I overreacted before. This is your home for as long as you want it.'

'Oh, thank you, my lord.' To his horror, she looked as if she were about to burst into more tears. 'And I just want to say—'

'Later.' He put his hands on her shoulders. 'Where's Anna?'

'Anna?' Her eyes widened again. 'Oh, yes... I'm afraid to say... The thing is...she's gone.'

'What?' His heart slammed to a halt. 'When?'

'Yesterday afternoon when she came back from the...' her cheeks darkened slightly '...the place where you were. She left straight away.'

'Did she leave a message?'

'In a manner. That is, she said...' She winced, as if she were considering the wisdom of telling him.

'What?'

Clarissa looked apologetic. 'She said that if you tried to follow her then I should tell you that a marriage between you would never have worked and that by the time you reach Bath she'll be Mrs Etton.'

'*Etton?*'

'Yes, but I have to say she didn't look very happy about it.'

'What time did she leave exactly?'

'It was just before three o'clock yesterday. She took the carriage.'

'Three o'clock.' Samuel glanced at his pocket-watch and calculated. It was almost noon now, which meant that a carriage travelling in daylight would have a six-or, at best, seven-hour start. A big enough lead to reach Bath ahead of him, though surely not to arrange a marriage, as well. He still had time.

'Are you going after her?' Clarissa called out as he raced back down the front steps.

'Yes!' He stopped, considered and then turned back, removing his hat and making a bow. 'Staunton is yours in the meantime, Lady Staunton. I know you'll take good care of it.'

Chapter Twenty-Two

Home. Anna pushed open the front door of Belles, set down her bag and breathed a heavy sigh of relief. She was home. There were no customers at that moment, nor any sign of Henrietta either, allowing her to look around uninterrupted. So much had happened over the past few weeks that she'd been vaguely apprehensive that things might have changed here, too, but everything was just as she remembered. The counters were gleaming, the tins neatly stacked and, judging by the empty trays on the shelves, they were nearly sold out of biscuits, too. It all looked and smelled comforting and reassuring—exactly what she needed.

'Anna!' Henrietta must have heard the bell because she came through from the kitchen after a few moments, rushing to embrace her. 'You're here!'

'Yes.' She hugged her back, feeling a rush of affection for her assistant. After Lady Staunton's bristly companionship it felt good to be greeted so warmly.

'I didn't expect to see you for another week at least.'

'I felt homesick.' Anna smiled, looking Henrietta up and down in surprise. There was something different about her, as if she'd grown in stature. She seemed older and more competent, exuding a new air of confidence, too. Maybe a few things *had* changed after all... 'You look very well.'

'Do you think so?' Henrietta smoothed a hand over her hair in her old familiar gesture. 'My brother said the same thing.'

'Managing a shop obviously suits you.'

'I've enjoyed it. Not that I didn't miss you, of course, but I was so pleased when the Baroness came and said you were going to marry Captain Delaney. I *knew* he was smitten with you. I could tell, right from the start. Is he back in Bath, too?'

'No, he has business to attend to in Staunton.' Anna shrugged her shoulders awkwardly, hurrying to change the subject as Henrietta's face fell. 'Now tell me everything that's happened here.'

'Oh... Well, mostly we've just carried on as usual, except that Nancy—you know one of Lady Jarrow's maids—has been taking a basket around town every morning and we've made a small fortune outside the Pump Rooms. I think people want something to take away the taste of the water. And then some afternoons we've taken a basket to Pulteney Bridge, too...'

Anna listened with half an ear to the details, half pleased, half perturbed that everything had run on so smoothly in her absence. She was starting to feel discomfited altogether. As much as it all looked and smelt like home, it no longer felt quite the same. *She* didn't feel the same, as if she'd somehow become redundant in her absence. Worse than that, she wasn't sure she belonged there any more, either.

'But that's all business.' Henrietta seemed to become self-conscious suddenly. 'Isn't your mother with you, either?'

'No. She decided to stay in Feversham for a while.'

'So she and your grandmother are reconciled?'

'Yes, it all went very well. As well as we could ever have hoped for, really.' She pressed her lips together as tears stung the backs of her eyelids.

'Anna?' Henrietta peered at her anxiously. 'Are you all right?'

'No.' She gave a loud sniff and shook her head. 'No, I don't think I am. Oh, Henrietta, I don't know what I'm going to do...'

Anna stood in the drawing room on the Circus, waiting for the Baroness to arrive. After pouring her heart out to Henrietta the night before, she'd decided to grasp the bull by the horns and report to Samuel's grandmother before she heard what had happened and came to the shop herself. At least that way *she* could be the one to announce that her engagement was over and explain why it was for the best. She could try to defend Lady Staunton, too, although she doubted the Baroness was going to be much more forgiving than her grandson.

'Anna.' Lady Jarrow swept into the drawing room finally and pressed a kiss to her cheek. 'How good to see you again, my dear, especially now that we're practically family.'

'Oh...' She steeled her resolve at the unexpected welcome. 'Yes.'

'But something tells me my congratulations are precipitous.' The Baroness fixed her with a steely eye. 'What's the matter?'

'It's just that we're not...going to be family, I mean. I

came to tell you that my engagement to Samuel is over. It was all a mistake.'

'Ah. In that case you'd better sit down. Do you drink brandy?'

Anna threw a startled glance at the clock on the mantel. It was only just after nine o'clock in the morning. 'No-o.'

'Pity. I hate to drink alone and after the night I've had, I could do with something stronger than coffee.'

Anna took a closer look at the Baroness. Her features were pale and drawn and there were grey shadows beneath her eyes. 'Is something the matter, my lady?'

'I'm afraid that my husband's condition has worsened since you left. He had another bad turn last night.'

'I'm sorry.'

'It is how it is.' Lady Jarrow sat down on the sofa beside her. 'Now tell me what happened with Samuel.'

'Well…' Anna folded her hands in her lap and proceeded to give a brief, though she hoped sympathetic, account of Clarissa's behaviour and the outcome.

'So the foolish woman was pretending to be pregnant the whole time?'

'I'm afraid so, yes.'

'And Samuel took it badly?'

'Yes.'

'What about you? Did you take the change in his circumstances badly, too? Is that why you ended the engagement?'

'No.' Anna bristled, offended. 'I gave him my word that I'd marry him and I meant it, but he wanted to elope and be married in Scotland.'

'And?'

'And I couldn't do it.' She lifted her hands as if it ought

to be obvious. 'Not when I was hiding the truth about the Baron's health. I know how close he is to you both.'

'He would have understood that I'd sworn you to secrecy.'

'No.' Anna shook her head. 'He told me that he valued my honesty. It would have been hypocritical of me to marry him while I was keeping such a big secret.'

'Pshaw!'

'But that's not the only reason.' Anna lifted her chin, annoyed by the other woman's dismissive tone. 'When I said that I wanted to marry him in Bath he became quite dictatorial. Just like an aristocrat.'

'Or a naval captain, perhaps? He's accustomed to giving orders.'

'They weren't *just* orders. He threatened to throw Lady Staunton out of the house and to dismiss all of the servants who'd helped her.'

'So you broke your engagement over a few foolish words?'

'No, *he* did. *He* walked away. The last I saw of him he was drunk and brawling in the local tavern.'

'I don't believe it. Samuel never drinks to excess.'

'Well, apparently he's changed now he's the *Earl* of Staunton.'

'I see.' Lady Jarrow stood up and walked across to the window. 'By the way, I received your correspondence. I wrote back and gave you permission to tell Samuel everything. You probably passed the letter on your way here.' She sighed. 'In light of what's happened I wish I'd replied sooner.'

'It doesn't make any difference now that he's shown his true colours.'

'One night of foolishness doesn't make him his father.'

'No, but it's a start. In any case, our engagement is over and I've come home. My mother is happy staying with her family for a while, but that's her life, not mine. I should never have left Bath in the first place.'

'And you intend to have nothing more to do with my grandson?' Lady Jarrow turned to face her again. 'Is that what you're telling me?'

'I think it would be for the best.'

'I see. You didn't love him, then, when you agreed to marry him?'

'I didn't say that.'

'But you can't have, to walk away so easily. I never thought of you as defeatist before.'

'It *wasn't* easy.'

'Yet you chose the easiest option of all, running away as soon as things became difficult. I'm disappointed. I thought you were the kind of woman who could face a challenge, but you've simply reverted to all your old prejudices. Personally, I don't believe that a woman in love would ever do such a thing.'

Anna leapt to her feet, stung by the words, especially the grain of truth behind them. *Was* that what she'd done? Jumped on the first excuse she could find to flee back to Bath? She didn't want to think so, but then she hadn't given herself much time to consider. She'd left Staunton as soon as she'd got back from the tavern without giving Samuel a chance to explain himself. Without even waiting to find out if he was all right. Now that she thought about it, the fight might have been dangerous. *Was* he all right?

She tossed her head at the Baroness anyway. 'That may be your opinion, but you've no right to say so.'

'I have every right. I'm his grandmother and I shall speak

as I find. It seems to me that he's had a lucky escape. After everything he's been through, Samuel deserves someone who'll love him no matter what.'

'I *do* love him!'

'Good.' Lady Jarrow's accusatory manner fell away instantly. 'I thought it was about time you said so. Now sit down again, my dear, and let's start at the beginning. You accepted my grandson's proposal when you didn't know whether or not he'd inherit, is that true?'

'Yes.' Anna subsided back down onto the sofa. 'We were preparing to come back here together when we found out about Clarissa.'

'That must have been a terrible shock.'

'Yes, but Samuel's behaviour afterwards...'

'Was irresponsible, but perhaps understandable given the circumstances. He found himself trapped in a future he didn't want and doubtless afraid that you might have changed your mind about marrying him. People can behave out of character at such times.'

'Well, yes...'

'As for his threat to throw Clarissa out of Staunton—did he go through with it?'

'No.'

'And the servants who went along with the deception?'

'No.'

'Then it seems to me his behaviour consisted of a few angry words and some foolishness in the local tavern.'

'You weren't there.'

'No, I wasn't.' Lady Jarrow's voice softened. 'And I'm not trying to condone his behaviour either, but before you come to any decision, tell me, what do you know of Samuel's childhood?'

'His childhood?' Anna drew her brows together. 'Not a great deal, except that his father left his mother for another woman and was killed in a duel.'

'That's true. He and his mother came to live with Hector and me afterwards, but I'm afraid it was a difficult situation. I don't like to criticise my daughter, but she wasn't the most attentive of mothers. She felt humiliated by the scandal, you see, and Samuel looked so much like his father that she found it hard to be around him. Consequently, she spent most of her time in London. That's where she met her second husband, Lord Hammerton. They were married a year after she was widowed and went straight to his estate in Cumberland. Samuel wasn't invited to join them.'

'He said he was sent to boarding school.'

'Yes, and spent his holidays with Hector and me, though I believe he was deeply hurt by his mother's rejection. When he was sixteen he ran away from school and went to find his father's family in London.'

'Oh?' Anna leaned forward, intrigued. 'He never told me that. What happened?'

'According to Samuel, nothing. When I asked he said no one was at home so he went to a gambling club and forgot all about it. In reality, he spoke to his grandfather.'

'But why would he lie?'

'Because of what happened next. His grandfather offered him money, a sizeable amount, to go away and never darken his doorstep again. He suggested that he go to the colonies, I believe. Naturally, Samuel refused both the suggestion and the money.'

'But that's awful!' Anna's heart wrenched at the thought. 'How did you find out?'

'Because his grandfather wrote to me, expressing his

outrage at my having allowed the *boy*, as he called him, to visit him. There were other comments, which I shan't deign to repeat. Suffice to say, Samuel never attempted to contact his father's family again.'

'And you've never told him you know what really happened?'

'No, he was miserable enough. I let him keep his pride, but I believe that Samuel has been made to feel second-best and rejected for most of his life. By his father, who ran away with some silly woman, by his mother, who chose a fresh start over him, and by the whole of the rest of his family who didn't want him.'

'*You* didn't reject him.'

'No. Hector and I did our best to make him feel wanted and loved, though he was quite a handful at first. There were times when I feared he might follow in his father's footsteps after all, but he had the strength of character enough to choose the opposite path. He determined to find his own place in the world and to prove his worth without help from anyone. As much as I disliked him joining the navy, it gave him something he'd never had before: a sense of self-worth and belonging. He found a place where he wasn't judged for being his father's son. When this inheritance situation arose it must have felt as though his family were trying to take that life, the one he'd striven so hard for, away from him. But then he met you and you gave him a reason to *want* to stay on shore.'

'But our engagement happened so quickly.' Anna had to swallow the lump in her throat. 'Maybe it was a response to all of that? Maybe he was just looking for a distraction?'

'Nonsense. My grandson may be impulsive, but he always knows what he's doing. He inherited that trait from me.'

'Yes, but…'

'However, if you really can't abide the thought of being a countess, then you're quite right to say so now. And don't worry about Samuel turning out like his father, either. He has more backbone than either of his parents, I'm relieved to say, only I hate to think of him feeling rejected again, or of you ending your engagement just because you were both too much in shock to know what you were doing.' A grey eyebrow arched upwards. 'By the way, what did your mother think of all this?'

'I…' Anna looked to one side sheepishly '… I don't know. I left a note, but I didn't see her before I left.'

'Because you were in such a rush to get away?'

'Yes. I wanted to come home.'

'Because you panicked?'

'I did *not* panic.' Anna thrust her chin out. 'I never panic.'

'Goodness me—' Lady Jarrow rolled her eyes '—you really might be the most stubborn woman I've ever met, Miss Fortini, present company excepted, of course. Once you get an idea in your head it seems remarkably hard to dislodge it. Now that you've run away, I wouldn't be at all surprised if you've talked yourself into doing something dramatic and final solely for the purpose of justifying your decision for years to come.' She pursed her lips speculatively. 'Travelling to Italy, perhaps?'

'No, actually.' Anna dropped her gaze at the thought of Thomas Etton. She *had* been planning on visiting him first thing that morning, only somehow she hadn't been able to go through with it…

'Then what?'

'It doesn't matter. I didn't come here to be insulted.'

'Then why did you come here?'

'To tell you that my and Samuel's engagement was over.'

'Or perhaps you were hoping I'd talk you around?'

Anna opened her mouth to retort and then sighed. 'Maybe I was. I *do* love Samuel, but maybe love isn't enough.'

'Your mother thought that it was.'

'I'm not my mother.'

'No, you're not.' Lady Jarrow's tone was kindly. 'To be honest, your mother was a young and foolish girl with romantic notions. She was lucky your father turned out to be the man that he was. Not everyone who follows their heart is so lucky. You have a great deal more common sense, I'm pleased to say, but you do have a similar choice to make. If you follow your heart, then it will mean turning your life upside down, leaving your shop and starting all over again. It will be difficult. A lot of people will say you can't do it. Some of them will call you names. So tell me, Anna, do you love my grandson enough to stand by him whatever the future brings? Can you be Countess of Staunton?'

Chapter Twenty-Three

Samuel dismounted beneath the familiar white-and-yellow-striped awning of Belles. It was the middle of the afternoon and he was exhausted. No doubt he was covered in dust and looking a mess, too. As a gentleman, he really ought to go and wash and change his clothes before doing anything else, but then Anna didn't particularly want him to be a gentleman and, as for everyone else…he passed a startled-looking couple on their way out of the shop…well, everyone else could go hang for all he cared.

He reached for the door, then stopped and peered in through the window. In place of the usual arrangement of tins, the display inside was a model of a house complete with roof and windows and turrets, all made entirely of biscuit. He leaned forward to make sure he wasn't imagining things and bumped his forehead against the glass. If he wasn't mistaken, it was a perfect model of Staunton.

Feeling slightly dazed, he pushed on the door and went inside.

'Good afternoon, my lord.' The assistant bobbed a curtsy when she saw him, her whole face lighting up with a look of excitement. *Excitement?* 'We've been expecting you.'

'You have?' He couldn't keep the surprise out of his voice.

'Oh, yes.' She scurried around the edge of the counter, turned over the sign on the door so that it read closed, and then drew a bolt across the top. 'If you can just wait here, I'll fetch Anna.'

'She's here?' He could have kissed her for the words.

'Yes, although she was starting to worry you weren't coming. I knew that you would, but I was still afraid you might be too late.'

'Too late for what? What did Anna—?'

He caught his breath as the woman in question appeared in the doorway that led to the kitchen. She was dressed in the periwinkle gown that she'd worn to his grandmother's party, although somehow, impossibly, she looked even more beautiful than she had that evening.

'Samuel.' Her brown eyes were warm and welcoming, the very opposite of what he'd expected.

'Anna.' He took a few steps towards her as Henrietta made a discreet exit. 'I'm sorry. The other day in the tavern…it wasn't what you think.'

'I know.' She gave a quick shake of the head. 'You were in shock and I made things worse. It's understandable that you felt in need of a drink.'

'But I wasn't drunk. I'd barely touched my ale and as for the fight…well, that was a matter of honour. The couple involved are engaged to be married now.'

'Oh.' She blinked with a look of confusion.

'I've promised them some land as a wedding present, too. I suppose I should have checked there was some available first, but I'll find something. What's the point of inheriting an earldom if you can't give away a few acres?'

'I suppose so.'

'And I would have come after you sooner, but the doctor wouldn't let me.' He removed his hat, unveiling a large, purple bruise on his temple.

'Oh!' She rushed forward, lifting her fingers to his forehead. 'Someone hit you?'

'I'm told it was a chair. In the chair's defence, it wasn't meant for me, but I got in the way.' He rubbed his face against her palm, revelling in the warm caress of her fingers. 'I sent a note to Staunton, but when I got back, Clarissa said you'd already left.'

'Yes. Your grandmother says that I panicked and ran away.'

'Did you?'

'I think perhaps I did, but it wasn't what *you* think, either. There was a reason I couldn't go with you to Scotland. It's about your grandfather.'

'You mean because of his illness?'

'Yes.' Her mouth fell open. 'You *know*?'

'I've suspected for a while. My grandmother never leaves Rutland unless she has to. I knew as soon as she said she was coming to Bath that it must be serious.'

'She says he hasn't even told her.'

'He probably knows that he doesn't have to.'

'I'm sorry.'

'So am I. He's been more of a father to me than my real father ever was.' He lifted an eyebrow. 'But why did that stop us eloping to Scotland?'

'Because I promised your grandmother that I wouldn't

tell you and I couldn't marry you while I was keeping secrets, especially when you said you valued my honesty.'

'So it wasn't because you'd changed your mind?'

'No.' She shook her head, threading her arms around his neck and teasing her fingers through his hair. 'It was only when I saw you drinking that I panicked. I thought...'

Her voice trailed away and he gave a wry smile. 'You thought that I was turning into my father?'

'At the time, yes, but your grandmother made me see I was just looking for an excuse to run away. Then she asked if I was brave enough to leave my old life behind like my mother did.'

He felt as if his heart had just stopped. 'And what did you say?'

'That I'd never abandon you again.'

'Anna...' He folded her into his arms, crushing his lips against hers and kissing her with several days' worth of relief.

'But we have to hurry.' She pulled away after a few moments, looking at his bruise anxiously. 'How are you feeling now?'

'Absolutely fine now that I'm here with you.'

'Good. Then we need to get ready.'

'For what?'

'Our wedding.' She paused. 'If you still want to marry me, that is?'

'If I still...?' He caught her about the waist, pulling her back towards him again. 'Anna, I love you. Of course I still want to marry you. I've spent the whole journey here worrying that you might be Mrs Etton already.'

'I could never have gone through with that. Not when I was in love with you.' She hung her head apologetically and then smiled. 'Now your grandmother's arranged everything at short notice. I don't think anyone dared to refuse her. A common licence, a supper afterwards...'

'Please tell me she hasn't invited guests, too.'

'None except me.' Henrietta poked her head into the shop again. 'Can I give you my wedding present now?'

'Another one?' Anna laughed. 'I thought the house in the window was our wedding present?'

'Oh, that was just for fun. This is your real present...' Henrietta walked towards them holding a plate piled high with diamond-shaped biscuits. 'They're a different shape and flavour to Belles so I thought they should have a different name. Maybe Countess biscuits, if you don't object?'

'I think that's the best wedding present anyone could wish for.' Samuel reached for a sample. 'Except...what about Contessa biscuits? That's Italian for countess, isn't it?'

'Perfect.' Anna clapped her hands together. 'I think my father would have approved of that, too.'

'They're savoury.' He took a bite and nodded appreciatively. 'With salt?'

'Just a hint. I thought it was fitting.'

'They're delicious.' Samuel popped the entire rest of the biscuit into his mouth. 'Can I have another? I've been riding for hours.'

'You can have them all.' Henrietta beamed and then tipped the whole plateful into one of his greatcoat pockets. 'Here, you can eat them on the way to the ceremony.'

'Wait.' Samuel held a hand out amid a flurry of activity as both women started to pull on bonnets and shawls. 'I just have to make a quick journey to the Circus first. I left some of my belongings there.'

'First?' Anna looked anxious. 'We're running out of time.'

'There's one last thing I need to do.' He bent his head, kissing her softly on the cheek. 'It won't take long, I promise.'

As wedding days went, Samuel reflected afterwards, it had certainly been eventful. After his headlong rush from Staunton back to Bath, he'd expected to have to apologise, plead and possibly beg for Anna to forgive him, but instead here he was, less than two hours since he'd reached Belles, standing in his grandparents' drawing room, a glass of champagne in one hand, his new Countess's waist in the other.

'I'm glad you wore your uniform.' His grandmother looked him up and down approvingly.

'So am I. You look very dashing.' Anna's eyes twinkled. 'If you'd told me that that was what you were hurrying back to the Circus for, then I wouldn't have protested.'

'Now you tell me.' He grinned down at her. 'I thought I ought to say goodbye to the navy properly.'

'To the new Earl and Countess of Staunton.' His grandfather lifted his glass, his hand shaking slightly though his voice was firm. 'Anna, I'm delighted to welcome you into the family. I wish you both as much happiness in marriage as I've found.'

'Pshaw,' his grandmother snorted. 'There's no need for sentiment.'

'I wish for that, too...' Anna answered, 'and we're grateful for everything you've done.'

'You mean arranging a wedding in less than a day? Yes, I rather impressed myself.' The Baroness drew herself up to her full height. 'Now I need to retire to the countryside for some peace and quiet. We'll be leaving Bath tomorrow.'

'So soon?' Samuel looked between his grandparents anxiously.

'Yes.' The Baron nodded. 'I'm missing my books. You know I enjoy nothing more than sitting in my library while this one booms in my ear.'

'I do not *boom*!'

'You'd put Wellington's cannons to shame, my dear, but I wouldn't change you for the world.' He winked at Samuel and then fixed him with a sombre look. 'I'd like to go home, my boy, you understand?'

'I do, Grandfather, but if you need me...'

'Then I won't hesitate to summon you, but you'll be heading north again soon, too, I imagine. Your place is there now.'

'In a few days, once a few things are settled at the shop. Anna's gifting it to her apprentice.' He gave a proud tug on her waist.

'Gifting?' The Baroness looked scandalised.

'Not exactly,' Anna corrected him. 'The building will still belong to my mother, but Henrietta will be free to live there and run the business for as long as she chooses. Sebastian never had any interest in the shop and it would be a shame to close Belles just because I'm leaving. I'm positive my mother will approve and you know that Nancy has asked if she can move in and continue working there? Apparently she enjoys baking.'

'Yes, I heard you wished to steal one of my maids.' Lady Jarrow's lips twitched. 'Naturally I've agreed.'

'We'll come and wave you off in the morning, of course.' Samuel leaned in to kiss his grandmother on the cheek.

'No, my boy.' His grandfather patted him on the shoulder when they went to shake hands. 'Let's say goodbye now.

I couldn't possibly be happier than I am at this moment. I was always proud of you as a boy and I'm even prouder of you as a man. Now take care of your wife, you understand? Or you'll have your grandmother to deal with.'

'Then you leave me no choice.' Samuel smiled through the lump in his throat and turned towards Anna. 'We'll take care of each other.'

Chapter Twenty-Four

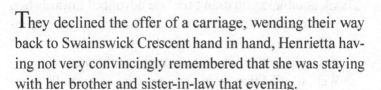

They declined the offer of a carriage, wending their way back to Swainswick Crescent hand in hand, Henrietta having not very convincingly remembered that she was staying with her brother and sister-in-law that evening.

'What do you think people would say if they knew the Earl and Countess of Staunton were spending their wedding night above a biscuit shop?' Anna asked, peering shyly over her shoulder as she unlocked the front door. 'It's not very grand.'

'But it's where we met.' Samuel came to stand close behind her, placing his hands on either side of her waist. 'That seems fitting for our first night together.'

'About that…' She pushed the door open, removing one of his hands and using it to lead him inside. 'I'm not sure whether…'

'It's all right.' He lifted her fingers to his mouth, kissing the backs of her knuckles reassuringly. 'I don't have any expectations tonight. I'll be happy just to hold you in my arms if you don't feel ready for more.'

'I'm ready.' She smiled at the obvious relief in his face. 'But you've had a hit on the head and you must be exhausted after such a long day. Maybe you should—'

'I'm ready, too.' He cut her off, closing the shop door and drawing the bolt firmly behind them. 'It'll take more than a bump on the head to keep my hands off you.'

'As long as you're certain.' She hesitated. 'Only the truth is that I'm not entirely sure what I'm ready for. I would have asked my mother, but she's not here, and as much as I like your grandmother...'

'She's not the kind of person you can talk to about *that*. Thank goodness you didn't try.' He advanced towards her, smiling in a way that set butterflies fluttering in her stomach. 'Remember what we did in the plunge pool?'

'Yes.' She felt her cheeks turn pink at the memory.

'Well, it's like that, only warmer, drier and usually more horizontal.'

'Oh... I see. Would you like some tea first?'

'No.' His lips quirked. 'No tea.'

'Wine?'

'Nothing.' He reached for the tasselled ends of her shawl, slowly peeling it from around her shoulders and dropping it onto the shop counter. 'I want you, Anna. Nothing else.'

'Oh...' She swallowed at the touch of cold air on her skin. It was a relief since the room seemed to have become ten times hotter all of a sudden. His hands surrounded her waist again, his gaze dark and hungry-looking, holding her own so intently that the fluttering sensation in her stomach felt more like flapping now, as if the butterflies had somehow transformed into birds. She took a faltering breath, her thoughts spinning as he lowered his lips against hers, softly and searchingly at first, then kissing her so deeply that she felt as if all the blood in her body had rushed straight to her head. She curled her arms around his neck, though she didn't realise they were moving until her back touched the counter.

'Samuel?' She tipped her head back, breaking the kiss to catch her breath. 'Should we go upstairs?'

'Probably,' he murmured against her neck, covering her skin with hot, open-mouthed kisses. 'While I still can walk.'

'Why wouldn't you—?' She opened her eyes wide as the lower half of his body pressed against her. 'Oh.'

'Oh,' he repeated, a smile in his voice as he slid his hands over her hips and bunched his fingers in the folds of her skirts. 'I've wanted to do this from the first moment I saw you.'

'Not the *first*,' she protested.

'The very first. I was standing just outside that window and you were scowling from behind the counter.'

'I was trying to scare you away.'

'I know. You have a very attractive scowl.'

He pressed a kiss into the hollow at the base of her throat. It felt so tender that she heard a moan escape her lips even before she'd opened them. Mercifully, the flapping in her abdomen had stopped, only it seemed to have been replaced by a throbbing sensation instead, making her legs so unsteady that she doubted she could make it up the stairs now, either. And he certainly couldn't carry her in his...*condition*. Which left only one alternative...

She braced her hands on the edge of the counter behind, pulling herself up to perch on the edge.

'Anna?' Samuel's gaze looked arrested.

'You said like the plunge pool.' She frowned. 'Or does it *have* to be horizontal?'

'No...' There was a raw edge to his voice as if he were struggling with the question himself. 'But this is your first time. It might be better if we...' He didn't finish the sentence as she leaned forward, pressing her breasts against his chest and skimming her lips along the curve of his ear with a small shushing sound. For a moment his whole body seemed to tense at the contact, but then he reached up, cupping her face in his hands and kissing her even more deeply than before. 'I want you.'

Moving by instinct, she wriggled forward until there was no space left between them, wrapping her legs around his waist while his fingers unfastened the hooks at the back of her gown, tugging it down over her shoulders. His mouth fell to her breasts, and she pushed her hands beneath his shirt, feeling the muscles of his shoulders flex as she smoothed her fingers greedily over the hard contours of his body.

'Anna.' His voice sounded guttural, making her heart clench with anticipation as he unfastened the front of his breeches and then slid a hand between her legs, touching her so intimately that she sucked in a breath of surprise. 'I don't want to hurt you.'

'You're not,' she gasped as hard flesh pressed against the entrance to her body. 'I want you, too.'

Determinedly, she clutched hold of his shoulders, moving her hips forward so that she slid on to him herself, biting her lip to hold back a cry at the new sense of intrusion. Samuel groaned, too, a low exclamation followed by a muffled oath as if she were the one hurting him.

'What's the matter?' She started to move back in alarm, but he grabbed at her waist, holding her where she was.

'Nothing's wrong.' He closed his eyes. 'You just feel too good.'

'How can it be *too* good?' She slid farther along his length, feeling a hot burst of pain followed by a tingle of pleasure.

'Wait.' He made a sound at the back of his throat, something between a laugh and a growl as he tightened his hold on her. 'You'll find out if you're not careful.'

'Maybe I want to find out.' She tried moving again, writhing her hips despite the arm clamped around her waist. Somehow the movement caused a fresh spasm of pleasure.

'Anna…' He sounded as if he were speaking through clenched teeth, pushing himself even deeper.

'Mmm…?' The spasm felt so good that she couldn't stop herself from moving again, bucking against him as she pursued the feeling. He didn't protest this time, bracing one hand on the counter as he moved with and against her, faster and deeper while the spasms seemed to build in intensity, one upon another, sending vibrations of feeling out along every nerve and through every limb. At last they all seemed to join together at once, mingling into one extended burst of feeling that wrenched a cry from her lips and left her feeling dazed and satiated. She let her head fall backwards, her body turning limp as Samuel thrust one last time and then shuddered inside her.

'Anna?' He pressed his face into her neck, gasping for breath.

'Yes?'

'Are you all right?'

'Yes.' She laughed at the question. 'I'm *very* all right.'

'Good.' He sounded relieved, letting out his own ragged laugh. 'So much for horizontal.'

'Horizontal is definitely more comfortable,' Anna sighed, tucking her head into the curve between Samuel's neck and shoulder after their second lovemaking, this time in bed. 'Although there's something to be said for shop counters, too.'

'I'll never look at one in the same way again,' Samuel murmured, stroking a hand over her hip and drawing one of her legs up over his body.

'Me neither. It's probably a good thing I'm leaving or I'd never be able to sell biscuits again without blushing.'

'No regrets?'

'None, except...'

'What?' His hand stilled instantly.

'Part of me wishes my mother could have been at our wedding, after all. And then there's Sebastian. I wish I even knew where he was.'

'It's not unusual for ships to be out of contact with the Admiralty for this long, but I'll write and ask if there's been any word.' He raised a hand to her hair, looping his finger around a stray curl that hung over her forehead. 'He—and your mother, too—can come to Staunton and celebrate with us as soon as he gets shore leave.'

'Thank you.' She nuzzled closer. 'You know, I always hoped that if I married then it would be a love match like my parents, but I never thought I'd be so lucky.'

'Certainly not with an earl.'

'*Definitely* not with an earl, but nobody's perfect.'

'How flattering.' He tugged gently on the curl. 'Are you sure you don't mind leaving Belles? It's going to be a big change.'

'Yes, but at least I have a manager I can rely on. Henrietta's enthusiastic and she seems to genuinely love baking. I think she'll make a bigger success of the place than I ever did.'

'She ought to. You're paying her twice as much as my steward with free lodgings to boot.'

'Do you object?'

'Not a bit. I'll have to raise my steward's wages to match. I'm just glad you're not closing the doors altogether. Belles is a Bath institution, after all, and you're the original Belle.'

'The Countess who smells of the shop.' She smoothed a hand over his chest. 'Of course, that's only an insult if you don't like the smell of biscuits.'

'And who in their right mind doesn't? Personally speaking, I adore it. I'm going to need a supply of Contessas just for the journey north.'

'Are we going to share a carriage this time?'

'What do you think?' He raised his eyebrows. 'I'm a newly married man. It would be remiss of me *not* to seize the opportunity of being in a closed carriage with my wife for two days. There are all sorts of things we can do to entertain ourselves.'

'All sorts?'

'Well, one sort really, with several variations.'

'Mmm.' She smiled lazily. 'In that case, when are we leaving?'

'Just give the order. Are you ready to start a new life with me, Countess?'

'If you're ready to leave the sea behind, then yes, Captain Delaney, I believe that I am.'

'Well, then…' he murmured, pressing a kiss onto the top of her head. 'Clear the decks and anchor aweigh.'

Epilogue

Six months later

Henrietta bolted upright with a gasp, startled awake by the sound of a thud from downstairs. As she listened, there was another, and another, all in quick succession, muffled but unmistakable. She judged, by the pitch blackness outside her small window in one of the attic bedrooms above Belles, that it was still the middle of the night, which meant that whatever, or whoever, it was shouldn't be there.

She tossed her blankets aside and flung her legs over the side of the bed, palms sweating and heart pounding like a drum, which was both terrifying and inconvenient since it made it impossible for her to listen for anything else. Slowly, she crept out into the hallway, pausing at the top of the stairs as she considered whether or not to wake Nancy, the Baroness's former kitchen-maid-turned-shop-assistant. Much as she wanted some moral support, however, she decided against it. There were no sounds coming from below now, making her wonder if she'd dreamt the thuds, after all. She'd been *so* certain, but what if...?

Just to be sure, she descended the wooden staircase to the parlour, feeling her way as her eyes grew accustomed to the dark, taking care not to creak any floorboards, but that room was so still and silent and looking so much like normal that she began to relax and feel foolish. It was typical of her wayward imagination to run away with her. Thank goodness she hadn't woken Nancy or she'd have to explain herself and...

A shiver raced down her spine at the sound of another distinct thud from below. Instinctively she reached for the nearest weapons, a pair of tongs and a metal shovel poking out of the coal bucket, before carrying on downstairs. Each step seemed to go on for ever, giving her sufficient time to terrify herself about what she might find. Thieves? Cutthroats? Probably not highwaymen since she wasn't on horseback *or* in a stagecoach, though the image of a masked man still popped into her mind with startling clarity.

For the first time in months she wished she had a husband there to protect her. Once upon a time she'd thought of marriage as the answer to all of her problems, but after several upsetting episodes she'd come to realise that commitment wasn't what most men had in mind when they looked at her. Now she was older and wiser, she understood the world a bit better and a husband was the last thing she wanted.

She was married to Belles now—and if there were thieves below stairs then she'd deal with them herself!

She braced herself, tightening her fingers around her makeshift weaponry as her foot touched the bottom step. The shop itself was completely swathed in darkness, which meant that the thuds had to be coming from the kitchen.

Which struck her as odd since there wasn't much there to steal except for a few sacks of flour and sugar and assorted baking utensils, but perhaps the thieves were hungry? She pressed her ear against the door to listen, stifling a yelp of alarm at the sound of footsteps inside. They seemed to be coming closer, too, as if whoever it was had heard her approach. If she didn't act quickly, then the door would open and she'd be caught.

Unless she caught them first.

Without pausing to reconsider, she grabbed hold of the handle, gave it a quick twist and then shoved as hard as she could, knocking the wooden door against something large and heavy. There was a thwack, followed by a volley of expletives and then another thud, as if she'd just knocked someone off their feet. Seizing the advantage, she pushed again and jumped inside, swinging the shovel up over her head and thrusting the tongs out in front of her.

'Get out!' She tried to sound as threatening as possible, relieved to find that the *thieves* were in fact just one *thief*, sprawled on the flagstones behind the door.

'What the blazes...?' The man stared up at her with one hand clamped over his face. In the shadowy light of the still-glowing hearth, it made him look like the masked highwayman she'd envisaged. All she could make out were dark eyes, black hair and what looked like a red trickle streaming between his fingers.

'Oh!' She started forward and then stopped. Just because he was injured didn't mean she should help him. If anything, it served him right!

'You might give a man some warning when you're about to open the door.' He pulled his hand away, revealing a handsome, albeit bloodstained and somewhat swarthy, countenance. 'I think you just broke my nose.'

'Good! That'll teach you to break into people's property in the middle of the night! Now get out or I'll scream for the night-watchman.'

'Wait!' He reached into his jacket pocket and pulled out a white handkerchief, waving it in the air like a flag of surrender before using it to wipe the blood off his face. 'I didn't break in. I have a key and I was trying *not* to make noise, if you must know, only things seem to have moved around since I was last here. Where's Anna?'

'You know Anna?' Henrietta blinked in surprise, lowering the coal shovel a few inches.

'All my life.' He looked her up and down speculatively. 'By the way, would you mind putting those tongs down? I'm afraid to ask what you intended to do with them, but they're making me want to cross my legs.'

'Oh.' A hot flush rushed through her body at the implication. The look of bemused interest on his face made her feel hotter still, as well as acutely conscious of the fact that her only clothing consisted of a plain cotton nightgown that stopped halfway down her calves. Thank goodness for the dark. 'No! Not until you tell me how you know Anna.'

'Well…' He jumped to his feet so abruptly that she took an instinctive step backwards. 'I believe that we first met in the cradle. She used to sing me lullabies, as I recall. Allow me to introduce myself. Sebastian Fortini, at your service.'

'Anna's little brother?' Now that he mentioned it, she could see the resemblance. His dark hair was wavy and dishevelled rather than curly, but he had the same square-shaped jaw and soulful, deep-set brown eyes. Judging by the crinkles around them, she had the impression that he laughed a lot. They held a mirthful glint now that made her want to smile, too.

'The one and only.' He winked good-naturedly and made an elaborate bow, flourishing the now bloodstained handkerchief out in front of him. 'As for you, I assume that you're a figment of my imagination caused by the blow to my head.'

'Oh, dear.' She put the tongs and shovel down by the fireplace. 'Sorry about that. I really thought you were a burglar.'

'Perfectly understandable.'

'My name's Henrietta Gardiner.'

'Delighted to meet you, even under the circumstances.' His sudden grin was dazzling. 'So, Miss Gardiner, has my sister employed you to guard the shop against night-time marauders?'

'Not exactly. I'm the new manager.'

'Manager?' His gaze sharpened. 'Why is Anna employing a manager?'

'Because she's...' She hesitated, looking at him askance. 'Wait, didn't you get any of her letters?'

'No. My ship's been stuck out in the Pacific for the past year. I haven't heard anything from home in the whole time. What's happened? Is she all right? Has something happened to our mother?'

'Oh, no, everything's all right.' Henrietta hastened to reassure him. 'They're both perfectly well, only...' She sucked on her bottom lip, wondering where to begin. 'I think I'd better put the kettle on. Are you hungry? There are some leftover biscuits somewhere.'

'You mean Belles?' He sat down at the table with a nostalgic expression. 'I can't remember the last time I had one of those. I hope Anna hasn't been messing around with the recipe.'

'You might be surprised by what Anna has done.' Henrietta stifled a smile. 'Welcome home, Mr Fortini, we have a lot to talk about.'

* * * * *

Unexpectedly Wed To The Officer

Author Note

Unexpectedly Wed to the Officer is the second book in my four-part Regency Belles of Bath miniseries, a collection inspired by my grandparents, the city of Bath, and my own profound and enduring love of biscuits. It also references the huge amount of maritime literature I read at university by featuring a naval hero, although I've made Sebastian's experiences quite tame by comparison to real-life events.

When the first book in the series, *An Unconventional Countess*, came out, a number of readers requested more of the indomitable Lady Jarrow. Having just finished the third book, I promise you she'll be back!

To my own little chatterbox.

Chapter One

Belles Biscuit Shop, Bath—November 1806

The door hit Sebastian Fortini squarely on the nose.

It was, he considered, a case of monumentally bad timing. If he hadn't been looking sideways, wondering why the dresser that had spent two decades in one particular corner of the kitchen had suddenly moved to the wall opposite, then he wouldn't have turned so sharply at the creak of a floorboard in the hallway, which meant that the door, when it opened, would have had only its own and not his additional impetus to wield against him. But unfortunately he had, and he was, so it did.

If only the chain of catastrophes had ended there...

Alas, his nose proved to be just the first victim as the full and somewhat considerable weight of a heavy oak door being violently rammed rather than gently pushed open knocked the rest of him off his feet and into an inelegant heap on the floor.

Between the impact of the wood on his face and the stone flagstones on his posterior, it was actually difficult to tell which was the most painful, a fact that did nothing to curb the flow of expletives that immediately burst from his lips, which appeared to be coated in some warm, sticky substance.

He reached a hand to his nose, felt blood and sucked in a breath, readying himself for a fresh burst of eloquence, when a female figure suddenly sprang out of the darkness of the hallway, armed with what appeared to be the contents of a coal bucket.

'Get out!'

Sebastian raised himself up on his elbows, squinting at his attacker through the murky flickers of light cast by the still-glowing hearth. Unexpected as it was to find himself being threatened in the dead of night by a shovel and pair of fire tongs, he was frankly more perplexed than alarmed. His sister's voice, he was further surprised to notice, had developed something of a west country burr in the two years since he'd last been home on shore leave. More bizarrely, she'd grown in height, too. In fact, her whole appearance had undergone some kind of radical transformation…

'What the blazes?' He drew his brows together, belatedly acknowledging that she was not, in fact, his sister after all. Not unless the blow to his head had affected his sight, which seemed unlikely since there was nothing blurry about the vision of golden loveliness before him. She was about as different in appearance to Anna as it was possible to be—willowy, golden and, at that moment, clad in a white nightgown short enough to reveal a pair of slender, shapely calves and positively minuscule ankles. In other circumstances he might have been quite delighted to find himself lying beside them. Unfortunately, she'd just knocked the sense out of him and the words racing through his mind were a great deal less than charitable. Ankles be damned, his nose felt as though it was about to explode.

'Oh!' She started forward at the sight of blood and then checked herself, jerking her chin upwards and scowling defiantly instead.

'You might give a man some warning when you're about to open the door.' He scowled back, clenching his jaw against the impulse to swear some more. He'd barely scratched the surface of his extensive sailor's vocabulary. 'I think you just broke my nose.'

'Good!' Her grip on the shovel only tightened. 'That'll teach you to break into people's property in the middle of the night! Now get out or I'll scream for the night-watchman.'

'Wait!' He reached into his jacket pocket and pulled out a handkerchief, waving it in the air like a flag of surrender before using it to wipe the blood off his face. After two days of travelling in a series of cramped stagecoaches from Plymouth, the last of which had arrived three hours late thanks to a loose wheel, being hit in the face by a door wasn't the welcome home he'd been hoping for, but, injured party or not, the last thing he wanted was to be hauled off to gaol in the middle of the night. 'I didn't break in. I have a key and I was trying *not* to make any noise, if you must know, only things seem to have moved around since I was last here.'

He threw another speculative look around the kitchen. The pale yellow walls, oval-shaped oak table and threadbare armchair by the hearth were familiar, but actually quite a *lot* had changed since he was last there. To begin with, there was the broom he'd knocked over when he'd opened the back door, then there was the sack of flour he'd stubbed his toe against, then a set of shelves he *definitely* hadn't seen before, not to mention the dresser... Presumably his sister had decided to move a few things around, but where was she anyhow?

'Where's Anna?' He cocked his head to one side enquiringly.

'You know Anna?' The woman blinked, apparently surprised enough to lower the shovel a few inches.

'All my life.' He glanced from her face to her makeshift weapons and then back again. It didn't seem as though she had any real intention of using them, but considering the various sharp edges and their potential uses, it was probably best to be sure. 'By the way, would you mind putting those tongs down? I'm afraid to ask what you intended to do with them, but they're making me want to cross my legs.'

'Oh.'

His lips twitched as a furious blush spread across her cheeks. Now that the pain in his nose was receding, it occurred to him that if he really *had* to be hit in the face by a woman, then she might well be the one he would have chosen to do it. Even scowling and wielding a pair of tongs, she was quite stunningly pretty. Beautiful in fact, with delicate, elfin features set in a peaches and cream complexion, albeit one that was currently claret-coloured.

'No!' She was adamant despite her embarrassment. 'Not until you tell me how you know Anna.'

'Well...' He braced his hands on the floor, pushing himself to his feet so abruptly that she leapt part way into the air, the tongs wobbling precariously in her grasp. 'I believe that we first met in the cradle. She used to sing me lullabies, as I recall. Allow me to introduce myself. Sebastian Fortini, at your service.'

'Anna's little brother?'

'The one and only.' He winked and made an elaborate bow, enjoying her gasp of surprise as he flourished the now bloodstained handkerchief out in front of him. 'As for you, I can only assume that you're a figment of my imagination caused by the blow to my head.'

'Oh, dear.' A horrified expression crossed her face. 'Sorry about that. I really thought you were a burglar.'

'Quite understandable.' He lifted his shoulders, conceding that it was, in fact, *entirely* understandable since he hadn't sent any advance notice of his arrival. There hadn't seemed much point when he could travel in person just as fast as a letter, but then he hadn't reckoned on his coach's late arrival. That *had* struck him as somewhat unfortunate, coinciding as it did with the middle of the night, but he'd assumed that he could simply let himself in, sleep in the armchair by the hearth and wait to surprise his sister in the morning. What he *hadn't* expected was to trip over half the kitchen furniture and wake anyone else up.

'My name's Henrietta Gardiner.' The woman placed the tongs and shovel down by the hearth and clasped her hands together primly in front of her.

'Delighted to meet you, even under the circumstances.' He suppressed a smile at the primness. There was something charmingly incongruous about it when she was standing in front of him wearing nothing more than a white nightgown, particularly one that, whilst not exactly sheer, did only a partial job of concealing the luscious curves beneath. He allowed himself a few seconds of appreciation before pulling his gaze reluctantly back to her face. 'So, Miss Gardiner, has my sister employed you to guard the shop against night-time marauders?'

'Not exactly. I'm the new manager.'

'Manager?' He forgot instantly about the nightgown, seized with a rush of panic. 'Why is Anna employing a manager?'

'Because she's—' She stopped mid-sentence, regarding him askance. 'Wait, didn't you get any of her letters?'

'No. My ship's been stuck out in the Pacific for the past year. I haven't heard anything from home in the whole time. What's happened?' He took a step forward impatiently. 'Is she all right? Has something happened to our mother?'

'Oh, no, everything's all right. They're both perfectly well, only—' She stopped for a second time, sucking her bottom lip between her teeth in a way that made him acutely conscious of her nightgown again. 'I think I'd better put the kettle on. Are you hungry? There are some leftover biscuits somewhere.'

'You mean Belles?' He pulled a chair out and settled himself down at the table, feeling relieved by her assurances. The thought of one of his family's famous biscuits was comforting, too, telling him he was finally home at last. 'I can't remember the last time I had one of those. I hope Anna hasn't been messing around with the recipe.'

There was a conspicuous pause before Miss Gardiner answered, a glint of amusement in her eye as she deposited a plate of biscuits on the table in front of him. 'You might be surprised by what Anna has done. Welcome home, Mr Fortini, we have a lot to talk about.'

* * *

'Let me get this straight. My sister—*my sister Anna*—who despises the aristocracy and everything they stand for, married an earl and now she's a countess?'

Sebastian wasn't sure how many times he'd repeated the question—or repeated the same combination of words in a variety of different ways. He'd started off with the vague idea that if he kept *on* repeating them, then they might start to make sense, but the tactic seemed to be having the opposite effect. Everything that he'd heard over the past half an hour was so bewildering and unbelievable that he was seriously wondering whether he ought to consult a doctor about the blow to his head, after all.

'I know it's a lot to take in and it sounds far-fetched, but I assure you it's all true, Mr Fortini.'

Miss Gardiner was regarding him across the table with an expression of tolerant sympathy, her delectable figure now modestly hidden beneath a green woollen dressing gown, more was the pity. *She* struck him as somewhat unbelievable, too, and not just because he'd been living among men for so long. If he'd tried, he could hardly have dreamt up a more exquisite-looking specimen of femininity, although, considering the circumstances, she surely *had* to be real. If she were a figment of his imagination, then they'd be doing a lot more than drinking tea and eating biscuits at midnight. They'd be on the same side of the table for a start, if not on top of it, and she wouldn't be wearing that dressing gown either. Not to mention that he'd be far more intimately acquainted with those ankles…

'But a *countess*?' He dragged his mind back to the subject in hand.

'Of Staunton, yes.' In addition to her more obvious attractions, Miss Gardiner appeared to have limitless amounts of patience. 'They held the wedding here in Bath six months ago. I was a witness.'

'You were?' He leaned forward. 'Tell me, how did Anna seem?'

'Very happy.'

'Are you certain? Forgive me, but I know how Anna feels about the aristocracy. She detests the whole lot of them. Are you sure she wasn't coerced into anything?'

'Coerced?' Miss Gardiner looked baffled. 'I believe that she had mixed feelings at first, but I've never heard of a shopkeeper being *coerced* to marry an earl.'

'No, but perhaps there was some compelling reason…?'

She stared at him blankly for a few seconds before emitting a high-pitched squeak of indignation. 'Absolutely not!'

'What about financial reasons, then?' Sebastian wasn't prepared to let the subject drop so easily. 'Perhaps she felt she needed the security?'

'Anna would *never* have married for money!' Miss Gardiner pushed her chair back, apparently on the verge of storming away. 'Or for any reason except affection and respect! It's insulting that you would even suggest such a thing!'

'I would never insult my sister.' Sebastian held his hands up in a placatory gesture. 'I just need to be sure that she got married of her own free will and that she was happy about it. I'd hate to think of her being forced into anything because I wasn't here to help her in a difficult situation.'

'Mmm.' She sat down again, her expression softening slightly as she tucked her chair back under the table. 'Well, in that case, you can put your mind at ease. Anna's marriage was a love match. She married the Earl despite his rank, not because of it.'

'That's a relief. Still, a countess...' He shook his head. 'You have to admit, it sounds pretty unbelievable and not just about Anna, but my mother, too. How is it possible that after twenty-five years of being disowned by her family, she's gone to live with her mother, my so-called grandmother? A dowager duchess, of all people?'

'I don't know, but she has, at your uncle's house, Feversham Hall in Yorkshire. Anna says they're all very happy together. As is she.'

'Well, damn it all.' He winced. 'Pardon me, Miss Gardiner.'

'That's all right.' She gave him an arch look. 'It's really nothing compared to the things you said earlier.'

'Ah...you mean when the door hit me? Sorry about that, although, to be honest, I've forgotten what it was exactly. Nothing too shocking, I hope?'

'That would probably depend on how easily a person is shocked, but I've chosen to regard it as educational. I never realised that my vocabulary was so lacking before.' One corner of her mouth curved upwards, revealing a dimple in her left cheek. 'But you're forgiven. All of this must have come as quite a shock.'

'That's an understatement.' He tipped his chair on to its back legs. 'You know, as pleasant as tea is, I believe that the situation might call for something stronger.'

'You mean to drink?' The dimple disappeared as two spots of colour blazed across her cheekbones. 'I'm afraid we don't have anything like that.'

'Not even some port? There always used to be a bottle tucked away on the top shelf in the pantry.'

'Ye-es.' Her gaze flickered to one side. 'There *was* a bottle, only I took it down a few months ago. I believe I might have poured it away.'

'You poured it away?' He dropped his chair back to the floor in surprise. She was looking curiously guilty, too, although, considering her healthy complexion, he found it difficult to believe that she was a hardened port-drinker or anything-drinker. Probably the opposite was true and she disapproved of alcohol entirely, which given his current desire for a drink was more than a little unfortunate. Still, since it couldn't be helped... 'Never mind. I can see that you've made quite a few changes.'

'Yes. Anna said that I could do whatever I liked and I thought that the dresser—'

'It wasn't a criticism, Miss Gardiner,' he interrupted as her spine stiffened defensively. 'Just an observation. Now that I look at it, I wonder why my mother never thought to put the dresser over there herself. It makes the whole kitchen look bigger.'

'That's what I thought.' She looked pleased, the vivid red of her cheeks fading to a dusky and extremely fetching shade of pink. 'And with the table here, we can see through to the shop when we're baking.'

'*We?* You have an assistant, I presume.'

'Nancy, yes. She was a kitchen maid, but the Earl's grandmother sent her to help with the baking for a while and she liked the work so much that she stayed. Now she lives here, too.'

'She's a deep sleeper, I take it?'

'*Very.*' The dimple made a fresh appearance. 'And she hates to be disturbed. That's why I didn't wake her tonight. I thought perhaps I was just imagining noises down here.'

'I'm relieved that you *didn't* wake her.' He lifted a finger to his nose and pushed it tentatively from side to side. 'You're quite ferocious enough on your own.'

'Oh, dear. Do you really think that it's broken?'

'Probably.' He felt a twinge of guilt at her contrite expression. 'But not to worry. It's not the first time and I doubt it will be the last. I actually forget how my face looked originally. For all we know, this might be an improvement.'

She gave a low, throaty laugh and then leaned across the table suddenly, her eyes alight with curiosity. 'Did you break it before in the navy? Anna said that you were a lieutenant.'

'Only *acting* lieutenant, I'm afraid. I was promoted by my captain, not the Admiralty, and I never got an opportunity to sit any exams. Now, thanks to Trafalgar, the navy has a surplus of officers so I've been discharged from duty. Not that I'm complaining about our victory, but it might have been easier to swallow if I'd actually been there instead of...' He bit his tongue. 'In any case, I'm back.'

'So you're not going back to sea?'

He lifted his shoulders in a shrug. It was a good question. He'd finally come home to help Anna run Belles, but apparently that ship had sailed, too. He wasn't needed here any more than he was in the navy. Which was ironic considering how guilty he'd felt about being away over the past few years. Now it appeared he was a completely free man. Free from family obligations, naval orders *and* commitments. It was a strange, somewhat exuberant feeling. He could do anything he wanted, go anywhere he wanted. He was still only in his early twenties, young enough to find another career. He could...

'Mr Fortini?'

He started. 'Forgive me, I was just thinking. To be honest, I've no idea what I'll do yet. Maybe I'll just enjoy my freedom for a while.'

'Anna and your mother will be thrilled to see you again. They've been so worried. The Earl even went to the Admiralty to ask about your ship.'

'Really?' Sebastian had to make a conscious effort not to clench his jaw at the words. If that were the case, then it was possible his new brother-in-law already knew what had happened to the *Menelaus*. The question was whether or not he would have told Anna. He hoped not, and fortunately Miss Gardiner seemed to have no idea…

'I'm afraid there was no way for me to send word any earlier.' He shifted forward in his chair, splaying both of his hands out on the table in what he hoped was a masterful way of steering the conversation. 'But I'm here now. Only it appears that I've come to the wrong place.'

'Not *wrong*. It's still your family's shop. They're just…'

'Not here?'

'No.' She smiled apologetically. 'I'm afraid not.'

Their gazes locked across the table and he found himself instinctively smiling back. Her eyes were a luminous and vibrant blue, he noticed, as clear and enticing as the tropical seas he'd seen on the other side of the world, like warm pools he might willingly dive into. Something about them made him completely forget what they were talking about. If he hadn't known better, he would actually have thought they had some kind of hypnotising effect… He couldn't take his own off them.

'More tea?' She broke the spell, reaching for the teapot. 'I think there's a little left.'

'No, thank you.' He stood up, suddenly aware of the impropriety of their situation and wondering if her eyes weren't perhaps a little too enticing for their own good. 'I ought to be on my way.'

'You're leaving?' She looked startled. 'But it's the middle of the night!'

'True, but under the circumstances I can hardly stay here. It wouldn't be proper, or so my mother would tell me anyway.'

'No, I suppose not.' A series of expressions passed over her face before settling into one of resolve. 'But I can't possibly throw you out into the cold. Belles belongs to your family, which makes it your home even more than it is mine.'

'Miss Gardiner…'

'I admit that the circumstances aren't ideal…' she spoke over him '…but it's not as if Nancy and I are ladies. Nobody cares what we do. There's really only the shop's reputation to think about, but as long as we smuggle you out discreetly in the morning, then who's to know you were ever here?'

'I still don't think…'

'But I *insist*.' Her chin jutted upwards mutinously. 'Most decent establishments will be closed at this time of night and, even if they aren't, it's likely to be freezing outside. Improper or not, I'd never be able to look Anna in the face again if anything happened to you. No, Mr Fortini, I simply cannot allow you to leave, not when there's a perfectly serviceable sofa in the parlour.'

'The green one? I remember.'

'Good. Because I'm putting my foot down.'

'So I see.' He rubbed a hand over his chin, recalling his earlier glimpse of ankle and feeling rather impressed by her speech. It seemed a shame to gainsay her after all that—besides, who was he to argue when a beautiful woman insisted that he stay for the night? Even if it wasn't *quite* in the way he might have preferred. An image of lithe female limbs wrapped around his own floated into his mind... He didn't want to think about how long it had been since *that* had last happened...or since he'd done anything with a woman for that matter. No wonder he was fantasising about ankles!

'Well then...' He cleared his throat huskily. 'I appreciate your hospitality, Miss Gardiner.'

'You do?' She looked vaguely surprised by her own success. 'I mean, good. I'll go and fetch some blankets and meet you in the parlour in a few minutes.'

'I'll see you there.'

Sebastian watched her go, dropping back into his chair to take stock of the events of the night. His nose was possibly broken, there were going to be bruises on sensitive areas of his body, he was no closer to being reunited with his family and he was about to sleep on a sofa that, if memory served, was a good foot too short to be comfortable. He *ought* to be wishing he'd stayed in Plymouth. Instead, he felt quite unexpectedly happy.

It must be the shop, he reasoned in bewilderment. Only that could explain this powerful, strangely profound sense of being home.

Chapter Two

The scream cut through the silence of the early morning like a knife. Not a blunt butter knife either, more of a blood-thirsty dagger, piercing Henrietta's eardrums and bringing her back to consciousness with a start.

Heart thumping, she flung her quilt aside and leapt out of bed, remembering to grab her dressing gown this time as she sprinted out of her small attic room and down the stairs. After making up a bed on the sofa for Mr Fortini, she'd returned to her own, confident in her ability to wake up early enough to tell Nancy what had happened during the night, not to mention who to expect in the parlour, but her nocturnal adventure had obviously caused her to over-sleep. Now the muffled exclamations and thuds coming from below made it sound as though a wildcat had been let loose in the parlour, which she had to admit was a pretty accurate description of her flaming-haired, flaming-tempered assistant.

'Stop!' She burst into the parlour just in time to snatch a

vase out of Nancy's hands and prevent her from hurling it like a missile across the room. 'He's a guest!'

'What?' Nancy spun around indignantly, still looking ready to do battle with her fists.

'A guest! This is Mr Fortini, *Anna's* brother. He arrived in the middle of the night and I said he could sleep here.' Henrietta looked around the parlour with dismay. The sofa was lying on its side, there were books and ornaments strewn everywhere and a porcelain figurine of a cat was balancing precariously on the edge of a coffee table. 'He didn't know that Anna and his mother have moved out.'

'How could he *not* know that?'

'Because he's been at sea and he never received any of their letters!'

'Oh.' The fiery light in Nancy's eyes dimmed slightly. 'Well, how was I supposed to know that?'

'You weren't.' Henrietta sighed. 'I was going to tell you when I woke up, but I slept longer than I expected and... Mr Fortini?'

She looked across the room to where the object of Nancy's wrath was bending over, hands pressed against his knees, apparently struggling and failing to contain a burgeoning sense of mirth. He was also, she noticed with a quickly stifled gasp, in a state of considerable undress. Thankfully, he was still wearing breeches, but his jacket, waistcoat and cravat were all neatly folded to one side, while his plain white shirt was unbuttoned and gaping open to reveal an expanse of broad and muscular chest, liberally sprinkled with hair the same midnight shade as the dishevelled and curly locks on his head.

'Are you *laughing*?' She gaped at him in disbelief.

'Just a little.' He let out what could only be described as a guffaw.

'But why?'

'Why?' It was several moments before he could answer with anything resembling calmness. 'Because I've spent the past five years in His Majesty's Navy and I've been attacked more in the past six hours than I have in almost the whole of that time. You two are more dangerous than the French.'

'I should think so.' Nancy folded her arms belligerently. *'I* could deal with Napoleon.'

'I'm sure you'd be a worthy opponent. The Emperor wouldn't stand a chance.' Mr Fortini pushed himself upright and wiped his eyes. 'I don't think I've ever been tipped out of a bed before. Not even a hammock.'

'Oh, dear.' Henrietta winced. 'I hope it didn't hurt.'

'Not too badly. Fortunately, I was distracted from the pain by the avalanche of books on my head.'

'They were the first things that came to hand, but if you really are Anna's brother then I'm sorry.' Nancy slid the porcelain cat back to safety. 'By the way, I think I might have damaged your nose.'

'No, that was me.' Henrietta shook her head miserably. 'I hit him with a door in the night.'

'Really?' Nancy looked impressed.

'Really,' Mr Fortini confirmed. 'She threatened to impale me with some tongs, too, though fortunately she relented. Altogether, it's been a somewhat strange homecoming, but I'm delighted to meet you, Miss...?'

'MacQueen. Nancy MacQueen.'

'Sebastian Fortini, at your service.'

'Hmmm.' Nancy gave him a long, interrogatory stare. 'No hard feelings, then?'

'I wouldn't dare.'

'Good. In that case, I'd better go and get breakfast started. We won't get the baking done on an empty stomach.'

Henrietta shuffled her feet self-consciously as Nancy disappeared down the lower flight of stairs to the kitchen and shop floor. It felt strange to be alone with Mr Fortini again. To be alone with any man for that matter. She'd made a point of avoiding situations like this for the past eight months and yet she'd spent at least an hour in *his* company during the night without any anxiety at all. She'd felt instinctively comfortable with him, probably because he was Anna's brother—so much that she'd actually asked him to stay! It seemed so unlike her, these days anyway, that if it hadn't been for her rude awakening then she might have suspected him to have been part of some dream. The whole situation was bizarre, but he looked too large and robust to be anything *but* real. Not to mention that there was an overturned sofa at his feet.

'I really am sorry.' She peered across at him sheepishly. 'I'm usually the first one to wake up. It never occurred to me that I'd sleep longer.'

'Since I was responsible for you being tired, I can hardly blame you for that.' He lowered his voice conspiratorially. 'Just promise there aren't any more assailants lying in wait. I'm not sure my nerves could take it.'

'I promise.' She caught her breath as he leaned in towards her, one hand on his chest as if he were genuinely concerned about his nerves, which only drew her attention back to that part of his body, not to mention the row of powerful-looking stomach muscles underneath… Quickly, she lifted her gaze to his face, though that was hardly much better. He looked rugged and rumpled and, well, *bruised*, with a masculine appeal that went beyond merely handsome, not to mention a roguish glint in his eye that made her feel as if she'd just been running. Which to be fair, she had down the stairs, but that had been several minutes ago.

'Well then...' She bent down, grasping one end of the overturned sofa in an attempt to hide her face while she got her breath back. The whole parlour seemed somehow smaller and airless with him in it. 'Perhaps you'd like to sleep some more? We'll try not to make too much noise in the kitchen.'

'Allow me.' He flipped the sofa over as if it were just a piece of toy furniture. 'No, I'll get up now, too. I should probably be going before your neighbours arrive to see what all the commotion was about.'

'If anyone asks, I'll tell them a cat got into the house.' She gathered up the books and stacked them back on the shelves, struck with a combination of relief and regret at the thought of him leaving. It seemed impossible to decide which was dominant. There was something both appealing and unsettling about him, something about his bare chest and playful, slightly lopsided smile that caused a peculiar fluttering sensation in her stomach. She wasn't sure whether she liked that either, but surely good manners compelled her to offer him some refreshment?

'Would you care for some breakfast before you go?' The words were out of her mouth before she could stop them. 'It's the least we can do after attacking you twice in one night.'

'That's a good point.' He smiled in a way that made her heart perform a somersault in her chest and her head instantly regret the offer. 'I'd be delighted, Miss Gardiner.'

* * *

'I didn't think I had a choice, especially after I hit his nose,' Henrietta explained to her assistant ten minutes later. 'He needed somewhere to sleep and this *is* his family's shop.'

'Did he demand to stay?' Nancy looked suspicious again.

'No-o. He was going to leave actually, but I offered to make up the sofa.' She reached for a piece of toast and smeared butter across it. 'Do you think I shouldn't have?'

'Not necessarily, but did you ask him for any proof?'

'Proof of what?'

'That he's who he says he is.' Nancy lifted her eyes to the ceiling. 'He doesn't look much like Anna, except for dark curly hair and brown eyes, but a lot of people have those.'

'He has a similar way of speaking, too, and his lips are *exactly* the same shape as Anna's.'

'You've obviously been paying more attention than I have.' Nancy gave her a quizzical look. 'I can't say I've looked that closely at his lips.'

'Neither have I.' Henrietta felt a wash of colour spread over her cheeks. 'I just think they look similar, that's all...'

She applied another, unnecessary layer of butter to her toast. Now that the shock of the night and that morning had worn off, she was starting to think that perhaps she *had* been somewhat foolish in encouraging Mr Fortini to stay. Even if he was Anna's brother, which she was inclined to believe he was—either that or a very convincing impostor—who was to say that he was the kind of man she *ought* to have let stay under the same roof? Neither Anna nor her mother had ever told her anything untoward about him, but then he'd been away at sea for five years! If there was anything bad, they might not have known about it. And it had never even *occurred* to her to ask for proof of his identity! Instead, she'd been so taken aback by his arrival that she'd let her guard down and gone back to her old ways. She'd been too trusting. Too stupid. Too naive. More unworldly than ever. Good grief, even *he'd* thought that his staying was a bad idea! What must he think of her now, especially after the way she'd been staring at his chest that morning? What if she'd given him the wrong idea about her and her motives for inviting him to stay? What if he thought—?

'Sorry about the books, by the way.' Nancy interrupted the rising tide of panic. 'I shouldn't have thrown them.'

'Don't worry.' Henrietta was too relieved by the interruption to scold. 'Anna took all of her favourites when she left. It's not as if we can read them anyway.'

'*You* can. You're still having lessons with Miss Pybus, aren't you?'

'Not recently. I haven't had time.'

'Humph.' Nancy's lips set in a thin, disapproving line. 'Your brother doesn't deserve you.'

'Yes, he does.' Henrietta dropped her toast back on to her plate. 'He practically raised me on his own and you know he's been in a terrible state since Alice died. It's as though he's broken inside.'

'I know he's not helping to mend himself either.' Nancy's expression was part-sharp, part-sympathetic. 'My stepfather's a drunk. I recognise the signs.'

'David's not a drunk. He's just having a hard time taking care of himself and the boys at the moment.'

'Well, I don't think it's fair the way he expects you to go every day and take care of them. My mother works herself to the bone for her worthless husband, too, and all she ever gets in return is misery. You'll never catch me throwing my life away on a man, father, brother, husband or whatever you want to call them. If you ask me, the whole lot are a thousand times more trouble than they're worth...' Nancy speared a hard-boiled egg violently on the end of her fork. 'Speaking of which, our guest needs to be on his way. It'll be bad for business if people think we entertain sailors at night.'

'Anyone who thinks us capable of that obviously has no idea what time bakers get up in the morning.' Henrietta sighed. 'But he said he'll be leaving after breakfast anyway, travelling north to see Anna and his mother, I expect.'

'My mother first.' The man in question appeared in the kitchen doorway suddenly, smartly dressed and with his curly hair swept back into a low, slightly dishevelled queue. His square jaw, on which there had been a veritable swathe of black stubble that morning, appeared to have been quite ruthlessly shaved, making the now infamous shape of his lips even more noticeable.

Henrietta turned her attention back to her plate before she could notice anything else. Even with a bruised and off-centre nose, he looked quite disconcertingly handsome. Words like *strapping* and *virile* sprang to mind.

'There's no rush, however,' Mr Fortini continued. 'I came straight here from Plymouth and I've no desire to be shut up in a stagecoach again too soon. I thought I might actually stay in Bath for a few days, although somewhere else, naturally. Is the Wig and Mitre still open?'

'Yes, but it's not very fancy.' Nancy lifted her eyebrows. 'Wouldn't a hotel suit you better?'

'Not really. I may be an officer, but I'm not exactly what you'd call a gentleman.' He winked. 'Now, if that coffee's sufficiently brewed, allow me to pour, ladies.'

'Thank you.' Henrietta took a deep breath as he placed a cup in front of her, trying to quell a fresh burst of fluttering in her chest now as well as her stomach. She'd felt quite comfortable with him during the night, except for one oddly intense moment when their gazes had locked over the teapot, but now it was downright unnerving, not to mention irritating, the way her body seemed to react whenever he winked or smiled or even so much as looked in her direction for that matter. She hadn't felt so unnerved since... well, since Mr Hoxley, and look how that had turned out! She'd learned her lesson about men eight months ago and learned it thoroughly, too, or so she'd thought. Only something about Mr Sebastian Fortini seemed to place her in danger of forgetting it.

She picked up her coffee cup and blew steam across the surface. Frankly, the sooner he left for Yorkshire the better for her peace of mind—and body—it would be.

'Well, this is pleasant.' He sat down in the chair next to hers, a discreet distance away, yet close enough to make the whole right side of her body tingle with awareness. 'You know, Anna told me about you, Miss Gardiner.'

'She did?' She looked around at the words. 'But I thought you said you hadn't heard from her for a year?'

'I haven't. It was before that, in the last letter I received. She'd said that she'd taken on a new assistant to replace the formidable Mrs Padgett and that you were a breath of fresh air. Now I can see why.' He tipped his head closer. 'I only hope she wasn't too much of a tyrant to work for.'

'Not at all.' She stiffened despite his teasing tone. 'I always loved working with Anna.'

'I'm delighted to hear it. What about you, Miss Mac-Queen? Do you know my sister?'

'A little.' Nancy gave him an appraising look before continuing. 'I got to know your mother quite well, too, when I first came to work here. She used to tell stories about you, like the time you and a friend climbed on to the roof and threw Belles at the houses opposite. She said that you were aiming for the chimneys, but the people in the street below thought it was raining biscuits.'

'Ah...yes.' Mr Fortini rubbed a hand around the back of his neck. 'I suppose I wasn't always the most responsible youth, but I promise to be perfectly well behaved today. In fact, I thought I might go and visit a few of my old haunts if the two of you would care to join me?'

'Us?' Henrietta almost poured coffee into her lap.

'Why not?'

'The shop...'

'Can be closed for one day. Anna and my mother might not be here, but I must have some kind of authority. I'll take the blame anyway.'

'I still don't think...'

'Why don't just the two of you go?' Nancy chimed in unexpectedly.

She felt her jaw drop in surprise. Considering her assistant's earlier comments, Henrietta thought it was the very last thing she would have expected her to say. 'But I couldn't possibly leave you to do everything. It wouldn't be fair.'

'It is when I'm offering and it would be silly for us both to miss a trip out. I can manage on my own as long as we get the baking done first.'

'And I can help with that,' Mr Fortini offered.

'You can bake?' Henrietta looked from him to Nancy and then back again. If she hadn't known better, she might have suspected them of conspiring together.

'I grew up here, didn't I?' He was already rolling his sleeves up. 'Admittedly, it's been a few years since I last wielded a rolling pin, but I haven't forgotten how. Between the three of us, we'll get it all done in no time.'

Chapter Three

Henrietta stared unhappily into her bedroom mirror. She'd changed out of the plain brown muslin she used for baking and into her best cotton day dress, but her reflection looked all wrong. The turquoise-blue shade of the fabric matched her eyes perfectly, complementing her skin tone and even somehow accentuating the strawberry threads in her hair, but those very things in themselves made her uneasy. She didn't *want* to match or complement or accentuate anything. And she didn't want to go for a walk either!

She stuck her tongue out at her reflection. It wasn't that Mr Fortini wasn't good company. On the contrary, he'd proven himself extremely *good* company that morning, chatting, joking and even singing a few verses of opera while he'd demonstrated his formidable skill in the kitchen. It wasn't that the weather was poor either. The world outside her window looked cold but sunny, surprisingly so for November. Annoyingly perfect for a promenade. It was just... *why* had he asked her to accompany him? *Why* did he want to go for a walk with her? What if she really *had* given him the wrong impression during the night and he thought she was the kind of woman who might welcome male attention? What if he wanted to flirt with her, or worse?

On the other hand, she reassured herself, he'd included Nancy in the invitation, too. *That* would have been acceptable, enjoyable even, if it hadn't been for her assistant's out-of-character suggestion that just the two of them should go. They'd have to discuss that later, Henrietta thought darkly, but right now she had more immediate problems. Such as the fact that she was going for a walk with a man, a gentleman even, which he *was* no matter how he described himself.

Anna had told her the story a few months before, about how their mother, Lady Elizabeth Holden, the only daughter of a duke, had run away with an Italian footman twenty-five years before and been disowned by her family right up until that past summer. *That* made Mr Fortini a gentleman, of sorts anyway, although whether he was or wasn't was beside the point since she no longer went for walks with *any* kind of man, no matter how ruggedly handsome she might find them.

No, she decided, unbuttoning her dress despite the fact that she'd already wasted five minutes simply staring and worrying, she *couldn't* wear anything so flattering. Or *anything* that might enhance her appearance at all! As much as she wanted and strove to be modest, it was impossible to deny the effect her looks seemed to have upon men. If she could have given some of her beauty away, she would have done so—and gladly. Maybe *then* she would have stood a chance of knowing who was interested in her real self and not just her appearance. Up until a few months ago, she hadn't understood the difference, but now she knew that all most men saw or cared about was her face and figure. They all wanted the same thing, too, something she wasn't prepared to give, and it didn't take much for them to confuse friendliness for encouragement. She'd learned *that* from experience, too, and had no intention of making the same mistake again.

Quickly, she slid the blue dress over her hips and replaced it with the most shapeless item she owned, a scratchy grey woollen gown that irritated her skin, but was eminently sensible for a winter's excursion, then wrapped a dowdy old shawl around her shoulders and topped the effect with an even dowdier jockey cap bonnet. *There*, she thought with satisfaction, taking a second look in the mirror before starting down the staircase, that was much better. Or, if not better, then at least nothing that could be misinterpreted. If Mr Fortini was like most other men and judged by appearances, her outfit would tell him everything he needed to know about her. She looked like what she was determined to be: a serious and respectable shopkeeper, not someone to be flirted with and absolutely *not* the kind of woman who flashed her ankles while accosting men in her nightgown.

Of course, it was possible, she realised upon entering the shop, that she was somewhat overdoing the statement. Or definitely overdoing it if the roll of Nancy's eyes was anything to go by. If Mr Fortini hadn't already been leaning against the shop counter, waiting for her in a surprisingly thin-looking jacket and black top hat, she had a feeling she might have been marched back up the stairs and made to change. Again.

'Ready, Miss Gardiner?' Mr Fortini's own expression didn't waver as he opened the shop door.

'Quite ready, thank you.' She threw Nancy a pointed look and stepped outside, albeit wondering whether the eye roll was appropriate and she *was* overreacting a little. After all, Mr Fortini was Anna's brother and it wasn't as if he'd suggested anything scandalous. They were simply going for a walk around the city in broad daylight, a stroll down memory lane for him and a pleasant change to the daily routine for her. And Bath in the winter was more spectacularly beautiful than ever, the long rows of limestone buildings glowing a pale honey-gold shade wherever the sun kissed them. It would really be a shame not to enjoy such a gorgeous day while it lasted. There was nothing for her to be worried about and she really shouldn't—

'Shall we?'

The appearance of an outstretched arm made her shriek as if a wild animal with razor-sharp teeth and blood-stained claws had just hurled itself across her path.

'Miss Gardiner?' Mr Fortini looked justifiably confused.

'Oh, excuse me. I thought I saw a...snake.'

'A snake?' A pair of black eyebrows disappeared beneath his top hat.

'Yes.' She came down off her tiptoes and cleared her throat awkwardly. It was the first wild animal that had come to mind, but still, a snake in *Bath*? Even a slow-worm was somewhat far-fetched.

'I see...' The eyebrows showed no sign of coming down again. 'Well, stranger things have happened, I suppose. Fortunately it appears to have slithered away.'

'Perhaps I imagined it.'

'Or a trick of the light, maybe?' He extended his arm a second time, bending his elbow with what appeared to be deliberate slowness.

'Ye-es.' She lifted her chin and curled her hand cautiously around his bicep, trying to ignore the flicker of heat that immediately sparked in her abdomen and darted outwards, along her arms to her fingers and down her legs all the way to her toes. If she wasn't mistaken, even the top of her head was in danger of overheating. Her whole body felt strange, the way it had that morning when she'd caught a glimpse of his bare chest, a memory she'd intended to repress as quickly as possible, but which seemed determined to keep intruding upon her consciousness like one of those tunes that got stuck in your head. Or like a particularly quote-worthy line from a poem, not that his chest was inherently poetic, just unfortunately unforgettable... Oh, dear. Her thick woollen shawl was starting to feel somewhat redundant.

'Shall we head towards Pulteney Bridge?' He strode onwards, appearing not to notice any change in temperature, possibly because he hadn't even bothered to fasten his jacket. 'I want to see what's changed over the past few years.'

'Not too much, I think.' She hurried to keep up, relieved to put the subject of snakes behind them. 'But then I suppose you don't always notice changes when you live in a place from day to day. I suppose even Belles must seem very different to you.'

'Yes, although that doesn't necessarily mean the changes are bad ones.' He gave her a sideways smile. 'Some of them are actually quite pleasant. Once the initial pain has worn off, obviously.'

'Oh...yes. How *is* your nose?'

'*Not* broken.' His expression was faintly triumphant. 'You'll have to try harder next time.'

She blinked, uncertain about how to respond to the joke,

especially when she was still trying to regain her equilibrium and accept his arm for what it was, *just* an arm, no matter how sturdy or sinewy or astonishingly muscular it felt beneath her fingertips. None the less, she had the alarming impression that he was trying to compliment her, which meant that she needed to change the subject and quickly.

'Oh, look!' She was seized with a sudden burst of inspiration, pointing across Great Pulteney Street to the shop-front opposite. 'That's Redbourne's new general store. They moved premises last year. Now it's one of the largest shops in the city.'

'Is that so?' Mr Fortini sounded interested. 'Tell me, does old Mr Redbourne still manage the place?'

'No, his son took over a while ago.'

'Even better...' He acknowledged the words with a wicked-looking grin. 'Remember that story about me and a friend throwing biscuits across the street? Jem was my partner in crime.'

'Mr *James* Redbourne? But he always seems so...'

'Good and responsible? I know. His father always thought I was the bad influence, if you can believe that, but Jem was more than capable of getting into trouble on his own. He was just better at hiding it.' His grin widened. 'I'll have to pay him a visit and see if I can lure him back into old ways.'

'Maybe I ought to warn him.' She couldn't help but smile, unable to resist his good humour. 'I could send a message, only not with Nancy. They don't get along.'

'Really? Has she been throwing books at his head, too?'

'She probably would if she could, but I don't know what she has against him. It's a mystery.'

'Now that sounds like a challenge...but enough about

them. Tell me more about yourself, Miss Gardiner. I'm curious. Have you always lived in Bath?'

'No-o.' She stopped smiling and drew her brows together, wondering what to make of the question. She'd had similar enquiries from men before—not so much out of interest, she'd realised eventually, more to work out if she had some kind of protector—but Mr Fortini looked as if he were simply making conversation. And there was no harm in telling him a few details, surely? 'I grew up six miles away in Ashley.'

'I know the village. In fact, I believe I travelled through it yesterday, although it was hard to tell in the dark.'

'It's a pleasant place, but Bath is my home now.'

'Mine, too.' He looked around as if he were trying to take in every detail of the street. 'You know, it's funny. I spent most of my youth longing to escape and see the world, but I missed this place the moment I left. As much as I wanted to go, part of me has been homesick ever since.'

'That must have been hard.'

'Fortunately, I had plenty of distractions. The navy doesn't like to let grass grow under your feet. Or lichen anyway. So what made you leave Ashley and move to the city?'

'I had to. After our parents died, my brother and I needed to find work. That was ten years ago.'

'I'm sorry.' His voice softened. 'It's always hard to lose a parent, but you must have been very young, too. Eight? Nine?'

'Nine, but it was worse for David, my brother. He's eleven years older than me and had to take care of both of us. Fortunately, I found a job on a market stall, selling cloth. Then when I was seventeen I got a position in a dressmaker's...' She frowned at the pavement, wondering why she'd just told him that when she usually avoiding thinking about it herself. It wasn't a pleasant memory, one she had to shake her head to get rid of. 'Then I came to Belles.'

'I see. Why di—?'

'What made you join the navy?' She spoke before he could finish the question.

'Mmm?' He looked mildly surprised at the interruption. 'Oh, the spirit of adventure, I suppose. I always loved the idea.'

'Did the reality match up?'

'It wasn't quite what I'd expected.' A strange, inscrutable expression passed over his face. 'Some parts were better than others, but I got to travel, to find out what I was made of, too. Unfortunately, it came to feel somewhat tainted.'

'Tainted?'

'Yes. My father died not long after I joined, but when I got the news I was already at sea and couldn't come back.' He paused, his voice sounding rougher when he spoke again. 'By the time I had shore leave he'd been buried a year.'

'Oh.' She tightened her hand on his arm. 'I'm sorry.'

'So am I. Sometimes I think it was selfish of me to have left Bath in the first place.'

'What do you mean?'

'My father always worked too hard. I knew that. Maybe I should have stayed and forced him to retire.'

'But did he enjoy working in the shop?'

'He loved it. Belles was his pride and joy.'

'Then maybe you couldn't have forced him to stop.' She looked at him steadily. 'What about the navy? Did he object to your joining?'

'No, he was happy for me. He knew how much I wanted to get out on my own and travel like he had. My mother wasn't so enthusiastic, but at the time…well, Anna and my father were a good team in the shop and there didn't seem any need for me to stay. He seemed in perfect health, too. There was no way any of us could have known what would happen, but when it did…' He paused for a moment as they crossed Pulteney Bridge. 'Miss Gardiner, if I ask you a question, would you promise to give me an honest answer?'

'Of course.'

'Thank you. You see, after my father died, I felt that it was my responsibility to come back and help run the business. That was what he would have wanted, but it's not so easy to leave the navy, especially in wartime. There was nothing I could do to help except send money home, but I'd still like to know…how difficult have things been for Anna and my mother over the past few years?'

'Oh…' Henrietta sucked in a breath slowly. She didn't want to make him feel bad by admitting the truth, but that was what he'd asked for and what she'd promised to give. 'I believe that Anna *did* have a hard time running the shop on her own. The swelling in your mother's hands and feet got so bad that it became impossible for her to help with the baking and they couldn't afford to pay anyone else for the hours. Not for a while anyway.'

'So Anna had to do it all by herself?'

'Ye-es, but then she met the Earl and I moved in, so…' She tried to sound positive. 'It all worked out in the end.'

'No thanks to me, but I appreciate your honesty, Miss Gardiner.' A muscle clenched in his jaw. 'So, what happened at the dressmaker's?'

'What?' She almost tripped over her feet at the question. She'd thought they'd moved past that particularly unpleasant subject. 'What do you mean, what happened?'

'I just wondered why you left.' He reached his other hand out to steady her. 'Presumably you decided you preferred biscuits to dresses?'

'Not exactly. That is, I *do* prefer working at Belles, but I had other reasons for leaving. Anna understood them.'

'Ah.' He gave her a sidelong glance, seemingly on the verge of asking something else before changing his mind. 'Tell me about my new brother-in-law, then. Do you like him?'

'Lord Staunton? Yes, very much.'

'Good. Although he has another name, I presume?'

'Samuel, although I never dare to call him that no matter how many times he tells me to. I'll always think of him as Captain Delaney.'

'*Captain?*' He stopped walking abruptly.

'Yes. He was Captain of the *Colossus* at Trafalgar.'

Mr Fortini adjusted the brim of his top hat, let out a low whistle and leaned against a wall looking out over the River Avon. 'That was involved in some of the worst fighting. I like him better already, but how did a sea captain-cum-earl become acquainted with my sister in the first place?'

'He came to the shop. You could see that he liked her straight away, but she wasn't so sure.'

'Why not?'

'Well…' She hesitated, her stomach churning in the way it always did when she thought of that day. Life-changing as it had been for Anna, it had been well-nigh disastrous for her. 'She thought that he was a rake.'

'Was he?' His expression sharpened at once.

'No, but she thought so because of his companion, Mr Hoxley. As it turned out, she was right about him.'

'I see.' Mr Fortini held on to her gaze for a few seconds. 'You know, you provoke a lot of questions, Miss Gardiner.'

'Do I?' She laughed nervously. 'I don't think I'm that interesting.'

'On the contrary, I think you might be *very* interesting.'

'No.' She swallowed convulsively. There was a softness to his voice suddenly, an almost liquid quality that made her stomach twist and tighten even as it set alarm bells ringing in her head. 'You're mistaken. I'm really not.'

'Which is a polite way of telling me to mind my own business, I suppose.' He leaned slightly towards her. 'Forgive me. It's been a while since I've been in the company of a young lady.'

'A lady?' She shook her head at the description. 'I'm hardly one of those either.'

'And now you sound just like Anna. I've always thought that most people fundamentally misunderstand the word. Personally, I take it to mean honest, kind and thoughtful, all of which qualities you've already demonstrated. No, Miss Gardiner, I have to disagree. You seem quintessentially ladylike to me.'

Henrietta was aware of a strange duality of feeling, as if one side of her body were burning hot and the other icy cold. His words were unexpectedly touching, but she didn't want to be touched, either metaphorically or literally, and she didn't know whether to trust such a compliment either. He sounded sincere, but rakes always *sounded* sincere. Just because he was Anna's brother didn't mean that he wasn't just the same as Mr Hoxley underneath! Or Mr Willerby for that matter... Or any of the other men who came to the shop trying to flirt with her!

'Shall we go up to the Crescent?' He turned his head in

that direction, smiling again. 'I'd like to be seen by as many people as possible. It's not every day I have such a beautiful young lady on my arm.'

Beautiful? Henrietta took a step backwards, bumping into a pedestrian walking behind her as she tore her hand away from his arm. That did it! If there was one thing she'd made sure of that morning, it was that she did *not* look beautiful!

'Mr Fortini.' She apologised to the pedestrian before wrapping her shawl tightly around her shoulders like a suit of armour. 'I agreed to come for a walk because I thought you simply wanted a companion.'

'I do.' He looked faintly bemused by her indignant tone.

'Then I'd like to get one thing clear. No matter what impression I might have given during the night, I am not *that* kind of woman.'

'What kind of—?'

'I do not have loose morals!'

'The thought never entered my mind.' His bemusement faded instantly. 'Miss Gardiner, if I've offended you then I'm truly sorry. It was unintentional, I assure you.'

'You haven't offended me.' She blinked a few times to hide the lie in her eyes. 'But just to be clear, I invited you to stay last night as a favour to Anna, nothing more. I may be an independent woman, but I do not care to be flirted with and I'd appreciate your putting any thoughts of that nature aside.'

'Consider it done.' He sounded sombre, though with a hint of confusion, almost enough to make her believe that he meant it.

'Good… And no more compliments.'

'Understood.'

'Thank you.'

'Well then, shall we continue?' He cleared his throat after a few moments of heavy silence, disturbed only by the fierce torrent of the river over the weir below. 'Perhaps you'd allow me to buy you a cup of tea to make amends? As I recall, there used to be quite a good tea shop on Milsom Street.'

Chapter Four

'Here we are, Miss Gardiner.'

Sebastian found them a small, octagon-shaped table in one corner of the tea room and tried to think of some innocuous subject to talk about. His companion was pursing her lips so tightly that she resembled a strait-laced and highly strung governess, a look exacerbated by her frankly appalling taste in clothes. She'd seemed tense from the moment they'd left Belles—since he'd come down to breakfast, now he thought about it—but he'd believed that she'd been starting to relax in his company. Obviously not. Whatever camaraderie they'd established during their walk was now completely gone. She seemed a whole different woman from the one who'd accosted him with fire tongs at midnight and he had no idea what the hell had gone wrong.

He folded one long leg over the other and bit back a sigh. In all honesty, he was having regrets about inviting her to walk at all, but ironically, he'd *wanted* to spend more time with her. Hard as it was to believe or remember why at that moment, he'd *wanted* to enjoy his newfound freedom with her and a walk in the sunshine. Now he had the impression that she was regretting it, too. If he wasn't mistaken, she was actually counting the minutes until he took her back to the shop, which didn't say a great deal for his company, but then he supposed he was somewhat out of practice in talking to the opposite sex.

Months on end at sea with eight hundred other sailors tended to have a somewhat coarsening effect on a man's manners, which was probably why he'd ended up offending her, although calling her beautiful wasn't *such* a terrible thing to do, was it? Especially when he'd been entirely serious. She would have been stunning wearing a sack. And he didn't even know where to begin with her declaration about *loose morals.* She was acting as if he'd just tried to seduce her in the street in broad daylight!

Not that he would have been entirely averse to the idea...

'Thank you.' Miss Gardiner managed a half-smile as the waitress placed two cups of tea on the table in front of them. 'And you, too, Mr Fortini. This is very kind.'

'Don't mention it.' He nodded tersely. At least he'd got *one* thing right that morning. 'My mother always liked this tea shop. I'm glad it's still here.'

'Yes.' She took a sip and then placed her cup back in its saucer with a loud rattle. Or at least it seemed loud in the silence that followed since neither of them appeared to have any idea what else to say next.

'Tea in the navy is appalling.' He groaned inwardly as the words emerged from his own lips. Why not just talk about the weather?

'Really?'

'Yes, the leaves get weaker and weaker over the course

of a voyage. We had to give up on them eventually on my last ship. Quite a calamity for an Englishman.'

'I suppose so.' Her lips un-pursed slightly. 'Nancy and I were thinking about selling tea at the shop. Or coffee, perhaps, to go with the biscuits. I thought I might suggest it to Anna the next time she visits. Of course, we'll probably have to hire another assistant, but the shop's doing well enough that I think we can afford it...' Her voice trailed away as if she thought she'd just said too much. 'We'll see.'

'It sounds like an excellent idea to me.' He shifted forward in his seat. 'Miss Gardiner, about before—'

'It's quite all right,' she interrupted quickly. 'Perhaps I overreacted. In fact, I probably did. It's just that I prefer *not* to be complimented.'

Sebastian resisted the urge to raise his eyebrows at such a curious statement. Surely a woman who looked the way she did received dozens of compliments every day? And compliments were generally considered to be good things, weren't they? Why would she object? Then again, why would a beautiful woman deliberately dress herself in a garment that resembled nothing so much as an old coal sack? Not to mention a bonnet that seemed intended to drain all the colour from her complexion. Unless she was wearing them deliberately to discourage him from offering any form of flattery? Because she didn't want to look attractive? He thought back to her earlier protest. *I'm not* that *kind of woman...* What the hell kind of impression did she think she'd given him during the night?

He gave a jolt, realising that she was still waiting for an answer. 'Of course.'

'In fact, I'd prefer it if you'd speak to me as you would to Anna, as if I'm your sister.'

This time he had to wrench his eyebrows firmly back into place. Apparently, he really *had* lost his touch with the opposite sex if she was experiencing fraternal feelings towards him. Not that it ought to matter since he was leaving Bath soon anyway, but a man had his pride. Still, if fraternal was what she wanted, then fraternal was what he would give her. Which meant, first and foremost, that he needed to stop paying quite so much attention to her lips. Even pursed, they were still decidedly tempting: plump in the middle, with a peaked cupid's bow that he wanted to run his finger along. What would it be like to kiss her? he wondered. To slide his hands into her hair and bring her face to his, to press his own lips against her forehead and cheeks, maybe the tip of her nose, then finally her mouth…

'Very well.' He cleared his throat, feeling hot under the collar all of a sudden. 'But I should warn you this gives me licence to pull your hair and untie your apron strings.'

There was a faint spark in her eye. 'Then I'll just have to keep my bonnet on and be vigilant.'

'Excellent idea. You can't be too careful.' He leaned backwards, relieved that they'd cleared the air slightly at least. 'So where shall we wander to next? Up to the Circus?'

The spark faltered and then went out. 'I think perhaps I ought to return to Belles. I'm not happy about leaving Nancy to mind the shop all alone.'

'Ah…' He inclined his head. It seemed she really was counting the minutes, after all, although perhaps she was right and it *was* better to put their promenade out of its misery before they ended up talking about tea again. 'As you wish. In that case, I'll escort you back.'

'There's really no need.'

'There is to me.' He picked up his teacup with a terse

smile. 'I said I wasn't much of a gentleman, Miss Gardiner, but I do make a bit of an effort. We'll leave whenever you're ready.'

'Sebastian Fortini?' A strapping, chestnut-haired man wearing a leather apron put down the barrel he was carrying and strode across the shop floor to greet him. 'What are you doing here?'

'I came to visit an old friend, but I can't see him anywhere.' Sebastian made a show of looking around. 'You look a *bit* like him, but you can't be. The James Redbourne I knew was a scrawny lad, all skin and bones.'

'I was a late developer.'

'*Late?* You must have grown at least a foot since I left.'

'A foot and a half, actually.'

'Well, it's good to see you again.' Sebastian found himself enveloped in a bear hug. 'Even if you *are* taller and broader than me these days.'

'Without any obvious bruises either.' His old friend peered at his face. 'What happened to your nose? Have you been fighting?'

'No. For once in my life, I've been entirely innocent of wrongdoing. Unfortunately, that doesn't seem to make any difference to the result.'

'Then I want to hear all about it. Come on.' James draped an arm around his shoulders, jerking his head at one of the women behind the counter as he steered him towards a small and pristinely tidy office.

'Take a seat.' James gestured towards a green leather-backed chair in front of a mahogany desk and then sat down behind it, extracting a bottle and two glasses from one of the drawers. 'Whisky?'

'I wouldn't say no.' Sebastian eased himself into the chair with a contented and approving sigh. 'The place looks good.'

'It's a new start.' James poured amber liquid into the two glasses and nudged one across the table. 'Our old premises were getting cramped so, once I took over the business, I decided we had to move.'

'I'm impressed. I thought your father would never retire.'

'So did I, but in the end my mother made the decision for him. Something to the effect of waiting fifty years for his attention and it was either her or the shop. Now they have a cottage in the country and are both happier than I've ever seen them. He's even taken up gardening. Delphiniums are his speciality.'

'Good for him. And even better for you. You're obviously a hands-on kind of manager.'

James glanced down at his leather apron and grinned. 'We had a delivery of brandy this morning.'

'I'll drink to that.' Sebastian raised his glass. 'Apparently I came home at just the right time.'

'Cheers!' James swallowed a mouthful and then gave him a searching look. 'But what are you doing in Bath? Shouldn't you be in Derbyshire, visiting Anna? Or the Countess of Staunton, I suppose I should call her now.'

'*That's* going to take some getting used to.' Sebastian rolled his eyes. 'The truth is I didn't know that she'd left, or that she'd got married either for that matter. I only found out when I got back to Belles last night and my mind is still boggling.'

'You only got home last night?'

'*During* the night, yes. That's how I ended up with this bruise.'

'Don't tell me, the charming Miss MacQueen?'

'Miss Gardiner actually.'

'Miss Gardiner?' James spluttered on his drink. '*She* hit you?'

'Not directly. She used a door. Then she threatened to castrate me with a pair of fire tongs.'

'You must have made quite an impression.'

'She thought I was a burglar, though in all fairness, she saved me from having a vase smashed over my head this morning. That *was* Miss MacQueen.' He put his glass down on the table for a refill. 'It was an eventful night.'

'It sounds like it.'

'Do you know her at all?'

'Miss MacQueen?'

'Miss Gardiner.'

'Oh.' If he wasn't mistaken, his old friend's cheeks flushed slightly. 'No, not very well. She was quite friendly when we first moved in, but she's been a lot more reserved since she took over Belles. One of my men tried flirting with her once and she almost bit his head off. Now they call her the ice queen, but no one really knows what to make of her any more.'

'I'm glad I'm not the only one.'

'Anna trusts her anyway.'

'What makes you say that?' Sebastian paused with his glass halfway to his lips.

'Nothing.'

'Nothing means something. I know you, James. What is it?'

His friend swallowed another mouthful of whisky and sighed. 'There were some rumours a while ago. Something to do with her previous place of employment. A milliner, I think.'

'A dressmaker. What kind of rumours?'

'I don't like gossip, Seb.'

'Neither do I, but if she's running my family business then I have a right to know.'

He winced inwardly, feeling a twinge of guilt at the words. They sounded pompous, not to mention faintly hypocritical given that he hadn't been involved in the business for so many years. In retrospect, Miss Gardiner *had* seemed somewhat defensive when he'd asked about her previous employment earlier, although she'd also told him that Anna knew her reasons for leaving. All of which meant that it was none of his business. In this case, however, curiosity appeared to outweigh conscience.

'All right, but it doesn't go outside this room.' James stood up and closed the door. 'They say there was some kind of scandal involving her and the owner's son.'

'*They* say?'

'One of my staff heard a story. Something about the mother accusing her of being a fortune hunter, of trying to seduce and trap him into marriage, but as to whether it's true...' He lifted his shoulders. 'In any case, she was sacked without references. That part's definitely true because I remember she came to the old shop looking for work. Unfortunately, my father wasn't sympathetic.'

Sebastian frowned into his glass, swirling the liquid around as he mentally negotiated his way through a confusing blend of emotions—indignation, surprise and something else he couldn't quite put his finger on... He didn't want to pay any heed to gossip and it was frankly hard to believe that the guarded and prickly woman he'd spent the morning with could ever have done something so scandalous, but it put her words about loose morals into some kind of perspective, especially if she'd been accused of them before...

If that were the case, however, then she'd either been unjustly accused or she was a reformed character, but surely *something* must have happened for her to be sacked without references...and damn it if the other emotion wasn't jealousy!

Jealousy? How could he be jealous over a woman he hadn't even met this time yesterday? The very idea was outlandish. Laughable, really. And yet something about it rang true.

'So, are you back on dry land for good?' James seemed eager to steer the conversation into a different channel. 'Or are you still restless?'

'Not as much as I used to be. To be honest, I'd reconciled myself to the idea of coming back to help Anna with Belles, but it appears I'm surplus to requirements. It's been taken over by two attractive, but extremely violent females.' He made a wry face. 'It could have been worse, I suppose. As for the navy, I'm pretty sure my chances of finding another post were scuppered alongside Napoleon's fleet.' He frowned. 'Although I'm not entirely sure I'd want to go back anyway.'

'So, what next?'

'Next I'll go north to visit Anna and my mother. After that...who knows? The world's my oyster apparently, although I thought I might loiter in Bath for today.'

'I was hoping you'd say that.' James grinned. 'In that case, you should stay with me tonight. I have rooms upstairs.'

'You're inviting me to stay in a building that's just received a fresh delivery of brandy?'

'Actually, when you put it like that...'

'Too late. I accept.' Sebastian laughed, resolving to put all thoughts of Miss Gardiner, fortune-hunting seductress or not, out of his mind. Aside from her obvious lack of interest in *him*, her past was none of his business and he had other things to think about. What to do with his future for a start. His sister was happily married, his mother ensconced with her family in the north and Belles appeared to be running smoothly. The world really *was* his oyster...and the last thing he needed was to be distracted by a woman, especially an ice queen.

He lifted his glass and tossed back the last of his whisky. He'd go and pick up his bag from Belles later, but after that...well, he doubted he'd be sharing anything more than pleasantries with Miss Gardiner again.

Chapter Five

'What went wrong?'

Henrietta's heart sank as Nancy confronted her, hands planted firmly on hips, at the bottom of the stairs. She'd been relieved to spy several customers in the shop when she'd come back in through the kitchen earlier, allowing her to sneak up to her bedroom and change into her yellow shop dress unnoticed, but now it seemed she wasn't going to escape an interrogation so lightly. Which was the very last thing she wanted, especially after she'd just made such a fool of herself in front of Mr Fortini.

'I don't know what you mean.' She smoothed her hair, making sure it was tucked neatly behind her ears while she maintained a calm and collected expression. 'Nothing went wrong.'

'*Something* must have happened for you to be back here so soon.' Nancy looked unconvinced. 'I said that you should take your time and enjoy yourself. Where *is* Mr Fortini anyway? Why didn't he escort you back?'

'He escorted me to the end of the crescent, if you must know, but I insisted on walking the rest of the way by myself. I'm sure he has better things to do than spend his time with me.'

'He seemed pretty keen on your company this morning.'

'I'm sure he was just being polite.'

'I doubt it.' Nancy gave a sceptical snort as they made their way through to the shop. 'Men are never that polite to me.'

'He invited both of us.'

'He was looking at you while he said it. I'm not blind. It was perfectly obvious it was you he wanted to walk with, just like every other man who comes in here, I might add. It's a good thing I *don't* want a husband or working with you could prove extremely frustrating.'

'You shouldn't put yourself down. You're very pretty.'

'No, I'm not, but you're a good friend to say so.' Nancy removed her hands from her hips finally. 'My hair is too red, my face is covered with freckles and I have an awful temper. Men don't like any of those things, or so my mother tells me.' She grimaced. 'Not that she's an authority on men, but my aunt said it, too. And my grandmother.'

'I'd rather that men *didn't* look at me.' Henrietta sighed. 'Or at least it would be nice if one of them could actually see *me*, the real me, I mean.'

'Is that what that awful outfit was about? You know you can be the real you without dressing like a scarecrow.'

'I dressed for the cold.'

'It's not *that* cold. I'm surprised birds didn't peck at you.'

'Well, they didn't.' Henrietta braced her hands firmly on the counter. 'I might have looked a bit severe, but I didn't want any misunderstandings, that's all.'

'And why do you always assume misunderstandings are your fault? You're not responsible for what other people think. If men get the wrong impression, then that's their problem, not yours.'

'I know. Or I sort of know. I just don't want to make any more mistakes or feel stupid again.'

'I understand.' Nancy placed a supportive hand on her arm. 'But you're *not* stupid, you never have been and you don't need to hide away or pretend to be anyone other than who you are. You don't see me pretending to be calm and patient, do you?'

'Not often, no.' Henrietta found her lips twitching. 'Only you're not getting out of this argument so easily. I didn't *want* to go for a walk with Mr Fortini and you shouldn't have suggested it. You were the one who said that men were more trouble than they're worth!'

'Most of them are.'

'Exactly! You weren't even convinced that he was Anna's brother this morning.'

'Yes, but once I looked closer, I could see that you were right about the resemblance. And if he's her brother, then that means he won't be anything like...' Nancy paused and clucked her tongue '...like some men whose ears I'd like to box and will if I ever see them. Even *I* can accept there are a few exceptions to the rule. Besides, I thought you liked him.'

Henrietta gawked in surprise. 'What on earth made you think that?'

'Like I said, I'm not blind. You kept sneaking glances at him over breakfast.'

'I did not!'

'Yes, you did *and* you were fidgeting, but if it makes you

feel any better, he was doing the same thing. It was putting me off my breakfast watching the pair of you.'

'You were imagining things.'

'I never imagine things. I'm not an imaginative person.' Nancy looked infuriatingly smug. 'And I'll admit that he's handsome in a rough kind of way. Is he coming to say goodbye?'

'I've no idea.' Henrietta started to tidy an already neat pile of boxes on the counter, chiding herself for the way her stomach clenched and then seemed to perform a jig at the thought. 'Although he left his belongings upstairs so I suppose he'll be back to—'

'What?' Nancy clamped her eyebrows together as she stopped mid-sentence.

'There she is again.' Henrietta pointed towards the window.

'Who?'

'The woman I told you about yesterday. She's been out on the pavement every day this week, just standing there or walking up and down. She's peered in at our window a few times, but she never comes in. I think she might be hungry.'

'She's dressed like a lady.' Nancy moved to one side of the window, peering out surreptitiously. 'Odd that she's wandering about without a maid, though. Maybe she's in some kind of trouble.'

'She keeps looking up at the boarding house as if she's waiting for someone to come out.'

'*Definitely* in trouble, then.'

'In that case, we should help her.' Henrietta nodded decisively, wrapping half a dozen Belles in a muslin cloth before heading for the door.

'Wait a minute.' Nancy put a restraining hand on her arm. 'For all we know, she might be a dangerous criminal.'

'I don't think so. She only looks about the same age as us.'

'*We* could be dangerous criminals if we wanted.'

'I'm still going to talk to her.' Henrietta lifted her chin, holding the door open for a group of septuagenarian ladies, then waited on the edge of the pavement for a few moments while a cart rolled past before crossing the road. The woman was facing in the other direction, a large, heavy-brimmed bonnet obscuring her face so effectively that Henrietta had to go and stand directly in front of her just to make eye contact.

'Excuse me.' She smiled, trying to look friendly as the woman let out a startled gasp. 'I don't mean to bother you, but I wondered if you'd like a biscuit?'

'I'm sorry?' The woman's face, which looked altogether too gaunt and pale against her sombre outfit, appeared panic-stricken.

'They're a new variety,' Henrietta lied, opening up the muslin. 'We're asking people what they think. Please… take them all.'

'I really shouldn't.' The woman lifted a hand hesitantly, as if she suspected some kind of trap.

'You can come into the shop, too, if you like?' Henrietta offered as the hand wavered in mid-air. 'It's cold out here.'

'No.' Her voice was the barest of whispers. 'No, thank you.'

'We might be able to help. Perhaps if there was someone in particular you were looking for?'

'How do you know—?' The woman's large, hazel-hued

eyes widened like saucers before she grabbed two of the biscuits, spun on her heel and ran.

'Maybe he's forgotten about his bag.' Nancy sank down on a stool behind the counter and sighed wearily. It was the end of the day and there was still no sign of Mr Fortini. 'It seems an odd thing to forget about, though.'

'Mmm.' Henrietta turned the sign on the door over to *Closed*, wondering if perhaps she'd been too severe with him earlier and he didn't *want* to come back. Apparently she was scaring everyone off today.

'But I'm sure he'll remember it eventually,' Nancy continued. 'Then you can fix whatever happened between you.'

'I told you, *nothing* happened.'

'I know what you told me, but admit it, you *want* to see him again.'

'I admit nothing of the kind.' Henrietta straightened her shoulders. 'Anyway, I ought to visit David this evening.'

'Again?' Nancy scowled. 'You shouldn't be wandering about the city on your own. It's dark already.'

'I've done it plenty of times and...' she paused awkwardly '...well, I've been thinking that perhaps I ought to move back in with him.'

'What?'

'I know it's not ideal, but he's struggling and he needs me. His neighbour, Mrs Roper, has been helping to look after the boys in the afternoons, but I can't expect her to do it for ever.'

'And you've been paying her too, I expect?'

'Just a little.'

'Oh, Hen, I don't want to sound harsh, but *he's* their father and you already spend most of your free time there. Not

to mention your money—and don't tell me it's *just* a little.'
She threw her hands up in the air with a look of exasperation. 'Why is it always women who are supposed to drop
everything whenever a man needs them? As if they think
we don't have lives and ambitions of our own!'

'Because most of them *do* think that.' Henrietta sighed.
'But David's different. He needs me.'

'What about Belles?'

'I could still work here. I'll just have to be a bit more organised.'

'You couldn't *be* any more organised. You'll work yourself into the ground just like my mother. Besides, you can't
be traipsing across the city before dawn to do the baking
every morning. I won't allow it. No, we'll have to think of
something else.'

'I've tried, believe me, but I *do* need to go now. I want to
be sure the boys have a proper meal before bed.'

'All right, but don't be too long or I'll worry.'

'I promise.' Henrietta planted a kiss on the top of her
head. 'What would I do without you?'

'Break men's noses with doors? You'll have to teach me
that trick.'

Henrietta laughed, scooping up a bonnet and shawl before heading out of the back door and retracing the steps
she'd walked earlier that day with Mr Fortini. Her brother
had a small house in the Avon Street district, only a quarter of an hour away, less if she walked quickly, which she
did, weaving her way through the other pedestrians so that
she was tapping on the front door in less than ten minutes.
To her dismay, however, there was no answer.

'David?' She lifted the latch and pushed the door open
cautiously, but there was no sign of anyone inside, only a

solitary rushlight flickering on a scratched and severely battered old table.

'He's asleep,' a small voice piped up through the gloom, though it was impossible to tell where it was coming from.

'Peter?' Henrietta looked around in consternation. 'Is that you?'

'It's Michael.' A head poked out from beneath the table. 'Peter's watching Papa. He said he ought to do it because he's two years older than me.'

'Why is he watching your father?' She crouched down, holding her arms out for a hug.

'He's been drinking again.' Michael's eight-year-old voice was matter of fact. 'All day, Mr Roper said. He brought him home and said that we should watch and be sure to roll him over if he's sick.'

'Oh, Michael.' She tightened her arms around her nephew, feeling nauseated herself at the words. 'I'm sorry.'

'It's all right. Mr Roper said he'll be right as rain in the morning, but we should talk quietly.'

'Ye-es.' Henrietta frowned as a new thought occurred to her. 'But how can your father have been drinking all day? Wasn't he at work in the mews?'

'Um…' A guilty expression crossed the little boy's face. 'I'm not s'posed to tell you.'

'Tell me what?'

'He lost his job.' Another voice emerged through a hole in the ceiling, closely followed by a pair of legs descending the ladder. 'Two days ago. They said he was a disgrace.'

'What?' Henrietta looked between the two boys in dismay. 'But I was here that evening. Peter, why didn't you tell me?'

'Papa said not to.'

'Oh.' She frowned. 'Well, that's not your fault. Where's Oliver?'

'Asleep in his cot.' Peter looked as if he were struggling to maintain a stoical expression.

'Aunt Henrietta?' Michael's tone turned wheedling. 'Did you bring any biscuits?'

'What kind of aunt would I be if I hadn't?' She reached into the folds of her cloak and drew out a small bundle. 'Cinnamon Belles for you, Comptessas for Peter and one of everything for Oliver.' She glanced towards the hatch in the ceiling, tempted to go up and deposit a bucket of cold water over her sleeping brother. 'Have you had a proper meal today?'

'Mrs Roper gave us some toast and cheese.' Michael shook his head as he dived into the parcel of biscuits.

'Right.' Henrietta straightened up, looking around the frigid and messy room with a burst of determination. She was going to have to break her promise to Nancy, but she'd deal with that later. 'First, we're going to stoke up the fire, second I'm going to make us all a nice meal and third… Well, third, I'm going to decide what to do with you.'

Chapter Six

'Good evening, Miss MacQueen.' Sebastian removed his hat and bowed as he entered Belles through the back door into the kitchen. 'I trust that you've had a pleasant and profitable day?'

'We've sold out of biscuits, if that's what you mean.' The pugnacious redhead glanced up from where she was polishing a brass plate beside the hearth.

'It wasn't, but I'm glad to hear it.' He threw a subtle look towards the hallway.

'If you're looking for Henrietta, she's not here.'

'And why would I be looking for Miss Gardiner specifically?' Maybe not so subtle, after all… 'It's a delight to see you again, too, Miss MacQueen.'

'If you say so.' She gave him an openly sceptical look. 'Your bag's over there. I brought it downstairs, but I was starting to think you'd left it for us as a souvenir.'

'Sorry about that. I spent the day with an old friend and lost track of time.' He reached down and swung the sack containing his few belongings over his shoulder. 'However, thank you again for your hospitality. If you need me, I'll be staying at—' He stopped, puzzled by the way she was chewing her bottom lip between her teeth as if she were worried. She didn't strike him as a particularly nervous person, but he had the distinct impression that she was preoccupied with something.

'Is everything all right, Miss MacQueen?'

She looked up again, holding his gaze for a few seconds before shaking her head. 'No.'

'No?'

'It's Henrietta. She promised she wouldn't be gone long, but that was two hours ago.'

'What do you mean *gone*?' The words caused his stomach to drop almost painfully. 'Do you know where she went?'

'To visit her brother over the bridge. She helps out with her nephews most evenings, though I keep telling her she shouldn't be walking around in the dark.'

'Do they live far away?'

'Around Avon Street.' The crease between her brows deepened. 'It's not the most salubrious area. I grew up there, so I ought to know.'

'I see.' Sebastian put his bag down again, gripped with a new sense of urgency. 'Then perhaps you and I should take a walk in that direction? Hopefully, we'll meet Miss Gardiner on her way home. Otherwise, you can direct us to her brother's house.'

'I knew it!' Miss MacQueen was already on her feet and reaching for her hat and bonnet.

'Knew what?'

'That you like her!'

'Of course I like her—as an acquaintance,' he added

hurriedly. 'At this moment, however, I'm mainly concerned about her.'

'*Because* you like her and not just as an acquaintance.'

'Miss MacQueen, if I've given you the wrong impression...'

'Oh, don't start with all that.' She gave the ribbons on her bonnet a vigorous tug. 'Only a word to the wise. If you *do* like her, don't comment on her appearance or give any compliments if you can help it. I know it sounds odd, but she doesn't like them.'

'I noticed. This morning I told her she looked beautiful and—'

'*Never* say that!' Miss MacQueen practically hissed, shoving past him towards the door. 'That's the *worst* thing you could possibly say!'

'That she's beautiful?'

'Yes!'

'But why?'

'Because...' She opened her mouth and then clamped it shut again. 'That's *her* business. Just remember not to— Oh!'

He never discovered what not to do as the back door flew open suddenly and the woman in question herself bundled in, flanked by two young boys and carrying another, smaller one in her arms.

'What on earth...?' Miss MacQueen's mouth fell open. 'What happened?'

'David's lost his job.' Miss Gardiner sounded breathless. 'And when I got to his house he was—' She stopped, her eyes widening in surprise as they settled on Sebastian.

'Sozzled.' One of the boys finished her sentence for her.

'Bosky. Three sheets to the wind. Stewed. That's what Mr Roper said.'

'Mr Roper's one of the neighbours,' Miss Gardiner explained with a pained expression. 'I gave his son a shilling to stay and keep an eye on David tonight, but I didn't want to leave the boys. I was going to make them a meal, but...'

'It looked like a pigsty,' the same boy piped up again. 'That's what Mrs Roper said.'

'It *was*.' Miss Gardiner looked faintly mortified and then sighed. 'I thought about tidying up, but there was so much to do and it was getting late so I decided to bring them here for a bath and something to eat instead. They can sleep in my bed tonight.'

'And you can share with me.' Miss MacQueen had already removed her outdoor clothes and was rubbing her hands together briskly. 'Right, boys. Come with me and I'll show you where you can put your things.'

'Let me help, too.' Sebastian stepped forward, holding his arms out for the sleeping child in Miss Gardiner's arms and feeling somewhat shaken by the intensity of his emotions. He'd been so relieved at the sight of her that he'd actually found himself unable to speak for a few moments. 'This one looks heavy.'

'I'm not!' a sleepy voice protested from over her shoulder.

'Only because you're such a strapping young man.' He smiled as a youthful face turned to peer at him. 'You'll soon be carrying ladies about yourself, I'll wager. How old are you? Fifteen?'

'Five.'

'No! That's incredible.' He turned back to Miss Gardiner as the boy giggled. 'Please? You look as though you're about to collapse.'

'I admit I am a little tired.' She hesitated for another moment before handing the boy over with a sigh of relief.

'Your nephews, I presume?'

'Yes. This is Oliver and the other two are Michael and Peter.' She gave a tentative smile. 'Michael's the talkative one, but I'm sorry for bringing them here. I hope you don't mind.'

'Why would I mind?'

'Because Belles belongs to your family. You should know, I would never have brought them if it hadn't been necessary.'

'Miss Gardiner.' Sebastian bounced Oliver up on one arm. 'I abnegated responsibility for Belles when I joined the navy. You're the manager now and this is your home, which means that you may treat it as you see fit. If my sister trusts you, then so do I. That's all there is to it.'

'Thank you.' The expression in her eyes softened in a way that caused an abrupt lurch followed by a warm glow in his chest.

'Now let me find somewhere cosy to put this young man and I'll help to prepare that bath.'

'You don't have to do that.'

'Ever hear the phrase "all hands on deck"?' He arched an eyebrow. 'You're the captain here tonight, Miss Gardiner. Just give me your orders and I'll endeavour to see them fulfilled.' He flashed a quick grin. 'Anna will have my head if I don't.'

'I never thought of that.' Her lips curled and the dimple he'd noticed the previous night appeared for the first time that day. *Aha!* he thought with a definite sense of triumph, there she was. *There* was the woman he'd met during the night, the one he'd *wanted* to walk with that morning. She was back and she couldn't have looked any less like a fortune-hunting ice queen. And maybe, just maybe, Miss MacQueen was right.

Mr Fortini, Henrietta decided, was going to make an excellent father some day. His light-hearted, easy-going manner seemed infectious, so much so that her nephews took to him instantly. During bathtime, an event that had soaked a considerably greater area of the kitchen floor than she would have liked, he'd regaled them all with stories about fantastical sea monsters, each one of which he claimed to have confronted, outwitted and finally defeated in hand-to-fin or hand-to-tentacle combat. After that, he'd bundled them into clean sheets and then sat them down at the kitchen table for steaming hot platefuls of pie and gravy while she'd washed their clothes in the remaining bathwater. Despite her concern for David, it had proved a strangely enjoyable and entertaining hour's work. Even Nancy had laughed on more than one occasion.

All in all, she had to admit that it was possible she'd misjudged Mr Fortini's character. He seemed to genuinely want to help—surely a man who was only interested in flirtation wouldn't inconvenience himself to such an extent? It was hard to imagine either Mr Willerby or Mr Hoxley going to so much trouble. Maybe he was a man who could be trusted, after all...

'There we go,' she announced finally, pegging the last pair of trousers up on a rack above the hearth. The boys' stockings, she noticed, were almost threadbare in places, though she'd only darned them again a couple of weeks ago.

'Anyone for a glass of milk before bed?' Nancy stuck her head out of the pantry.

'Yes, please!'

'That doesn't mean you have to wolf down the rest of your pies,' Henrietta admonished them quickly. 'The milk isn't going anywhere, we promise.'

'Is there anything else I can do to help?' Mr Fortini stole a chunk of pie crust from Peter's plate and popped it into his mouth with a wink.

'You've already done more than enough.' Henrietta shook her head, feeling self-conscious again as he got up and came to stand before her. 'I'm very grateful. We all are.'

'It's been my honour to serve.' He reached for his jacket and drew it over his shoulders. 'Now, if you need me, I'll be staying at Redbourne's store tonight.'

'Redbourne's?' Nancy's head poked out of the pantry again.

'Yes. James Redbourne and I were best friends growing up. He's given me a bed for the night.' One of his eyebrows quirked upwards. 'I believe the two of you are also acquainted?'

'We've met.'

'Well…' He shrugged when no more comment appeared to be forthcoming. 'That's where I'll be.'

'Just for tonight?' Henrietta was dismayed by how awkwardly high-pitched her voice sounded.

'Yes. I'll be taking the stagecoach north tomorrow.'

'Oh.' Somehow the words made her feel deflated inside, as if she'd just lost something important. If she could have gone back to that morning, then she had a feeling she would have behaved very differently, but it was too late now. The opportunity was gone and the realisation felt like a cold lump in her stomach. 'Then I suppose this is goodbye.'

'I suppose it is.' He inclined his head though his eyes never left hers. 'It's been a pleasure to meet you, Miss Gardiner.'

'You, too, Mr Fortini.' She was horribly aware of colour rising up her throat and over her cheeks. Even with Nancy and the boys in the kitchen, the situation felt too intimate, as if some unspoken communication were passing between them. Only she wasn't sure what exactly they were trying to say either. It was less of a conversation and more of an awareness…one that was raising goose pimples on her skin and causing more fluttering than ever. 'Sorry again about your nose.'

'What happened to his nose?' Michael chirruped from the table.

'I hit it with a door.'

'For perfectly good reasons.' Sebastian averted his gaze finally. 'Your aunt thought I'd broken into the shop to steal all the biscuits.'

'Like a pirate?'

'*Exactly* like a pirate. But now I can leave safe in the knowledge that she has three young men to protect her.' He lowered his voice confidentially. 'Can I trust you all to act as my marines?'

'Yes, sir!' Peter and Michael both sat up straighter at once.

'Very good. Carry on then, men.' He raised a hand in a salute before bowing to Henrietta and Nancy. 'Miss Gardiner, Miss MacQueen. I'll leave through the shop if you don't mind?'

'Of course not.' Henrietta smiled, though for some reason she felt more like crying. 'Goodbye, Mr Fortini.'

'Goodbye,' Nancy added, waiting until he was out in the hallway before giving her a sharp nudge in the ribs. *'Well?'*

'Well what?' Henrietta lifted her chin.

'You know very well what *well* means!'

'What does it mean?' Michael looked between them both quizzically.

'Nothing. Finish your milk.'

'Go after him.' Nancy wasn't so easily put off. 'Say goodbye properly.'

'I just did.'

'With about as much warmth as an icicle!'

'*Don't* call me an ice queen!' Henrietta whirled on her. 'You know how I hate that.'

'All right, but he deserved better and I don't say that about any man very often. He was very worried about you earlier.'

'He was?'

'Yes! We were going to go and search for you when you arrived.'

'I still don't think...'

'Go!' Nancy pointed an imperative finger towards the hallway. 'Say it properly and *without* an audience. You'll regret it if you don't.'

'Mr Fortini?'

Sebastian had one foot out of the door and on to the pavement when Miss Gardiner came hurrying through the shop towards him. After all the commotion of the evening, she was looking somewhat dishevelled. Still beautiful, but with a few golden tendrils hanging loose around her face.

'Miss Gardiner?' He shifted his weight back over the threshold. 'Did I forget something?'

'No, but I...' She stopped a few feet away and clasped her hands together, seemingly reluctant to meet his eyes. 'I had a message for Anna.'

'Indeed?'

'Yes. If you don't mind, that is?'

'Not at all.' He waited a few seconds. 'Only you might have to tell me what it is first.'

'Oh…of course… Just tell her that everything's all right here. With Belles, I mean. And please give her my best wishes.'

'I'll be sure to pass that on.'

'Thank you.'

'Was there something else?' He lifted an eyebrow when she didn't move.

'I… Yes.' She pulled her shoulders back and looked at him finally. 'I wanted to say thank you for being so kind to my nephews. They've been through a great deal over the past few months.'

'Peter told me about their mother, that she passed away in the summer. I'm sorry.'

'But the way that you spoke to them tonight, telling them to take care of me like that… I think you've made them feel ten feet tall.'

'I hope so. There are a lot of boys in the navy around Peter's age. Powder keggers, cabin boys, servants… It's not uncommon for them to feel lost away from home, but giving them a sense of purpose always helps.'

'Well, you've helped them—and me.' She cleared her throat. 'Which is why I also want to apologise for the way I behaved this morning. There are certain subjects that I'm a little sensitive about. Oversensitive, perhaps. I thought that you…' She stopped and gave her head a small shake. 'It doesn't matter what I thought. What matters is that I misjudged you and I'm sorry.'

'I see.' He regarded her steadily for a few seconds before

closing the door softly behind him. 'Then shall we shake hands and be friends?'

Her shoulders seemed to sag with relief. 'Yes. I'd like that very much.'

'As would I.' He extended a hand and she took it, placing her fingers in his with a smile that seemed to spread and then falter abruptly. Which was strange, he thought, because he was aware of his own smile doing the same thing at the exact same moment. The very ambience in the room seemed to shift suddenly, as if some of the air had been sucked out of the door when he'd closed it.

Standing all alone, cocooned together in the dimly lit shop, he had the bizarre impression that they were the only two people in the world and that something significant and irrevocable was happening. The mere touch of skin against skin seemed to have set all of his nerves thrumming, so much so that he could actually hear blood rushing in his head. It was like the feeling before a thunderstorm, the atmosphere stretching and crackling with tension. If he'd been on board a ship, it would have been time to start battening down the hatches. On dry land, he didn't have the faintest idea what to do.

All he knew was that he couldn't look away from her or move his gaze even an iota to one side, as if she were hypnotising him the way she had on that first night. Not that she *had* actually hypnotised him, obviously, but whatever strange effect she'd had then seemed to be happening again... He had a powerful urge to wrap one of her golden tendrils around his fingers and draw her closer.

Fortunately, she blinked first. Several times, in fact, enabling him to look away.

'Do they have any family on their mother's side?' He

cleared his throat, deafeningly loudly, or so it seemed in the silence.

'Not close by. Alice came from Taunton and I'd hate to send the boys so far away.' Miss Gardiner's throat appeared to need clearing as well. 'They can be quite a handful, but they're good boys really. My brother just isn't able to pay them much attention at the moment.' Her chin wobbled slightly. 'I'm afraid he grieves for his wife very much.'

'Ah. You mean that he drinks often?'

'Yes.' Her whole face seemed to crumple. 'More and more since Alice died. I've been telling myself that he'll stop eventually, but now he's lost his job and I can't see any way for things to get better.'

Sebastian started to reach a hand out and then stopped himself. The atmosphere still hadn't quite returned to normal and, after that morning, he didn't want to risk any more misunderstandings between them.

'What happened to your sister-in-law?' he asked softly instead.

'She thought it was another baby at first, only she got thinner instead of bigger. The doctor was never sure why.'

'Poor woman.'

'It was dreadful. She was so young and such a good mother. She'd be horrified if she knew how David was behaving now.' She wrapped her arms around her waist, hugging herself as if she were cold. 'I try to help as much as I can, but it's not enough. I know that I ought to do more, that I should go and live with him and take care of the boys and the house, but...'

'But you have your own life?'

'Yes!' Her eyes shot to his, a glimmer of pain swirling in the depths. 'I feel so torn. I don't see how I can do that and run Belles properly, but they're my nephews and I love them, too. And who will take care of them if I don't? It's wicked of me to want to do otherwise.'

'It's not wicked at all.' This time he couldn't stop himself from reaching for one of her hands, clasping it tight between both of his. 'I understand about feeling torn. I don't know your brother, but I expect he is, too. Sometimes people drink to forget their pain. I've seen it happen more times than I can count. Maybe your brother's not ready to face reality yet.'

'But he *needs* to be ready!' An angry expression crossed her face before she clapped her other hand over her mouth. 'Oh! I shouldn't have said that.'

'Why not? It's the truth. He has three sons to care for and a sister who's desperately worried about him. You've every right to be angry, but he's only human. Knowing how we ought to behave and actually doing it are often very different things. He'll face reality when he's ready.'

'What if he drinks himself to death in the meantime?' Her voice caught as her expression turned anguished again.

He squeezed her hand, unable to find an answer for that and unwilling to voice empty platitudes. He wanted to comfort her, if only he knew how...

'I'm sorry. I didn't mean to burden you with any of this.' She drew her fingers away abruptly, her eyes welling with tears as she took a few steps backwards, retreating towards the kitchen before he could say or do anything to stop her. 'Goodbye, Mr Fortini. Have a good journey.'

Chapter Seven

'What now?' Nancy rolled a lump of cinnamon-flavoured biscuit dough out on the table. 'I don't mind the boys staying here, but we can't look after them *and* manage the shop.'

'I know.' Henrietta drew a flour-stained wrist across her forehead. 'They go to the charity school in the mornings and then Peter and Michael used to go and help David in the mews, but now he's lost his job…' She heaved her shoulders and cut out a row of perfectly square Comptessa biscuits. 'I'll go and speak to him after I take them to school, before he has a chance to start drinking again.'

'Good idea.'

'Hopefully it won't take long, but I'm sorry to leave you alone again.'

'Pshaw.' Nancy waved a hand dismissively. 'Don't worry about me, but what will you say?'

'I'm not sure yet.' She began to arrange the biscuits on a baking tray. 'Mr Fortini said that some people drink when they're not ready to face their pain, but David can't go on as he is and I can't take the boys home until I know that he's better. I need to make him understand that. In any case, I'll bring the boys back here this afternoon.'

'I'll find them some jobs to keep them out of trouble.' Nancy looked thoughtful. 'Maybe we could offer complimentary shoe-shining with every bag of biscuits?'

'I'm not sure how Mr Redbourne would feel about that, considering he has a shoe-shiner outside his store.'

'Does he? I hadn't noticed.' Nancy's tone was altogether too uninterested. 'Speaking of Mr Redbourne, I wonder if Mr Fortini has left yet. Did he say what time his stagecoach was leaving?'

'Does it matter?'

'Not to me, no.'

Henrietta kept her eyes on her dough. She'd been trying, unsuccessfully, not to think about Mr Fortini for most of the night and since she'd woken up that morning, still mortified by her near tears the previous evening. He'd been so sympathetic and understanding that she'd been strongly tempted to rest her head on his shoulder and start sobbing. Strangely enough, she had a feeling that he would have let her, too, despite the way she'd behaved on their walk. What would he have thought of her then? What would he have reported to Anna? That she was an emotional mess, most likely…which she was starting to think wasn't so far from the truth.

'If he hasn't left by now then I'm sure he'll be on his way soon.' She tipped her head to one side as if she expected to hear a stagecoach rolling past at any moment. 'I don't suppose we'll be seeing him again.'

'Breakfast is served.' James set two plates of sausages and egg on the table with a flourish.

'You know, I could get used to this.' Sebastian lifted his feet off a neighbouring chair and picked up his fork with a grin. 'Don't you have a maid to cook for you?'

'No. I can't see the point when I can manage perfectly well by myself.'

'Spoken like a true bachelor. It's funny, but I would have thought you of all men would be married by now.'

'Why me of *all men*?'

'You always seemed like the marrying type, that's all.'

'Maybe I just haven't met the right woman.'

'Really?' Sebastian paused in the act of spearing a sausage. There was something distinctly evasive about his friend's tone. 'Why don't I believe you?'

'Because you never could mind your own business.' James gave him a swift kick under the table. 'As it happens, I *thought* I had met the right one once, only it turned out the feeling wasn't reciprocated.'

'Well, plenty more fish in the sea.' Sebastian stopped and put his utensils down again. 'What a ridiculous phrase that is. I wonder who came up with it?'

'A sailor?'

'Probably, but it's not true, is it? I mean, there are fish and then there are *fish*.'

'Succinctly put.'

'What I mean is that it makes women sound interchangeable when they're clearly not.'

'True. I suppose some of them are mackerel and some are sharks.'

'You're not bitter, then?'

'Maybe a little, but I can't blame her for what happened. She never gave me any encouragement, I just hoped, that's all.' He laughed ruefully. 'So the stagecoach leaves at nine. It goes to Bristol first, I presume?'

'I think so, but the truth is, I was wondering whether you'd mind me staying for a few more days?'

'Not at all.' James gave him a searching look. 'I'd like to think it was for the pleasure of my company, but something tells me it has more to do with Miss Gardiner. Is the ice thawing a little?'

Sebastian didn't answer, vaguely surprised by his own request. He really ought to be heading north. He *wanted* to see his mother and Anna again and to start enjoying his newfound freedom, too, yet he couldn't quite bring himself to leave. Miss Gardiner needed his help and somehow that seemed more important. He wasn't quite sure what she'd meant when she'd said she'd misjudged him, but they seemed to be friends again and he couldn't just abandon a woman in trouble, especially one who worked in his family's shop. In the absence of Anna, it was *his* responsibility to help, surely?

Yes, that was it, he reassured himself. He felt compelled to stay because she was Anna's employee and Anna would want him to help. It had nothing to do with *her* specifically. He was attracted to her—it would have been frankly ridiculous to pretend otherwise—he liked her, even, but that had nothing to do with his decision, especially since she'd made it clear that flirtation was out of the question. He would have helped Miss MacQueen in a similar situation, too. Probably.

'It's not that difficult a question.' James gave him a puzzled look. 'The food's going to get cold if you keep staring at your plate much longer.'

'Sorry.' Sebastian came back to himself with a jolt. 'It *is* to do with Miss Gardiner, as a matter of fact, only not in the way that you think. She needs help.'

'With the shop?' James looked surprised.

'No, some trouble with her brother and nephews.' He picked up his knife and fork again. 'It'll probably only be for a few more days, just until I know that she's all right. The end of the week at the most. It's what Anna would want me to do.'

'Naturally.' James smirked over the rim of his coffee cup. 'What other reason could there possibly be?'

'Do we *have* to go to school?' Michael complained as Henrietta marched him and his brothers out of the shop and along Swainswick Crescent. 'Can't we stay and help you sell biscuits?'

'No. Learning is more important.' She clutched Oliver's five-year-old hand firmly in hers. 'Besides, it's only for the morning. Then you can come back and do some jobs for me.'

'Will you teach us to bake?'

'If you like.'

'I'd rather learn about life in the navy,' Peter interjected. 'I'm going to be a sailor one day.'

'Really?' Henrietta glanced at him in surprise. 'I didn't know that you liked the water.'

'He wants to run away to sea like Sebastian when he grows up. He said so last night.' Michael smirked, elbowing his brother in the ribs and earning himself a fist in the arm back.

'No fighting, the pair of you!' Henrietta jabbed a hand between them. 'And it's *Mr* Fortini to you.'

'He said that we could call him Sebastian.'

'That's not the point.'

'But he said so!'

'It's true, I did!' a familiar deep voice called out from behind them. 'As may you, Miss Gardiner, if you wish?'

'Oh!' Henrietta whirled around in surprise, spinning Oliver along with her. 'Where did you...?'

'Come from?' He grinned lopsidedly. 'The same place as you, only I went into Belles through the back way and Miss MacQueen told me you'd just left through the front. I have to admit, it was quite a challenge to catch up with your fast pace.'

'We're late for school,' Michael informed him.

'But I thought you were leaving?' Henrietta gasped and then winced at the sound of her own words. 'Not that I wanted you to leave. Or to stay,' she added quickly. 'I just...' She shook her head, wondering what was the matter with her tongue. Not to mention her stomach, which seemed to have bounced all the way up to her chest, lifting her spirits along with it. Even her pulse seemed to be accelerating, pounding so fast it was actually hard to draw enough air into her lungs. Despite the embarrassment of the previous night, she felt quite ridiculously, ludicrously happy to see him again—and somehow unable to stop smiling. 'Forgive me, I'm just surprised, that's all. I thought you'd be on your way north by now.'

'So did I.' He shrugged in a faintly bemused manner. 'Only I decided I wasn't quite ready to leave yet. I have a few old friends I'd like to catch up with, as well as three young cadets to train.'

'Really, sir?' Peter's face lit up. 'Will you teach us to be sailors?'

'As long as you go to school first and *without* any complaining.' Sebastian winked at him. 'I actually wondered if you'd allow me to walk with you, Miss Gardiner? To signal the start of our new friendship?'

'You should call her Henrietta,' Michael interjected. 'If she's allowed to call you Sebastian. It's only fair.'

'I wouldn't presume…'

'But Michael's right. It *is* only fair.' She found herself smiling even wider in agreement. 'I'd be delighted if you'd escort us… Sebastian.'

'Then it would be my pleasure.' He tilted his head to one side, his dark eyes gleaming with what looked like satisfaction. 'I'd offer you my arm, but it appears this young gentleman has beaten me to it. What do you two say?' He held his hands out to Peter and Michael. 'Will you walk with me instead?'

'Yes, Sebastian!'

Henrietta led the way, laughing softly as he was immediately bombarded with questions about life in the navy. Just like the evening before, however, he seemed completely relaxed and at ease, impressing his young audience so much that she was half afraid they might both enlist before the end of the week.

She was so preoccupied with listening that she almost walked straight into another woman hurrying around the railings at the corner of the street.

'Pardon me.' She looked up, straight into the eyes of the woman from the pavement the day before.

'Oh! No, it was my fault.' The woman hesitated, her lips parting as if she wanted to say something else, before she noticed Sebastian and scampered quickly onwards again.

'An acquaintance of yours?' he asked quizzically when she was out of earshot.

'Not exactly.' Henrietta looked back over her shoulder

for a few seconds and then carried on walking. As much as she wanted to help anyone in distress, her nephews needed to get to school and she needed to speak to David. At that moment, she had more than enough problems of her own to deal with.

Chapter Eight

Henrietta found Sebastian exactly where she'd left him, leaning casually against a red brick wall opposite the school-yard. In broad daylight, he looked even more ruggedly handsome than she'd remembered. His coat was hanging open as usual and his dark hair was swept away from his face, all except for one black curl that seemed determined to take up residence over his nose. That appendage was also looking noticeably less bruised today, allowing her to focus on his twinkling dark eyes as she approached.

There was something slightly wicked about them, she thought as she came closer, or, if not wicked, then definitely mischievous. Yes, that was a much better word. There was no malice in them, although now that she'd got past the initial pleasure of seeing him, she wondered if she was simply being naive again.

He'd said that he was staying longer in Bath to visit old friends, but then why was he here with her? She thought she'd addressed the issue of potential misunderstandings the day before, but why was he helping her if he didn't expect anything in return? They might have decided to be friends, but she still couldn't help feeling a little suspicious. Not to mention alarmed when just the sight of him made her stomach start fluttering as if there were a swarm of butterflies inside looking for a way out.

'So where next? Your brother's house?' He uncrossed his ankles and pushed himself upright to greet her.

'Yes, although I've no idea what I'm going to say.' She felt instantly anxious again. 'I want to help him get better, but I feel so powerless.'

'Maybe just tell him that.' He looked sympathetic. 'Is it far?'

'Just a few streets away.'

'Then let's go.' He bent his elbow and she curled her hand around it, without hesitation and without mistaking it for a wild creature this time either, which was definitely progress, she thought ironically as they made their way through the backstreets. His arm felt just as big and solid as it had the day before, although there was something reassuring and supportive about it now, too. Reassuring *with* butterflies. She wouldn't have thought it possible to feel tense in two such different ways at the same time and yet she did, her concern for David vying with a new sense of repressed excitement with Sebastian.

'Here we are.' She stopped outside a small two-storey wooden building, squeezed between two equally ramshackle others. 'Would you mind—?'

'Waiting outside? Of course not.'

'I don't know how long I'll be.'

'Take all the time you need.' Sebastian squeezed her arm gently before releasing her. 'I'll be right here.'

'Thank you.' She opened the door without knocking and stepped inside, only to find the room just as she'd left it. Messy, freezing and apparently deserted.

'David?' she called softly as she made her way through the downstairs, but there was no answer, not as much as a murmur of acknowledgement. Carefully, she climbed the steps up into the loft space, but that was empty, too, rumpled bedsheets the only evidence that her brother had ever been there. Everything else was eerily still and quiet and forbidding somehow. A lump of dread started to form in her stomach, apprehension getting the better of her nerves. If David hadn't gone to work, then where was he? Surely he couldn't have started drinking again already?

'Henrietta?' Sebastian's shout summoned her back down the steps.

'What is it?' She hurried towards the front door, flinging it open and then stopping dead at the sight of her brother's neighbour confronting Sebastian. 'Oh! Is everything all right?'

'So he *is* with you then?' Mrs Roper's belligerent expression bore a strong resemblance to Nancy's. 'He said he was, but you can't be too careful.'

'No, I suppose you can't.' Henrietta closed the door behind her, unable to mask her disappointment. 'Mrs Roper, do you have any idea where my brother is?'

'Not exactly.' The neighbour looked as if she were suddenly keen to leave again. 'My boy came back this morning saying David was awake and feeling a bit worse for wear, but sober enough.'

'Oh.'

'He was muttering some strange things though, my boy said, all about going away and making a fresh start.'

'Going away?' Henrietta felt as though she'd just been slapped in the face.

''Course we thought it was just the headache talking so I made him some tea and bacon, but by the time I brought it over, he was gone. So, I checked in his coffer, I hope you don't mind, and it was empty.'

'Empty...' Henrietta swallowed, trying to maintain an outward appearance of calm when her insides felt like a butter churn. 'But... I don't understand—what about his sons?'

'He *did* ask where they were, my boy says, so he told him they was with you and...well, David said something about it being for the best.'

'What?'

'But I'm sure he didn't mean it like that. He loves his boys, there's no doubting that. No matter how much he drinks, he won't abandon them...not for ever, anyways.'

'Didn't he give *any* clue about where he was going?'

'No, but if I hear anything I'll send word straight to the shop. In the meantime, you take care of 'em boys and I'll keep an eye on the house. I'll give it a good clean up, too. Ready for when he comes back again. It's the least I can do for Alice.' Mrs Roper gave a loud sniff. 'She was a lovely girl.'

'She was.' Henrietta found herself blinking furiously. 'Thank you, Mrs Roper. I'm grateful for everything you've done.'

'And you take care of *her*—' Mrs Roper turned fierce eyes on Sebastian '—whoever you are.'

'Oh, forgive me, this is Anna's brother,' Henrietta murmured, having forgotten about introductions until that moment. 'Mr Sebastian Fortini.'

'The *Countess's* brother?' Mrs Roper's expression turned instantly to one of dismay. 'I do beg your pardon, sir.'

'Don't mention it.' He inclined his head. 'You were absolutely right to be suspicious. I'm sure Mr Gardiner would be most obliged.'

Henrietta reached for his arm before he could offer it, glad of the support as he led her back towards Belles. Now that the initial shock had passed, she felt as though she were walking through a cold fog, unable to see what was going on around her and feeling numb all over. It was taking all of her energy just to put one foot in front of the other. As for her mind... The same questions kept swirling around her head. Where was David? How could he have got up that morning and just left? Or had he been planning to do it for weeks, simply waiting for an opportunity to leave the boys with her? No, surely he wouldn't have done anything so calculating? *Surely* he wouldn't have done this deliberately to her, to his sons, to all of them?

'Can you think of any place he's likely to go?' Sebastian's voice jolted her back to the present and thankfully out of the fog. They were already turning the corner on to Swainswick Crescent, she noticed, though she had no memory of even crossing Pulteney Bridge. 'Do you have any other family?'

'No, it's been just the two of us, and then Alice, for years.'

'It still might be worth paying a visit to Ashley.' He looked thoughtful. 'With your permission, I'll take a ride out there and see. If he's walking that way, then I'll likely pass him on the road. If not, I can leave word at the local tavern to contact you if he makes an appearance.'

'No.' She shook her head. 'There's no need to involve yourself any more in my troubles. I've put you out enough.'

'Not at all. I want to help and it's a nice day for a ride.'

'You don't have a horse!'

'But I *do* have friends with horses.'

'Mr Fortini—'

'Sebastian.'

'Sebastian… I'm very grateful for your help, but you said that you were staying in Bath to catch up with old friends. How can you do that if you're chasing after my brother?'

'There's plenty of time for both.'

'Is there? Because I don't want to inconvenience you or to keep you from your family either. They don't even know that you're back in England. They'll still be worried about you.'

'Ah, but not for much longer. I wrote to both Staunton Manor and Feversham Hall this morning. That should put Anna and my mother's minds at rest.'

'Good.' She let out a heartfelt sigh of relief. 'I'm sure it will.'

'Although I admit it felt slightly absurd to be writing to such addresses, never mind to a countess.'

'But why should it? Your grandfather was a duke, wasn't he?'

'He was.' His steps faltered briefly as his brows snapped together. 'Did Anna tell you that? We hardly ever spoke about it growing up.'

'Ye-es.' She was faintly perturbed by the stern change in his demeanour. 'She told me just before her wedding to the Earl. All about your mother eloping with a footman, too. It sounded very romantic.'

'I suppose it was, until her family cut her off without a penny. Or has she forgotten that part?' He clenched his jaw, his throat working silently for a few seconds. 'Now, what time do your nephews finish at school?'

'Midday.'

'Then I'd better hurry if I'm going to get to Ashley and back in time. With your permission, I thought I'd take them to Sydney Gardens this afternoon. They need to start cadet training in earnest if they're going to be captains by the time they're twenty.'

She hesitated, still uncertain about accepting his help, but they were friends now, weren't they? And if it helped to find David… The thought decided her.

'I think they'd enjoy Sydney Gardens very much. Definitely more than whatever jobs Nancy has planned, but I'd like to come, too, if she doesn't mind looking after the shop. I need to tell them that they'll be staying with me for a little while and they're bound to have questions.'

'Good point.'

'I was actually wondering whether it might be better to tell them that David's unwell? Then if—*when*—he changes his mind and comes back, they'll never know that he left.' She paused. 'What do you think?'

'I can see why you might want to, given the circumstances…' Sebastian made a face.

'But?'

'But if he doesn't come back and they think that you deceived them… It might make things worse in the long run. They seem like bright boys and you don't want to lose their trust.'

'So, you think that honesty is the best policy?' She chewed her bottom lip thoughtfully. 'Maybe you're right. I just can't bear the thought of them being hurt any more or feeling they're not wanted.'

'But they have an aunt who loves them.' He stopped outside Belles and turned to face her, his dark gaze boring into hers so intently that she could almost feel it like a touch on her skin. 'Don't underestimate that.'

She felt her breath catch, her legs feeling slightly unsteady all of a sudden, unable to think of a response. There it was again, that temptation to lay her head on his shoulder, only not to cry this time, just to be close, to wrap her arms around him and feel his arms around her. What would his shoulders feel like beneath her fingertips? What would it be like simply to be held?

'Now, if you'll excuse me.' His gaze dropped to her lips for a fleeting moment before he moved away. 'I need to go and see a man about a horse. I'll see you this afternoon.'

She nodded, feeling oddly disorientated as he bowed and walked away. She still wasn't entirely sure why he was helping her, but at that moment she was extremely, possibly foolishly, glad that he was.

Chapter Nine

'So, he's just abandoned them?' James summarised, holding on to the horse's bridle while Sebastian climbed the mounting block.

'That's what it looks like. He left sometime this morning.'

'Poor Miss Gardiner, but if he doesn't want to be found then he's not likely to go anywhere familiar, is he?'

'Probably not,' Sebastian conceded, throwing one leg over the saddle. 'But it's still worth a try. Thanks for the horse, by the way.'

'Don't mention it. Dulcie's a docile old creature, but she'll get you there all right.'

'Docile is good.' Sebastian picked up the reins with a grimace. 'It's been five years since I last did this. Where are the oars again?'

'The same place as the mast.' James looked mildly concerned. 'Are you sure you wouldn't prefer to take the cart?'

'I'd *much* rather take the cart, but it'll take too long. I said I'd be back by early afternoon.'

'I'm sure she'd prefer to have you back in one piece, but it's up to you. Good luck.' James gave him a pointed look. 'Try not to fall off.'

'I'll do my best.' Sebastian nudged his legs and set off. It was approximately six miles to Ashley, just over an hour's ride if he took it steady, which between him and Dulcie was probably the only way he *could* take it. Then he'd need an hour in the village to look around and make friends with the local innkeeper, followed by another hour to ride back. He wouldn't get back to Bath in time to collect the boys from school, but they'd still have plenty of time to spend in Sydney Gardens.

He rubbed a hand over the mare's neck, vaguely wondering what on earth he was doing. He was *supposed* to be visiting his family and enjoying his newfound freedom, not volunteering to ride around the countryside on behalf of a woman who'd asked him to treat her like a sister, in search of a man he'd never met. It couldn't *just* be because it was what Anna would want him to do, could it? He didn't know, but then he was finding it hard to think clearly about anything involving Henrietta.

In truth, his mind was still preoccupied with the smile she'd given him that morning. He hadn't been certain how she'd react to seeing him again, but the way her face had come to life when she had, as if she were genuinely happy, had turned her from beautiful into…what? He couldn't even think of a word to do her justice. Radiant, exquisite, ravishing, *pulchritudinous*? It had started with a gleam in her eyes and then the rest of her features had followed suit and before he'd known it, her whole face had lit up as if she were glowing from within.

The sight had stolen his breath away and apparently addled his senses, too, because he'd volunteered to ride out to Ashley without even asking what her brother looked like! But it was too late to turn back, even if doing so wouldn't have made him feel just a little bit foolish. All he had to do was keep his eyes open for a man who looked as though he might have a hangover—and probably one with fair hair, too, if Henrietta and the boys were any indication.

On a more positive note, at least the weather was co-operating. It wasn't particularly sunny, but the roads were dry and navigable. The views were like a balm to his soul, too, the rolling hills and arable valleys familiar and comforting. They made him want to start quoting poetry or break out into song. He'd missed these views over the past five years, he realised. In all of his travels, he'd never ever seen anywhere to compare, not because the landscape was particularly dramatic or spectacular, but because it was home.

Not that he'd waxed quite so lyrical two days ago during the interminable stagecoach ride from Plymouth, but now he seemed to be viewing the world in a whole different light and there was only one reason he could think of to account for it. A reason with golden hair and a willowy figure that, despite the unfortunate circumstances, had struck him as even more attractive on the second day of their acquaintance. He wondered how she would look on the third and fourth and fifth…and fiftieth.

It was tempting to remain in Bath to find out, but they were *just* friends, he reminded himself sternly, just friends who exchanged long and intense looks on the street—or had he imagined that? Not that it mattered. He was only staying a few more days, no matter how attractive she looked or how poetically inclined he found himself. Hopefully her brother would have turned up by then. Because after that, he really *had* to go.

It was three hours precisely before Sebastian opened the back door of Belles and raised his hand to his forehead in a salute. Henrietta's nephews were all sitting fidgeting around the kitchen table, looking ready to burst out of their seats at any moment.

'Who's ready for some naval training?'

'I am!' Peter was the first to his feet.

'Not so fast.' Henrietta came through from the shop, wiping her hands on her apron as she looked at him enquiringly. 'I need to speak to Mr Fortini in the parlour first. You can be getting your shoes and coats on in the meantime.'

'I won't be long.' Sebastian threw Peter an encouraging smile before following her up the stairs. He wished he had better news to impart, but unfortunately all he could do was shake his head the moment they were alone. 'I'm afraid there was no sign of him.'

'Oh...' Her eyelashes dipped as she pressed her lips together. 'I told myself not to hope, but I still wondered...' She put a hand to her throat and rubbed gently. 'Thank you for trying.'

'He might just want to lie low for a while.' He couldn't resist the impulse to reassure her. 'I doubt that he's gone far.'

'Then he's probably still in Bath.' She looked hopeful again. 'Maybe I ought to go and look for him? I could visit a few of the taverns.'

'Absolutely not.' He closed the distance between them in two strides, putting his hands on her shoulders without thinking. The very idea of her visiting a tavern made him feel suddenly, fiercely protective. 'It could be dangerous.'

'I have to try.'

'You can let me do it.'

'No. You've done enough.'

'Visiting a few taverns isn't exactly a hardship. I can be more discreet and I'm a lot less likely to be groped.' He slid his hands over her upper arms, vaguely appreciating the irony as his fingers skimmed across bare skin. 'Only I forgot to ask what your brother looks like. It would be useful to know.'

'Oh, I never told you that, did I?' Her voice caught as she glanced down at one of his hands, as if she were uncertain what to make of its presence. 'Just like Michael, only a larger version. They're almost identical.'

'Well, that should make life a bit easier.' He smiled and released her, his fingers still tingling with her body heat. 'I'll go tonight with James. If your brother's still in Bath, then we'll find him, I promise, but first you and I have an expedition to the park to enjoy.'

'Yes, but please don't feel obliged. You must be tired after your ride...'

'Any more objections and I'll make you join in cadet training, too,' he interrupted sternly. 'I keep telling you, I *want* to help.'

'But *why*?' Her eyes flashed with a look of suspicion. 'It can't just be because of Anna.'

'Actually it can, although not just because it's what she would want me to do.' He paused. It was the same question he'd asked himself earlier, but suddenly the answer seemed a lot clearer. 'The truth is, I wasn't here when Anna needed me after our father died and I've always felt guilty about that. She had to run the shop almost single-handedly. And now she's married, she doesn't need me at all and there's no way I can make it up to her. But I still *want* to make it up to her. I thought perhaps I could help you and your nephews instead, if you'll let me?'

'I see.' Her brows knotted, as if she were thinking the idea through. 'So, you want to help me to make amends to Anna?'

'Yes.' He nodded. It was the truth, too, or at least the part of it he understood. 'And because there was a time in my life when I felt utterly futile and helpless. It was a horrible feeling and I hated it. Now that I *can* help, I want to. You'd be doing me a favour, giving me a chance to redeem myself, if that makes any sense?'

'It does.' Her gaze softened again. 'In that case, I'd be honoured by your help, Sebastian.'

'As I am to give it.' He bowed his head, feeling a flicker of heat in his chest at the words, a flicker that built into a glow, then flared into a blaze, until he felt hot all over.

'Well then...' She turned towards the stairs, mercifully oblivious to the inferno now raging inside him. 'I'd better fetch my bonnet.'

Sebastian took a few deep, though not particularly cooling, breaths before following and they were on their way in a matter of minutes, Peter and Michael walking on either side of him, chattering excitedly, while Henrietta walked hand in hand with Oliver. It was a strange feeling, Sebastian thought, to be jealous of a five-year-old, but he was, especially when said five-year-old was also hugged and kissed on numerous occasions. Just *one* hug would have sufficed for *him*, he thought, watching covertly, although perhaps he was deluding himself and keeping his hands away from Henrietta was the wiser course of action... Truthfully, there was no *perhaps* about it.

* * *

He insisted on paying their entry to Sydney Gardens and led them inside, past the maze and faux castle to a secluded corner that was more woodland than manicured lawn. At this time of year there were hardly any people on the paths and none at all after the first few minutes, which was exactly what he wanted.

'How are we going to train as sailors here?' Peter looked confused. 'The lake's over that way.'

'Yes, but the oak trees are here.'

'What do oak trees have to do with ships?'

'Aside from the fact that most ships are made from oak?' Sebastian put his hands on his hips and craned his neck backwards. 'Ever climbed a mast?'

'Oh!' Henrietta let out a worried exclamation. 'That doesn't sound very safe.'

'Children ought to climb trees. I always did. So did Anna for that matter.' He grinned as Peter and Michael's faces lit up with excitement. 'I'll look after them, don't worry. As a matter of fact...' He tossed his hat carelessly to one side. 'I think I'll join in.'

'I'm exhausted!'

Sebastian threw himself on to the ground beside Henrietta. Fortunately, she'd brought a blanket to sit on, although one corner of it was covered with a collection of pine cones that Oliver had obviously gathered for her. The young boy had tired of climbing after only a few minutes.

'I'm not surprised.' She smiled down at Sebastian, the winter sunshine catching the hair beneath her wide-brimmed bonnet so that it shone like spun gold. 'I feel exhausted from just watching you. That was nerve-racking.'

'I didn't let them go so high, although they're pretty good climbers already.' He lifted his head and looked around. 'Where's Oliver?'

She gestured to a nearby shrub. 'Building a den inside that. You're invited to visit, but apparently girls are forbidden.'

'How ungentlemanly.'

'I thought so.'

'That was fun!' Michael and Peter came running over to join them. 'What next?'

'Next you need to give an old man a rest.' Sebastian laid his head back down again.

'You're not old. Nancy says you're younger than Papa.' Michael dropped down on to the blanket and crossed his legs. 'Where *is* Papa anyway?'

'About that...' Henrietta threw Sebastian a swift glance before continuing. 'How would you feel about staying with me for a bit longer?'

'Why?' Peter sounded suspicious.

'Well...the truth is that your father's gone away for a little while.'

'You mean, he's left us?' Peter's voice hardened.

'He doesn't want us.' It was Michael who spoke this time. 'He loved Mama, but now she's gone he doesn't want us any more.'

'No, it's nothing like that.' Henrietta put her arm around the little boy's shoulders. 'He loves you very much.'

'He doesn't if he's left us.' Peter answered belligerently, turning on his heel and stalking away.

'Does he really love us, Aunt?' Michael's eyes were suspiciously bright.

'Of course he does. I promise.'

Sebastian waited a few moments before giving her a single nod and getting up to follow Peter. The boy was standing off to one side, his back turned and shoulders hunched, obviously trying not to cry.

'Permission to join you?' Sebastian came to a halt beside him, looking out over the park.

'You don't have to ask. You outrank me.'

'But you were here first. I don't want to intrude.' He paused, but there was no answer. 'You know, I used to come and climb here with my friend James when we were boys. The park attendants used to yell and chase us.'

'He's not coming back, is he?'

Sebastian turned his head. It was obvious the boy wasn't talking about James. 'I don't know.'

'Michael's right. He doesn't want us any more.'

'It's not as simple as that.'

'Why not?'

Sebastian rubbed a hand over his chin, trying to think of a way to explain. 'You know, in the navy each man is given a single tot of rum a day. Just one, mind, so that they don't fall off the rigging.'

Peter looked at him strangely. 'What does that have to do with Papa?'

'Nothing directly. I suppose what I'm trying to say is that too much drink is dangerous. It makes men forgetful and encourages them to take risks, but sometimes, when a man *wants* to forget something, it can be a means of escape, too. Then he can come to prefer that feeling to real life. It becomes an illness and he doesn't know how to stop drinking.'

'So, Papa is sick?'

'I think so, but I know that he hasn't left because of you. It's more likely because he loves you and he doesn't want you to see him the way he is now. Sometimes people need to go away in order to get better. And he made sure to leave you in good hands, didn't he?'

'Aunt Henrietta needs to run the shop. I heard her and Nancy talking. She doesn't know how she's going to manage.'

'But she will.' Sebastian glanced over his shoulder to where Henrietta was now holding a crying child in each arm. 'I haven't known your aunt long, but if there's one thing I'm certain of it's that she won't let you down.'

Peter looked pensive for a moment. 'Are you going to marry her?'

'What?' He let out a startled cough. Suddenly the solid ground beneath his feet felt ten times more precarious than the branches he'd just been swinging from.

'Is that why you're helping Aunt Henrietta to take care of us?'

'No-o.' He cleared his throat. 'We're friends, that's all.'

'But you won't leave, too?'

Sebastian tensed. Staying beyond the end of the week wasn't what he'd intended, but something about Peter's anguished expression at that moment reached inside him and pulled at his heart strings... He'd seen that look on other boys' faces before, but at least this time he could do something about it.

He put a hand on his shoulder and squeezed. 'I'll stay for as long as your aunt needs me. How about that?'

'Thank you.' Peter nodded stiffly.

'Now, do you know what we need?'

'No.'

'A cricket bat. You need to vent those feelings.'

'We don't have a cricket bat.'

'But we do have branches and pine cones.' He looked around, searching the ground for suitable candidates. 'That's another trick you learn in the navy. Improvisation.'

And that, Sebastian realised, was that. He'd just made a promise to a ten-year-old boy that he wasn't going any-where. Oddly enough, he couldn't even bring himself to regret it.

Chapter Ten

*K*nots.

Henrietta wandered slowly around the gazebo, listening with amusement as her nephews were tutored on the apparently ancient art of knot-tying inside. Overhand knots, square knots, granny knots, bowline knots, oyster knots, reef knots, thief knots, figure-eight knots... So many that she'd quickly forgotten the names of the rest. She'd declined the offer of instruction herself, preferring to enjoy the winter sunshine than play with bits of string—a choice of words that had earned her a stern look and lecture from Sebastian.

She laughed softly to herself at the memory of his outraged expression, though he'd been unable to maintain it for more than a few seconds. He seemed almost incapable of *not* smiling for long, as if his sense of humour were irrepressible. Somehow, it suited his general air of dishevelment, the way he never tightened his cravat or fastened his coat, as if he were too busy being cheerful to notice or care about such details.

Now they'd reached a clear understanding about his reasons for staying in Bath to help her, it was surprising how much she enjoyed his company. She'd known he'd felt guilty about leaving Anna to run Belles alone, but she hadn't realised quite *how* much, and his honesty endeared him to her more than she would have expected. As did his behaviour generally. They'd come to the park together with the boys for a couple of hours every afternoon that week, after which she took over the running of the shop and gave Nancy the rest of the day off, and his good nature had never once wavered.

After a week, there was still no sign or word of David, but Sebastian seemed determined to stop her from worrying, distracting both her and the boys with his so-called nautical training. Overall, it was surprisingly pleasant to have him as a friend. She felt as relaxed with him now as she had on the first night they'd met, so much that she was even wearing her blue dress today, having eventually decided that Nancy was right and it wasn't her fault or responsibility how anyone chose to interpret her clothes or behaviour. So why *shouldn't* she wear her favourite dress if she wanted? As for Mr Fortini specifically, she felt safe with him. She trusted him. Which meant that she could wear her best bonnet, too, for good measure!

She propped her shoulder against one of the gazebo columns and peered in through the archway. The boys were all sitting cross-legged on the floor while Sebastian crouched beside them, making corrections and smiling encouragement—*of course smiling*! He wasn't classically handsome by any means. His features were far too rough hewn and irregular for that, yet his lopsided smile made his face a thousand times more attractive than that of any other man she'd ever met. Which was exactly the sort of thing she ought *not* to think about a friend!

'Look, Aunt Henrietta!' Michael scrambled to his feet when he saw her, holding aloft a piece of string with a triumphant expression. 'It's called a cat's paw.'

'What a lovely name.' She bent over to admire it. 'That looks tricky.'

'*This* is the most important knot!' Peter held up his own piece of string. 'A bowline.'

'They're both very good.'

'And wait until you see this…' Sebastian gave Oliver a nudge. 'It's an overhand knot. One of the best I've ever seen.'

'Goodness me.' She made a show of examining each in turn. 'I hope you aren't planning to tie my feet together.'

'Umm…' Michael and Peter exchanged looks as if that was exactly what they'd been planning.

'Oh, dear.' She shook her head, looking around the gazebo at each of them in turn before her gaze settled on Sebastian and she smiled. It was a smile that seemed to come from deep within, as if her very heartstrings were tugging at the corners of her mouth. Maybe it was contagious, she thought, all this smiling. Despite her worries about David, at that moment she couldn't have stopped if she'd tried. She was aware, too, of a strangely dizzy feeling, as if the gazebo itself were spinning around. She actually had the bizarre impression that all her thoughts and feelings were up in the air, rearranging themselves somehow, and that when she stopped spinning and they settled down again, as they eventually had to, then nothing would ever be the same again.

It was outlandish and unexpected and alarming. And yet here she was, *still* smiling. And so was Sebastian. They were both smiling at each other. For almost a whole minute before Michael asked what they were doing.

'I enjoyed that.' Sebastian chuckled to himself as they walked home an hour later, the boys scampering ahead, still comparing and competing over who'd tied the strongest knots. 'It was just like old times.'

'They enjoyed it, too.' Henrietta turned her head to smile at him, that genuine smile that made him feel as if his lungs couldn't draw in enough air. She was looking exceptionally pulchritudinous today, he thought, like a rare and precious orchid escaped from a hothouse. She was dressed far less sombrely than on any of their previous excursions, too, in a blue-green gown the exact same shade as her eyes, not that he'd said so. Or allowed anything even remotely resembling a compliment to pass his lips, though it was getting harder and harder to stop himself. He must have thought at least a hundred complimentary things since he'd collected her a couple of hours before. Frankly, he was starting to wonder if he had masochistic tendencies, agreeing to simply be her friend.

'I'm afraid you're making life at sea sound far too appealing,' she went on, *still* smiling. 'No offence to the navy, but I'd rather keep the boys closer to home.'

'I recall my mother once saying something similar.'

'I'm not surprised. It must have been very hard for her when you left.' She winced. 'Sorry. I'm not trying to make you feel any guiltier.'

'I know. I suppose I just hoped she'd get used to the idea eventually. They say sailors' wives do.' He blinked at his own words. What on earth had made him say that? They'd been talking about mothers, not wives.

'Really?' She gave him a sideways look, so quickly that he couldn't catch her eye.

'They say it gets easier anyway.'

'I suppose it's just a different way of life.'

'Yes.'

'But it must still be lonely.' She seemed determined to look straight ahead now.

'I suppose so. Of course the men miss their wives, too.'

'Of course.'

'So it's hard for both of them.' He paused. 'I'm not sure it's the kind of marriage that I'd want for myself...' And why was he telling her that? 'Although my naval days are behind me.'

'They are?' This time, she *did* look at him. 'Have you decided for certain?'

'Yes.' He nodded firmly. 'I don't know what I'm going to do next, but it won't be the navy.'

'Oh.' There was a faint crease between her brows. 'I see.'

'You sound disappointed.'

'No, just surprised. Anna said you were so desperate to join.'

'When I was seventeen, yes, as soon as I could convince my father to let me go.'

'And you're an acting lieutenant already? You must be good at what you do.'

'It's easier to be promoted in wartime. My captain thought I had a talent for navigation so he made me a midshipman. Then, when we were short of officers, he promoted me to lieutenant.'

'Why were you short of officers?'

'Enemy action.'

'You mean in a battle?'

'Not quite. We were set on by a French Squadron a couple of years ago. Fortunately Captain Marlow hid us in a fog bank, but we sustained a lot of damage.'

'How frightening.' She shuddered. 'Is that why you were out of contact with the Admiralty for so long?'

'Not because of that, no.' He hesitated, tempted to tell her the truth, the things he hadn't told anyone, even James, but it was hard to find the words to begin...

'Forgive me.' She seemed to notice his expression. 'It's none of my business.'

'No, it's not that...' He slowed his pace, suddenly *wanting* to tell her. 'The reason we were out of contact started a few months later when we were sent in pursuit of a Spanish frigate. She led us across the Atlantic and down the coast of South America.'

'Around Cape Horn? I remember you said you were stuck in the Pacific for the past year.'

He grimaced, swallowing against a sudden constricting sensation in his throat. 'That wasn't *quite* true, I'm afraid. That is, we did round Cape Horn, but then the frigate turned around again. We never did find out why.'

'Oh.' She looked faintly puzzled.

'Forgive the deception. Only the truth is difficult to talk about.'

'Then you don't have to.'

'But I think I'd like to. You see, our Captain fell ill just off the coast of Brazil not long afterwards and we were forced to berth in the West Indies for him to get medical treatment. He was a good captain: honourable, strict, but fair, too. Unfortunately, his replacement, Captain Belton, was the opposite. He had no honour at all. He was a bully and a fool, determined to find the lost frigate and prove himself no matter what the cost. He got information that it had gone north so we followed, all the way up to Lower Canada, never mind that it was nearly winter and we were all practically freezing to the masts.'

'Couldn't you object?'

He made a face. 'Objecting isn't really an option in the navy. Naval vessels have a strict hierarchy. Obeying the chain of command is everything, even when the commands in question don't make any sense. There's only one punishment for mutiny.'

'But surely if he was endangering your lives...?'

'That's not something for the crew to decide. A ship's doctor can diagnose madness, but stupidity isn't the same thing, not in the Admiralty's eyes anyway.' He shook his head. 'We were off the coast of Newfoundland when a blizzard set in. We were blown off course into a bay and trapped. *Literally* trapped. When the storm abated, the ship was held fast by ice.'

'How terrifying.'

'As I recall, I was too cold to feel a great deal of anything except numb. Fortunately, at that point our worthy captain decided to barricade himself in his cabin.'

'Fortunately?'

'It left smarter men in charge. We'd restocked on provisions in the West Indies so we had enough food to wait for a thaw and we all stayed below deck together, trying to keep warm and desperately hoping the ice wouldn't crush the ship. It wasn't easy. Some of the men came close to despair. Most of the boys, too. They tried to act like men, but they were frightened.'

'Like Peter is now?' She tightened her grip on his arm.

'No wonder you're so good with him. I think those boys were lucky to have someone like you with them.'

'I don't know. I tried my best to keep their hopes up, but I felt so powerless, as if I were failing them. But we were lucky and survived. Any further north and we'd have been done for. A few men lost fingers and toes to frostbite, but after a few months, we were able to escape.'

'So that's why Anna didn't hear from you for so long?'

'Yes. We made it back to the West Indies eventually, but needless to say, the Admiralty wasn't impressed. We were forbidden from sending messages home while there was an investigation, but in the end the whole thing was hushed up.'

'But wasn't your captain punished?'

'Retired.' He gave her a pointed look. 'His brother is a marquess.'

'Ah... So then you came home?'

'*Then* we had to wait for the ship to be repaired, but, yes, then I came home.'

'Well, that explains it.'

'Explains what?'

'Why you always dress as though it's the middle of summer.'

He chuckled. 'I believe there are parts of my body now permanently immune to the cold.'

'You still shouldn't be careless about it,' she scolded him. 'I'm going to knit you a scarf.'

'Really?' He felt both surprised and pleased by the idea. 'I'd like that.'

'Yes. What's your favourite colour?'

'Blue,' he answered without hesitation. Which was funny because up until that moment he'd always thought it was red. And they were standing outside Belles, he realised suddenly. He hadn't even noticed that they'd reached it, although he'd seen the boys go inside.

'Blue it is.' She moved closer to him, so close that every inch of his body seemed to tingle with awareness. He was vividly aware of the heavy thud of his own heartbeat. Any closer and she would be, too. 'I'm glad you made it back to England safely.'

'So am I.' He made a conscious effort to keep his voice steady. 'Although I'd rather not share the details with my family, at least not yet. Since I wasn't here to help them, I'd rather they thought I was away doing something useful. I don't want them feeling sorry for me either.'

'I understand.' She smiled softly. 'Thank you for telling me.'

'Well... I ought to be going.' He inclined his head, reluctant to leave after sharing something so personal, although he hated saying goodbye to her in general, he realised, even when it was only for an hour or two. If the past week was any indication, he'd be craving her company again in a few minutes, but she had a business to run and he had more taverns to visit and they were *just friends*, dammit. All of which meant that he ought to be going.

Gently, he untucked her hand from the crook of his arm and lifted it to his lips. He did it every time he left, but this time he did it more slowly than usual, half expecting her to pull away, but she didn't. Instead her eyes widened and flickered with a distinctly *un*friend-like expression, the pupils swelling slightly as his lips touched the back of her glove. And why kissing fabric felt so damnably erotic at that moment, he had no idea.

'Yes.' Her voice sounded breathy. 'Until tomorrow then.'

He took a step backwards and nearly ran down the street.

Chapter Eleven

Henrietta watched Sebastian through the glass pane of the shop door as he walked, surprisingly quickly, down the street. The dizzy, disorientated sensation she'd felt in the gazebo was back and stronger than ever. When he'd kissed her hand she'd actually felt as if her insides were trembling, a rush of heat coursing wildly through her veins straight to her abdomen. It felt new and exciting and shockingly wanton. As wanton as she'd once been accused of being. As wanton as...no, she'd never been wanton with Mr Hoxley. As wanton as she imagined a woman might feel for a man she cared about. Whatever she'd felt in the past was nothing compared to this. She didn't even know what *this* was, but she had a suspicion it might be desire...

She placed her forehead against the glass to cool down. Even now, her pulse was still racing, hard and fast, and her legs were shaking, as if she'd been sitting on them for too long and they'd gone numb. She only hoped that Sebastian hadn't noticed the effect he'd had on her limbs. It would be too mortifyingly ironic after the way she'd behaved towards him on that first day. It already *was* too ironic. She'd condemned him because she'd thought he'd been trying to flirt with her and now here she was tempted to flirt with him!

She didn't know which was worse, the irony itself or the fact that she'd been wrong about his intentions and he was only helping her to make amends to his sister and because of the boys he thought that he'd failed on his ship. Both of which were even more reasons to like him! It was all such a tangle...

'Nancy?' she called out, unable to unravel the skein at that moment. Maybe she'd try later, when she was in bed and had time to think, although thinking about him in bed probably wasn't such a good idea either... 'Are you in the kitchen?'

'I'm here.' Nancy came hurrying through from the hallway abruptly, marching up to the shop door and turning over the *Closed* sign before drawing one of the bolts. 'But we need to close for a while.'

'Why? Are you all right?'

'I'm fine. Only somebody else isn't.'

'David!' Henrietta gasped and started towards the kitchen.

'Not him.' Nancy caught at her arm, lowering her voice to an undertone. 'Remember the woman from the street?'

'Ye-es.'

'She says you offered her help.'

'I suppose so, but she ran away.'

'Well, apparently she's changed her mind.'

'Oh.' Henrietta took a deep breath. Her meeting with the woman seemed like such a long time ago now, but an offer was an offer... 'Where are the boys?'

'I sent them upstairs to play.'

'Right.' She straightened her spine. 'Well, hopefully it won't be anything too difficult.'

'Oh, I don't know. I thought we could do with some fresh challenges.'

Nancy threw her a speaking look before striding back through to the kitchen. The woman was sitting at the table, twisting her fingers together and looking more than a little nervous, although she'd removed her cloak and bonnet, Henrietta noticed, which at least suggested she wasn't about to run away again.

'Hello.' She gave a warm smile as she sat down opposite. 'I understand that you'd like to take up my offer of help?'

'Yes.' The woman bobbed her head so vigorously that a couple of sable-coloured tendrils escaped from her bun. 'If you're still willing, that is?'

'Of course. Might I ask your name?'

'Bel...' the woman hesitated '...linda. *Belinda.* It's not my real name, but...'

'But it's the one we'll use. I understand. I'm Henrietta and you've already met Nancy. Now, why don't you tell us what we can do to help?'

'Well...' The woman put her hands flat on the table as if she were bracing herself. 'I'm looking for a lady who lives in the boarding house opposite, a Miss Foster. She's a former governess, *my* former governess, and this is the last address I have for her. I've been waiting outside, hoping to catch her one day on the street, but it's been almost two weeks and I haven't had as much as a glimpse. I waited for five hours yesterday.' She paused for breath. 'Do you know her?'

'I'm afraid not.' Henrietta threw a quick glance at Nancy, who also shook her head. 'Forgive me, but why don't you simply ask the proprietor?'

'Because I can't.' The woman dropped her gaze to her hands. 'There's a chance that they've been told to look out for a woman like me asking questions and if they were to report back on my whereabouts...' She swallowed and looked up again. 'I haven't done anything criminal, I promise, but I can't take the risk of being seen. It's hazardous enough waiting on the street. Now I don't know what to do. I had it all planned out when I...' She stopped and bit her lip.

'When you ran away?' Nancy prodded her.

'Yes,' she admitted, rubbing a palm over her cheek as tears trickled down her face. 'I made my way here by stagecoach, but I only had enough money for a couple of weeks. Now it's almost run out and there's still no sign of Miss Foster.'

'Right then.' Nancy clapped her hands together. 'Give me five minutes.'

'What?' Belinda got halfway up from the table. 'Where are you going?'

'To find out if she's still there.'

'But if you ask questions they might get suspicious.'

'Not of me they won't. I'll take a basket so it looks as though I'm making a delivery and it's not as if they'll mistake my description for yours.' Nancy tugged at her copper-red curls. 'Don't worry.'

'It'll be all right.' Henrietta gestured for Belinda to sit down again as Nancy tramped out through the back door. 'She's one of the cleverest people I know and she doesn't take no for an answer. Now let's have some tea while we wait, shall we?'

'Thank you.' Belinda gave her a tremulous smile, her cheeks still damp, when Henrietta came back with two cups. 'I truly am sorry to involve you.'

'There's no need to be sorry.' She shook her head reassuringly, recalling something similar she'd said to Sebastian. 'We all have our burdens. It helps to share them if we can.'

'I don't want to get you into any trouble.'

'You mean with your family?'

'No.' Belinda gave a short laugh. 'I doubt my family care where I am. They won't want to see me again, not now.'

'Then who?'

'I...' She sounded hesitant. 'I'm afraid I can't say. All I can tell you is that I did something foolish.'

'Ah.' Henrietta slid a hand across the table. 'Well, we all make mistakes sometimes.'

'Yes, but this was a very big one.' Belinda sobbed and then hiccupped. 'I'm sorry. I'm not usually so emotional. It's just been such a worry, waiting and watching and—'

'She's not there!' Nancy flung the back door open dramatically.

'What do you mean?' Henrietta squeezed their new companion's hand, alarmed by the way all the blood seemed to have drained from her face.

'I mean that she left a month ago, only not as Miss Foster. She's Mrs Sheridan now, and who knows where on her honeymoon.'

'Oh, no!' Belinda's face turned positively ashen. 'She was my last hope. What will I do now?'

'Don't panic for a start.' Nancy deposited her basket on one of the counters. 'That never does any good at all.'

'But how can I not?'

'Where are you staying?' Henrietta tried a more sensitive approach.

'At another boarding house on Tibberton Street. I've told

the proprietor that I'm a governess between jobs, looking for a new position, but I think he's suspicious about me.'

'Of course he's suspicious.' Nancy gave a snort. 'Your cloak alone must be worth twenty pounds.'

'Is it so obvious?'

'Yes. Everything you're wearing is much too expensive for a governess.'

'Oh, dear.' Belinda looked crestfallen. 'I've never run away before.'

'Obviously.'

'Nancy.' Henrietta gave her a chiding look. 'It's not Belinda's fault.'

'I never said that it was, but it's obvious she's not going to survive on her own—and I'm not saying that's her fault either.' She held her hands up as she flopped down into a chair. 'Ladies aren't taught how to survive because men don't want them to find out the truth: that they can live perfectly happy and independent lives without them. *That's* why they're taught embroidery and opera instead of anything useful. I mean, what use is piano playing in the real world?'

'Nancy, this might not be the best time...'

'So, as far as I can see, there's only one thing we can do.'

'What?' Henrietta and Belinda asked together.

'We can give her a job here in the afternoons.' Nancy spoke as if the answer ought to be obvious. 'It's actually the perfect solution now you have the boys to take care of. Then I won't be working on my own and she'll have the money to pay her rent until...well, until she learns how to stand on her own two feet.'

'But she's a lady! Sorry.' Henrietta threw Belinda an apologetic look. 'But a lady like most of our customers. What if one of them recognises her?'

'They won't,' Belinda chimed in eagerly. 'I don't know anyone.'

'Anyone?'

'*Hardly* anyone.'

'There you go.' Nancy folded her arms with a look of satisfaction. '*Problem* solved.'

'Can I really have a job?' Belinda's expression was pleading.

Henrietta opened her mouth, closed it again, considered and then gave an exasperated laugh. 'Oh, very well, the more the merrier. Welcome to Belles.'

Chapter Twelve

'And *that's* how Nelson escaped the polar bear!' Sebastian concluded his story with a bow in the middle of the street.

'That *can't* be true.' Michael turned to Henrietta for support. 'He just made that story up, didn't he?'

'Upon my honour as a sailor, it's all true.' He put a hand on his heart. 'Or at least that's what I've heard.'

'So his musket misfired and he fought it with the other end like a club?'

'Exactly! I'm not saying it was one of his better ideas, but he was only fourteen so we ought to make allowances.'

'It seems very convenient that the ice broke up and he was able to escape.' Henrietta looked somewhat sceptical, too. 'Are you certain Nelson didn't make that story up himself?'

'Embellished, maybe. Who knows, but he was certainly brave enough for it. Ask anyone who served with him at the Battle of the Nile. *Or* Copenhagen. *Or* Trafalgar. He was wounded in combat three times.'

'Did he really lose an eye?' Michael's expression turned slightly bloodthirsty.

'No, just the sight in it, but he did lose most of one arm. That's enough, don't you think?'

'I want to be just like him,' Peter announced, somewhat incongruously. 'But I have to hurry. He was a captain before he was twenty-one.'

'You have ten years.' Henrietta laughed. 'That sounds like plenty of time to me.'

'But we'll accelerate your training anyway. This afternoon's subject: map-reading!' Sebastian winked and then grinned at the boy's happy expression. A week and a day into his new routine, he was surprised to discover that despite his *friend* status, he was actually enjoying himself. Being a nursemaid wasn't a career he'd ever contemplated before, but it felt good to be doing something useful again.

In the mornings he picked up the boys from Belles, escorted them across the city to school, then collected them again for excursions in the afternoons, usually accompanied by Henrietta. In his spare time, he visited old acquaintances, helped James in his store and continued to make enquiries about David, so far without any success. Although he hadn't yet told Henrietta, it seemed increasingly likely that her brother had left Bath altogether.

'Will you teach us to row?' Peter asked as they approached the school yard.

'Yes, as soon as you've learned how to swim. Unfortunately, November's a little cold for that.'

'Then will you teach us in the spring?'

'Mr Fortini has other places he needs to visit.' Henrietta leaned forward. She'd joined them that morning to do some shopping and was walking on Sebastian's other side with Oliver holding on to each of their hands and swinging between.

'But he said he'd stay as long as you needed him!'

'He *did*?'

'I did,' Sebastian confirmed, trying to sound casual despite her obvious surprise.

'Oh…well…here we are.' She gestured towards the front door of the school. 'Have a good morning.'

'Yes, Aunt.'

'Goodbye!'

'Sorry about that.' Henrietta looked apologetically at Sebastian after they'd all scurried inside. 'You know, you mustn't feel obliged to stay and help us.'

'So you keep saying.'

'But surely you want to go and visit your family soon?'

'Ye-es.' He felt a stab of guilt at the words. He really ought to be heading north, but somehow he couldn't bring himself to leave Bath either. 'I've had a letter from my mother, as it happens.'

'Oh? How is she?'

'Very well. Only it seems that Anna isn't in Derbyshire at all. The Earl's grandfather is ill and they've gone to stay with him.'

'Oh, dear. I'm afraid that sounds serious. He seemed very frail the last time I saw him.'

'Apparently it is. So Anna is in Retford, although my mother still urges me to visit her and my…' he clenched his jaw, steeling himself to say the words '…my grandmother and uncle in Yorkshire.'

'Don't you want to?' She looked at him curiously.

'I suppose so.' He pressed two fingers against the bridge of his nose and squeezed. 'It's just that I never imagined a reconciliation was even possible. It's hard to accept a family I've never met before, especially given the circumstances.'

'From what Anna told me, your grandmother never wanted the estrangement in the first place, but your grandfather was very proud.' She placed a hand on his arm with a sympathetic expression. 'There may be more to the story than you think.'

'Perhaps.' He resisted the urge to put his own hand on top of hers. 'But it's still hard to feel enthusiastic, especially when...' he paused, trying to think of a way to finish the sentence that didn't involve mentioning her '...when Bath is my home. I feel as though I'm just settling back in.'

'I'm sure— Oh!' She came to a halt abruptly.

'Henrietta?' He turned to her in alarm. Her expression looked strained all of a sudden, as if her skin was pulled too tightly across her cheekbones. 'Are you all right?'

'Yes. No. I just didn't realise we were walking this way.'

'I thought it would make a nice change.'

'Yes, but...' She looked up at him and then quickly away. 'Can we take another route?'

'Of course, but what's the matter?' He looked up and down the street, trying to work out what had upset her. Everything looked perfectly normal to him.

'The shop where I used to work is over there.' Her voice sounded noticeably smaller than before.

'Ah.' He followed the direction of her gaze. 'I understand. In that case, we'll go another way.'

'Thank you.'

'So...what do you need to buy?' Sebastian asked, discreetly changing the subject after a few minutes of walking in silence. 'Now that we're out shopping.'

'Hmm?' She sounded preoccupied. 'Oh, new stockings for the boys. I've given up on Oliver's.'

'Redbourne's, then?'

'Yes. I thought I might buy us something nice for tea, too. You're obviously invited, only…'

'James isn't?'

'I'm afraid I wouldn't dare.' She made an apologetic face. 'Once Nancy makes up her mind about a person, there's not much anyone else can do about it.'

'It's strange. I've tried asking what she's got against him, but he won't say a word.'

'I'm sure it's all a big misunderstanding. I can't imagine him doing anything hurtful.'

'Neither can I. And speaking of James…' Sebastian raised a hand as they entered the shop.

'You again?' His old friend looked up from a ledger book and grinned. 'I thought you were out for the day?'

'Stockings.'

'I beg your pardon?'

'I need them for the boys,' Henrietta interjected. 'I'll just be a moment.'

'So…' James gave Sebastian a subtle nudge in the ribs as Henrietta walked across to a different counter. 'Still *just* friends?'

'Trying to be. It's not easy, but it's all she wants.'

'Ah. Well, I'm not the man to give advice about unrequited affection, I'm afraid, although spending so much time with her might not be the best thing for your sanity.'

'I know. Only I'm not sure leaving would do me any good either. *And* I made a promise.'

'To her?'

'To one of her nephews. So…' He spread his hands out in a futile gesture. 'I can't go anywhere, sane or not.'

'All done.' Henrietta came back with a full basket and a smile. 'I'm glad we bumped into you, Mr Redbourne. Sebastian told me you've been helping him look for David.'

'Yes. I only wish we'd had more success.'

'You still tried and I'm grateful.'

'Well then…' Sebastian found himself offering his arm, vaguely irritated by the way she was smiling at his friend. 'We'd better get back to Belles.'

'And I'd better get back to work.' James lifted an eyebrow before smiling at Henrietta. 'Good day, Miss Gardiner.'

'Mr Redbourne.'

Henrietta gave Sebastian a quizzical look as they stepped back on to the pavement. 'Are you in a hurry?'

'Me? No, but I thought you might want to check up on your new assistant. What does she call herself again? Belinda?'

'Yes… Wait! How do you know that's not her real name?'

'Bel-linda?'

'Oh… All right, it's not.'

'Belinda Smith, by any chance?'

'No.' Her lips twitched. 'Belinda Carr. And she's doing very well in the shop. As for the baking…she's learning.'

'As bad as that?'

She lifted her shoulders as if she were trying to be charitable. 'She's doing her best, but it might take a while. Nancy and I are taking turns to give her lessons, but we haven't had much success so far. I don't think she's ever set foot in a kitchen before, let alone prepared any food.' A small giggle escaped her. 'You should have seen her face the first time she saw the rolling pin. I think she thought Nancy was about to attack her.'

'Knowing Miss MacQueen, that's surely a reasonable assumption?'

'Nancy wouldn't hurt a fly.'

'I beg to differ. She tipped me off a sofa, remember?'

'Only because she thought you were a burglar.'

'A burglar who takes a nap on the job?'

'She probably didn't have time to consider that. What I mean is that Nancy wouldn't hurt a fly unless the fly deserved it. Which she thought you did at the time.'

'True.' He chuckled. 'Fortunately Belinda seems to have got off to a better start. I suppose there's no point in my telling you she might be a fugitive?'

'She's not a fugitive. She says she hasn't broken any laws.'

'And you believe her?'

'Yes. She's obviously in some kind of trouble, but if she doesn't want to tell us the details then I'm sure she has good reasons and I know Anna would think the same. Everyone deserves a second chance.'

'That's very trusting of you.' He gave her a sidelong glance as they approached Belles. 'But then I suppose you'd understand more than most.'

'What do you mean?' She froze mid-step.

'About second chances...' He could have kicked himself for the words. 'I mean because Anna trusted you.'

'Why *wouldn't* Anna have trusted me?' She pulled her hand away from his arm, twisting sharply to face him.

'No reason.' He cleared his throat when she continued to stare. 'Just a turn of phrase.'

'A turn of phrase...' She seemed to go very still as she repeated the words. Which was curious because she was

already still, but there seemed to be a new tension about her, too, suddenly, as if she were suppressing some powerful emotion. 'Then tell me this...' Her voice was clipped now. 'What did you mean about *understanding*?'

'Pardon?' He had an urgent desire to escape from the conversation.

'Ten minutes ago when I didn't want to walk past my old shop, you said that you understood, but I never told you why I left. So *what* do you understand?'

'I heard a rumour, that's all.'

'What *kind* of rumour?'

Sebastian glanced at the pavement, vaguely wishing a chasm might open up beneath his feet, big enough for him to hide in. 'Something about you and the owner's son.'

'Something such as?'

He groaned inwardly. Really, it didn't have to be a chasm. A reasonable-sized hole would suffice. 'All right. I heard that you were caught in some kind of indiscretion and that his mother accused you of being a fortune hunter and threw you out without references. Which is what I meant about Anna giving you a second chance, but I wasn't condemning you. I'm sure it wasn't as bad as it sounded and you must have been very young when it happened.'

'So you're *not* condemning me?' She lifted a finger and poked him hard in the chest, her whole body shaking as if she were cold. 'How *generous* of you, especially in the light of such overwhelming evidence as gossip and speculation.'

'I didn't say—'

'You've said quite enough! Forgive me if I don't care to listen to any more. Good day!'

'Hen—'

'I said good day!'

'Damn it.' He took a few seconds to vent his feelings before following inside, but there was already no sign of her. He judged by the sound of stomping footsteps, however, that she was already halfway up the stairs.

'Where do you think you're going?' Nancy jumped out from behind the counter, blocking his way as he went in pursuit.

'I need to talk to Henrietta.'

'Why? What did you do?'

'I said the wrong thing, obviously.'

'About?'

'About what happened, what she was accused of doing at the dressmaker's.'

'You mentioned *that*?' Nancy looked appalled. 'Why?'

'I didn't intend to mention it. We just happened to walk that way by accident and it came up and…please—' he gestured towards the staircase '—let me talk to her.'

'No. In case it isn't already obvious, she doesn't want to talk to you.'

'I need to apologise.'

'You need to do more than that.' Nancy's eyes flashed. 'Didn't it ever occur to you that the rumours you've heard *weren't* true?'

'I told her I was sure it wasn't as bad as it sounded and—' He stopped talking, struck with the distinct impression that Miss MacQueen was about to throw a fist at his head.

'If that's the best you can do, then you should turn around and leave right now.' From the sound of it, her teeth were gritted. 'If you weren't Anna's brother, I'd throw you out myself. Henrietta never set her cap at Roy Willerby. He was besotted with her! Only she wasn't good enough for his mother so once the old bat found out, she gave Henrietta her marching orders. Without references, too, just to make it look as though it was all her fault.

'And do you know what else?' Nancy advanced a few steps towards him, standing on her tiptoes to speak into his face. 'Even after his mother threw her out, Mr Willerby *still* wanted to marry her. She could have married him just to spite his mother and to have a place to live, too! But she didn't because she didn't care about him that way. Instead, she searched and searched for a job until finally your sister was smart enough to give her the benefit of the doubt. Unlike *some* people I could mention.'

'I see.' Sebastian felt his gut clench at the accusation. It was a fair one. He hadn't necessarily assumed that Henrietta was guilty, just that there had been some grain of truth in the rumours...

'Look...' Nancy's expression relented a tiny bit. 'You seem—*seemed*—different. You've been a lot of help with the boys and as far as I can tell you've behaved decently, too. Most men take one look at her and their minds go straight to one thing, and because she's a shop girl they think they can get it, too. That's why she doesn't like compliments, in case you were still wondering. She's learnt her lesson about men the hard way. So if that's all you're after—'

'It's not,' he interrupted her. 'We're friends.'

'Are you sure? Because I've seen the way you two look at each other. You may be helping her with the boys, but maybe it's time you started thinking about your intentions, too.'

'My intentions?' Sebastian ran a hand over his jaw. The whole situation struck him as ludicrous. Here he was, standing in his own family's shop, being challenged by a woman younger than him, barring his way with an expression as ferocious as Boudicca herself. As for the matter of intentions, Henrietta had made it very clear that anything besides friendship was out of the question, so unless she'd changed her mind... And what had Miss MacQueen just said? *The way you two look at each other*, not the way *he* looked at *her*...

'In any case...' Nancy continued as the shop door opened to admit an elderly couple '...you can go and do your thinking elsewhere. She doesn't want to speak with you at the moment.'

Sebastian bowed his head, feigning agreement before darting past the counter and up the stairs before Nancy could let out as much as a squeak of protest. He wouldn't have long, he knew, but if he could just find Henrietta before Miss MacQueen found him... *Had* she changed her mind? His pulse quickened at the thought. Because if she had, then he'd be more than happy to oblige. And he couldn't wait another minute to find out...

Chapter Thirteen

Sebastian reached the landing in less than three seconds. Unfortunately, there was no sign of Henrietta in the parlour so he carried on up to the next floor, the one he was least acquainted with. Despite growing up above the shop, he'd never spent a great deal of time in either of the two bedrooms—his own sleeping arrangements being a truckle bed in the parlour—but the staircase was still familiar enough for him not to feel strange about going there. Which, in retrospect, was probably a mistake, but then discretion had never been one of his strong suits.

'I'm sor—'

He skidded to a halt, stopped in his tracks by the sight of Henrietta standing just inside her bedroom door, the grey gown she'd been wearing that morning draped over a chair while her yellow shop dress was only halfway over her hips.

'What—?' She jerked her head up at the sound of his voice, her expression turning swiftly from anger to shock to anger again before she reached a hand out and slammed the door in his face. Fortunately, his nose was far enough away this time *not* to suffer injury, although he had a feeling she wouldn't have hesitated if it hadn't been. She might actually have preferred it.

Double damn. He closed his eyes and pressed his forehead against the wood. That hadn't been supposed to happen. He'd come to apologise, not to ogle, to tell her he wasn't like the other men Miss MacQueen had mentioned, but he had a horrible sinking feeling that he'd just lost the moral high ground on that one. Still, since it *had* happened, he couldn't quite bring himself to regret it either—and he definitely wasn't going to forget it any time soon.

Not only had she been half dressed, but her undergarments had been in a state of considerable disarray, in all the right places in his opinion. The way her breasts had been popping out of her chemise as she'd bent over had made the view nothing short of mesmerising. It was probably fortunate that he'd had only a few short seconds to appreciate it since his body had come dangerously close to combusting as it was. He had a feeling the memory alone was going to heat his blood for some time to come.

He was still leaning against the door, wondering what to do next, when it opened again abruptly, sending him toppling forwards into the room and on top of a now fully clad Henrietta, knocking her off balance like a domino and sending them both stumbling towards the bed.

'Wait!' It was a foolish thing for him to say, Sebastian thought, even as the word left his mouth. *Wait?* It wasn't as if there was anything she—or he—could do to arrest their fall, though he made a valiant attempt to minimise injury none the less, curling one arm behind her back and managing to twist them both sideways so that they landed side by side rather than with his full weight on top of her.

'Sorry.' It was his second useless word in a row, he realised, staring into her eyes, which he couldn't help but do since their noses were only an inch apart and their bodies were even closer, pressed intimately together with his arm squashed between her breast and the mattress. 'I was leaning against the door.'

'I noticed.' She skewered him with a look though her cheeks were flaming red.

'I didn't know you were changing your clothes.' He felt an additional need to explain. 'Are you all right?'

'It's a mattress.'

'Good point. Here, let me…' He shuffled his body backwards, trying not to notice the soft weight of her breast against his arm, and stood up, offering her a hand which she pointedly ignored.

He coughed, racking his brains to remember why he'd gone up there in the first place. 'I really am sorry.'

'So you said.' She rolled herself to a sitting position.

'Not just about that—about all of it. That's why I'm here, to apologise. Don't blame Nancy.' He held a hand up as she opened her mouth. 'I waited until she was distracted. She'll probably be here to throw books at me any second.'

'I would never blame Nancy.' She didn't smile at the joke. 'You shouldn't have followed me.'

'You're right, but I wanted to explain. I should never have listened to gossip.'

'No, you shouldn't have.' She turned her face away with quiet dignity. 'I trusted you. I *thought* we were friends.'

'We are.'

'Friends don't think things like that about each other. They're supposed to know each other better!'

'I didn't think about it, not really. It didn't matter to me what happened.'

'It matters to me!'

'I know. I'm not explaining myself well. What I mean is that I knew it wasn't who you were. *Are.*' He paused. 'Nancy says it was the other way round and Mr Willerby was in love with you.'

She gave a short laugh. 'No, he only thought that he was.'

'What makes you so sure?'

'Because we never had a single real conversation. All he ever did was stare at me and tell me how pretty I was. He never asked me a single question about where I came from or what I liked to do. It was as though I was just another mannequin in the shop window.'

'If his mother was the owner, then she ought to have done something to stop him.'

'She blamed me.' Henrietta pressed her lips together tight and then sighed. 'And maybe I wasn't entirely blameless. Maybe I was friendlier than I ought to have been, but I thought I was being polite. No one ever told me that smiling was a bad thing!'

'It's not. It wasn't your fault.' He reached for her hand, but she stood up, stalking across the room away from him.

'Yes, it was! Because I didn't learn my lesson even then. I kept on smiling because I was young and foolish and flattered by compliments. Anna tried to warn me it could get me into more trouble, but I didn't listen. I didn't understand that my appearance was all most men ever saw or cared about. I didn't realise that they'd take a smile for a promise either.'

He tensed. 'What do you mean?'

She looked back at him, her jaw muscles clenched tight. 'Do you remember what I told you about the Earl's friend, Mr Hoxley? He came to the shop a few times to see me. He was handsome and charming and I liked him better than any man I'd ever met before. I knew he was a gentleman, but I was still naive enough to believe in daydreams and I thought he truly liked me, too.'

'What happened?' Sebastian heard his voice darken. Hearing another man described as handsome and charming was bad enough, but he had a feeling he was about to get even angrier.

'One day he invited me to meet him alone. He said he had something important to ask me and stupidly I believed him. I even lied to Anna about where I was going. I felt terrible about it, but I was so excited. I thought that he wanted to marry me like Mr Willerby, only it turned out he had much baser motives. It never occurred to me that he meant to seduce me, but fortunately a lady, the Earl's grandmother, in fact, intervened. She made his intentions *very* clear.'

'I see.' He was clenching his fists, Sebastian realised, so hard he could feel his fingernails digging into his palms.

'So there it is. Yes, I've been foolish and naive in the past, but I changed on that day with Mr Hoxley. I *stopped* smiling at men. I stopped doing anything that could be taken for flirtation or encouragement. I've done everything I can to prove I'm not the woman the rumours paint me as and yet people still want to believe the worst! I'm not a flirt and I would *never* try to seduce a man into marriage.'

'I know.' Several aspects of her behaviour all made sense at once. 'That's why you objected to me calling you beautiful that first day, wasn't it? You were afraid I was trying to flirt with you?'

'Yes.' Her chin jutted upwards a notch. 'I thought that maybe I'd given you the wrong impression during the night and that was why you'd invited me to walk with you.'

'And the clothes?'

Another notch. 'They weren't so bad.'

'They weren't good either.'

'That was the whole point!' She glared at him. 'I didn't want to look good. I didn't want to be flattered. Sometimes it feels as though I'm wearing a mask that no one wants to take off because they don't care what's underneath. As if there isn't anything underneath.' Her eyes glinted, but with pain, not anger. 'You know, when enough people treat you like that, you start to wonder if they're right and you *are* empty inside. But I'm not. I'm more than my face. I've made myself more than that and I won't be treated like an ornament to be possessed or used ever again. I want to be seen for my whole self.'

'I *can* see you.' He moved towards her, but she swayed backwards. 'Henrietta, I'm not like those other men, I promise. I don't want to possess or to use you.'

She shook her head sadly. 'When we became friends I thought that maybe I'd been too suspicious and you really were an honourable man, but now it turns out you've been thinking the worst about me this whole time!' Her eyelashes quivered. 'Tell me the truth. Is *that* the real reason you're still here?'

'You know that's not true.'

'Do I? Or did you think that if you helped with my nephews then I'd repay you somehow?'

'No! I've told you why I want to help.'

'So you *don't* want anything else?'

'No.' He stopped and frowned, compelled to be honest. 'Yes, but not like that. Truthfully, I've wanted to kiss you from the first moment I saw you, but you made it clear that you only wanted friendship and I would never abuse that, but it doesn't stop me from finding you attractive. *You*, that is, not just your face. Yes, you're beautiful. That night when we first met, I thought you were the most perfect-looking woman I'd ever seen. I thought that it was impossible to imagine anyone more beautiful, but none of that would matter a damn if it wasn't for who you are inside. Your beauty is in your heart and soul. It's in the way you care for your nephews, the way you let Nancy rant whenever she wants to, the way you help strangers who stand outside your shop looking hungry. *That's* the real you. That's why you're even more beautiful to me now.' He paused. 'But you're not perfect.'

She blinked and then stared at him, her eyes wide with a look that he couldn't interpret. 'I'm not?'

'No, I only thought so at first.' He took a cautious step forward, only this time she didn't move away. 'The fact is, one of your eyes is a slightly greener shade than the other, your laugh can be a little too high-pitched and you smooth your hair much too often.'

'What's wrong with smoothing my hair? I like to be neat.'

'I've noticed, but some people could argue that you're a little *too* neat, especially when you're standing next to a ruffian with a bruised nose. It's enough to make a man feel self-conscious.'

'Oh.' Her lips parted slowly. 'And you're not just saying all this to make me feel better?'

'Yes and no. I can want to make you feel better and mean it, too, can't I?'

She frowned as if the idea had never struck her before. 'I suppose so.'

'Just like I can think that you're beautiful and see more than your face?'

'Ye-es.' Her breathing sounded erratic now, almost as ragged as his own. 'Then you really want me? The real me?'

'Yes. Quite a lot, in fact, but I thought you only wanted friendship?'

'I did.' She swallowed, drawing her tongue lightly across her top lip. 'Before...'

'Before?' His pulse thudded at the word.

'Before I got to know you.' Her eyes widened even further, as if she were trying to hypnotise him again. 'But how do I know you're telling the truth? I couldn't bear to make another mistake.'

'Then I won't be a mistake.' He lifted his hands to her face, cradling her cheeks between his fingers. 'I promise you, Henrietta, but I won't kiss you unless you want me to...'

Henrietta caught her breath, trying to get her swirling thoughts into some kind of coherent order, though it seemed impossible when Sebastian was standing so close, his lips within a hair's breadth of hers, his gaze smouldering with desire and the promise he'd just made her. The feeling of his hands on her cheeks raised gooseflesh on her skin, making her mouth feel dry and her heart skip one, if not several, beats. He'd just said that he liked her. He'd just said that he wanted to kiss her, too. The words ought to have sent her running and yet, for the first time in what felt like a long time, they didn't. Because she trusted him. She knew that in as much as she knew anything at that moment—so much that the whisper was past her lips before she even realised she was speaking.

'I want you, too.'

She didn't have to wait long for his response. The words were barely out of her mouth before his lips brushed against hers, soft and warm and gentle, as if he half expected her to pull away. Instead she kissed him back and it was more, much more, than the moderately pleasant feeling she'd experienced the one time she'd kissed Mr Hoxley. She felt as though her body had just come to life, as though she really were an ice queen and her frozen limbs were melting to liquid.

Her heart was racing a mile to the minute, too, making her feel vulnerable and strangely powerful at the same time, and she was aware of a strange mewling sound in the back of her throat as Sebastian's hand moved to the small of her back, drawing her body against his and kissing her even more deeply... It was bliss, it was perfect, it was how she'd always imagined being kissed...

They both jumped, his arm tightening protectively around her waist at the sound of a thud, followed by a splash and two loud squeals from below.

'*What—?*'

They both exclaimed in unison, exchanging startled glances before rushing down the stairs and through the hallway to find Nancy and Belinda standing side by side in the middle of the kitchen, the former soaking wet and the latter covered from head to toe in white powder.

'Oh!' Henrietta slapped a hand over her mouth in surprise. 'Oh, dear.'

'I dropped the flour,' Belinda explained, unnecessarily, putting her hands to her cheeks and making them look even worse. 'I didn't notice Nancy come in and I turned around and we bumped into one another and...' Flour-covered hands moved to her forehead. 'I'll clear it up, I promise, every last speck.'

'Don't worry. There's no point in crying over spilt...you know.' Henrietta gave a reassuring smile, though unfortunately Sebastian was less charitable, his laughter clearly audible behind her.

'*You.*' Nancy pointed a finger accusingly. 'This is all your fault.'

'Me? How?' He sounded faintly aggrieved.

'Because I was rushing to get a bucket of water to hurl over *you*! You had no right to run past me!'

'Then this serves you right, doesn't it?' He chuckled again. 'I'd call that poetic justice.'

'Do you know what else you can call it?' Nancy started forward, arms pumping as if she were about to throw more than a bucket.

'Wait! You'd better go and change.' Henrietta stepped swiftly between them. 'And Belinda should go outside and brush herself down. I'll start to clean up.'

'While I watch the shop,' Sebastian volunteered.

'No!' Nancy stopped and folded her soggy arms. 'This is the last straw. We can't go on like this, what with looking after the boys and teaching Belinda to bake and *him* visiting every five minutes.' She threw another belligerent look at Sebastian. 'The shop isn't big enough for all of us.'

'I know.' Henrietta sighed. 'But what's the alternative?'

'You can come north with me.'

'What?' She spun towards Sebastian, uncertain about which of them had just gasped the loudest, her or Belinda or even Nancy, as they all stared at him in amazement. It would have been a surprising enough offer even before what had just happened upstairs, but now...

'Come with me,' he repeated, more firmly this time. 'Anna might be away, but my mother's in Yorkshire. You can bring the boys, too. It'll be a holiday for them.'

'What about David? What if he comes back?'

'Then he'll come here and Miss MacQueen will tell him where you are.'

'But I can't just go to Yorkshire with you!'

'Why not?'

'Because...' She gaped at him. There were almost too many reasons to name! The first and most obvious being, 'It wouldn't be seemly!'

'We'll be staying with my mother, grandmother and uncle. It won't exactly be sordid.'

'But your grandmother was a duchess!'

'And?'

'I can't stay in the same house as a duchess!'

'A dowager duchess.'

'That's not the point. What will she think if you turn up with a shop girl and three children in tow? It could ruin your chances of a reconciliation.'

'If it does, then I don't believe she's someone I want to reconcile with.'

'I won't fit in!'

'Neither will I, most likely. I'm a sailor whose father was a footman-turned-baker, remember?'

'It's different and you know it. You're a blood relation. I'm just...'

'Don't.' He lifted a hand, his dark eyes flashing so brightly it was as though lightning had just streaked across them. 'Whatever you were about to say, don't. You're not *just* anything. If other members of my family have a problem with you, then we'll turn straight around and come back.'

Henrietta swallowed. Ten minutes ago she'd resolved to throw him out of her life for believing gossip about her. Five minutes ago she'd been clasped in his arms, kissing him with a quite shameless amount of enthusiasm. *Now* he was asking her to go away with him. She felt as though time were accelerating. She'd only just accepted the possibility of their being more than friends...

'This is ridiculous.' She shook her head against the temptation to say yes. 'Nancy, tell him how ridiculous he's being.'

'Personally, I think it's the most sensible thing I've ever heard him say.' Nancy unfolded her arms. 'I presume he's apologised?'

'What?' Henrietta looked between the two of them in consternation. 'You wanted to throw a bucket of water at him a few moments ago!'

'Yes, well, the cold water's given me a chance to reconsider and now I think it's the perfect answer. You could do with a rest after the past couple of months and it would take the boys' minds off their father.'

'What about the shop?'

'Belinda can move in.'

'Oh! Can I?' Belinda clapped her hands so enthusiastically that a cloud of white dust billowed into the air, making them all cough.

'Yes,' Nancy spluttered as she waved her arms around. 'I'll make a baker of you if it's the last thing I do. Which will be *much* easier without so many people under my feet.'

'But what will people say?' Henrietta drew her brows together at her own question. The gossips would no doubt say that she was up to her old tricks again, trying to seduce yet *another* employer's son. She might as well confirm everything bad they'd ever said about her. Mrs Willerby would be particularly delighted. And the worst of it was that this time there'd be some truth in the accusations. She'd kissed Sebastian. If it hadn't been for the interruption, she would have kissed him some more. Given the opportunity, it was entirely likely she'd kiss him again. Which made travelling north with him probably the worst idea in the world. And yet, insane as it sounded, she wanted to go.

I won't be a mistake... She didn't know what the future held, but she knew those words at least were true. If she trusted any man, it was him.

'I'll go a day ahead and meet you in Bristol,' Sebastian offered. 'Then no one in Bath will know that we're travelling together. You can say that you're going to visit Anna.'

'No.' She pulled her shoulders back. 'I've wasted enough time caring about what people say about me. They'll never change their minds anyway. In their eyes, I'll always be either a fortune hunter or an ice queen and I don't want to be either. From now on, I'm going to be myself and let people interpret that however they please.'

Sebastian's gaze warmed. 'Then you'll come to York-shire with me?'

She sucked in a deep breath, struck with the feeling that the whole of her future depended on this one moment. 'Yes. We'll go together.'

Chapter Fourteen

'Are we there yet?' Michael flung his head back against the seat with a loud sigh. 'We've been in this stagecoach *for ever*! It must be time to stop soon.'

'I told you the journey would take a few days.' Henrietta gritted her teeth, trying to sound sympathetic, although if he asked the question one more time, she thought she might open the door and jump out from sheer exasperation. It wasn't as if she was any more comfortable than he was! In fact, she was undoubtedly a lot *less* comfortable. Oliver and Peter had both fallen asleep, one on her knee, the other leaning against her shoulder, making it impossible for her to move for the last hour. Belles in biscuit tins were treated better than this, she thought, ironically. At least *they* came individually wrapped in tissue paper, something she might have used to make the headrest more comfortable. Every part of her ached or was numb with fatigue, but at least Michael was right about one thing. *Surely* it had to be time to stop soon... 'Are you warm enough?'

'Yes.' Michael scowled at the blanket tucked over his lap. 'But I'd rather ride up top like Sebastian.'

'It's far too cold for that.'

'It's not too cold for *him*!'

'Yes, well…he's a grown man.' Henrietta pursed her lips. She wasn't particularly happy about Sebastian riding on the roof of a violently swaying stagecoach in the middle of winter either, but unlike her three charges, she had no right to tell him what to do—besides, there hadn't been any alternative. Between her and the boys squeezed on to one side and a middle-aged couple and their teenage daughter on the other, the carriage was already bursting at the seams.

'Sebastian said a good sailor doesn't complain.' Peter mumbled sleepily across her. 'I bet he was talking to you.'

'He was not!'

'No arguing!' Henrietta felt as though her temper were hanging by a single, extremely frayed thread. 'Or we'll get off at the next inn and go straight back to Bath.'

'But…'

'Not *one more word* until we stop again!'

Incredibly, the threat worked, allowing her twenty minutes of rare, comparative peace, listening to the sound of Oliver's snoring and looking out at the darkness encroaching over the landscape outside. From what she could see through the carriage windows, Derbyshire had a wild, untamed kind of beauty, filled with wild-looking moors and jagged rock formations. Unfortunately for them, however, it *wasn't* Yorkshire, which meant that they still had another day of cramped conditions and moaning ahead before they reached Feversham. Which also meant another day of gradually building trepidation and dread.

It had seemed like a good idea at the time, leaving Nancy

and Belinda in peace and giving herself and the boys a holiday, but now she was starting to wonder if she'd taken leave of her senses by agreeing to come. It wasn't just that she was going to stay in a manor—*a manor*! She knew Sebastian's mother well enough to know that she wouldn't be turned away, no matter what his uncle and grandmother might think of her. It wasn't even that she was afraid of being in the same company as a dowager duchess. Anna was a countess, after all, and one of her best friends.

It was that she'd kissed Sebastian! Right after she'd told him that she wouldn't be used or possessed by any man ever again! She'd kissed him and now she had no idea what it meant. In all the commotion of packing and organising, there hadn't been any chance to discuss it and it wasn't as if they could talk in front of her nephews. Which had left her with three days, trapped inside a carriage, with little to do except think.

What did it mean? More to the point, what did his invitation to come north mean? She knew that he wasn't the kind of man who would act dishonourably, but that didn't mean he'd thought their situation through. In fact, he *definitely* hadn't, considering that he'd both kissed and invited her on impulse. And even if he *had* felt serious about her at the time—serious enough to invite her to meet his family— surely he'd change his mind once he had time to reflect?

For a start, and no matter what he said, they were too far apart socially. For another thing, there were the boys. It was one thing to *help* her look after them, but to take responsibility and become a surrogate father if David didn't come back, which she was starting to accept as a real possibility, was a different matter entirely. In which case, it was foolish to even contemplate a future together and better to remain as *just friends*…wasn't it?

The situation wasn't helped by the fact that they were sharing a chamber at night. It had actually been her idea to pretend they were a man and wife travelling with their sons. In her defence, she'd had a sneaking suspicion that Sebastian had charged her only a fraction of the real price of stagecoach tickets, despite her own insistence on paying, and she hadn't wanted him to spend any more money on her and her nephews than necessary. Besides which, as she'd explained with increasingly red cheeks, it was safer for them all to be in one room and it would save the bother of explaining the situation to every innkeeper they met.

She must have had children at a very young age, Sebastian had teased her, but he'd agreed readily enough, telling the boys that it was all part of a game. Consequently, every evening after dinner, he left the chamber to allow them to wash and change into their nightclothes before coming back and settling himself into either a spare truckle bed or an armchair by the fire. It was an eminently practical arrangement, but one that had left no opportunity to talk privately, something she really wanted to do *before* they reached Feversham, if only to work out how they ought to behave.

And all this thinking was giving her a headache…

She was just attempting to adjust her position when the carriage swung sideways abruptly, lurching to a halt in front of a small coaching inn and jolting Peter and Oliver awake at the same moment.

'Here we are.' Henrietta gave them both a squeeze, letting the middle-aged couple and their daughter descend first before climbing out of the carriage and stretching her arms above her head with relief.

'I'm hungry,' Michael grumbled beside her.

'We're all hungry.'

'I don't know about you, but I could eat a cow.' Sebastian jumped down from the roof, landing with a heavy thud beside them. 'Only let's start with something smaller, shall we? Some stew, perhaps?'

'I like stew.' Oliver grinned.

'Excellent!' He reached down, scooping her youngest nephew up under one arm before grabbing hold of their travelling bag with the other. 'Now let's go and find a room, shall we? You boys can carry that chest between you, I hope?'

'Yes, sir.'

Henrietta watched with amazement as Michael and Peter transformed into young cadets before her eyes, trotting behind Sebastian as he led them first into the taproom and then up a creaking staircase into a cosy, wood-panelled bedchamber.

'I'll order some dinner before it gets too busy.' Sebastian dropped a giggling Oliver on to the bed and the bag on to the floor alongside.

'Let me do it.' Henrietta showed the boys where to put the chest. 'You should warm yourself by the fire. You must have been frozen on that roof.'

'I've felt worse, believe me, although I have to admit the wind was bracing. I have no cobwebs left, but at least we're done with stagecoaches now. Feversham's only a few miles from here. If it wasn't so late, I'd hire a cart to take us there tonight.'

'Just a few miles?' Henrietta's voice emerged as a croak. Suddenly she wished they had a week of cramped carriages ahead of them. 'But I thought we were still in Derbyshire?'

'Only just. Yorkshire's over the next hill.'

'So we'll arrive tomorrow?'

'Before lunch, I should think.' His smile faltered briefly. 'Now, I'll be back in a few minutes. Stew all round!'

'Wait…!' Henrietta hastened into the corridor after him, pulling the door half closed behind her to block out the chorus of cheers from within.

'What's the matter?' Sebastian turned around at once. 'Would you prefer something else?'

'No, it's not the food, it's about tomorrow. I've been thinking—perhaps it isn't such a good idea our coming with you to Feversham, after all. Maybe we could just stay here for a few days? Or somewhere close by? I don't want us to be in the way.'

Sebastian's brow furrowed. 'If you think I'm just going to abandon you here, then you're very mistaken. We've come this far together and that means we stay together.'

'But it's not your house. It's your uncle's. He might think that you've taken a liberty by inviting us.'

'He might. In which case, our visit will be a short one.'

'Sebastian.' She adopted the stern voice she used occasionally with the boys, exasperated by his refusal to see any problems. 'What I'm trying to say is that if you're having any second thoughts about any of this then I would understand. I don't want you to feel any obligation.'

'Obligation?' He mused over the word. 'No, I can't say that I do.'

'*Especially* considering what your family might think of us travelling together. I wouldn't want them to get the wrong impression.' She was starting to think that she might need to hit him over the head with a stick to make him understand. 'They might think there's more between us than friendship.'

'Probably.'

'Probably?' She blinked.

'It's the likely conclusion.' He looked remarkably unbothered by the idea. 'And it's the truth, isn't it?'

'I...' She hesitated. 'I don't know. We haven't talked about what happened. We've been so busy...'

'Ah.' He looked faintly relieved, reaching for her hands and twining their fingers together in a way that made goose pimples rise on her skin. 'The truth is, I was afraid you might change your mind if we talked too much. And I suppose I've been preoccupied, too. I'm not thrilled about the idea of meeting my family. Seeing my mother, yes, but *her* mother and my uncle?' His brows contracted. 'I can't help but feel as though I'm betraying my father.'

'Oh, Sebastian.' She slid her thumbs around so that they were on top of his hands. 'Surely if your mother can forgive them...?'

'Then I should, too, I know. Even Anna seems to have made peace with it all, but if it wasn't for them...' A muscle tightened in his jaw. 'My father spent his whole life trying to make up for what my mother lost by marrying him. He never wanted her to regret their elopement. She didn't and she told him so often enough, but the worry was always there underneath. I think it's part of the reason he worked so hard. I'm not saying that her family were responsible for his death, but it's hard not to resent them. And now it's as though my mother's gone backwards, as if my father never even existed. I know that's not fair, but all of this has happened so quickly.' He shook his head as if to clear it of unpleasant thoughts. 'But I'm glad that you're with me. I can't think of anyone I'd rather be with. Truly, Henrietta.'

'Then I'm glad to be here, too.' She caught her breath, her chest feeling too tight all of a sudden.

'But I don't want you to feel any obligation either.' He looked serious again. 'If you're not happy or you want to leave for any reason, just say the word and I'll take you back to Bath. You have my word on it.'

'Thank you.' She jumped at the sound of a loud thud from the chamber behind her. 'In that case, while we're staying with your family, I think that we ought to remain as just friends. I might not care what the shopkeepers of Bath think of me any more, but I do care about your mother.'

'*Just* while we're staying there?' He quirked an eyebrow.

'Until we can talk about things…properly.'

'Ah.' He glanced at the partially open door behind them, his expression inscrutable. 'As you wish. Now I'd better let you go. It sounds like a herd of cattle in there.'

Chapter Fifteen

It was a perfect winter morning, Sebastian thought, the kind you might get only once or twice in a season. The December sun was blindingly low, gleaming off the river that ran behind the inn and bathing the trees alongside in bright yellow light. Aside from their bare branches, however, there were almost no signs of winter, just a light frost gilding the scattering of stones beneath. He stood by the window, admiring the scene for a few moments before turning around and clapping his hands together enthusiastically.

'Shall we go for a stroll?'

'Right now?' Henrietta gave him a surprised look. They'd eaten breakfast and she'd just finished repacking their chest. 'I thought you wanted to go and hire a cart?'

'I do, but it's such a lovely morning and the boys could do with some exercise.'

'Of course, if you like.' She appeared to bite her tongue as she wrapped a shawl around her shoulders. 'That would be very pleasant.'

He watched as she bundled her nephews into their caps and jackets. *Just friends.* The words had rankled and rattled around his brain all night. They weren't exactly what he'd been hoping to hear, though perhaps she had a point about not scandalising his family. Still, he was starting to regret his *friendly* behaviour over the past few days.

After what she'd told him about her previous romantic experiences, he hadn't wanted her to feel under any pressure, especially when they were sharing a chamber, or to change her mind about accompanying him, but now it appeared, ironically, that he'd been *too* well behaved. She'd got used to them being just friends again. His only consolation was that she hadn't said she *never* wanted to kiss him again...only while they were in Yorkshire, until they could find some time to talk...which made him want to get this visit over with quicker than ever.

They were halfway down the staircase when Michael let out a yelp and a small tin fell from his fingers, spilling marbles all over the corridor below.

'Oh, no!' Michael and Peter immediately sprang after them.

'Careful!' Henrietta kept a firm grip on Oliver's hand. 'Don't slip!'

'Do you know how many you had?' Sebastian went to help, crouching on his haunches.

'Twenty altogether.'

'All right. Where's the tin?' Quickly, he scooped up a handful of marbles and dropped them in one by one. 'That's eight.'

'I have another five!'

'I've only got two.'

'Keep looking.'

'I can't find them!' Michael wailed after a few minutes. 'Maybe they rolled outside?'

'Are these what you're looking for?' A grey-haired gentleman with a round, friendly face and wispy hair appeared in the taproom doorway, holding the last five marbles. 'Wouldn't do to lose them.'

'Thank you, sir.' Michael darted forward with a grin.

'Here. I'll carry them in my pocket from now on.' Sebastian gave a nod of thanks and reached for the tin. 'So that we don't have any more accidents.'

'Sorry, Sebastian.'

'Come on.' He ruffled Michael's hair. 'Let's go for that walk. Good morning.'

He tipped his hat to the gentleman, surprised when the man only stared quizzically back, and went outside. The stagecoach had already departed and the courtyard was relatively peaceful now, most people preferring to stand in the sunshine of the main street. That was wider than he'd given it credit for the previous evening, with several shops interspersed with neat-looking grey houses. A number of shoppers were out and about, too, milling around and chattering. Altogether it was a pleasant place for a stroll, he thought, made even pleasanter by the touch of Henrietta's hand on his arm.

He couldn't help but watch her out of the corner of his eye, wondering whether she was having regrets about kissing him at all. Her words the previous evening implied it. Or maybe she was simply having more doubts about whether or not she could trust him. Or maybe she was genuinely worried about what his family might think? Or was it about his intentions in general? And what were they anyway?

He tipped his hat to a group of ladies as they walked by,

considering the question. He probably ought to have thought about it sooner, especially after the way Miss MacQueen had chided him, but everything had happened so quickly. What *were* his intentions? Honourable, yes, but *how* honourable? Marriage? Was he really prepared to tie himself down just when he'd become a free man?

He sighed. Whatever his intentions, he was back in *friends* territory just when he wanted to kiss her more than ever.

They had made their way through the town and along a path to the river. The water was fast, but not particularly deep, and there had been stones to throw, branches to race under the bridge and stepping stones to jump across, after which the boys had been so hungry that Henrietta had had to pop into a bakery for some bread for them to share. All of which meant that it was past noon by the time they headed back to the inn to collect their bags.

'Sebastian?' Henrietta lowered her voice as they wandered back.

'Mmm?' He liked the way she said his name. *Sebastian...* with an emphasis on the *B*. Nobody else said it like that.

'You know it might just be better to get it over with?'

He gave her arm a small nudge. 'Are you suggesting that I'm delaying the last leg of our journey on purpose?'

'It crossed my mind.' She nudged him back. 'Although I wouldn't blame you if you were.'

'I'm not saying you're wrong, but I've run out of excuses anyway. I'll go and ask the innkeeper about that cart n—'

'*Sebastian!*'

He stopped mid-stride at the sound of his name, looking up to see two women emerging from an apothecary's just ahead of them. Quickly, he let go of Henrietta, opening his arms just in time for one of the women to launch herself at him, moving faster than he'd ever seen her move in, well— *ever.* If he hadn't taken a moment to brace himself, they would surely both have been sent sprawling into a puddle.

'Sebastian!' the woman repeated, pummelling him in the face with her bonnet as she tightened her grip on his neck. 'I thought you were still in Bath. Why didn't you tell me you were coming?'

'It was a last-minute decision.' He tipped his head back with some difficulty and smiled. His mother had a few more wrinkles and grey hairs than the last time he'd seen her, but her face was just as kind and loving as he remembered. 'It's good to see you again, Mama.'

'You've no idea how good it is to see you.' There were tears in her eyes now. 'It's been so long!'

'I know, but I'm here to make up for it now.'

'Yes, you are. I can hardly believe it. Oh!' She noticed his companion finally, a surprised expression passing over her face. 'Henrietta? How lovely to see you, my dear.'

'Miss Gardiner and her nephews accompanied me,' Sebastian announced, deciding to dive straight in before anyone could start asking questions. 'We decided we were all in need of a holiday. Mama, meet Peter, Michael and Oliver.'

'What fine-looking young men.' His mother gave them all a wide smile. 'Now, let me introduce you to my mother, Her Grace the Dowager Duchess of Messingham.'

Sebastian tensed as he looked towards that formidably titled personage. Small and white-haired as she was, it was impossible to doubt the family relation. She looked so much like his mother they might as well have had mother and daughter stamped across their foreheads.

'My friends call me Ottoline.' The woman smiled. 'I'm so pleased to finally meet you.'

'Your Grace.' He bowed politely, unable to agree with anything resembling honesty, though fortunately he was saved by the arrival of the gentleman from the inn.

'Tobias!' His mother waved. 'Look who we found.'

'My nephew, I presume?' The man beamed as he shook his hand. 'I wondered when I heard your name, but I couldn't be sure. It's a pleasure to meet you.'

Sebastian exchanged a quick glance with Henrietta. She and the boys were standing off to one side, huddled together and looking faintly bewildered by the number of greetings being exchanged. He was experiencing a similar feeling himself. As first meetings after long estrangements went, it was frankly bizarre. Everyone seemed so...*happy.*

'Would you do me the honour of introducing your companions?' His uncle turned towards Henrietta, still beaming.

'Of course, forgive me. Lord Tobias, this is Miss Henrietta Gardiner.' He paused, rebelling at the thought of referring to her as *just* a friend. 'She's the current manager of Belles.'

'Miss Gardiner, I'm delighted.' His uncle bowed over her hand. 'I hope that you're coming to visit us at Feversham Hall, too? And I presume these young marble-players belong to you?'

'Yes, they're my nephews.'

'Then you must all come to stay. How jolly!'

'I...' She looked somewhat overwhelmed. 'Thank you. If it's not an inconvenience?'

'Balderdash! Where are your bags?'

'At the inn.'

'Then let's go and fetch them! Ah.' Lord Tobias took a

few steps before stopping and clucking his tongue. 'It occurs to me, we're not going to fit everyone in one carriage.'

'Sebastian was going to hire a cart.' Michael found his voice again.

'What a splendid idea!' Lord Tobias snapped his fingers. 'In that case, why don't we fellows go and organise that while the ladies go ahead?'

'If that's all right with Henrietta?' Sebastian threw her a questioning look.

'Ye-es…' She looked from him to her nephews and back again. 'If you think it is?'

'I'll collect the bags and keep an eye on the boys.' He gave her a reassuring smile. 'And I'll see you soon. *Very* soon.'

'Well, that's settled. Come along, my dear.' His mother slid her hand through Henrietta's arm. 'The carriage is just over here.'

It was the first time Henrietta had ever been in a private carriage, but despite the cosy leather interior and silk cushions, she fervently wished that she might have got out and walked—or at least travelled in a cart with Sebastian and the boys. Mrs Fortini and her mother were both perfectly pleasant, but she found herself answering their questions in awkward monosyllables, far too aware of the questions *behind* the questions. They were both much too polite to ask outright, but they *had* to be wondering what on earth she was doing there, never mind her nephews! They had to be wondering about her relationship with Sebastian, too, but it wasn't as if she had any answers to give them, not yet anyway. It was a huge relief when the carriage finally drew to a stop, less so when she climbed out and saw a grey brick manor house roughly twice the size of the Bath Assembly Rooms.

'This way.' Sebastian's mother took hold of her arm again, leading her up the steps as a footman came to escort the Dowager Duchess. 'Let's get you settled.'

'I'm so sorry to intrude, Mrs Fortini...' Henrietta glanced over her shoulder, already hoping for a glimpse of the cart following behind. 'It was all such a rush and there was no time to send a message ahead. If we're causing you any inconvenience, then please say so.'

'It's nothing of the sort.' Mrs Fortini smiled benignly. 'And you used to call me Elizabeth, remember?'

'Ye-es, but it's been several months and so much has changed.'

'But not *me*, I hope.' Mrs Fortini—*Elizabeth*—squeezed her arm. 'Do you remember when you made that beautiful evening gown for Anna to wear at Lady Jarrow's party? And then you fixed up one of my old ones so that it looked as good as new? Well, if memory serves, I said that I was indebted that day. Now I'm thrilled to be able to repay you.'

'Thank you, but I would never have dreamed of intruding if... Well, if things hadn't been so difficult recently.'

'At Belles?'

'Oh, no, the shop's in good hands. It's just a situation involving my brother. You see, his wife died and now he's run away and I've no idea where's he's gone and there's nobody else to look after my nephews and—' She stopped short, feeling horribly short of breath and as though she were about to start crying.

'Oh, my dear.' Elizabeth led her in through the great doors. 'How terrible.'

'But Sebastian's been a great help. Honestly, I don't know what I would have done without him.'

'Good! Now let's go into the sitting room and you can tell me all about it.'

Chapter Sixteen

'There's a lake!' Michael bounced to his feet with excitement.

'Careful!' Sebastian swung around, grabbing hold of his waist. 'If you break your leg falling off this cart, then I won't let you go anywhere near it.'

'Sorry.' Michael settled back down again. 'But it's huge!'

'Full of trout, too.' Lord Tobias grinned. 'Excellent for young boys to fish in.'

'We don't know how to fish.'

'You don't? Good gracious. Well, I'd be happy to teach you. A boy ought to know how to fish.'

'Sailors need to know, too.' Peter spoke up this time. 'Don't they, Sebastian?'

'It can definitely come in handy.'

'And there's Feversham.' Lord Tobias pointed ahead towards a large grey house.

'That's huge, too!' Michael sounded thunderstruck.

'I built it myself. Not brick by brick, of course, but I designed it with an architect friend of mine about fifteen years ago. My father wanted to keep the bulk of the estate together for my older brother, but he gave me enough money to be independent so I decided to build this. It gives me plenty of room to indulge my interests.'

'It's a fine-looking house,' Sebastian answered honestly. The building was large, but not imposing, blending discreetly into the landscape instead of fighting against it. 'Is the Messingham estate close by?'

'Don't you know?' Lord Tobias looked surprised.

'No. I made a point of never being interested.'

'Ah. Well, there are properties all over the country, of course, but the bulk of the estate is in Kent.'

'Kent?' Sebastian looked at his uncle properly for the first time. 'That's a long way from Yorkshire.'

'Exactly. Far enough away that I'm not required to visit too often.' Lord Tobias shrugged. 'It's not that I don't love my brother. I do, but we get along much better at a distance. Besides, I always loved this part of the world.'

'What about your mother? Wasn't there a dower house in Kent for her?'

'Yes, but she preferred to come and live here with me. We were always very close.'

'Really?' Sebastian couldn't keep the sarcasm out of his voice.

'Forgive me, I didn't mean to be tactless. I know that she and Elizabeth were close, too, before…well…'

'Before she cut her off without a penny.'

'That was our father's doing.' His uncle's voice took on a harder edge. 'Our mother had nothing to do with it.'

'She still went along with it.' Sebastian threw a cautious glance over his shoulder, but the boys were too busy chattering to be paying any attention to their conversation at that moment.

'Actually I don't believe that she did.' Lord Tobias's knuckles tightened over the reins. 'I was only thirteen and away at school when it happened, but the next time I came home I could see that everything was different. My mother was deeply unhappy, but she was also powerless to defy my father. He was a controlling man at the best of times, but his temper was worse than ever after Elizabeth ran away. I was terrified of him.'

'You were?' Sebastian lifted his eyebrows.

'I'm not saying that we were blameless, my mother and I. Maybe we should have done more, but at the time there didn't seem to be anything we could do. Then, after my father died, we thought of contacting Elizabeth, but it had been so long and we assumed she wouldn't want to hear from us. I thought about visiting Bath and Belles several times, but I never summoned up the courage. Now I wish that I had. I know this situation must be very disconcerting for you and I wouldn't blame you for being angry, but I can't tell you how pleased I am to meet you finally. You're welcome to stay as long as you wish, all of you.'

'You know that I'm a sailor, Henrietta's a shopkeeper and the boys' father is a stable hand?'

'I do now.'

'Then are you *sure* that you want to invite us? Some people might say we're not fit company for a dowager duchess.'

'Some people might. *I* wouldn't. I stopped caring about what society thought a long time ago, around the same time as I lost my sister, as it happens.'

'We might be a handful.'

'I'll enjoy it. I'm an old bachelor myself, but it'll be nice to hear children's voices about the place.' Lord Tobias pulled on the reins, bringing them to a halt in front of the house. 'You can keep trying to deter me as much as you like, but you won't dampen my enthusiasm.'

'What about the Duke?' Sebastian lifted an eyebrow. 'The new Duke, I mean? Has *he* reconciled with my mother, too?'

'No.' A shadow crossed his uncle's face. 'I'm afraid that my brother takes after my father in that regard.'

'Meaning he doesn't approve of her living here?'

'I'm afraid not. He's written to me about it in no uncertain terms.'

'And?'

'And I've replied in a similar vein.'

Sebastian smiled his approval. 'I'd like to have been a fly on the wall when he opened that letter.'

'Nobody should be told who they can or can't share their lives with, or who they can love either.'

'I agree.' Sebastian looked up at the house and rubbed his chin thoughtfully. 'If you were away at school when my mother ran away, then I don't suppose you ever met my father.'

'No, although I wish that I had. From what Elizabeth tells me, he was a very special man.'

'He was.' Sebastian nodded, starting to suspect that his uncle might be, too. 'Now, I ought to go and find Henrietta.'

Pouring her heart out to Elizabeth had been soothing, Henrietta realised, as Sebastian walked into the drawing room half an hour later alongside his uncle and her nephews. Now that her tears had dried, her mind felt ten times easier than it had that morning. Surprisingly, *he* looked more relaxed, too, albeit a little confused, as if he were trying to make sense of something.

'We're going to learn fishing!' Michael announced, already hurtling across the room.

'Are you?' She gave him a pointed look that only just stopped him from leaping on to the sofa beside her.

'Oh!' He skidded to a halt and sat down gingerly. 'Yes, Lord Tobias said that he'll teach us.'

'With your permission?' Sebastian's uncle looked towards her with a smile.

'Of course.' She smiled back. 'That's very kind.'

'And we're allowed to call him Uncle Toby!' Michael blinked. 'Only I just forgot to.'

'I see.' She glanced uncertainly at Sebastian, who only lifted his shoulders.

'We decided it would be easier, didn't we, young man?' His uncle's smile grew even wider. 'Lord Tobias sounds much too formal.'

'I've asked Mrs Lancaster to prepare the nursery,' Elizabeth commented, speaking to her brother, though her gaze was focused on Sebastian, Henrietta noticed.

'The nursery?' His uncle chuckled. 'You know, my architect insisted on calling it that, but I never thought I'd have a use for it. The rooms will need a good airing.'

'I'm sure Mrs Lancaster is seeing to it now.'

'In the meantime...' His uncle caught his sister's eye and took a tactful step backwards. 'Perhaps I could take the boys into the library and have a marble tournament? I'll send for some refreshments, too.'

'What a good idea.' The Dowager Duchess reached for her walking stick. 'I think I'll join you.'

'Maybe I should, too...' Henrietta started out of her seat.

'No. You stay.' Sebastian turned sharply towards her. 'If you don't mind,' he added more gently.

'If that's what you want...' She sat down again, looking between him and his mother anxiously.

'Henrietta's just been telling me about Belles.' His mother spoke first. 'I'm glad that the shop's doing so well, although I never doubted she'd do a good job.'

'Yes. Has she told you her idea about selling tea?'

Henrietta shook her head quickly. 'It's still just an idea.'

'But it sounds like a very interesting one.' Elizabeth smiled. 'I'm sure Anna would love to discuss it when she comes back from Retford, but I'm afraid that may not be for a while. The Earl's grandfather died last week and they don't want to leave his grandmother. I doubt we'll be seeing her before the new year.'

'Oh, how sad.' Henrietta felt genuinely sorrowful. 'He was such a kind man. He used to talk to me about bees.'

'I remember. Anna was very fond of him.' Elizabeth turned to her son as he sat down in the chair just vacated by the Dowager Duchess. 'And how was your ride with Tobias?'

'Fine... Enlightening... Good.'

'Good,' his mother repeated, leaning forward to place a hand on his knee. 'I can't tell you how wonderful it is to see you again. When I got your letter from Bath, I thought that my heart would burst. I've been so worried.'

'It's good to see you again, too.' His slightly perplexed expression turned to one of affection.

'But tell me, what happened? Why didn't we hear from you for so long?'

'It's a long story, one for another time. The main thing is that I'm here now.'

'Well, I can't argue with that. And will you stay?' Mrs Fortini looked between the two of them. 'Oh, do say you will, at least until after Christmas.'

'We'll need to talk about it.'

Sebastian caught Henrietta's eye and she bit her lip. Christmas was still several weeks away. Nancy had told her to take as long as she needed, promising to send word if there was any sign of David or any problems, and she knew that Sebastian would insist on accompanying her and the boys if they left any sooner. And how could she do that when Mrs Fortini was looking at her with large, distinctly moist eyes? But Sebastian was giving her a way out, she realised, giving her the power to say yes or no, as if her desires and comfort mattered more than his. In which case... how *could* she say no?

'I'd be delighted to stay.'

Until after Christmas... Henrietta sat on the edge of a large four-poster bed, looking around a bedroom larger than any she'd slept in in her life. And it was hers—*until after Christmas!*

She'd agreed to stay. *Of course* she'd agreed to stay. It would have felt cruel to Mrs Fortini not to, but what was she supposed to do for the next month? Especially now that the boys had been appointed a pair of housemaids to tend to their every need as if they were little dukes themselves! She'd insisted on reading them a bedtime story that evening, but she had no doubt that they were still wide awake up in the nursery, wondering what on earth had happened to their lives. She was wondering the same thing. It was as if her whole existence had been turned upside down from the moment she'd rammed her kitchen door into Sebastian's face.

Speaking of doors… She heard a light tap on hers and hurried across the room to open it.

'Ready for dinner?' Sebastian stood in the hallway, dressed in his regular clothes instead of the dinner suit she might have expected. Which was a relief. She'd been afraid that her best evening gown, a pink muslin with a lacy trim around the neckline, wasn't formal enough.

'I think so.' She smoothed a hand nervously over her hair. 'Do I look all right?'

'Am I allowed to give compliments now?' He leaned closer, his dark eyes twinkling. 'Because if I am, then I'd say you look as beautiful as always.'

'I meant, do I look smart enough? This is my best dress.'

'And it looks gorgeous on you.'

'*Sebastian…*'

'I mean it. You have absolutely nothing to worry about.'

'What should I talk about at dinner?'

'Damned if I know. I'm just glad that you're with me.'

She glanced at his profile as they made their way to the staircase, surprised by the apparent depth of feeling behind the words. He sounded as if he genuinely meant them, as if he were relying on her as much as she'd come to rely on him over the past couple of weeks.

'Your family seem very pleasant.'

'Yes. They're not what I expected.'

'They've been very welcoming. I don't think the Dowager Duchess has stopped smiling since she set eyes on you.'

'Does that mean you really don't mind staying?' He gave her a searching look, smiling when she nodded. 'Well then, I'm grateful to them for that. I couldn't tell from your expression earlier. I was afraid I might have to sleep outside your door to stop you running away in the night.'

'I promise that if I run away then I'll do it broad daylight.'

'Good. Because I have a very comfortable-looking bed down the hall and I'd like to make the most of it. Not that I didn't appreciate all the sofas and chairs I've been sleeping on recently, but a real bed makes a pleasant change.'

'Mmm.' She stared straight ahead, feeling her cheeks start to flush. It didn't feel quite right to be discussing beds with him. Or to be thinking about him in one either...especially when her imagination seemed determined to place her in the scene, too. 'Your mother seems very happy.' She changed the subject hastily.

'Yes. I'm pleased about that. As for the rest... I don't know quite how to feel yet.' He turned to face her as they reached the bottom of the staircase. 'All I *do* know is that I'm hungry. Ravenous actually.'

'Me, too. I was too nervous to eat earlier.'

'Then will you do me the honour of accompanying me into the drawing room, my lady?' He made a bow, sweeping his hand so low that it skimmed lightly across the floor. 'Although I doubt that we'll be able to find the dining room on our own without a map.'

'I'd be most obliged, my lord.' She laughed, sinking into an equally low curtsy before tucking her arm into his elbow and then immediately trying to extract it again as they entered the drawing room to find Mrs Fortini, Lord Tobias and the Dowager Duchess all waiting. Sebastian was faster, however, raising his other hand and clamping it down on top of hers.

'Good evening.' Lord Tobias stood up to welcome them. 'The boys are all settled, I trust?'

'Yes.' Henrietta dipped into a slightly less effusive curtsy. 'Thank you, Lord Tobias. They like the nursery very much.'

'Call me Tobias, please. Now, dinner's ready if we are?' His smile looked almost in danger of splitting his face. 'I never would have thought when I got up this morning that by tonight I'd be welcoming my own long-lost nephew into my home. I honestly couldn't be any happier.'

Henrietta nudged Sebastian lightly in the ribs when he didn't respond. Instead, his expression looked oddly tense for a few seconds before he let her go and reached an arm out. 'Here you are, Uncle. I didn't shake your hand properly before. It's a pleasure to meet you and, for the record, I'm happy, too.'

'Thank you. And Miss Gardiner...' his uncle continued. 'I do hope your nephews will be happy here, as well.' His laugh positively boomed around the room. 'There appear to be nephews everywhere these days!'

Chapter Seventeen

'What a beautiful day.' Elizabeth Fortini sighed happily as she walked arm in arm with Sebastian through Feversham's frost-covered garden. 'It looks as though the world is covered in sugar.'

'That sounds like something Father would have said.'

'It probably was.' She smiled nostalgically. 'He always made me look at the world in new ways and he saw the beauty in everything. It was one of the things I loved most about him, that optimism. You remind me so much of him, you know, even more than when you left, although I think you might be even more handsome.'

Sebastian bent to press a kiss on her cheek. After four days in his uncle's house, he was finally starting to relax, enough to talk about his father. It was the first time that he and his mother had done so since his arrival.

'Did you have any doubts when you ran away with him? He always said it was love at first sight, but it was a big risk.'

'It was both. I remember the first time I saw him, standing outside the drawing room at Messingham Hall. Footmen weren't supposed to look directly at us, but he was never very good at following the rules. I was eighteen years old and thought he was the most handsome man I'd ever laid eyes on. He quite took my breath away.'

'But how did you know that you loved him? You can't have spent much time together before you eloped.'

'No. We met in the gardens a few times, but never for long.'

'Then how could you be sure that he was the right man for you?'

'I'm not sure. I just *knew*.' Her brow creased slightly. 'I suppose you could say I had anxieties more than doubts. I was afraid of upsetting my mother, but I was young and impetuous and I hoped that my family would forgive me and accept him eventually. Deep down, I suppose I knew that would never happen, but I also knew that I'd never be happy with any other man. So we eloped. It was the only way. If my father had got even the slightest inkling of how we felt, then he would have made sure we never saw each other again.'

'So you never regretted it?'

'Being estranged from my family? Very much. Marrying your father? Never.' She stopped to smile up at him. 'I consider myself a very lucky woman. I miss him every day, but we had seventeen happy years and two wonderful children together.'

'And now you're happy here? Even with your ailments?'

'Yes.' She nodded emphatically. 'I still feel stiff most days, but I feel as though I can finally put the past behind me. Mainly because I know your father would have been happy for me. I've no doubts at all about that.'

'Then I'm glad, too. As much as it pains me to admit it, I like them, your mother and Tobias.'

'They like you, too. I can tell.'

'Which means that they would probably have liked Father.'

'Yes, but there's no point in regretting that now. When you get to my age, you realise life is too short to harbour ill will.' Her expression shifted as they started walking again. 'You know, they like Henrietta and her nephews, too.'

'Do they?' Sebastian fixed his gaze on the lake.

'Yes.' Her arm tightened perceptibly. 'As for myself, I understand your reasons for bringing her, but you must know how it looks.'

'What if that were the truth?'

'Then I'd be delighted. I've always liked Henrietta, but I'd also want to be sure that you have the right motives for pursuing her. She's a very beautiful woman.'

'Meaning?'

'Just that it can be hard not to be blinded by beauty. Some people might mistake that for love.'

'I know. So does she.'

'You haven't known her for very long.'

'How many times did you say you met Father before you eloped?'

'*Touché.* Then you truly care for her?'

'I do.' He didn't even need to think about the answer. 'Maybe I was dazzled by her beauty at first, but now she's just…' he gave an exaggerated shrug '… Henrietta.'

'Do you love her?'

'Love…' he hesitated '…is a big word, but I like her a great deal. She's caring and intelligent and much more than a beautiful face.'

'She's always been a great deal more than that.' His mother smiled her agreement. 'And if you can see that, too, then I wish you both joy. So...?'

'*So?*'

'Don't be obtuse. What are you going to do about it?'

'Oh, I don't know.' He lifted his eyes to the sky and whistled. 'There's no rush.'

'*Sebastian Fortini!*'

'I'm going to propose, obviously.'

'Good, although if her brother doesn't come back——'

'He's not going to.'

'What?' She put a hand over her mouth in surprise. 'How do you know?'

'Because of a letter I received yesterday.' He glanced over his shoulder, making sure there were no small boys around to overhear them. 'I asked James Redbourne to listen out for any news of Henrietta's brother and he finally heard some. Apparently David Gardiner didn't run away on his own. He went to Bristol with one of his friends, only when the friend sobered up he changed his mind about their plans and came home again. Her brother didn't. He took a ship for America instead.'

'So he's really gone and left his sons?'

'Yes. He knew that Henrietta would take care of them, probably *better* care of them, but, yes, he's gone.'

'Have you told her?'

'Not yet.' He shook his head. 'She needs a holiday and I don't want to spoil it. I thought maybe I could tell her after Christmas.'

'Absolutely not.' His mother lifted her chin. 'She's not a child and she won't thank you for keeping it from her. She has more of a right to know than you do.'

'Yes, but...'

'You *know* you have to.'

Sebastian gritted his teeth. 'I suppose so. I just don't want her getting hurt.'

'I think that's unavoidable at this point.' His mother quirked an eyebrow. 'But I hope you understand what this means. Henrietta will be their mother from now on, so if you marry her...'

'Then I'll be their father.' He nodded. 'It had occurred to me.'

'It's a lot to take on.'

'I know, but I want to.'

His mother reached a hand to his cheek. 'You really have grown up.'

'I suppose so. A little sooner than I'd hoped, but I don't seem to be able to do anything about it.' He grinned. 'You know, this will make you a grandmother.'

The caress turned into a light pat. 'I think I might enjoy that.'

'You'll be wonderful at it. You were a wonderful mother, after all.'

'Come on, let's go inside.' His mother gave a suspicious-sounding sniff. 'You need to speak to Henrietta and then comfort her. The sooner that's done, the sooner you can propose.'

'Don't tell me...' Sebastian leaned against the doorframe of the nursery, rubbing his chin thoughtfully. 'You're a snowman?'

'A polar bear!' Oliver peered up at him through two holes in a white sheet.

'Ah.' He clicked his fingers. 'Of course, silly me. Might I enquire why?'

'We're rehearsing a play.' Michael jumped down from a chair, wielding a wooden sword. 'It's all about Nelson fighting the polar bear.' He straightened his shoulders proudly. '*I'm* Nelson.'

'Naturally.' Sebastian inclined his head and then looked across the room towards Peter. 'And you are…?'

'A pirate.'

'In the North Pole?'

'I challenge Nelson to a duel after the polar bear escapes.'

'Well, that all sounds excellent. I'm looking forward to it already.' Sebastian nodded approvingly. 'Now I don't suppose you happen to know where your aunt is?'

'In there.' Michael gestured towards a door in the opposite wall. 'She's making up our beds. So we don't make any more work for the maids, she says.'

'Ah.' Sebastian looked pensively towards the door. After dragging his feet up three staircases, he'd been hoping for an excuse to postpone the task for another day or a few weeks, but his mother was right, Henrietta had a right to the truth.

'I tell you what…' he jerked his head at the boys '…why don't you run down to the kitchens for something to eat?'

'We just had breakfast.'

'Then it must be time for a snack.'

'Biscuits?'

'Naturally.'

He stepped aside, letting them scurry past before making his way reluctantly to the bedroom.

'You know you don't have to do that.' He gestured to the coverlet Henrietta was smoothing over the furthest of the three beds.

'I know.' She straightened up with a smile. 'But it makes me feel better.'

'I'm glad I found you anyway. I have some news.'

'Oh.' A hand crept to her throat. 'About David?'

'Ye-es.' He pulled the letter from his coat pocket. 'My friend James heard a rumour and went to investigate.'

'And?'

'And...' He cleared his throat, unable to find any way of softening the blow. 'It seems that when your brother left he went to Bristol and...well, according to what James has heard, he took a ship for America.'

There were several moments of absolute silence as she stared at him, so pale and motionless that it was hard to tell if she were still breathing. She looked frozen.

'Henrietta?' He moved back towards her, alarmed by the silence, but she held a hand out, holding him back.

'He's gone to America?' Her voice was different, high-pitched and laced with hurt. The sound of it made his heart wrench.

'Apparently so.'

'America...' Her expression seemed to waver between shock and hurt. 'I don't understand.'

'Maybe you ought to sit down?'

'Why?' She stared at him as if he'd just told her to go for a swim. 'What good will that do? How could he just go to America? How could he abandon his sons?'

'I don't know. He must have thought he had no choice.'

'I can't... I don't... Argh!' She swung around, wrenching the quilt and pillows off the nearest bed and stomping on top of them. 'If he were here, this is what I'd do to him!' She moved to the next bed, punching her fist into the pillow before hurling it across the room. 'And this!'

'And he'd deserve it, only...'

'His own sons!' She dropped heavily on to the bare mattress behind her. 'What am I supposed to tell them?'

Sebastian sat on the adjacent bed, facing her. 'Maybe nothing for now.'

'Nothing? You were the one who told me to be honest with them before.'

'I know, but you need time to come to terms with this first.'

'Maybe you're right.' She dropped her head into her hands, golden hair spilling over her fingers. 'You know, I wondered, but I kept telling myself that he'd come back. I really thought it was just a matter of time.'

'I know.'

'Thank you for telling me.' She sat upright again after a few seconds, dragging the palms of her hands across her cheeks.

He made a face. 'To be honest, I didn't want to. My mother said you had a right to know, but I didn't want to upset you.'

'It's not your fault I'm upset.' Her jaw tightened. 'But at least now I can make plans.'

'What do you mean?'

'Plans for the boys. I have to be their mother from now on. That means I need to be practical and find a job that works around their schooling.'

'What? No, you don't have to leave Belles.'

'Yes, I do. It wouldn't be fair on Nancy to carry on as we've been doing. The shop demands a lot of time, you know that as well as anyone.'

'There's Belinda now, too. *And* me.'

'You?' Her whole body seemed to tense. 'But I thought

you wanted to enjoy your freedom? You said you didn't know what you wanted to do next.'

'I think I've decided. Now that I'm back on dry land, I want to stay. More than that, I want to stay with you and help to take care of the boys properly.' He hesitated, the next words hovering on the tip of his tongue. This probably wasn't a good idea. It wasn't the time or place for a proposal. She'd just had a shock and he'd planned to wait for a few days. It wasn't the least bit romantic, but suddenly he couldn't stop himself from dropping down on to one knee. 'Henrietta Gardiner, I'd consider it a great honour if you'd consent to be my wife.'

Chapter Eighteen

'What did you just say?' Henrietta stared at Sebastian open-mouthed. It sounded as though he'd just proposed to her.

'It was a bit long-winded, to be honest.' He looked faintly abashed. 'Not like something I'd usually say at all.'

'But what *was* it?'

'Ahem…' He cleared his throat and tipped his head to one side, almost apologetically. 'I asked if you'd marry me.'

'That's what I thought you said…' If she hadn't been sitting already, she was quite certain her legs would have collapsed beneath her. Her knees already felt as if they were trembling and her ankles…well, they'd surely have twisted from shock. 'Are you mad?'

'I don't think so, although I've wondered occasionally.' Sebastian rubbed his chin. 'But I don't *feel* mad. Not at the moment anyway.'

'You must be.' She leaned forward to put her hands on

his shoulders, ready to talk some sense into him. '*Think* about it. I'm a shopkeeper.'

'As was my father. As I would have been if I hadn't joined the navy.'

'You're the grandson of a duke.'

'This again?' He rolled his eyes. 'Haven't we been through this enough times? I don't care who my grandfather was or wasn't.'

'But the world will. Sebastian, I have no family and no money. Nothing in the world except three little boys to take care of. You should be marrying up, not down. Look at Anna. She's a countess now.'

'Anna married for love, or so you and my mother keep telling me. Rank had nothing to do with it.'

'Yes, but...' She gulped, feeling an almost electric jolt at the mention of love. Was he saying that he *loved* her? No, he was comparing them to Anna and the Earl, but not in that way...

'And since my grandfather disowned my parents and by extension me, I don't see what his vaunted position has to do with anything.'

'All I'm saying is that you could marry a lady if you wanted.'

'*If* being the operative word.' He sounded almost angry at the suggestion. 'Or are you saying that I should marry a lady on some kind of principle?'

'No-o, I just think...'

'I think you are.' He tore himself free from her hands and stood up, pacing the room as he spoke. 'You're suggesting that I ought to make up for my mother's so-called "mistake"! That I ought to act as if my father never existed and take up some kind of position in society.'

'Not necessarily, but maybe you ought to meet a few more ladies before deciding against them.'

'I've met ladies. I've served them in the shop enough times and trust me, there's no difference between them and any other woman except for clipped vowels and expensive clothes. I told you the first day, that's not my definition of a lady.'

'It's not just about vowels and clothes! It's about all of this!' She waved her arms around in a circle. 'This house. This estate. This is the world your family lives in now! That makes it part of your life, too, and how could I ever be a part of it? I don't belong here.'

'And you think that *I* do? Henrietta, I may have a tenuous connection to this place by birth, but in case you hadn't noticed, this isn't my world either. I'm glad to be here with my family again, but as a guest. I'm not a gentleman.'

'But you *could* be.'

'I doubt it. Honestly, I can't think of anything more boring. People expect you to make calls and wear damned dinner jackets every day!'

'Sebastian.' She couldn't help a burble of laughter from escaping her lips.

'I'm not saying that there wouldn't be compensations. Good food, a feather-filled bed, servants catering to my every whim and cigars after dinner, but none of that's who I am. I could never live in a place like this. Whereas a house in Bath, close to Swainswick Crescent, maybe next to the park where the boys could play, with a woman who knows how to work for a living, a friend and an equal, someone I like and respect…well, that sounds pretty close to perfect to me.'

She swallowed again, staring into his eyes as they bored

into hers, unable to think of a single thing to say. He was right, it *did* sound pretty close to perfect...

'Henrietta...' He crouched down, his knees touching against hers. 'I know who I am and who I want to be. There have been moments in my life when I've felt guilty and help-less, but I finally feel as though I'm making up for those times now. I feel as though I'm doing something useful and worthwhile again. Most of all I want to do the right thing.'

The right thing? She blinked at the words. He was talk-ing as if she were a lady and he'd compromised her. Which, if she *had* been a lady, she supposed would be true. He'd kissed her and slept in the same room, albeit chastely, on several occasions over the past week. But she wasn't a lady and there was no need for him to do the right thing. Nei-ther she nor the boys were his responsibility. Besides, what about love? she wanted to ask, but somehow she couldn't bring herself to do it. How could she expect him to answer a question she didn't know the answer to herself? She liked him, she enjoyed his company far more than she'd ever ex-pected to enjoy any man's company, but surely it was too soon for love? And wasn't what he was offering her enough? Friendship, mutual respect and a home, not just for herself, but for her nephews, too. It would have sounded greedy to ask for more.

'I'm not saying I can afford a house immediately.' He looked faintly sheepish. 'In fact, I'm not even sure where we'll live, but I'll work something out. I have some sav-ings and I'll earn the rest. I was thinking about your idea of serving tea at Belles. Maybe we could expand the prem-ises? Or better still, find somewhere new and call it *Hen-rietta's*. What do you think?'

'I don't know.' She closed her eyes and then opened them

again, trying to stop the room from spinning around her. 'I'm speechless.'

'Then just nod your head. Or shake it, but I'd prefer a nod.'

'Sebastian...'

'Wait.' He reached for her hands, clasping them firmly between his. 'If you're going to say no, then let me say one more thing first. I know this is a bad time to ask. In fact, it's a terrible time, probably the worst I could possibly have chosen, but I want you to know that you don't have to face the future alone. I want to be there for you—all of you.'

'But you don't *have* to.' She shook her head. 'You don't have to marry me just to be useful and make amends for the past.'

'It's not just that. Yes, I still feel guilty about Anna, but not enough to propose, I promise you.' He lifted one of her hands and kissed the pulse at the base of her wrist. 'It's not *just* a question of feeling guilty. It's you, too.'

Her breath stalled. 'What about your freedom?'

'I'll still be free. So will you. We'll make our own decisions together and with our own crew. Me, you and the boys.' He grinned. 'I'm happy. Right here and now, I'm happy and a large part of that is due to you. I think we could be happy building a life together.'

'Oh.' She felt her lips part, though for the life of her she had no idea how to close them again. Or how to form words for that matter.

'We're friends, aren't we? Maybe even a little more than that? You kissed me once.' His dark eyes glinted. 'It wasn't *such* a painful experience, was it?'

'No.' She let out something between a laugh and a hiccup, the joke unlocking her tongue. 'No, it wasn't painful.'

'Damning with faint praise...' The top half of his body swayed forward. 'In that case, maybe you'd let me try to persuade you again?'

He brought his face slowly to hers and she moved to greet him until they met somewhere in the middle. It wasn't that she'd intended to move, she thought with a vague sense of surprise, just that she couldn't help it, as if there were an invisible rope tied around them, drawing her closer and binding them together. It was a perfect moment, tender and serene and somehow just *right*, lasting for several heart-stopping seconds before something seemed to catch fire between them and she found herself moving again, trying to press even closer towards him.

Sebastian gave a low, surprised-sounding murmur before curling his arms around her waist, his lips clinging to hers as if he felt the same fire, too. She reached her own arms around his neck, absorbing the heat of his chest with her breasts in a way that made her stomach clench and contract with tingles of pleasure. She felt as though she had one of his knots inside her, being pulled tighter and tighter, although surely it had to stop at some point? If you pulled on a knot hard enough, then eventually, surely *eventually* it had to unravel. Or the string would snap. Or...well, *something* would happen! Only she had no idea what.

'I must be mad, too.' She panted as they came apart finally, foreheads pressed together as they each struggled to regain their breath.

'Does that mean you're considering my proposal?' He laughed huskily, one of his hands sliding across the small of her back and up to her shoulder blades.

'No.' She shook her head, smiling back. 'I've already

considered. Yes. Yes, I'll marry you. I still think it's madness, but I—'

She didn't get any further as his lips seized upon hers again, kissing her so deeply that she felt a wave of heat rush all the way from the top of her head to the tips of her toes in a cascade of sensation. If this was madness, she decided in the split second before coherent thought abandoned her, then sanity was vastly overrated.

Sebastian had always thought of kissing with ambivalence. It wasn't that he didn't enjoy it, just that there were other, similar and yet slightly more energetic activities that he preferred. Kissing Henrietta, however, was different. Words like 'new' and 'exciting' were far too mild to describe what they were doing. It was an utterly engrossing, nerve-tinglingly heady sensation, unlike any kiss he'd ever experienced before. It was, quite simply, bliss. He could have happily done it all day. Two days. A whole week if he could have gone that long without food and water. Her lips were the smoothest he'd ever felt, the sweetest he'd ever tasted, the most exquisitely shaped...

'Wait!' She pulled back abruptly. 'The boys! They're next door.'

'No, they're not.' He trailed his mouth over her cheek, across her jaw and down the delicate column of her throat. 'I sent them to the kitchens.'

'They might come back.'

'We'll hear them coming, believe me.'

'But I might not have time to straighten up.' She lifted her hands to his chest. 'You've unfastened my hair.'

'Have I?' He lifted his head, surprised to find that she was right. Somehow he'd managed to unpin and unravel her hair without even noticing. Now it was lying over her shoulders in a pale golden torrent. And if she thought that drawing attention to it was the way to convince him to let her go then she was extremely deluded... He gave a low moan and buried his face in the tresses.

'Mmm.'

'What are you doing?'

'Breathing you in.' He inhaled deeply as her body sagged against him. 'It smells different from usual.'

'It does?' Her voice sounded breathless.

'Just a little. Usually it smells of sugar and baking. Now it smells of...' He drew in another deep breath. 'Apricots?'

'The maids gave me a soap.'

'I like it. I like both. Have you ever considered making an apricot-flavoured Belle?'

'I think we have enough to deal with at the moment.' She laughed huskily. 'But we really should stop.'

'All right.' He pressed one last kiss to the tip of her nose before moving away. Truth be told, it *would* look somewhat incriminating if they were disturbed now and not just by the boys. Both his uncle and grandmother had paid visits to the nursery over the past couple of days and if they discovered him and Henrietta together like this...well, it wasn't just her loose hair that would give them away. He was going to need a few minutes to recover himself.

Henrietta pressed her lips together, watching him through her lashes as she coiled her hair up and then looked around for the pins.

'Here.' He reached down, picking a handful off the floor.

'Thank you.' She fixed the roll into place and folded her hands in her lap. 'Just so you know, it wasn't that I didn't like it. Kissing you, I mean.'

'Glad to hear it.' He grinned. Her pose reminded him of the first time they'd met, when she'd clasped her hands so primly in front of her. 'Because if you didn't, then I'm afraid you'll find marriage to me somewhat tedious.'

'Really?' Her eyelashes fluttered. 'Do you intend to kiss me a lot, then?'

'If you mean do I intend to wake you up with kisses every morning then, yes, yes, I do. For the record, I also intend to lull you to sleep the same way.'

'I don't think that will work.' The corners of her lips tugged upwards, her dimple more pronounced than ever. 'It doesn't seem to have made me very sleepy.'

'Wait and see.' He winked, barely resisting the urge to pull her into his lap. 'In the meantime, let's go and share the good news.'

'Right now?' She looked startled.

'No time like the present. Then we'd better start packing.'

'You mean you want to go back to Bath?'

'No. The other direction, actually.'

'What? Sebastian, what are you talking about?' She shook her head at him. 'Where are we going?'

'Gretna Green. *Today.* I'm not giving you a chance to change your mind.'

Chapter Nineteen

'Are you sure you've got enough blankets?'

'Yes, as well two hot bricks and five layers of clothing. If we take any more, the horses won't be able to pull us.' Sebastian chuckled as his mother peered anxiously inside the carriage. 'We'll be fine.'

'I still think it's a ridiculous time of year to be heading to Scotland. What if it snows when you're up on the hills?'

'If it looks like bad weather, then we'll stop somewhere, I promise. It's not as though we're in the middle of the ocean.'

'Don't even joke about that.' His mother gave him a stern look before surrendering to the inevitable. 'Oh, very well. In that case, travel safely and don't worry about the boys. They'll be perfectly safe here.'

'Are you sure you don't mind me going away for a few days?' Henrietta crouched down in front of her nephews.

'We don't mind,' Peter answered. 'Lord Tobias says he'll carry on our cadet training. He's going to teach us about ich…icthy…'

'Ichthyology?'

'That's it!'

'And we'll have our play ready for when you get back,' Michael added.

'Will you still be our aunt when you're Mrs Sebastian?' Oliver sounded anxious.

'Of course. I'll *always* be your aunt. I'll just be Mrs Fortini, too.'

'Good. In that case you can go.' He grinned as she kissed him on the cheek.

'Now take care of each other and be good.'

'I'm sure they will be.' Elizabeth smiled warmly. 'We're going to have fun, aren't we, boys?'

'And *we'd* better be going.' Sebastian gestured towards the carriage door. 'The sooner we get there, the sooner we can get back again.'

'Try to be a little more romantic, dear.' His mother rolled her eyes. 'It is your wedding, after all.'

'You're right.' He winked and then bowed to Henrietta. 'Your carriage awaits, my lady.'

'Thank you, my lord.'

She gave the boys one last hug each and then climbed inside, burying herself beneath a pile of his mother's blankets.

'Off we go.' He took a seat beside her and banged on the roof. 'No second thoughts?'

'None, but how long will it take to get there?'

'A couple of days, I should think. We'll be back with the boys by the end of the week, don't worry.'

She nodded and then looked anxious again. 'What do your family really think?'

'They're happy for us. They said so.'

'It's just so hard to believe, considering everything.'

'Considering nothing.' He gave her a sharp look. 'You know my mother said something earlier about life being too short to carry ill will. I think my uncle and grandmother know it's too short to judge a person by where they come from, too. At the very least, they know it's foolish to stand between two people who care about each other.' He paused briefly. 'As we do.'

'As we do.' She met his gaze with a smile. 'I wonder what Anna will say?'

'That you're too good for me, I expect.' He slid across the bench, nudging his shoulder against hers. 'Now, are you warm enough?'

'You sound like your mother.'

'I know, but she made some good points. It *is* colder than it was last week. I don't want a frozen bride.' He twisted his head as she laughed. 'What?'

'Some people do call me an ice queen.'

'There's no need to live up to it.'

'Then you'll be glad to hear that I'm feeling quite toasty. Almost too warm, actually.'

'You do look a bit flushed, now that you mention it. Are you feeling all right?'

'Perfectly. It's probably just the hot brick. I'm only worried about the poor coachman.'

'For a start, there are two poor coachmen and I've said they can take turns travelling inside if they want to. For another thing, they're both being paid a small fortune.'

'Good.'

'Then we're all set.' He slid his hand into hers, lacing their fingers together and tipping his head back with a sigh. Maybe his mother was right and it *was* foolish, racing off to Scotland in the middle of December, but now that they were on their way, he couldn't wait to be married.

'We're here.'

'Not yet...' Henrietta shook her head as she felt Sebastian's hand on her shoulder. 'I'm sleeping.'

'I know, but we have an anvil to get married over.'

'Oh!' She prised her eyelids open and looked out. After two days, most of which time she'd spent asleep, both in the carriage and the inn where they'd stayed for the night, it seemed they were finally over the Scottish border and in Gretna. Which was a relief in more ways than one. She'd gone from feeling slightly warm to quite ill the morning after they'd left Feversham. Not *very* ill, just aware of a tightness in her throat and behind her eyes, not to mention an overwhelming sense of exhaustion, all of which suggested she was on the verge of a bad cold.

Naturally, she hadn't shared any of this information with Sebastian. She had a feeling that he would have turned the carriage around if he'd known the truth and now that she'd agreed to marry him, she wanted to do it as quickly as possible. As it was, she could tell that he'd been watching her more closely than usual.

He'd tried not to be too obvious about it when she was awake, but the tilt of his head, facing straight ahead but with his chin turned slightly sideways, gave him away. Every time she'd sniffed, which had started to happen more and more frequently, his fingers had twitched beneath hers. There had been moments when she would have given a large proportion of her meagre savings just to be able to blow her nose without him noticing. Instead, she'd tried to angle her face away from his scrutiny and towards the window, but after a while it had made her neck stiff.

'Are you sure you're not feeling unwell?' He asked, climbing out of the carriage.

'I'm fine.' She stifled the urge to sneeze. 'So what do we do now?'

'Now I'll go and speak to the blacksmith and see if he can marry us.' He paused. 'Are you sure—?'

'I'm *fine.*'

'Hmm.' He sounded unconvinced. 'Come into the inn so you can wait in the warm.'

'Good idea.' She looked around and shivered. The village of Gretna was covered in a thin layer of white. 'Snow!'

'Just a little. It won't stop us from leaving again tomorrow.' He spoke briefly to the coachman and then reached for her hand, leading her into an old and cosy-looking inn.

'Wait here.' He found her a vacant armchair by the fireplace, his expression still full of concern. 'I'll be as quick as I can.'

Henrietta fumbled in her purse for a handkerchief and sank into the armchair with a sense of relief. It was old and tattered and stained in places, but she didn't care. All she wanted was to bury herself in its warmth and close her eyes again. Her nose was running, she was finding it increasingly difficult to swallow and, overall, she was starting to suspect that she was a great deal sicker than she'd initially thought—certainly more than she'd let on. Feverish didn't seem like a strong enough word for the hot tremors now coursing through her body. Even so, if she were going to collapse, she was determined to do it as a married woman. If anything happened to her, then what would become of her nephews? Sebastian would take care of them, but it would be much easier if he was already legally their uncle.

'You are *not* all right.'

She opened her eyes with a jolt to find him leaning over her, looking as though there was a lot more he wanted to say.

'No, I'm not.' She lifted her head with an effort. 'What did the blacksmith say?'

'That he won't marry women who are sick.'

'He did not!'

'He'll probably say something about you needing to be in your right mind.' He placed a hand on her forehead. 'You're burning up.'

'That doesn't mean I'm not in my right mind.'

'You have a fever.'

'I'm just a bit hot.'

'It's more than—'

'No, it's not, not yet.' She pushed his hand away. 'It probably will be, but I can still say *I do* without sneezing. After that, I admit I might require some kind of medicine, but right now I'd like to get on with it.'

It was a good argument, she thought—authoritative, firm and determined—although it would have been a lot more effective if she hadn't decided to add gravitas to the words by standing up and then immediately veering off to one side.

'That's it.' He caught her elbow, stopping her from tumbling over. 'You're going to bed.'

'I'm not. We didn't come all this way to give up now.'

'We're not giving up. We're postponing.'

'No!' She grabbed his shoulder, trying not to lean too heavily against him. 'Did the blacksmith *say* he'd marry us now?'

'Yes.'

'Then we're getting married now or I'll change my mind.'

'Is that so?' He lifted an eyebrow. 'You wouldn't be trying to blackmail me by any chance, would you?'

'Yes,' she lied. 'It's now or never and right now I'm perfectly capable of making my own decisions. You said we were equals, remember?'

'We would be if we could both stand upright.'

'*Please*, Sebastian.'

His jaw set, as if he were still going to refuse, before he muttered something she wasn't sure she wanted to understand. 'All right.' He tightened his grip on her arm as if he were afraid she might topple over again at any moment, which she had to admit was a distinct possibility. 'But I'm summoning a doctor now. Hopefully he'll be here by the time we get back.'

'Fine.'

'And you're going to stop pretending you're not ill and tell me the truth from now on.'

'Whatever you say.'

'Do you need me to carry you?'

'No, thank you.' She lifted her chin, unwilling to make a scene. 'I believe that, traditionally, the bride makes her own way.'

'I'm not feeling very traditional. Let's just make this quick.'

Hardly the most romantic sentiment for the occasion,

Henrietta thought, but at that moment exactly what she wanted to hear. Then, after they were married, he could carry her wherever he wanted.

Chapter Twenty

'Here you are, wife.' Sebastian held out a cup of steaming hot tea. 'Drink up.'

'Thank you.' Henrietta lifted a hand and then sneezed.

'Maybe I'll just hold on to it for now.' He sat down on the edge of the bed with a smile. 'Just tell me when you're ready for a sip.'

'Thank you. *Atishoo!* Oh, dear... I'm sorry.'

'What for?'

'Because this is our wedding night and I... I... *Atishoo!*'

He gave her a pointed look. 'Are you *feigning* sickness?'

'What?' She opened her eyes wide. 'No!'

'Exactly. So don't apologise. If anyone should say sorry it's me, for dragging you halfway across the country in the cold.'

'You weren't to know I'd get sick and it was for a good reason.'

'Yes, but the truth is I've always been impulsive. Once I decide on something, I like to do it as soon as possible.'

'Oh.' She felt a vague sense of alarm. She wasn't sure she liked to be thought of as an impulse, though hopefully that was only an expression...although her head felt much too hazy to think about it now. 'Can I have some of that tea?'

'With pleasure.' He passed the cup over carefully. 'You're still a bit pale. How does your head feel?'

'Like the time I drank the last of the port in the pantry.'

'What?' He looked at her in disbelief. 'You said you poured it away! I thought it must have been because of your brother.'

'No-o.' She screwed up her lips with embarrassment. 'Nancy and I drank it after she had a bad argument with her mother. It happens quite often, I'm afraid.'

'You amaze me.'

'No, it's not like that. I think a lot of Nancy's anger is because of her mother. She doesn't usually drink because of her stepfather, but...well, that night she said she needed to drown her sorrows and I wanted to support her. What? Why are you smiling?'

'It's just unexpected, that's all.'

'Never again.' She shuddered and drank her tea in a few swallows. 'This is much nicer. I didn't realise I was so thirsty.'

'Anything else I can get you?' He put the cup aside.

'I'm a little chilly.'

'Then come here.' He shuffled up the bed, swinging his legs up and reaching an arm around her shoulders before drawing her head back against his chest.

She closed her eyes instinctively. It felt lovely, blissful even, to be lying so close, encircled in his arms. As if she were exactly where she wanted to be.

'This is nice.' He pressed a kiss on to the top of her head.

'Mmm.'

'Now get some more rest,' he murmured into her ear, his breath warming her neck and making her skin tingle. 'I'll be here when you wake up.'

'A bull escaped, trampling several gardens including that of Lord and Lady Pewter. This reporter has it on good authority that a row of prize-winning hydrangeas...'

Henrietta rolled on to her side, surprised to find herself dreaming of escaped bulls and crushed flowerbeds. Only it wasn't a dream, she realised gradually, more of a voice.

She opened her eyes to find her husband—bizarre as it still seemed to call him that—sitting beside her with one leg draped casually over the other, reading aloud from a local newspaper.

'Sebastian?'

'Ah.' He lowered the paper and smiled. 'And how's the patient today?'

'*Much* better.' She smiled back, pushing herself up on to her elbows as she realised it was true. She felt considerably better than she had when she'd last closed her eyes.

'Here.' He tossed the paper aside and leaned forward, rearranging the pillows before helping her sit up against them. 'Let me help.'

'I can manage.'

'You need to build your strength back up. You've barely eaten for two days.'

'*Two days?*'

'Since you got into this bed, yes.'

'You mean I've been lying here for *two days*?'

'Yes.' He chuckled tenderly. 'You did seem a bit confused.'

She opened her eyes wider, looking at him properly. He

had two days' worth of stubble on his chin, enough to qualify as a beard, and his eyes were circled with shadows, making them look even darker than usual. Now that she thought of it, she had a vague memory of drifting in and out of consciousness. There had been someone else in the room occasionally, but Sebastian had always been there, speaking to her in reassuring tones as she'd tossed and turned. When she'd been shivering, his arms had been around her. When she'd been burning up, he'd pulled the covers away and dabbed at her forehead with a damp cloth. When she'd been neither, well…he'd been there then, too.

'Have you been here the whole time?' she asked even though she already knew the answer.

He winked. 'I'm thinking of a new career as a nurse. The doctor thinks I show a lot of promise.'

'I agree. What else did the doctor say?'

'That it was a fever exacerbated by nervous exhaustion.' He leaned over, brushing the backs of his fingers across her cheek and beneath her jaw until his hand cradled the side of her face. 'So no more worrying. Doctor's orders. Your husband's, too.'

'I'll do my best.' She smiled and lifted her hand to cover his, trapping it against her skin. 'I didn't dream it all, then? We really are married?'

'We really are. Notice the ring. It was my mother's.'

'Oh!' She gasped in surprise, holding her other hand out to study it. 'Why didn't you tell me at the blacksmith's?'

'I thought you'd appreciate the gesture more when you weren't about to collapse.'

'I can't believe that she gave you her wedding ring…'

'Actually she gave *you* her wedding ring. She said she knew you'd take care of it.'

'It's beautiful. I don't know what to say.'

'You said yes. That's enough.'

He smiled into her eyes, his own darkening almost to black before he cleared his throat huskily.

'I apologise for the reading material. There wasn't much else, I'm afraid.'

'That's all right.' Her own throat felt somewhat dry, too. 'The bull was captured, I presume?'

'Yes, though at the cost of several prize-winning hydrangeas.'

'Oh, dear.' She started to laugh and then let out a shocked shriek.

'What?' Sebastian looked panicked. 'What's wrong?'

She pointed across the room to a mirror sitting on top of a dresser. 'I just saw my reflection!'

'Your...?' He practically sagged with relief. 'And?'

'I look *terrible!*'

'Actually, you're looking much better.'

'What?' Shock turned to horror. 'How bad did I look before?'

'Not bad, just...sick.'

'Swollen?'

'A little. That reminds me. May I?' He slid his hands around her throat, prodding gently. 'Good. You can hardly feel any swelling today and you're definitely not green any longer.'

'*Green?*' Any pleasure she might have found in his touch evaporated instantly.

'It's perfectly normal when you're sick.'

'Yes, but...' She stiffened. 'Wait, if you've been nursing me, what about my...' she closed her eyes, reluctant to even voice the thought aloud '...needs?'

'Ah.' He drew his hands away, rubbing one of them over his bristly-looking chin. 'To be honest, you were sweating so much that you didn't have many of those.'

'None?'

'Well, *some*...' He made a show of picking up the newspaper and folding it neatly. 'But nothing to concern yourself about.'

'Oh!' She flung herself over, burying her face in her pillow.

'Henrietta.' He laid a hand on her back. 'I've seen and dealt with much worse, believe me. Eight hundred men on one ship, some of them seasick...'

'I'm not a sailor!'

'True.' His hand moved in a slow circle over her back, rubbing gently. 'But you know, one of the advantages of *not* marrying a gentleman is that we're not so squeamish. I wouldn't have left you even if the doctor had brought a nurse. I wanted to take care of you. Besides, maybe this is a good thing?'

'How?'

'You were afraid of me seeing you as just a pretty face, weren't you?'

'That doesn't mean I wanted you to see me sweating, swollen and...*green*!' She groaned and pressed her face deeper into the pillow. 'Never mind anything to do with a chamber pot!'

'It doesn't make me look at you any differently.'

'How can it not?'

'Because I don't care about things like that. You were sick and you needed my help so I gave it.' She felt the bed shift as he lay down beside her. 'You're still as beautiful now as the first day I saw you.'

'Liar!'

'I was referring to inner beauty. *That* never dims, not according to the poets anyway.'

'Oh…' She twisted her head to one side. 'Maybe I'm more vain than I realised.'

'I won't tell anyone.'

She sniffed. 'In that case, do you think maybe myself and my inner beauty could have a bath?'

'I think that could be arranged.' He pressed his lips lightly against hers before leaping up and heading for the door. '*Then* you need to eat. It's about time we had our wedding breakfast.'

Chapter Twenty-One

'Just a few more mouthfuls.'

'No more!' Henrietta protested as Sebastian pushed his own, barely touched bowl of soup across the table towards her. 'I've had plenty.'

'Are you sure?' He gave her an appraising look and then relented. She was looking almost like her old self again, he thought, her still-damp hair trailing over the front of her nightgown in silken coils as she sat by the fire in their chamber. Altogether *too much* like her old self, tempting him to forget that she was still weak and recovering. Both his thoughts and eyes already kept straying dangerously close to the bed, which had been stripped and then remade with fresh sheets, but it was much too soon to even consider anything like that.

He couldn't forget how frightened he'd been just two days before, acutely aware of her breathing, of every soft inhalation and whisper of sound that passed her lips. He'd been terrified that the fever might attach to her lungs. His whole world had seemed to contract to that one bedchamber and the woman inside it.

'Sebastian?'

'Mmm?'

'You look tense.'

'Do I?' He shook his head quickly. 'It's been a worrying couple of days, that's all. I'm glad you're feeling better.'

'So am I. We can probably make a start back to Yorkshire tomorrow.'

'No.' He intended to stand firm on this point. 'Not for another day at least. I don't want you falling sick again.'

'I'm sure I won't.'

'I'm still not risking it.'

'Well, I'm not staying in bed *all* day tomorrow. How will I pass the time?' She gave him a pointed look that turned suddenly speculative. 'You know, you look different with a beard.'

'I ought to shave.'

'Do you have to? I quite like it.'

'You *do*?'

'Yes.' Her expression turned faintly mischievous. 'You look like a pirate.'

'You know, that really isn't a compliment for a naval officer.' He rubbed a hand over his jaw with a grimace. 'Have you met many pirates?'

'None that I'm aware of, but it's how I imagine a pirate might look. And I *do* mean it as a compliment.'

She tipped her head to one side and then sat forward, her eyes glittering with an expression he'd never seen in them before. It wasn't one he recognised either, or at least not exactly. It seemed to be playful and inquisitive and sultry all at the same time, each one of which made him feel at least ten degrees hotter.

'Can I touch it?'

'My beard?' He blinked, both at the request and the jolt of excitement that shot through him. 'If you want.'

'Thank you.' She stood up and moved slowly around the table to perch on the edge of his chair. 'Although it's hard to know where to begin...' She leaned close enough for one of her breasts to brush against his shoulder, making his breath catch and then quicken. 'There's just so much of it.'

'If there's one thing I excel at, it's growing hair.' He tried to swallow, but his face muscles felt unusually taut.

'Maybe here.' She skimmed her fingers across his cheekbone and down to his jaw. 'It's softer than I expected.'

'Is it?' Because the touch of her fingers was making another part of him quite the opposite. 'Not scratchy?'

'No.' Her eyelashes fluttered as she bent her head and laid her own cheek against his, rubbing back and forth gently. 'Not at all.'

Sebastian shifted in his chair, ordering himself to get up and go outside to cool down, but his legs seemed unable to move. Apparently only one part of him was still capable of movement and that wasn't obeying his commands either. Meanwhile, Henrietta's fingertips were trailing a path across his chest, making his body temperature soar even higher.

'You know...' she murmured, her cheek still pressed against his, 'you never kissed me after our wedding. Isn't the groom supposed to kiss the bride?'

Sebastian thought about flags. Naval flags. National flags. Any kind of flags... Maybe if he concentrated hard on remembering those then he could ignore the warm caress of her breath against his ear. It made his skin tingle, not just there, but all over, like ripples on a pond spreading outwards. He gritted his teeth to repress a shiver of pleasure, glad that she couldn't see his face. Or vice versa. If she looked at him just one more time with those big blue eyes, then he had a feeling he might lose his resolve completely. He felt as if he might go mad if he didn't touch her soon, but she was sick, she was recovering, she was...*kissing his ear*?

He couldn't have identified a single damned flag if his life depended on it.

'The bride was sick.' Somehow he pushed the words out.

'But she's not any more.' Her tongue touched his earlobe. 'Or are you afraid of catching my fever?'

'No.' He turned his head slightly, catching a glimpse of her pulse at the base of her throat, just above the buttons of her nightgown. It appeared to be pounding almost as fast as his. 'If I were going to catch it, I think I would have done so by now.'

'That's what I thought.'

Her lips curved against his skin as if she were smiling and he swallowed a groan. One of his hands was clenching the arm of his chair so hard he was afraid of snapping the wood, the other was lying in his lap, itching to curl itself around her waist and pull her fully into his lap. He could do it so easily, too. It would only take a second.

'You still need to rest.' It was actually becoming painful to talk.

'I'm not tired.'

'Henrietta...' He tipped his head to one side, dragging his ear away with what surely had to be the last ounce of his self-control. Men had received medals for less. 'We can't do this.'

'Oh.' She sat back on his chair-arm, digging her teeth into her bottom lip.

'It's not that I don't want to.' His heart wrenched at the look of hurt on her face. 'I just don't want you to overexert yourself.'

'I only asked for a kiss.'

'It might become more than a kiss.'

'I know.' She released her lip again. 'But…would that be so bad?'

Every muscle in his body seemed to go into some kind of collective spasm. 'Do you know what that means?'

'Yes.' Her cheeks darkened as she nodded. 'My sister-in-law told me.'

'Ah.' His chest heaved as his mind raced. If she knew what she'd be letting herself in for, then it wouldn't be so bad, would it? But then knowing in theory was very different from knowing in practice…

'You didn't answer my question.' She was holding her bottom lip between her teeth again. 'Would it be so bad?'

'Not bad.' He swallowed. 'In fact, I think it would be very good, but it's just not a good idea at the moment. I think I should go down to the taproom and you should go back to bed.'

'I'm not an invalid!' She jumped up, taking a few steps away before whirling around again, arms folded around her waist. 'You said that the past few days hadn't affected how you saw me.'

'They haven't.'

'The other day you couldn't wait to kiss me and now you can't wait to get away!'

'Not because I don't find you attractive!' The idea was so absurd that it gave him the impetus to stand up. 'I don't want to leave, Henrietta, but I have to! If I start to kiss you, then I won't want to stop.'

'Then you don't have to.'

'Don't say that. We should wait until you're completely recovered and you've got all your strength back. Then we can—'

He didn't get any further as she kissed him. She moved so quickly that he barely had time to react before her lips were pressed against his, and she wasn't gentle about it either. On the contrary, she was rough, as if she were determined to show him just how recovered she was. It was the fiercest, most potent kiss he'd ever experienced, so unexpected and mind-spinning that it rendered him utterly powerless to do anything but kiss her back. And then she pulled away and stared up at him, hands gripping the front of his shirt as her eyes blazed a challenge and that was it, he realised—he was lost.

The next few seconds were a frenzied blur. He was vaguely aware of reaching for her, of catching her up in his arms as her own curved around his neck, until her feet were trailing along the floor and they were both stumbling towards the bed. And then his clothes were being discarded, scattered in all directions at once, and her nightdress was being pulled over her head, and they were lying side by side, only not *quite* side by side. He was lying half on top of her, one of his legs draped across hers while he kept his weight on one arm, trying to keep from crushing her.

'Mmm…' He kissed her again, one of his hands smoothing a path over her stomach and up her ribcage until he found her breast and cradled it. 'Mmm.' He slid his tongue inside her mouth as he drew his thumb across the bud, swallowing her moan of pleasure. She was a perfect handful, he thought, even more perfect than he'd imagined, and if she moaned like that again, she might just unman him before they could get any further...

'Tell me...' He broke the kiss. 'If you change your mind. If you want me to stop...'

'I will...' she arched her back as his hand slid downwards again, curving gently around her hip '...but I won't.'

'But if you do...' He almost growled the words, needing her to know she could trust him, before he moved downwards, placing his mouth where his hand had left off.

'Oh!'

She cried out as his lips closed around her nipple and suckled. It was beyond any shadow of a doubt the most seductive sound he'd ever heard. It made him feel an even greater need to hurry, although he didn't want to rush her or do anything before she was ready. Which meant that he was going to have to think of something powerfully *un*-seductive to hold himself in check, though frankly it was a wonder he could still think at all when all the blood in his body appeared to have sped straight to his groin.

Flags again?

'Sebastian...' She placed her hands on either side of his head, lifting his mouth back to hers, her breathing fast and erratic. 'I want you.'

'I want you, too.' He rolled on top of her, nudging her legs apart and settling his body gently between her thighs. 'But it might hurt at first.'

'I know.'

He smiled. 'You know a lot.'

'I know that I trust you...' her eyes were wide and intense '...and I can't wait any longer.'

There was only one way he could think of to reply, holding her gaze as he pushed inside her. She gave another gasp, one that sounded like pain this time, and he stopped at once, counting to ten as he tried to remain completely still. He was only part way sheathed. Maybe if he pulled back, it would...

'No.' She moved beneath him suddenly, as if she'd sensed his retreat, pushing upwards until he was fully embedded.

'Hen...' He couldn't even finish her name, pressing his face into the curve of her neck and breathing heavily as they both lay completely still for a few seconds.

She felt so, so good, her body moulded against his, her inner muscles clenching around him so tightly he could have groaned aloud. She was his, his wife, his Henrietta, and she fitted him as if they were made for each other. And then they both started moving, pressing together and pulling apart in an awkward and then less awkward and then almost flawless rhythm. He wouldn't have believed the feeling could get any better and yet it did, so close to perfection that he didn't think he could hold on for much longer. He tried stopping, pushing himself up on his arms to cool them both down, but her breasts were slick with a sheen of perspiration and one of her legs was around his hip and there was nothing he could do. He sank back into her, thrusting one last time before he found his release.

'Sebastian?'

It took him a few oblivious moments to realise that she was speaking to him.

'Are you hurt?' He rolled quickly away from her.

'No.' She placed a hand on his chest and gave a low laugh. 'Stop worrying.'

'Says the woman who collapsed due to nervous exhaustion.' He fell on to his back, raking one hand through his hair. He could still feel his own heartbeat, beating so hard it felt like a drum inside his chest. It was no wonder. The last half-hour—he *hoped* he'd at least lasted that long—had been the most intense experience of his life. He had a feeling it might take him the rest of the night and then some to recover.

'Well, I've learned the error of my ways.' Henrietta laid one arm across his chest and rested her chin on top. 'That was as good as any medicine.'

'It didn't hurt at all?'

'A little at first, but then I forgot about it.'

'Good.' He wrapped his arms around her waist, holding her tight. 'Although I still don't think the doctor would have approved.'

'The doctor isn't a newlywed.'

'True.' He laughed. 'And given the circumstances, I think he would have understood. You're hard enough to resist at the best of times, but in a nightdress it's well nigh impossible. I thought that the first night I met you.'

'You did?'

'Yes. I remember being particularly taken with your ankles.'

'These ankles?' She kicked her legs up in the air behind her.

'The very same.' He regarded them thoughtfully. Exhausted as he was, the sight was irresistible. 'I haven't given them nearly enough attention tonight. Here.' He sat up, turning her over until she was lying on her back with her legs draped across his lap. 'I hate to be neglectful.'

'Sebastian…' She giggled as he ran a hand gently across her calf.

'Don't tell me you're ticklish?'

'No, it's just…' She drew the bed sheet across her waist. 'I'm naked.'

'I noticed. So am I.' He bent her knee and pressed kisses all the way down to her ankle. 'You know, I've never been seduced by a woman before.'

Her mouth dropped open. 'I did *not* seduce you!'

'I beg to differ. I offered to go to the taproom and let you recover in peace.'

'All *I* did was kiss you.'

'There was no *all I did* about it. There are kisses and then there are *kisses*.'

'And the way you're kissing my ankle right now would be?'

'Definitely the latter.' He pressed his lips to each of her toes in turn before putting her leg down gently. 'But you're right. It's too soon.'

'I never said…'

'But it is. I'll just have to dream of your ankles. Now close your eyes and I'll tuck you back in.'

'Oh, all right.' She snuggled against him as he lay down beside her again, hoisting the blankets up to cover them both. 'I suppose I did seduce you a bit, but you *were* going to seduce me at some point, weren't you?'

'As soon as possible, yes.'

'That's all right then.' She smiled and yawned. 'I only sped things up a little bit.'

'I hadn't worked out all the details yet, but it was going to be very romantic.'

'How nice.'

'You would have enjoyed it.'

'I'm sure. Did I spoil things, then?'

'What do you think?'

She laughed and snuggled closer. 'Sebastian?'

'Yes?'

'Do I really have to spend the whole day in bed again tomorrow?'

'Absolutely.'

'Good.' She pressed a sleepy kiss against his chest. 'Because I'm looking forward to it now.'

Henrietta lay back against the pillows and stretched her arms above her head, feeling like the cat who'd got the cream and was basking in sunshine to boot. As horrified as she'd been by her sickbed appearance the previous day, she was starting to think that perhaps having Sebastian as a nurse wasn't such a bad thing, after all. All things considered, she would be perfectly content to lie in bed all day long. Not only was he extremely attentive, but his methods of keeping her there were surprisingly pleasurable. She didn't think there was a single square inch of her body that he *hadn't* kissed that morning, though he'd paid particular attention to her ankles, she'd noticed.

She supposed she ought to feel embarrassed by some of the things they'd done, but instead, every time she looked at him, she felt a fresh flurry of stomach tingles. They were beyond friendship now, quite a long way beyond, and, although neither of them had mentioned love, they had a new kind of relationship. One based on honesty, affection, respect and undeniable mutual attraction. And if that didn't feel like quite enough, a tiny voice at the back of her mind argued, it was still better than a lot of marriages.

No, she had no regrets, she decided, watching the ripple of Sebastian's shoulder blades as he drew a knife across his cheeks and frowned into the mirror on the dresser that had given her such a shock. None except that she hadn't been able to persuade him to keep the beard, but he'd claimed it was too itchy, promising to compensate in ways that made her imagination run riot.

'There.' He put the knife down and rubbed a piece of cloth over his face. 'All done. What do you think?'

'I *think* I miss my husband.'

'Ah, I forgot, you like pirates.' He placed his hands on his hips. 'I'll just have to save that look for special occasions. Now, am I allowed to get undressed and come back to bed?'

'I don't know.' She tapped a finger against her bottom lip. 'I *would* say yes, but I thought I was supposed to be recovering?'

'That was yesterday.' He was already removing his trousers. 'The doctor's given you the all-clear today.'

'Oh, yes.' She giggled. 'He said I looked quite invigorated.'

'I hope you didn't tell him why.'

'No, although he did tell me I was most fortunate in my choice of husband.'

'And you agreed?'

'I might have.' She glanced at the window. 'What's the weather like outside?'

'Wet and cold.'

'No more snow?'

'Not at the moment.' He gave her a quizzical look. 'You sound disappointed.'

'I am a little. Part of me was hoping we'd get snowed in.'

'That sounds blissful.' He jumped on to the bed and climbed on top of her. 'Although I thought you wanted to get back to Feversham as quickly as possible?'

'That was before I discovered what we could do indoors.'

She smiled provocatively. 'Besides, if we were snowed in, then it wouldn't be our fault, would it? A delay would be out of our control. And we'd have to fill in the time somehow.'

'I see.' He nuzzled the side of her neck. 'You wouldn't be trying to seduce me again, would you, Mrs Fortini?'

'No. It's your turn.'

'Challenge accepted.' He grinned wickedly and dived under the covers.

'Sebastian?' She let out a squeal of surprise. 'What are you doing?'

'Ankles.'

She laughed at his muffled reply and settled back against the pillows again. Only it wasn't just her ankles he was kissing, she realised quickly. It was her toes, too, and her calves and the backs of her knees, the insides of her thighs...

'Sebastian!' She thrust her hands under the covers, grabbing his shoulders. 'You can't!'

'I can.' His hands wrapped around her waist, pinning her down again.

'But *what* are you doing?'

'It's much better if I show you.' His head appeared from beneath the covers, one eyebrow raised. 'Let me?'

She hesitated briefly and then nodded, squeezing her eyes shut as curiosity battled with modesty. She probably ought to protest some more, she thought, only she couldn't quite bring herself to do it, not when everything he did, every way and place he touched her felt so good, and even better when he slid up the bed and entered her, thrusting gently until she gave a low moan and started to rock against him, too. It was better than the first time, as if they were truly one body, moving together in total harmony.

And then he reversed their positions, holding on to her

hips and rolling them both over until she was positioned on top of him, naked and exposed and feeling more powerful than she ever had in her life. For a moment she wasn't quite sure what to do, but then the sensations seemed to intensify until she was moving to her own rhythm, sliding back and forth, faster and faster until at last she felt a trembling, shuddering sensation in her abdomen as if something had burst inside her, leaving her whole body quivering and shaking. It was a few minutes before she rolled over and came back to herself.

'You really do like my ankles.' She stared up at the canopy in wonderment.

He gave a ragged laugh, though she could tell he was staring at the canopy, too. 'You have no idea.'

Chapter Twenty-Two

Mornings had officially become Sebastian's favourite time of the day. He'd woken up in the same room as Henrietta several times while they'd been travelling north, but he'd quickly discovered that waking up *beside* her, with her face next to his on the pillow, was completely different. Just looking at her while she slept, watching her eyelashes flutter and her chest move slowly up and down made his heart clench with a sense of gladness and contentment. And when she woke up, all tousled and wide eyed... It made it phenomenally difficult to get out of bed, though after two days of so-called rest and recuperation, the continued absence of snow left them no choice but to board the carriage again and head south.

On the other hand, being cuddled up together in a carriage beneath a pile of blankets had its own cosy charm. Henrietta seemed happy, too, which made him even happier. With her arm tucked into his and her head resting on his shoulder, the sense of contentment he'd been afraid might end with the honeymoon only seemed to grow deeper and more intense with each passing mile. He insisted they make regular stops to prevent the coachmen from freezing, as well as to make sure she showed no signs of a relapse, so that it was three days before they eventually came within sight of Feversham.

It was clear from the moment they climbed down from the carriage that it was going to be some time before he got Henrietta to himself again. The boys were like a litter of puppies, rushing down the front steps to hurl themselves at her legs and jump about with excitement. His own greeting was only slightly less enthusiastic: hugs from Oliver and Michael and a firm handshake from Peter, and then his mother and Lord Tobias were welcoming them back, too, while the Dowager Duchess stood at the front door, smiling.

After the comparative peace and tranquillity of the journey, it was a frenetic half an hour of excitement, naturally succeeded by tea in the drawing room as everyone clamoured to hear about the wedding.

'Did you really get married in a blacksmith's shop?' As always, Michael was the most voluble.

'We did.' Sebastian tousled his hair. 'The blacksmith hit the anvil with his hammer when we said "I do".'

'So this means you're really my uncle?'

'It really does.' He reached for Henrietta's hand and squeezed it. Even sitting on the chair next to his, she felt too far away. He'd got accustomed to sitting close beside her, to always touching her. Now it felt wrong to be as much as a foot away.

'And are we all going to live at Belles?'

'I think Miss MacQueen might have a few things to say

about that.' Sebastian laughed at the boy's persistence. 'We haven't worked out all the details yet, but you'll be the first to know once we come up with a plan. Right now we'd like to know what you've been up to.'

'We've set up a proper stage for our play!' Oliver bounced enthusiastically.

'And we painted some backdrops,' Peter added.

'That sounds very professional.'

'I helped to make curtains,' his mother joined in. 'It's become quite a production. Tobias even has a small part.'

'A good one, I hope?' He lifted an eyebrow at his uncle.

'They needed another villain...' Lord Tobias spread his hands out. 'Sorry to say, I'm fairly quickly despatched.'

'No match for Nelson obviously. Another pirate, then?'

'Napoleon, actually.'

'Indeed? That sounds...original.'

'It's artistic licence.' His mother smiled serenely. 'All great playwrights have to bend the truth a little.'

'Of course.' Henrietta nodded in agreement. 'It sounds as though it's going to be spectacular.'

'I'm certain of it. They've worked very hard, haven't you, boys? But now it's time for you to go and clean up for dinner.'

'Yes, Mrs Fortini.' Michael looked puzzled. 'Or should we call you Great-Aunt Fortini now?'

'How about Aunt Elizabeth? If that's all right with everyone?'

'It is with me.' Henrietta beamed at Sebastian. 'I think it's lovely.'

'Aunt Elizabeth.' Peter threw his brothers a superior look as they trooped out of the room. 'I told you so.'

'I'm so relieved that you're back,' his mother continued

once they'd gone. 'We expected you a couple of days ago. Was the weather bad?'

'Not very, but—'

'I caught a bit of a chill.' Henrietta interrupted. 'Not much of one, but I didn't feel up to the journey home straight away, so we stayed in Gretna for a few days. I'm sorry if we caused you concern.'

'Ah, well, I'm just glad you're back safe and sound, especially now. The weather's taken a turn for the worse over the past couple of days.' His mother held on to his gaze for a few moments longer than necessary. 'In any case, I'll let you get cleaned up before dinner, too. We'll eat a bit early since I'm sure you're exhausted after your journey.'

'A little. All that sitting and bumping around is surprisingly wearing. Give me a ship any day. Come on, wife.' Sebastian stood and tugged on Henrietta's hand, pulling her to her feet. 'We'll see you at dinner, Mama.'

He kept hold of her fingers as they climbed the stairs, not saying anything until they were inside their bedchamber—previously *her* bedchamber.

'A *bit* of a chill?' He spun around, catching her by the waist.

'Yes.' She laughed up at him. 'Your mother would only scold if she knew the truth, and that's my job from now on.'

'Scolding me?' He walked her backwards towards the closed door. 'Is that what you intend to do?'

'Among other things. Fortunately for you, I'm in a good mood at the moment.'

'What a coincidence.' He pressed his lips to the side of her neck, smiling as she tipped her head back against the wood, arching her neck to allow him greater access. 'So am I.'

'Sebastian...' Her breath caught in her throat.

'Mmm.' He slid his hands down, pulling slowly on the fabric of her gown until it was bunched up around her hips.

'It's almost time for dinner.'

'No, it's time to get dressed for dinner. I believe that involves a bit of undressing first.'

'Ye-es, but...' She gasped as he pressed his tongue against the hollow at the base of her throat and then blew softly against it. 'I suppose we *are* newlyweds...'

'Exactly.' He grinned. 'Is that going to be your excuse for everything from now on?'

'For a few months definitely. Shouldn't we move to the bed?'

'Not necessarily.' He held her dress up with one hand, unbuttoning his trousers with the other while his mouth drifted back to capture hers. 'Unless you want to?'

'No, but how...?'

'That...' he pressed closer, sliding one hand behind her back '...is what we're about to work out.'

Chapter Twenty-Three

'So, at the risk of sounding like Michael, what *are* your plans?' Lord Tobias leaned back in his chair at the dinner table, peering at Sebastian through a cloud of cigar smoke. 'Your mother told me she's giving you Belles as a wedding present.'

'Yes...' Sebastian drew on his own cigar, knitting his brows together at the reminder. His mother had taken him aside when he and Henrietta had finally come downstairs for dinner, in even better moods thanks to some very effective manoeuvring, although he still hadn't been quite sure what to make of her announcement. It seemed wrong not to at least share Belles with Anna, especially considering the years she'd put into the business, but as his mother had explained, as Countess of Staunton, his sister didn't have any need of the income. In fact, she'd already approved the plan when his mother had drawn up her will.

'Sebastian?' His uncle looked faintly worried.

'Sorry, Uncle, I was wool-gathering. I'm very grateful. I'm just not sure I deserve it.'

'Your mother thinks you do, but if it makes you feel any better, it's for you *and* Henrietta. You wouldn't say that *she* doesn't deserve it, would you?'

'Good point. The truth is, I want to keep Belles in the family, but I don't want to put anyone else out of work and I'd like to build something of my own, too. I have some money saved and I think a tea room would make Henrietta happy.' He gave a low chuckle. 'That appears to have become my main purpose in life these days.'

'As it should be.' Lord Tobias rested his cigar on an ashtray. 'I'd like to invest.'

'Really?' Sebastian almost dropped his own cigar in surprise. 'You mean like a business partner?'

'A *silent* business partner. The money will be yours one day anyway.'

'It will?'

'Yes. I intend to make you my heir.'

'Your heir?' It was a good thing he'd tightened his grip on the cigar, Sebastian thought, or he would *definitely* have singed his trousers. 'Me?'

'You're my nephew.'

'Yes, but...'

'I've no children and I'm not likely to marry now.'

'Still... I don't know what to say...' Sebastian felt vaguely dumbstruck. 'Did you never want to marry, Uncle?'

'No, I was always more interested in my studies. Of course, I was forced to endure a few London Seasons in my youth, but fortunately my brother married and let me off the hook quite early.'

'But won't he mind if you make me your heir?'

'He won't be happy about it, but if you knew my brother then you'd know he rarely experiences that emotion anyway. For once, however, there'll be nothing he can do.'

'Does my mother know about this?'

'We discussed it while you were in Scotland.' Lord Tobias sat forward. 'Sebastian, I'm not trying—I would never try—to replace your father, but this way you'll have a legacy from both sides of your family. It would make an old man very happy, too. So, what do you say?'

'I can hardly refuse.' Sebastian held a hand out to clasp his uncle's. 'Thank you. I'm honoured.'

'Then it's agreed. With only one condition...' Lord Tobias smiled. 'That you're not allowed to leave before the new year. I'd like a chance to introduce you to my friends and neighbours. I want everyone to know that you're my heir with my blessing.'

'I'll need to speak with Henrietta, but I'm sure we can stay.' Sebastian nodded thoughtfully. 'We're not allowed to go anywhere until after the play anyway and I'm told it needs a few more rehearsals. I'm actually starting to think—'

He didn't finish the sentence as the butler cleared his throat from the dining room doorway.

'Yes, Dennison?' Lord Tobias glanced up expectantly.

'Forgive the intrusion, sir, but there's someone at the servants' entrance asking to see Mrs Fortini. The younger Mrs Fortini, that is.'

'Henrietta?' Sebastian got to his feet in surprise. 'Did they give a name?'

'Yes, sir. I believe he called himself David Gardiner.'

'What?' He made a grab for the back of his chair. 'Are you sure?'

'Perhaps you could invite our guest to join us in here?' Lord Tobias stood, too, addressing the butler before turning to Sebastian. 'Should I call Henrietta?'

'No.' He was vaguely aware of his fingers tightening around the wood. 'Not yet. I need to be sure he's who he says he is first.'

'Of course.' Lord Tobias agreed, waiting at his side for what felt like an interminable period of time until the butler returned, leading a man with untidy blond hair and such an uncanny resemblance to Michael that it left not the tiniest shred of doubt about his identity.

'Mr Gardiner.' Lord Tobias spoke when Sebastian just stared.

'Yes, sir.' The other man darted a look between them, his expression somehow both defiant and apologetic at the same time. 'I'm looking for my sister and boys. I was told they were here.'

'They are.' Sebastian found his voice at last, though it sounded strange even to him. Harder and confrontational, but then he was feeling remarkably, uncharacteristically, belligerent. Coming so soon after his mother's gift and his uncle's announcement, the unexpected sight of David Gardiner made him feel as if the ground beneath his feet had just shifted, as if he were standing on a deck and a giant wave had just hit the side of his ship. He had the horrible feeling that if he did the wrong thing now then he might topple overboard, as if the life he'd envisaged for himself just a few minutes ago might disappear into thin air. He'd never experienced sea sickness, but at that moment he felt distinctly nauseated.

'Are they all right?'

'Your sons are upstairs in bed, safe and sound.'

'Thank goodness.' The man's mouth contorted before he let out a strangled sob and put his hands over his face.

'Sit down.' Lord Tobias pulled out a chair. 'Port?'

'No.' He shook his head, recoiling as if he'd just been offered poison. 'No, thank you. I'd like to see Henrietta.'

'Not yet.' Sebastian answered heavily. 'Not until you explain yourself and what you're doing here.'

'I'd rather speak to her. *She's* my sister.'

'But under *my* protection.'

'What does that mean? I've never met you before.'

Sebastian drew himself up, deriving a savage sense of satisfaction from the other man's shocked expression. 'I mean that *your* sister is *my* wife. We were married a few days ago in Gretna Green.'

'What?'

'Perhaps you could have a room prepared for Mr Gardiner?' Lord Tobias gestured discreetly to the butler still standing in the doorway.

'As you wish, sir.'

'I looked for you.' Sebastian narrowed his eyes accusingly. 'One of your friends said that you'd boarded a ship for America.'

'I did.' David Gardiner stared heavily at him for a few seconds before continuing. 'Although I did a lot of drinking first. Then I got all the way up the gangplank before I came to my senses. So I got off again.'

'Then where the hell have you been since?'

'I had no money left so I had to walk back to Bath.' David pushed a hand through his hair. 'I went to the biscuit shop and the woman there told me Henrietta had left with you and sent me to Redbourne's store. She said you were friends with the owner and that he'd be able to get a message to you.'

'And he sent you here instead?'

'He paid my coach fare, yes.'

Sebastian scowled. Typical of James to do the *right* thing, sending David to be reconciled with his family. It *was* the right thing to do, but now he was aware of an unreasonable surge of resentment. How dared David come back and just walk into Henrietta's life as if nothing had happened? As if she hadn't spent the past few weeks working and worrying and struggling before finally moving on with her life? How dared he come back and shatter their plans for the future? He'd given up his freedom for those plans and now David's arrival threatened to destroy everything.

All of which made him want to pick up the chair he was still clutching and smash it to pieces.

'Perhaps it's time to fetch my wife?' he said instead, forcing his fists to uncurl as he glanced at Lord Tobias. 'If you don't mind?'

'Of course not.' Lord Tobias looked as if he were eager for an excuse to flee the room. 'I'll send her directly.'

'Henrietta never mentioned you to me before.' David looked up from the table, sounding as combative as Sebastian felt.

'Really?' He folded his arms. Of course, it would have been impossible for Henrietta to have mentioned him since they'd only met at the same time David had left, but damned if he was going to tell him that. *He* wasn't the one with explaining to do… He took a step towards the open doorway to make sure that Henrietta would see him first.

'Sebastian?' She appeared after only a few minutes. 'Tobias said you wanted to see me.' She stopped at the sight of his face. 'What's the matter?'

'Come and see.' He reached a hand out, telling himself that he needed to hold her steady in case she swooned with surprise. Not that she'd ever swooned before, or seemed prone to swooning in general, but there was a first time for everything. It wasn't that he just wanted to hold her. To hold *on to* her...

'David!' Her fingers had barely grazed his before she tore them away again. It was necessary in order for her to run across the room to her brother, but for the life of him, Sebastian didn't think he could have released her if she hadn't pulled away first. It was all he could do not to clamp his fingers around hers in protest. Instead, he stood watching, half of him knowing that he ought to leave and give them privacy, the other half absolutely refusing to budge as much as an inch.

'Oh, David.' Henrietta clamped her arms tight around her brother's neck, though her voice had a definite tremor. 'You're here! You're actually here.' She pulled back after a few seconds, staring hard into his face as if she daren't believe the evidence of her own eyes. 'What happened? Why did you leave?'

'I'll explain it all later.' Her brother tried to take a step back, though she didn't let him go far. 'At the time I felt desperate, but it wasn't fair of me. I'm sorry, Henrietta, truly, but it won't happen again. I'm a different man now.'

'Then that's all that matters.'

She embraced him again, missing Sebastian's snort of disgust. Was that it? No argument, no condemnation, no judgement at all? He wanted her to rail at her brother, but instead she was all smiles, as if he'd only been away on a holiday. As if he'd never abandoned her in the first place!

'Come on.' Hard as it was to stomach, her smile spread even wider. 'I'll take you up to the nursery. The boys are probably asleep by now, but I can still show you they're all right.'

Sebastian stiffened as they passed. He had a horrible feeling that his wife had already forgotten he was there. *I*, she'd just said. *I'll take you up. I can still show you they're all right.* One glimpse of her brother and all of a sudden they'd stopped being *we*.

A horrible sinking sensation told him this was only the start of it.

'They've missed you.' Henrietta whispered, standing shoulder to shoulder with David in the doorway of the boys' bedroom.

'I've missed them.' He sucked in a breath and let it go again slowly. 'I don't know how I'm going to explain to them what I did.'

'I told them you were sick.' She gave him a sidelong look. 'Which was the truth, wasn't it? And now you're better?'

'Better than I was. I've given up alcohol. It wasn't easy, but it was the only way.'

'Good. Then all you need to tell them is that you love them and that you won't leave again.'

He wrapped an arm around her shoulders. 'I should probably say it to you, too.'

'Yes, you probably should.'

'I love you and I won't do it again. I promise.'

'Thank you. Now come away before we wake anyone.'

She stepped back into the nursery, closing the door to the bedroom softly behind them.

'Thank you for taking care of them.' David looked sombre again.

'It wasn't just me. Sebastian's been a great help, too.'

'Mmm.' David's face twisted. 'You never told me you had a beau.'

'I didn't before. It all happened very quickly.'

'How quickly?'

'Well… I met him the night before you left actually, but—'

'And you're already married?' David's expression turned into that of an angry big brother. 'Why? Just because you needed his help?' He shook his head. 'If I'd known you'd do something like this…'

'It's not something like anything.'

'It's all my fault.'

'It's nobody's fault!' She blinked at the harshness of his tone. 'That's entirely the wrong word. Your leaving brought us together, I don't deny that, but I'm glad that it did. Sebastian wanted to help me and we became friends and—'

'He didn't have to marry you to be *your friend*.' David's eyebrows snapped together ferociously. 'What else did he want? Are you certain you're really married?'

'Yes!' She put her hands on her hips. 'We decided that marrying was the right thing to do for the boys. We *thought* that you weren't coming back.'

'It still doesn't make sense. Why does a gentleman marry a shop girl just so that he can help raise her nephews? Why would he care?'

'Because he did! And he's not a gentleman. He's a sailor.' She frowned. 'Or he was anyway.'

'A sailor whose family live in a place like this.' David looked around at the nursery. 'My whole house is smaller than this room.'

'I know.' She felt vaguely uncomfortable at the observation. 'But Sebastian and I have decided to build a life together. We care for each other and we're equals.'

David gave her a sceptical look. 'You can't be in love, not after less than a month.'

Henrietta opened her mouth and then closed it again. Why *couldn't* she be in love after less than a month? Because she was, she realised suddenly. She was very much in love. Only she wanted Sebastian to be the first one to hear the words, not her brother.

'Does he treat you well? Is he good to you? Because if he isn't...'

'He treats me very well.' She folded her arms, struck with a sudden sense of foreboding. 'Trust me, in a few days, you'll be the best of friends.'

'All settled?'

Sebastian was standing beside the fireplace, hands clasped behind his back, as Henrietta entered their bedroom. He was wearing an entirely *un*-Sebastian-like expression. The lines of his face looked uncharacteristically tight and rigid.

'Yes. I didn't mean to take so long.' She closed the door and hesitated. She hadn't expected him to be frowning. She'd expected to come back to their room and for him to reassure her, to wrap his arms around her and tell her how happy he was for her and the boys, too, but unfortunately the sense of foreboding she'd felt with her brother grew even worse. 'David wanted to look at the boys for a while and then we talked.'

'Understandable.'

'Have you told the others?'

'Yes. They were very pleased, as no doubt they'll tell you themselves in the morning. They've gone to bed now.'

'Of course. It's late.' She took a few steps closer. 'I'm glad you're still awake.'

'I wanted to wait and see how you were.' He quirked an eyebrow. 'How are you?'

'Happy.' She smiled, though somehow both the word and action felt unconvincing. It wasn't that she was *un*happy. She *had* been happy, *very* happy just an hour ago. She was thrilled that David was back, but his obvious antipathy towards Sebastian, not to mention all of his questions about her marriage, had left her feeling tense, too. And now that she thought about it, Sebastian had been frowning downstairs, as well...

'What about you?' Something in his face stopped her from touching him. 'Are *you* happy?'

'Of course.' His smile looked just as unconvincing. His eyes were completely dark, without any sparkle at all. 'It's just come out of the blue, that's all.'

'Yes.' She forced her lips wider, though she had a feeling the effect looked more grotesque than genuine. 'The boys will probably think it's all a dream in the morning.'

'Quite.' There was a long pause before Sebastian cleared his throat. 'Did your brother say anything about his plans? Anything at all?'

'No, but it's too soon for all that, isn't it? He's only just arrived.'

'I suppose so.' Another awkward silence descended before he stepped away from the fireplace. 'Well... I'm tired. It's been an eventful evening.'

She nodded, avoiding his eyes as they both undressed in silence. *We thought you weren't coming back...* Those were the words she'd used to explain to David why she'd married Sebastian—to explain why he'd married her, too. They'd made a conscious decision to raise her nephews together, which meant that now David was back, the very cornerstone of their marriage was gone, knocked down in one fell swoop. Their reason no longer existed.

She still had no regrets about marrying him, especially now that she'd realised just how much she cared, but...did *he* regret it? His cold behaviour implied that she'd tricked or betrayed him somehow, as if he'd never really cared for her or thought of her as anything more than a pretty face, after all. As if making amends for his guilty conscience had been all that had mattered, had ever mattered... Apparently she was just as foolish and naive as she'd always feared, deep down. She'd truly thought their marriage had meant more than that.

She lowered herself on to the stool in front of her dressing table, staring at the reflection of their bed in the mirror with a new sense of bleakness. She felt cold inside, as if her heart had just frozen. Sebastian was already under the covers, lying on his back with his eyes closed. That was different, too. Usually he sat up, waiting until she came to bed before curling up in a spoon shape beside her.

She pressed her eyes shut to stop the tears from seeping out. How could an evening that had brought so much joy end so badly? She'd fallen in love with her husband just at the moment he seemed to have changed his mind about her.

Chapter Twenty-Four

'Will your brother be joining us?'

Sebastian threw his napkin aside, resisting the urge to glare at his mother as she smiled blithely across the breakfast table at his wife.

'Not this morning.' Henrietta shook her head apologetically. 'He went up to the nursery first thing and…well, there was a great deal of excitement.'

'I can imagine. I think I actually heard some of it. Not that I'm complaining—it was a lovely sound.'

'They're all breakfasting up there together, although David sends his thanks for the invitation. I'll go up again shortly, but I thought I should give them some time alone.'

'Harumph.'

'Is something the matter?' Henrietta twisted her head, lifting an eyebrow at the sound Sebastian hadn't intended to make quite so loudly.

'With *me*?' He put a particular stress on the word. 'Nothing at all. *I'm* perfectly fine.'

'Oh.' A look of confusion, mingled with hurt, flashed across her face. 'I thought the boys might like to show David around the gardens after breakfast.'

'It's a bit cold, isn't it?'

'We'll wrap up.' She paused. 'Will you join us? We could take a walk down to the lake?'

'No.' He didn't intend to be quite so brusque, only for some reason he couldn't seem to help it. 'I promised to take Mother into the village this morning.'

'That can wait.' His mother seemed determined to earn herself a glare. 'This is much more important and it would be nice for you and David to get to know each other. You're brothers-in-law now.'

'Yes... Very well, then. I'll be in the library when you're ready.'

He pushed his chair back and marched out of the breakfast room at a brisk pace. It was the same pace with which he'd marched out of the bedroom that morning and the one he intended to keep using until he got his emotions under control. He was behaving badly, he knew, but he couldn't seem to help himself. Just as he couldn't help the seething resentment he was experiencing towards his new brother-in-law. Even towards Henrietta. Every time she mentioned her brother he felt as if she were plunging a dagger into his heart and then twisting it for good measure.

Scowling, he threw himself into a green leather chair by the fireplace and picked up a book, reading the same page at least half a dozen times without taking a single word in.

'Mr Fortini?' The butler's voice sounded from the doorway in a tone he was starting to resent. 'Mrs Fortini asked me to inform you that she's ready.'

'Thank you, Dennison.'

He sighed and marched back out through the hall, pulling on a coat and hat before walking out of the front door. Henrietta was already outside, standing next to her brother, though she took a step towards him as he approached, her expression one of trepidation.

'Good morning.' He gave David a terse nod and received an equally terse one back.

'I'm so glad you're coming with us.' Henrietta looked relieved that he'd spoken first. 'Although I don't think we'll have long before it rains.'

'Father's home!' Michael bounced up to him, grinning so widely it looked as if his face might actually split in two. Obviously a forgiving type, Sebastian thought, stifling a rush of resentment. Only Peter looked as if he weren't enjoying himself, standing off to one side with his hands shoved deep into his pockets. That was more like it.

'So he is.' He forced himself to sound cheerful. 'You must be very pleased.'

'Now we're one big, happy family!'

'Let's get moving, then...' Henrietta held out her hand when neither he nor David responded '...before we all freeze.'

'So...' David gave him a sidelong look as she walked ahead. 'Peter tells me you've been teaching them about the navy. He says he wants to join when he's old enough.'

'It's not a bad career for a young man.' Sebastian set off at his earlier brisk march, vaguely irritated when David kept pace beside him. 'Although he's still young enough to change his mind.'

'I hope he does. I don't want any of my boys going to sea.'

'Is that so?' Sebastian gritted his teeth. 'Any particular reason?'

'I've just never trusted sailors, that's all.'

'Interesting. Fortunately, I'd say your boys have minds of their own.'

'Oh, look, some starlings!' Henrietta pointed, her voice unnecessarily loud in the crisp morning air.

'They can still be guided by their father, can't they?'

'Or are they blackbirds?'

'They can when their father is around.'

'I'm here now.'

'And there's a robin!'

'For the time being.'

'For good.'

Sebastian made a snorting sound. 'It still seems a little odd to be laying the law down so soon after abandoning them, wouldn't you say?'

'I didn't abandon them. I left them with their aunt.'

'Whom you abandoned, too. And you say that sailors can't be trusted?'

'You don't understand anything about it.' David glared and then veered off the path with a growl. 'Come on, boys. I think I'd rather see those woods than the lake.'

'What was that?' Henrietta stayed where she was, her hands clenched into fists at her sides as the others scurried away across the lawn, although Peter hesitated briefly before joining them, Sebastian noticed. 'How *could* you?'

'How could I what?' He squared his shoulders, feigning ignorance.

'How could you be so cruel? He knows what he did was wrong. You didn't have to make him feel any worse. This isn't like you.'

He felt a momentary twinge of guilt. The words *had* been cruel and she was right, it wasn't like him. He was rarely cruel, but he'd wanted to hurt David; wanted to hurt him more than he'd ever wanted to hurt anyone, Captain Belton included.

'He said he didn't trust sailors.'

'I heard. I'm not defending him, but—'

'It sounds like it.'

'Sebastian!'

'At least I'm not pretending nothing happened.'

She folded her arms, eyes flashing angrily. 'David and I have talked about it. I don't need to punish him as well.'

'Well, maybe you should!'

'Why? What good will it do?'

He ground his teeth, silently acknowledging the truth of it. What good *would* it do? Nothing, except to make him feel better.

'Henrietta, he abandoned you!'

'You abandoned Anna!'

'That was different. I would have come back if I could have, but there was nothing I could do.'

'And his drinking was a sickness that he couldn't help either. *You* were the one who told me that. Only you were a lot more sympathetic *before* you met him. Now you're just being a hypocrite. You wanted—you got!—a second chance. You abandoned your sister and you had a chance to make up for it by helping me. Well, David's back and he deserves a second chance, too.'

'So you choose him?'

'What? No, Sebastian, you're my husband...'

'A husband you don't need any longer. Now that David's back, you don't need my help any more, do you?'

'Is that why you're angry? Because you think his second chance means that yours doesn't count any more? As if it's all just been a waste of time and effort! As if our marriage is pointless!'

'No, of course not.' He stiffened, shocked by the expression on her face. She looked more than hurt. She looked distraught. And as if she wanted to hurt him back.

'I think that's what you *do* think.' Her eyes narrowed and then blazed suddenly. 'But really you ought to be glad. You *did* the right thing so you don't have to make amends any more. Now you can have your freedom back and without any guilt this time. You can go wherever you want, I won't stop you.'

She stormed up to confront him. 'I'm sorry I married you under false pretences. I didn't know they were false then, but they were. If I could turn the clock back for you then I would, but I can't. We're married now and there's nothing we can do about that. Just know that I won't expect anything from you ever again.' She turned away from him to follow David. 'We'll leave as soon as I can pack.'

Sebastian stared after her in shock, hardly able to take in the words. She was back at her brother's side before he could even rouse himself enough to open his mouth and then he wasn't sure *what* to say. All he could do was repeat her parting words over and over in his head. He could have his freedom back. He could go anywhere he wanted. She'd be leaving as soon as she could pack... She was leaving him! As if nothing they'd shared over the past few weeks meant anything to her at all!

He turned on his heel, marching away across the lawn until he reached the lake. Unfortunately, that didn't seem like far enough so he kept going, storming all the way around it in a large circle until he came to the top of a hill where an ancient oak tree stood like some long-forgotten sentinel all on its own. Then he stopped, relishing the feel of the cold wind biting his face. The sting of it seemed to match his mood. Hypocrite, she'd called him, talking to him as if he were the one in the wrong! *Him!* After he'd given up his freedom to help her! And yet...wasn't he a little in the wrong? Hadn't he just forced her into making a choice? Wasn't he acting like the most boorish, resentful, jealous fool in the world?

Jealous?

His stomach lurched. Damn it all, he *was* jealous. And not just jealous, but terrified, too. It had been David who'd brought them together—more specifically, his departure—and it was David who had the power to tear them apart. *That* was the reason he'd behaved so badly, because he was afraid she might love her brother and nephews more than she loved the idea of being married to him. The very thought of it turned his blood to ice. Because he loved her, he was in love with her, and he was desperately afraid that she didn't feel the same way.

Neither of them had ever said *I love you.* Until that moment, he hadn't even put a great amount of thought into the matter. There hadn't seemed any rush to do so. He'd been happy as they were, but now the realisation of how much he cared was making him lash out, not because he was angry at what David had done, but because he was afraid of what he could do—*was* doing—with his help! He could hardly have made matters any worse if he'd actually pushed Henrietta into her brother's arms!

He slammed his palm hard against the tree trunk, sending a spasm of pain shooting through his hand and up his arm. He ought to go back and talk to her, not least because his mother had been right about the change in weather and dark clouds appeared to be closing in fast. He'd been in too much of a temper to notice before, but now he was aware of snowflakes dancing in the air around him, slowly gathering in strength.

There was a murky-looking bank of cloud on the horizon, too, like a slate-grey wall heading towards Feversham. He *definitely* ought to go back. Then he could tell Henrietta how he really felt and hope that she felt the same, or something similar anyway. That would be the sensible thing to do—what he *would* do—and he was just about to when a voice called out to him suddenly.

'That looked as though it hurt.'

'Peter?' He tipped his head back, peering up through the bare branches of the oak tree until he caught sight of the boy sitting on one of the uppermost boughs, higher than he would have expected. 'What are you doing up there? I thought you were with your father.'

'I ran off.' Peter's tone was petulant. 'I wanted to be on my own.'

'I know how you feel.' Sebastian leaned his shoulder against the trunk. 'Only this might not be the best time or place.'

'Why not?'

'See those dark clouds? They're coming this way.'

'I don't care.'

'Well, I do.' He looked up again. 'Want to come down and talk about it?'

'I can't.' There was a hint of fear behind the defiance now. 'I don't know how to get down.'

'Ah. Well, in that case, I'd better come up.' He tossed his hat to one side and started to climb, moving up the trunk and swinging his legs over a neighbouring branch in a matter of seconds.

'That was fast!' Peter looked impressed.

'I've had a lot of practice.'

'Will you help me to get down?'

'Why do you think I'm here?' He gave a reassuring wink. 'We'll take it slowly, don't worry.'

'Thank you.'

'So... You ran off?'

'Yes. I told my father I hated him.'

'Ah.'

There was a brief pause. 'I don't.'

'I know. I'm sure he knows that, too.'

'I'm just angry.'

'I don't blame you.'

'Really?' The boy looked surprised. 'Then you don't think I ought to forgive him?'

'I didn't say that.' Sebastian feigned an interest in some nearby twigs. 'Sometimes it can be hard to understand what you're feeling. Sometimes a man needs to run away for a while in order to make sense of things.'

'Is that what you're doing?'

He made a wry face. 'Something like that, but perhaps it's better to forgive and forget and concentrate on what matters. You love your father really, don't you?'

Another pause. 'Yes.'

'Then that's what matters.'

'I suppose so... Uncle Sebastian?' Peter sounded anxious again. 'Now that my father's back, does this mean *you'll* go away?'

'I don't know.' He felt a stab of fear in his chest. 'I hope not.'

'I like having you as my uncle.'

'I like it, too. Very much.'

'And you love Aunt Henrietta, don't you?'

He smiled. 'You're a smart boy, but right now we need to get down before that storm hits. Put your foot here.'

He led the way, instructing Peter where to hold on and where to place his feet as they made their way slowly down the trunk. There were plenty of footholds, enough that they would probably have made it to the ground quite safely if it hadn't been for the rain making the bark slippery. Unfortunately for them, however, it had, a large chunk of it peeling away beneath Peter's fingertips and sending them both tumbling through the air to the ground.

'Oof!' Sebastian felt stunned for a few seconds. It wasn't so much the fall that hurt, or the root beneath his back, as the weight of a ten-year-old boy landing on top of his chest.

'Sorry.' Peter wriggled away to one side and then yelped.

'What's the matter?' He tried to sit up, then fell back as his ribs protested.

'My foot hurts.'

'Can you stand?' He rolled on to his right shoulder, using his arm to push himself up to a sitting position. That felt marginally better, though he was still aware of a searing pain in his side.

'Only on one leg, I think.'

'Damn—I mean, oh, dear.' He looked up at the sky, just in time for a large drop of freezing cold water to fall into his face. Only it wasn't quite rain—or snow either. It was sludge. Thick, wet, thoroughly drenching sludge that made it downright impossible for them to stay where they were. There weren't any leaves and nowhere near enough branches on the tree to provide shelter.

'We need to get back to the house.'

'But we'll get soaked!' Peter protested. 'Maybe we should wait here for somebody to find us.'

'Not in this weather.'

'We could shout for help.'

Sebastian looked around, but there was no one in sight to hear them. No doubt David was already looking for his son, but the Feversham estate was big enough that it could be hours before anyone came this way. Besides, the clouds in the distance looked even more threatening than the ones above them now. The last thing they wanted was to be huddled beneath a tree in a lightning storm.

'No, we need to move.' He held his hands out and they pulled each other up to their feet with an effort.

'Ow.' Peter hopped a few times on his good foot.

'It'll be all right.' Sebastian crouched down, steeling himself for a fresh burst of pain. 'Climb on to my back. Imagine I'm a mast.'

'But you're hurt.'

'Only a little. We'll manage.'

He clamped his teeth together as Peter clambered on to his back and then staggered forward, concentrating on putting one foot in front of the other and trying to ignore the sound of rolling thunder in the distance. It wasn't elegant and the pain was excruciating, but at least it was progress, albeit of the infinitely slow kind. If they followed the path around the lake, then it would take them back to the main lawn…provided his ribs could make it that far.

'Uncle Sebastian?' Peter sounded frightened.

'Yes?'

'I'm sorry.'

'What did I just tell you?' He twisted his head, managing to grin over his shoulder. 'Sometimes we just need to forgive. Now come on, cadet, we can do this.'

Chapter Twenty-Five

Bother, Henrietta thought. Bother and fiddlesticks and… She screwed up her face and let loose several of the choicest nautical phrases Sebastian had taught her—or said in close proximity to her anyway, usually under his breath. There hadn't been any *deliberate* teaching, but she had a good memory, especially when it came to such colourful metaphors. Under normal circumstances, she would never have dreamed of repeating any of them, but in this particular instance, the words made her feel better.

'Oh!' Mrs Fortini looked startled as she passed her in the hallway. 'Is everything all right?'

'Yes. I'm just going for a lie down.' Henrietta hurried past, attempting a smile, though she was afraid the effort made her look as though she had some kind of digestive problem.

'Of course. Are the boys still out walking?'

'I think so.' She nodded, though in all honesty she wasn't sure. She'd changed her mind about accompanying David and her nephews into the woods, stomping about the herb garden for half an hour by herself instead.

She ran up the staircase, into her room, and flung herself down on the bed. The fire was lit, but she still couldn't stop from shivering, as if the cold were coming from inside her. Which made sense since her argument with Sebastian had left her feeling as if a part of her had frozen. She'd told him to leave, to go back to sea, to go anywhere he wanted.

She folded an arm over her face, trying to blot out what had happened, but it was impossible. Her mind was a raging whirlwind of misery and self-recrimination and her chest felt tight, as if her heart were truly breaking. That was when she knew how stupid she'd been, spinning daydreams. She'd really thought they'd been more than friends, that he cared about her, that he might even love her, but he hadn't. His motives for being with her might have been more honourable than most other men's, but in the end they'd had nothing to do with the *real* her. Anything else he'd said had only been what she'd wanted to hear.

After what might have been ten minutes or an hour, she got up and went to the window. The weather was abysmal now, the pale grey of the morning replaced by a dark and threatening shade of lead. There were no gaps in the clouds any more, only one single dark mass for as far as she could see, blocking out the sun like a vast cloak across the sky. It was beautiful in a dramatic kind of way, the kind of scene she might have enjoyed watching with Sebastian, with her head resting on his shoulder, his arm around her waist, stroking her hip... She touched the ring on her finger, a lump rising in her throat at the realisation they would never stand that way again.

She swallowed and turned away from the window. David

and the boys had probably already gone back to the nursery, which meant she ought to go up and tell them to start gathering their things. She wanted to begin packing right away. If she was only Sebastian's wife in name, then she had no right to stay at Feversham any longer. Whatever the weather, they needed to leave.

She started towards the door at the sound of a knock, surprised when it opened before she could reach it.

'Is Peter here?' David didn't pause to exchange greetings.

'No. I thought he was with you.'

'He was, but he ran away!'

'What?' She felt a stab of panic. Peter hadn't seemed in a particularly celebratory mood when he'd seen his father that morning. Instead, he'd looked angry and guarded, but she'd thought some time alone together would help.

'I don't know what happened.' David pushed a hand through his hair. 'I was just trying to talk to him…'

'Which way did he go?' She grabbed hold of his arm. Why it had happened wasn't as important at that moment as finding him.

'I don't know. He charged off through the trees.'

'Tobias!' She ran out of the room and hurtled down the stairs, trying to think clearly and not panic. Despite the storm, there was still plenty of daylight left. It wasn't even time for luncheon. And Peter wouldn't have been foolish enough to go near the lake, not after everything Sebastian had taught him.

The thought of her husband made her heart contract almost painfully. If only he were there to help! If only they hadn't argued—and in front of Peter, too! The boy hadn't been within hearing distance, but it would have been obvious from their body language that they were arguing. He'd probably guessed that it was about his father. Which was probably why he'd gone on to argue with David himself...

'Henrietta?' Lord Tobias emerged from his library just as she reached the bottom step.

'It's Peter. He's run away.' She could hear herself panting, from barely controlled panic as well as her flight down the stairs. 'We need to organise search parties.'

'Of course. Dennison!' Lord Tobias started towards the servants' quarters. 'We'll send some men out at once.'

'Oh, my dear.' Elizabeth emerged from the drawing room and put an arm around her shoulders. 'I'm sure he can't have gone far.'

'I know. It's just that the weather's so terrible...' She winced at a roll of thunder outside. If the rain now lashing against the windows was any indication, the tempest was increasing by the minute. 'I'm going out to look for him.'

'Absolutely not. I'm sure Sebastian and your brother would both want you to stay inside.' Elizabeth looked around. 'Where *is* Sebastian?'

'I don't know. He went off somewhere, too.' Henrietta shook her head. 'But I *need* to go.'

'I really don't think—'

'But I *must*.'

'Very well.' Elizabeth sighed and unravelled her shawl. 'But at least wear this. I don't want you getting sick again. Now where are Michael and Oliver?'

'Up in the nursery.' David was already opening the front door.

'I'll go and keep an eye on them.'

'Thank you.' Henrietta flung the shawl around her shoulders and then followed her brother, almost blowing back inside the house again as the wind caught her on the front steps. There was no lightning yet, thank goodness, but the clouds were skidding by at a ferocious pace. It wouldn't be long before the centre of the storm was upon them.

'Where do we start?' she called after David, shouting to make herself heard over the roar of the wind. The outside world felt strange, as if she'd fallen into water and was fighting against the current, which, since she was already drenched, seemed an appropriate image. She had to bow her head and hunch over to make any progress at all.

'In the woods! That's where I last saw Peter!'

'Do you think—? *Look!*' She caught her breath, looking past David's shoulder towards a dark shape coming from the direction of the lake. It was roughly the same size as a horse, only it wasn't a horse. It had two heads and two of its legs were dangling in mid-air and it looked like...

'Sebastian!' she shouted, running across the lawn as fast as the wind would allow, which was still slower than David, who darted like a streak of lightning himself. He was already lifting Peter into his arms by the time she arrived.

'What happened?' She stretched her arms out, grabbing hold of Sebastian's shoulders as he sank to one knee, clasping his side with a groan.

'I fell out of a tree and landed on top of him,' Peter answered for them, water streaming down his small face.

'Out of a tree?' She looked between them in horror. 'Are you injured?'

'I hurt my ankle.'

'And I came to my senses.' Sebastian leaned forward, eyes like hot coals though his eyelashes held tiny droplets of water as he rested his forehead against hers. 'I don't want my freedom back, not from you. I don't want to go anywhere or lose you. I should never have expected you to choose. Whatever our reasons for getting married, I want to stay married.'

'Yes!' She pressed her lips to his wet cheeks, then his chin and nose, covering the whole of his face with kisses. 'Yes to all of that. Everything you just said, especially the part about staying married.'

'Good. Because I love you.'

'I lo— *Sebastian?*'

She tried to catch him, but it was too late. She never got to repeat the sentiment as he tumbled to the ground, unconscious.

'I thought she might want a cup of tea.' David hesitated in the doorway, looking surprised to see Sebastian awake and Henrietta sleeping soundly in a chair by the bed. 'I suppose you can have it if you like?'

'Thank you.' Sebastian answered in the same low undertone. 'I could do with one.'

'Well then…' David put the saucer down on the bedside table and took a few steps back. 'How are you feeling?'

'Better now I'm warm and dry. Well enough to know I owe you an apology.'

'You do?' His brother-in-law lifted an eyebrow dubiously.

'Yes. I haven't been particularly welcoming.'

'No, you haven't.' David frowned and then relented. 'But I would probably have behaved the same way if our positions had been reversed. You didn't say anything this morning that wasn't true.'

'It still wasn't my place to say it. I was afraid of what you coming back might mean for me, but I shouldn't have said those things, especially when I know a little something about abandoning sisters.' He shrugged at the other's enquiring expression. 'I'll tell you another time. How's Peter?'

'Lying on a sofa, enjoying the fuss.' David scratched his chin. 'Thank you for bringing him back safely.'

'He's a good boy. They all are. They'll grow into fine men.'

'I hope so. I never meant to hurt them. I just couldn't see past my grief.'

'And now?'

'It's still not easy, but from now on I'm going to behave the way Alice would have wanted me to. I've been as low as a man can go and I won't go back.'

Sebastian nodded sombrely. 'I'd shake your hand, but I'm not sure I can lift my arm.'

'I just need to know one thing. Do you really love my sister?'

'I do.'

'Then we'll shake hands later.' David jerked his head towards the chair. 'She hasn't moved from your side since they carried you up.'

'I know.'

'How long have you been awake?'

'Only ten minutes or so, but I know her.'

David smiled for the first time, revealing a familiar dimple in his left cheek. 'I'll leave you to drink your tea in peace, then.'

Sebastian leaned back against the bedhead, watching as Henrietta's eyelashes slowly fluttered and then opened.

'I must have fallen asleep.' She seemed surprised by the fact.

'You did.' He smiled. 'Fortunately, it gave your brother and me a chance to talk.'

'Oh.' She looked worried.

'And to make friends.'

'Oh!'

'I meant what I said on the lawn. I acted like a jealous boor before, but I was just so afraid of losing you.'

'I was afraid it was the other way round, that you thought you were stuck with me.' Her chin wobbled. 'I thought that maybe you didn't want the real me, after all.'

'I'll *always* want the real you. I love you, everything about you, but I was terrified you didn't feel the same way. I was afraid you'd want to go with the boys if they went back to live with their father.'

'I love them dearly, but they belong with David and I... well, I belong with you.' She tipped her head to one side, her gaze softening. 'Why didn't you just tell me how you were feeling?'

'I was too busy being righteously indignant. And I didn't realise how much I loved you until I thought that I'd lost you. That's when I knew the real reason I married you.'

She blinked. 'What do you mean?'

'That I was in love with you before we even left Bath. I already knew I wanted to spend the rest of my life with you.' He clenched his jaw. 'Henrietta, there's something else I should tell you. Something I've never told anyone before. Something I don't even like admitting to myself, about Anna and Belles.'

'What?'

He swallowed, shame-faced. 'When I got the news about my father's death, I was devastated, but a selfish part of me was also relieved that I was already in the navy. I didn't want to go back to Belles, not then anyway. I was relieved that I couldn't go back and help Anna, even though knowing that made me feel ten times worse. It sounds terrible, doesn't it?'

'You can't help your feelings.'

'No, but what I'm trying to say is, part of the reason I proposed to you was that I knew that with you it was different, that if I left you, I *wouldn't* feel relieved.' He reached for her hand and lifted it to his lips, kissing each of her fingers in turn. 'I knew I'd spend the rest of my life regretting it. So what do you think? Could you be happy with just the two of us?'

'Yes...' She turned her hand around so that their fingers were interlaced. 'Apart from David, you're the only man I've ever been able to trust. I was a little in love with you on our wedding day, too.'

His breathing stalled. 'And now?'

'Now, a little seems to have become quite a lot.'

'Just *quite* a lot?' He raised an eyebrow though his heart soared. 'Remember you're talking to an injured man. I need some motivation to get better.'

'You're bruised, not broken. The doctor said you'll be up and about in no time.'

'So I don't get any compliments, then?'

She leaned forward, smiling tenderly into his eyes. 'I love you, Sebastian Fortini, more than I ever imagined possible.'

'And I love you more than any ship.'

'What?'

'That's a deeply profound compliment from a sailor.' He grinned. 'But you know, this is all wrong. If this is our happily-ever-after, I shouldn't be lying here in bed. If anything, I should be tending to you.'

'You already did that, remember? Besides, wouldn't it be dull if all love stories ended the same way?'

'I still don't feel very heroic lying here.'

'Well, if you're the hero then that makes me the heroine and I don't want to be a damsel in distress. It should have become obvious by now that the women of Belles don't need rescuing. We might need a little help now and again, but we want equals, not knights in shining armour.' She reached up and stroked the side of his face. 'But you'll always be *my* hero.'

'Mmm. I still think there ought to be some kind of peril.'

'Oh, all right then.' She climbed up on to the bed to stretch out beside him. 'There you are.'

'Are you implying that being in a bed with me is perilous? I have bruised ribs, remember?'

'And why would you assume that *I'm* the one in danger? Now lie still and I'll be gentle...'

Chapter Twenty-Six

'How long until the curtain goes up?' Henrietta sat in front of a makeshift stage in the library next to David. 'I'm too excited to wait much longer.'

'Patience.' Her mother-in-law sat down on her brother's other side. 'Although I have to admit I'm quite excited myself. It's all been so secretive.'

'I thought you were involved in the preparations?'

'Only in set design, I'm afraid. I interrupted rehearsals this morning and I was practically thrown out.'

'Quite rightly, too.' Lord Tobias peered out from between two makeshift curtains draped from a wooden frame. 'However, you'll be glad to know that it's almost time. Lights!' He gestured to a footman who dutifully blew out all the candles except for those close to the stage. 'Where's Sebastian?'

'On his way.' The Dowager Duchess sat down next, arranging her skirts regally around her. 'He was late getting back from the village, but he says he only needs a few minutes to change his clothes.'

'I still can't believe this is all real.' David lowered his voice to whisper in Henrietta's ear. 'The boys seem almost at home here.'

'That's because they're a part of the family now. Just like you are.'

'I'm starting to realise that, unlikely as it seems.' He shook his head slightly. 'I'm grateful, but I'll be a lot more comfortable when we've moved into our new cottage.'

'I understand.' She squeezed his hand. 'Are you certain about staying in Yorkshire?'

'Yes.' He nodded decisively. 'Lord Tobias's offered me a good job in his stables. Head groom. I'd be a fool not to take it. Never mind his offer of tutoring for the boys.'

'I'll miss them, but you know you can visit whenever you want. You'll always have a home with us, too.'

'Who has a home with us?' Sebastian murmured in her ear a second before his lips found her cheek.

'Oh.' She gave a guilty start, then caught her breath at the sight of him dressed in pristine black and white evening clothes. He looked dazzlingly handsome, not to mention *almost* neat and tidy, for once. 'David and the boys. Obviously I would have asked you first...'

'No need.' He waved a hand as he draped himself over the chair on her other side. 'The more the merrier. I've found I rather like big families.'

'What's this?' His mother swayed sideways. 'Is there something you two want to tell me?'

'Not yet, Mama, but we're working on it.'

'Sebastian!' Henrietta dug her elbow into his ribs, eliciting a small chuckle from him and a placid smile from his mother.

'Good. Because it turns out I enjoy being a grandmother. I only wish that Anna was here to share the fun.'

'When is she coming home anyway?'

'Not for a while. Samuel doesn't want to leave his grandmother just yet. Understandably. Poor Georgiana isn't quite as indomitable as she seems.'

'Your attention, please!' Lord Tobias's head poked through the curtain again. 'Allow me to present the Gardiner brothers' production of *Nelson versus the Polar Bear and Other Adventures*!'

'Oh, good.' Mrs Fortini clapped her hands. 'Now hush, everyone.'

It was, Henrietta thought, linking her arm through Sebastian's as the curtains swept back to reveal several large, white-painted boxes obviously intended to represent icebergs, quite the most bizarre, unexpected and inventive dramatical performance she'd ever witnessed. At some point during rehearsals, Oliver the polar bear appeared to have stolen centre stage from Nelson, who was now relegated to a supporting role while a storm whipped up a blue piece of cloth, presumably representing the ocean, Peter the pirate sang a sea shanty, Napoleon, aka Lord Tobias, fell headlong into an icy crevice and, at one particularly surreal point, Michael turned into an octopus, waving eight woollen tentacles around his head before being finally vanquished by the aforementioned polar bear.

'What do you think the moral is?' Sebastian turned his head, pressing his lips into her hair.

'I'm not sure there is one, but the octopus and polar bear appear to have reconciled. They're embracing now.' She smiled happily. 'I do like a happy ending.'

'So do I. And here comes our young pirate, too.' Sebastian leapt to his feet, pulling her with him. 'Bravo! Encore!'

'Wonderful!' Henrietta clapped enthusiastically. 'A triumph!'

'Do you really think so?' Peter pulled his pirate's eye-patch away from his face.

'It's the best play I've ever seen.' David's voice had a crack in it.

'I agree.' Even the Dowager Duchess was beaming. 'I've seen a lot of plays, but that was spellbinding.'

'Does that mean we can have some cocoa now, Aunt Elizabeth?' Michael grinned cheekily. 'And biscuits, too?'

'Of course. You all deserve a reward.'

'You certainly do.' Henrietta bent to kiss each of her nephews in turn. 'But you'll need to have it up in the nursery. The guests will be arriving soon.'

'Can't we stay for the party?'

'It's not for children.' David interceded, putting an arm around Peter's shoulders and earning himself a wide smile. 'But *I'd* like to join you upstairs for cocoa and biscuits.'

'Are you certain?' Elizabeth gave him a kindly look. 'You're more than welcome to stay.'

'No, thank you.' David shook his head. 'I'd rather be with my boys, but I appreciate the invitation.'

'Very well, but if you're going to escape then I suggest that you hurry. I think I can hear the first carriages arriving now.'

'Come along then, the rest of you.' Lord Tobias tore off his French soldier's costume and made sweeping gestures towards the doorway with his arms. 'Let's go and greet them. It's about time I introduced my heir to the neighbourhood.'

'Feeling nervous?' Sebastian slid an arm around Henrietta's waist as they moved obediently towards the door.

'A little, but it's very kind of your uncle to want to introduce us.' She peered up at him. 'What about you?'

'Not nervous exactly, just slightly in shock. A month ago I was a single man heading home to run a biscuit shop with his widowed mother and unwed sister and now...' He shook his head slightly. 'It's hard to accept that all this is real.'

'I know. I still can't believe that Tobias made you his heir. We aren't really going to live here one day, are we?'

'There's no need to look so horrified.' He laughed. 'But who knows? Maybe I'll decide to become a gentleman of leisure eventually. Or we could turn it into a maritime academy?'

'I think it might be a little far from the sea. What about a baking school?'

'It's an interesting idea.' He stopped and tugged her towards him. 'Speaking of baking, I wrote to James a little while ago, asking him to look out for suitable properties for our tea shop.'

'And he's found one?' She stood up on tiptoes, clasping her hands to her chest in delight.

'He might have. Not on Swainswick Crescent, but only a few minutes' walk away. Next door to his store, actually, with rooms upstairs for us to live in.'

'That sounds perfect!'

'Which means there'll be no need to throw Nancy and Bel-whatever-her-name-is out into the street. They can stay and run Belles together if they want, with a wage increase naturally.'

'As if you would ever have thrown them into the street!'

'You're right. Nancy would have thrown me back.'

'At the very least, and you already have bruised ribs.'

'You know...' he slid his hands gently over her hips '... this will make an excellent story for the children one day. I offered your mother a manor, but she wanted a tea shop...'

'Just for now.' She drew in a breath and then smiled it out again, wanting to purr like a cat at his touch. 'But maybe I'll want to be a lady of leisure some day, too. You never know what the future will bring. I certainly never expected to find a sailor in my kitchen in the middle of the night.'

'And I never expected to find anyone as perfect as you.' He grinned. 'Not beautiful perfect, obviously. Inner perfect.'

She clucked her tongue. 'You know, you're allowed to give me compliments now that we're married. I only objected at first.'

'I don't believe you ever *officially* withdrew your objections.'

'Well, I'm doing so now.' She gave him an arch look. 'You haven't even mentioned how I look this evening.'

'Lovely, but I'm used to you now.'

'What difference does that make?'

'Quite a lot actually. When you love someone, you don't really notice what they look like any more. You only see the essence of them. You could be the most beautiful woman in the world—you *might* actually be, come to think of it— and I still wouldn't notice. To me, you're just Henrietta.'

'Thank you... I think.'

'I *did* just say that I loved you.'

'True.'

'And you love me, too?'

'Also true.'

'Excellent. In that case...' He reached into his pocket and

pulled out a red velvet box. 'I ordered this for Christmas, but I thought you might like to wear it tonight.'

'Is this why you went into the village?' She opened the lid to reveal a small padlock-shaped locket complete with a tiny key. 'Oh, Sebastian, it's beautiful.'

'It's so you never doubt that I'm yours. My heart belongs to you now, Henrietta.' He grinned her favourite lopsided grin. 'I couldn't have been happy giving up my freedom for anyone else.'

'It's the most wonderful present I've ever received.' She sniffed as he lifted the locket and fastened it around her neck, his fingers lingering briefly. 'Can I have the key?'

'Of course.'

'There…' She opened it up and pressed a kiss to the inside before holding it out for him to do the same.

'You want me to kiss it?' He looked amused. 'Aren't you supposed to put a picture inside? Or a lock of hair?'

'Maybe, but for now, I just want a kiss. Now hurry up before mine escapes.'

He pressed his lips to the metal. 'Will that do?'

'That's perfect.' She closed the lid and turned the key again. 'Only it makes my present seem a little unimpressive.'

'I'm sure I'll love it, whatever it is.'

'Well, it's in a similar vein… Remember how I once offered to knit you a scarf?'

'You've made me one?' His grin seemed to take over his whole face. 'Well, a handmade gift is even better. I'll treasure it for ever.'

'Just as long as you wear it.'

'Every day. Even when I don't go outside…'

'Are the two of you coming?' Lord Tobias poked his head back around the library door.

'Imminently.' Sebastian slid the key back into the box and inclined his head. 'I just need to kiss my wife first.'

'Again?' Lord Tobias rolled his eyes. 'The poor woman never gets a moment's peace. Make it quick, then.'

'Understood.' He gave a mock salute and then cupped her face in his hands. 'I'll take a lot longer about kissing you later, I promise.'

'Paying special attention to my ankles, I hope?'

'Naturally.' He lowered his mouth towards hers. 'Don't I always?'

'Oh!' She gave a start a split second before their lips touched.

'What?' His head spun towards the door. 'What's the matter?'

'I can hear music!'

'And?' He blinked. 'Is that bad?'

'It could be. Your mother said this was going to be an evening party, but I never thought... What if there's dancing?'

'Does it matter?'

'Yes! I don't know any steps. I've never danced before, not properly. I'm not a lady!'

'As it happens, I don't know any either. And I'm not a gentleman, as I believe I've mentioned a couple of times.'

'But people will be watching us!'

'Then we'll make the steps up as we go along...' He rubbed his thumbs tenderly across her cheekbones. 'That approach seems to have worked pretty well for us so far, don't you think?'

'You're right.' She thought about that for a few moments

and then laughed, her heart swelling at the thought. 'I suppose it has.'

'Now about that kiss…?'

'No time.' She twisted away, reaching for his hand and dragging him towards the door.

'But…'

'Your family are waiting.'

He shook his head with a mocking sigh. 'Is this what I gave up my freedom for? Not even a single kiss?'

She stopped at the door, blowing a kiss over her shoulder. 'You can't say I didn't warn you. You're mine now, Sebastian Fortini, and I intend to keep you.'

Epilogue

Bath—January 1807

'What did *he* want?' a belligerent voice called from the kitchen as Beatrix Roxbury—more familiarly known to the patrons of Belles as Belinda Carr—bolted the shop door behind the last customer of the day. Not that the man in question had been a customer, more of a friendly, helpful and, in her opinion, extremely handsome fellow shopkeeper, but there was no way on earth that Nancy would *ever* agree with that description.

'Who?' She smiled mischievously.

'You know very well who!' The voice sounded exasperated.

'*Do* I?'

'James Redbourne!'

'Oh, yes, of course.' She allowed herself a small giggle. 'Silly me.'

'Well?' Nancy demanded as she went through to the kitchen.

'He didn't *want* anything, actually, but you might want to brace yourself.'

'I'm always braced, especially where he's concerned.'

'So I've noticed.' Beatrix murmured, drawing her apron over her head and hooking it over a peg in the corner.

'*What?*'

'Nothing. He just brought a message from Mr and *Mrs* Fortini, that's all.'

'Sebastian and his mother?'

'No. Sebastian and Henrietta. They're married!'

'Married?' For the first time since they'd met, Nancy seemed unable to form an opinion.

'They went to Gretna Green and they'll be back here in a few days.'

'With the boys?'

'No. They're staying in Yorkshire with their father.'

'What's Henrietta's brother doing in Yorkshire?'

'I presume Mr Redbourne told him where to find them.' She paused slyly. 'I wouldn't be surprised if he paid for him to get there, too. It's just the sort of thing he'd do.'

Nancy's lips thinned. 'You seem to have a very high opinion of Mr Redbourne.'

'I do.' Beatrix kept her tone placid. 'I think he's a good man.'

'Harumph.'

'You might have to get used to him. I expect he'll be spending a lot more time here with Mr Fortini. Maybe it's time to—'

'Never!' Nancy glared and then grimaced. 'I suppose we ought to start looking for new positions then, not to mention somewhere else to live.'

'No need. Henrietta says they're starting a tea room and

they're going to live there, too. So they want us to stay and run Belles. Which makes you the new manager!'

'*I'm* the manager?' Nancy looked almost on the verge of tears before she cleared her throat briskly. 'Well, that's very good of them, I will say—*and* a relief. I didn't want to be sharing a house with a pair of newlyweds, thank you very much. Much better for us spinsters to stick together.'

'Mmm…' Beatrix chewed on her bottom lip for a few seconds before coming to a decision. 'About that, being a spinster, I mean… I think it's time that I told you the truth.'

'About who you are?' Nancy looked amazed for the third time that evening.

'Yes. I should have told you from the start, but I was scared and I didn't know who to trust. Now I know I could trust you with anything. My life if it came to it.'

'Well, it's about time you realised that.' Nancy appeared both pleased and embarrassed at the same time.

'I'm sure you must have wondered who I was.'

'Once or twice.'

'Which is why I'm so grateful that you never insisted I tell you. Here.' She pulled out a chair from the table. 'You might want to sit down.'

'This sounds serious.' Nancy made a show of seating herself. 'Let me guess. You're a runaway princess.'

'Nothing so romantic, I'm afraid. However, for a start, my real name isn't Belinda. It's Beatrix.'

'Oh.' Nancy looked disappointed. 'That's not so shocking.'

'That was the easy part. I'm not a spinster either. I was married two months ago.'

'*What?*' Nancy gave her a look that implied she'd just

taken leave of her senses. 'But you've been here for a month! And you said you were in Bath for a while before that.'

'I know. I can't say I have a great deal of experience of married life...or any, in fact. I ran away from my husband.'

'Why?' Nancy's eyebrows shot up, her expression shifting to one of outrage. 'What did he do?'

'Nothing. He never had a chance. I never even got to the wedding breakfast.'

'You mean you ran away on your wedding day?'

'Yes.' She pursed her lips, wondering how to explain. The only way she could think of was to go back to the beginning. 'The truth is that I am—*was*—quite wealthy. My mother died when I was a baby and my father a few years later. He was a merchant, dealing in tea mostly, and after he died, his entire fortune came to me.'

'So you're an heiress?' Nancy's eyes gleamed with excitement. 'How *much* of an heiress?'

'Sixty thousand pounds.'

Nancy's jaw almost hit the table. '*Sixty thousand?* And you're here making biscuits for a living?'

'I like making biscuits. Anyway, my father left me in the care of his brother, my Uncle Benedict, and his wife, Augusta, but neither of them were very pleased about it. All they cared about was the annual payment they received for allowing me a home under their roof. Maybe they'd expected more from my father's will and they considered the money as their due, because they certainly never went out of their way to earn it. They never liked me.'

'Why not?'

Beatrix lifted her shoulders. It was a good question, one that she'd asked herself countless times over the years. As a ten-year-old orphan, she'd wondered if it was because she was simply unlovable. Either that or inherently wicked somehow. Only the arrival of the kind-hearted Miss Foster had saved her from a lifetime of despair and self-loathing. Eventually, however, she'd realised that her family's behaviour had much less to do with her than themselves. Despite following his brother into trade, her uncle had never enjoyed anything close to her father's success and his wife and children never ceased to remind him about it. The whole house had reeked of bitterness, jealousy and ill will, most of it vented on her.

'Bel— Beatrix?' Nancy looked concerned. 'Was it so bad?'

'It was…unpleasant.' She shook her head, reluctant to dwell on the worst of her experiences growing up. 'My cousins were older than me and I was never accepted into the family.'

'But why didn't you just leave and set up your own house? Especially if you had so much money.'

'Because I didn't have the money. My father put my whole fortune into trust until I turned twenty-five. Unless I married, of course, but I could only do that with my uncle's consent. I couldn't do *anything* without his consent, not even leave the house.' She clenched her jaw at the irony. 'My uncle and aunt didn't want me, but they were terrified of me running away. After a few years, they even became afraid of my friendship with Miss Foster so they dismissed her and appointed a maid to guard me instead. Then once I turned twenty-two, they decided to find me a husband, one important and aristocratic enough to help my uncle's business interests, but impoverished enough to need my money.'

'Eurgh.' Nancy leaned across the table. 'Old and smelly?'

'No, actually, although I'm sure my aunt would have preferred that.' Beatrix drew her brows together as an image of her stern, raven-haired husband flickered into her mind. 'Quite handsome really, and only six years older than me.'

'Cold and cruel?'

'Cold, perhaps, but not cruel, I think. It was honestly hard to tell. I only met him twice, once when he proposed and then again at our wedding. I've barely spoken to him except to say *yes* and *I do*.' She shook her head. 'I know it sounds ridiculous that I would marry a man I didn't know, but if I'd refused my uncle, it would have meant another three years living like a prisoner under his roof. Marriage seemed like the only escape. I thought it couldn't possibly be any worse, especially after...well, something else.' She dropped her gaze, unwilling to specify what the other thing had been. It was mortifying enough to think about, let alone to tell anyone else. 'I was upset and confused and it was only after I'd said my marriage vows that I realised I'd made a terrible mistake. We went back to my husband's house for the wedding breakfast and I went up to my new room to freshen up and then...well, for once there was nobody about, nobody watching me. Before I knew it, I was running down the back stairs and out of the servants' entrance.'

'So that's when you came to Bath?'

'Not straight away. There was someone else...someone I thought I could go to, only it turned out I was wrong about them. Then I remembered the last address I had for Miss Foster and I came here. You know the rest.'

'Mmm, I can see why you were afraid to tell the truth.' Nancy leaned back in her chair, folding her arms over her chest.

'But I never lied. I told you I wasn't a criminal and as for hurting anyone, my uncle and aunt only cared about the money and my husband…well, it's not as if he ever had a chance to care about me, though goodness knows what he must think of me now. He probably hates me for humiliating him so badly.'

'Sixty thousand pounds probably softens the blow.' Nancy lifted an eyebrow. 'Still, if he finds out where you are…'

'He hasn't found me yet.' Beatrix glanced towards the back door as if she half expected a man to appear there at that moment. 'There was a time, when I first arrived in Bath, that I thought maybe he *had* tracked me down. I had a funny feeling that someone was following me, but I must have been imagining things and now…' She paused and bit her lip.

'Now?'

'Now I think that I'm safe, but I wonder if I ought to write to him.'

'What?' Nancy's voice was more of a shriek. 'Why?'

'Because I want to ask for a divorce.' Beatrix kept her voice calm. 'And I think it's a reasonable request. He won't want me back as a wife. Running away was scandalous enough, but these past months should have ruined my reputation beyond any repair. I've given him more than enough to divorce me with.'

'Wouldn't a divorce have to go through Parliament?'

'Yes, but he has the money to do it.'

'Only thanks to you.'

'True, but at least he'd be putting it to good use.'

'I don't know. A divorce would cause even more scandal. What if he decides it's easier to lock you up in a dungeon for the rest of your life?'

'I'm not sure he owns a castle, let alone a dungeon.'

'You said he's an aristocrat, didn't you? They all have

crumbling old castles hidden away on their estates. If you let him know where you are, then you could just be trading your uncle's imprisonment for his. At least here you're free.'

'I know, but I think it's a risk I have to take. I can't spend the rest of my life looking over my shoulder. Besides, he'll want an heir and he won't want one with a woman who's behaved the way I have. And he *seemed* reasonable.'

'Mmm.' Nancy still sounded uncertain. 'Well, I suppose I'll just have to rescue you if he *does* lock you up. Anna and Henrietta can probably persuade Samuel and Sebastian to help, too.'

'Thank you. It's reassuring to know I have friends.'

'What will you say in your letter?'

'That I accept all the blame and that I don't expect any money.'

'That's not fair!' Nancy smacked her hand on the table. 'First you spend years being bullied by your uncle and aunt and now you have to just *give away* your parents' fortune to some husband you don't even know!'

'But at least I'll still have you.'

Nancy snorted. 'I may be a good friend, but even *I'm* not worth sixty thousand pounds.'

'I disagree. A true friend is worth several fortunes. I've had a lot of time to think since I came here and I've made up my mind. This is just the price I have to pay to be free.' She nodded her head emphatically. 'I'll write to him tomorrow.'

'Fine.' Nancy let out a heavy sigh. 'Who is *he*, by the way? You haven't told me his name.'

'Oh…no, I didn't.' Beatrix paused. 'This is the part you might need to sit down for.'

'I'm already sitting.'

'Yes…' She gave a tight smile. 'Well… You see, the thing is his name is Roxbury. Quinton Roxbury.'

'Just Quinton Roxbury? No sir or my lord?'

'Your Grace, actually.' She took a deep breath, admitting the truth in a rush. 'Quinton Roxbury, Twelfth Duke of Howden.'

It was funny, Beatrix thought, rummaging in a drawer for some smelling salts a few minutes later, but Nancy was the last person she would ever have expected to faint…

* * * * *

Subscribe and fall in love with a Mills & Boon series today!

You'll be among the first to read stories delivered to your door monthly and enjoy great savings.

WE
SIMPLY
LOVE
ROMANCE

MILLS & BOON

JOIN US

Sign up to our newsletter to stay up to date with...

- Exclusive member discount codes
- Competitions
- New release book information
- All the latest news on your favourite authors

Plus...
get $10 off your first order.
What's not to love?

Sign up at **millsandboon.com.au/newsletter**